Georgia Le Carre

Contents

You Don't Own Me

Published by Georgia Le Carre
Copyright © 2016 by Georgia Le Carre

The right of Georgia Le Carre to be identified as the Author of the Work has been asserted by her in accordance with the copyright, designs and patent act 1988.

All rights reserved. No part of this publication may be reproduced, stored in a retrieval system, or transmitted, in any form or by any means without the prior written permission of the publisher, nor be otherwise circulated in any form of binding or cover other than that which it is published and without a similar condition being imposed on the subsequent purchaser.

All characters in this publication are fictitious, any resemblance to real persons, living or dead, is purely coincidental.

ISBN: 978-1-910575-37-6

Author's Note

This book is steamy. :)

Dedication

For my gorgeous muse, Snjezana Sute aka Snow.

Appreciations

I wish to extend my deepest and most
profound gratitude to:

Caryl Milton
Elizabeth Burns
Nicola Rhead
Tracy Gray
Brittany Urbaniak
SueBee★bring me an alpha!★

Russian Terms

Russian terms of endearment are different from English ones. Here are the translations for the ones that are used in this series.

lyubov moya" (my love), "**kotik**" (pussycat), "**kotyonok**" (kitten), "**zaika/zaichik**" (bunny), "**malysh**" (baby), "**lapochka**" (sweetie pie), "**zvezda moya**" (my star), "**zolotse**" (my gold). "**rybka**" (little fish), "**myshka**" (little mouse),

'YOU DON'T OWN ME'
'Yes, I fucking do"

- I'll tell you just how much a dollar costs
it is the price of having a spot in Heaven -

One

Dahlia Fury

'**O**h, my God, Dahlia, you have to help me,' Stella, my best friend and roomie cries. She has burst open my bedroom door and is standing at the threshold theatrically wringing her hands.

Stella is a well-known drama queen so I don't panic. I mute my video and turn towards her. 'Calm down and tell me what's wrong.'

'I have a massage client in less than an hour and I've just realized that I've also got another client coming here.'

See what I mean about drama. 'Just cancel one of them,' I suggest reasonably.

'I can't do that. The one who is coming here is that crazy rich bitch from Richmond who told me she is going to recommend me to all her crazy assed rich friends in Richmond. She's probably already on the train. And the other is a Russian Mafia boss.'

I frown. First of all, I didn't know she had a Russian mafia boss as one of her clients. Must

address that one later, but not yet. 'So what do you want me to do?'

'Can you stand in for me?'

I shake my head resolutely. 'Nope. Absolutely not. You'll just have to tell the Mafia boss that you can't make it.'

'I can't do that,' she wails. 'One of the clauses in the confidentiality agreement I signed was that I would never miss any of my appointments once I agreed it unless it was a life or death situation.'

'Huh?' I cock an eyebrow. 'He made you sign a confidentiality agreement?'

She makes an exasperated sound. 'Yes.'

'What kind of person puts an unreasonable clause like that into an agreement with their *masseuse*?' I ask, genuinely surprised.

'Dahlia,' she screams in frustration. 'Can you focus, please. I'm running out of time here.'

'It's simple. Go on to the Mafia boss, and I'll tell your other client when she arrives that she can have a free massage next week.'

'No, she can't come next week. She is away, and anyway, she's in pain and really needs me.'

'So tell the Mafia boss that you can't make it because you have a life and death scenario.'

'You want me to lie to Zane?' she asks incredulously.

'If that's what his name is,' I reply coolly.

She comes into the room and starts pacing the small space like a caged animal. 'I'm not going to lie to him. He'll know.' She stops and stares at me. 'He's got like the coldest most piercing eyes you ever saw. It's like they can see right through you.'

I laugh. 'I can't believe you said that.'

'I'm serious, Dahlia. Lying to him is out of the question.'

'Well, then you'll have to let the rich bitch down.'

'Did you not hear me? She's in pain. Oh, please, please, can you help me this time. You can have my fee and I'll owe you big time.'

'No,' I say clearly. The solution to her problem seems obvious to me —she should cancel the Russian guy.

'I'll do the dishes for a whole month,' she declares suddenly.

I pause. Hmmm. Then I shake my head.

'I'll do the dishes and clean the apartment for a whole month.'

I hesitate. 'Even the bathroom?'

'Yes, even the bathroom,' she confirms immediately.

'I'd love to help but—'

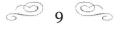

9

'Two months,' she says with a determined glint in her eyes.

My eyebrows fly upwards. I open my mouth and she shouts out, 'Three fucking months.'

To say that I am not tempted would be a lie. I HATE cleaning the bathroom. I am very tempted, but I can't actually take her up on her offer even if she offered me a year's worth of bathroom cleaning.

'Jesus, Stella. Just stop. You know I'd love to take you up on your offer, but I simply can't massage like you. I just about know the basics and rich bitch's problem sounds complicated. For all I know, I'll just end up making her back worse and instead of giving you a glowing recommendation to all her rich friends she will do the opposite.'

Stella fixes her hazel eyes on me. 'I wasn't thinking of her.'

I look at her, astonished 'What?'

'He just needs a simple basic Swedish. Just exactly what I've already taught you. You just need to put a bit more effort into it. He likes it really hard.'

'Like hell, I'm massaging your Mafia boss.'

She falls to her knees. 'Oh please, please, please.'

'If you're trying to make me feel guilty, it's not working,' I say.

She looks at me pleadingly. 'Pleeeeeeease. I promise you he's really easy to do.'

'Oh yeah. Is that why you're so terrified of him?'

She turns her mouth downwards. 'I'm not terrified of him.'

'Could have fooled me.'

She sighs. 'Actually, I'm a bit … in lust with him,' she confesses with a wry smile.

'A bit? You?' I explode in disbelief. This is Stella, the woman who turns a spider sighting in her bedroom into a shrieking Victorian melodrama.

'Yeah,' she says softly.

'In lust?'

'Yeah.'

I shake my head in wonder. 'Since when?'

'Since,' she shrugs, 'forever. I've always had a thing for him, but of course, he's way out of my league. The women he dates are all at least ten feet tall and totally perfect. I only register on his radar as a pair of strong hands.'

I stare at her suspiciously. 'Are you just making all this up so I'll go and massage him?'

She shakes her head. 'No.'

'Why haven't you told me about this man crush before?'

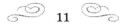

She looks down at her right shoe. 'There seemed to be no point. I've come to terms with it. The truth is it is way stronger than a crush, and it could even be love, but there's nothing I can do about it.'

Suddenly I realize why every time we go out she freezes out every man, even the ones that look like serious contenders, who come up to her. 'Oh, Stella!' I breathe. I had no idea she was suffering in silence.

She looks at me sadly. 'It doesn't matter. It'll pass, but right now I just need your help. I don't want to let him down or give him cause to fire me. Until I'm ready to let go of him I want to keep this job going.'

'But—'

She holds up her hand. 'Don't say it. I know. It's stupid and it's crazy, and I don't know where I'm going with this, but I can't let go. Not yet. One day I'll eventually leave, I know that, but just not quite yet, OK?'

'OK.'

One corner of her mouth lifts. 'So you'll do it?'

Now I am torn between feeling horribly sorry for her and not wanting to be manipulated into massaging her Russian. 'I do want to help, Stella, but I can't. I'm not

qualified. I wouldn't know what to do or say to someone like that.'

'You don't even have to talk to him. He never says a word. Just comes in and lies there, and after I've finished, I turn down the lights and leave. He doesn't even lift up his head to say goodbye.'

Ugh, sounds like a horrible man. I have a sinking feeling in my stomach. 'I think this is a really bad idea,' I say, but my voice is weak. Both of us know that she has won.

'Yes, you can. It's a plain massage. Nothing fancy. Just basic moves. You could do it with your eyes closed. All you have to remember is that he likes it hard.'

I stare at her indecisively.

'Remember three months of no cleaning.'

'Stella,' I groan.

'Oh, thank you. Thank you. I promise you'll never regret it. I owe you one.'

I sigh. 'I'm already regretting it.'

'Come on. Let's get you into one of my uniforms.'

We go into her room and I take my T-shirt off and slip into her white uniform. It has a black collar and black buttons all the way down, but because my boobs are so much bigger than hers I cannot button all the way.

'Now what?' I ask.

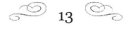

Her head disappears into her closet. She comes out with a scarf, hooks it around the back of my neck and tucks it into the front of her uniform.

I look at myself in the mirror.

'I really don't know about this, Stella,' I say doubtfully.

'Are you kidding? You absolutely look the part.'

'Are you mad? This uniform is too tight.'

'No, no, you look great,' she says quickly and bundles me out of her room. 'Look, you best get going or you'll be late. The car will be here anytime now.' She grabs my handbag from the dining table, presses it into my hands and practically pushes me out of the front door. Holding on to my elbow she rushes me down the corridor.

'Does he even know that I'm going in your place?'

'Not yet. Noah's phone was engaged, but I'll call again in a bit.'

We go into the lift together and as she said, there is a black Mercedes with tinted windows waiting outside. She opens the back door and manhandles me into it.

'See you later,' she calls cheerily as she closes the door with a thick click.

The driver glances at me in the mirror.

14

'You all right, Miss?'

'Yeah, I'm all right,' I say with a sigh. Looks like I'm massaging the man Stella is in love with.'

Hey, I heard you are a wild one, wild one, wild one.

Two

Dahlia Fury

The Mafia boss's house is in Park Lane. A dour, deeply tanned man in a black suit and a white shirt opens the door and raises his eyebrows. He is wearing an earpiece. Noah, presumably, and obviously Stella never managed to get him on the phone.

'Stella can't make it. I'm taking her place,' I explain shortly.

'We do body searches on people we don't know,' he says, his eyes travelling down my length.

'The fuck you are,' I tell him rudely.

He grins suddenly. 'I like you. You've got balls.'

'Whatever,' I say in a bored voice.

His grin widens. He's got good strong teeth. 'If you've got a weapon hidden in that tight dress you deserve to kill him.'

'It's a uniform,' I say stiffly.

'No kidding,' he leers.

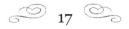

I look at him with raised eyebrows.
'Come with me.'

I step into the mansion, he closes the door, and I follow him into the Mafia Don's residence. What can I say? Wow? Crime really does pay. Yeah, must be nice to have so much. Polished granite, marble columns, fantastic lighting, touches of platinum, sleek black leather trimmings. Nope, not my thing, nevertheless very, very impressive in a cold, masculine sort of way.

He takes me down a curving staircase that appears to go down at least another three floors into the ground. I have heard of such houses. There are more floors underground than above ground. He stops after the second flight of stairs and walking down a corridor, opens the door to what looks like a dimly lit massage room.

He flicks his wrist, looks at his watch, and says. 'He'll be with you in five minutes.'

Then he winks and disappears. I look around the room. Opera music is being piped in through hidden speakers, and it is wonderfully warm. I walk towards the massage table. All the different oils are in a kind of bain-marie on a trolley next to it.

Shit. Suddenly I feel really nervous.

I've never massaged anyone other than Stella and my sister. I take a deep breath. No, I can do this. I will tell my grandchildren about the day I massaged a Russian Mafia boss. I smile to myself. I pick up a bottle of oil. I twist the cap and smell it. Oooo... lavender, musk and something else ... Rosemary?

I pour some on my palm and rub my hands together. The smell surrounds me. Very nice. I adjust my clothes. I know exactly why the black suit had been staring at me. The uniform is way too tight. I hear a sound outside the door and quickly put my hands to my sides and look towards it.

The door opens and this huge mountain of a man with a small towel slung around his hips comes in. Whoa! I inhale in slow motion. Jesus! No wonder Stella is all tied up in knots. He exudes pure sexual energy. Let me describe him to you. The first thing that hits me after his height and breadth are his incredible tattoos. They cover his body and they are not an untidy collection of random images, but each one subtly connected to the others. For example; an angel smiles at a tiger tearing into an impala, above their heads are intricate images of stars, demons and other strange creatures. On his shoulder a cobra hisses dangerously, its mouth open and hood flared.

The next thing that floors you are his eyes. You know those crazy drawings of Nordic aliens, with their hypnotizing ice-blue eyes? That's what his are like. Piercing and magnetic. Shit. I can't stop staring. Those crazy eyes slide over me, lingering on my breasts, and then pulling back, and narrowing on my face.

I want to smile, but I am frozen.

'Where is ...?' He makes a rolling motion with his big, powerful hand. Stella was right; after six months, twice a week, she has not even registered enough for him to even remember her name.

'Stella,' I supply helpfully.

'Where is ... Stella?' he asks quietly. His voice is deep and the accent is strong and actually extremely sexy.

I open my mouth to speak, and nothing comes out. I clear my throat. 'She couldn't make it. I'm here to take her place.'

He nods. 'Ok,' and going to the massage table lies on it face down.

I gaze at the splendid body, the muscles gleaming in the dim room, and think of Stella. God, I'm not surprised she's fallen for him. I can feel my blood throbbing in my veins. I want to touch him. My desire is so strong it's as unsettling as a fingernail on a blackboard. It sets my teeth on edge. It's almost like making love. I feel hot and excited. My face feels flushed and I pray he hasn't noticed my hesitation. I take a deep breath. Right. Swedish. Make it hard, Stella is saying in my head.

A light sheen of sweat starts on my body. I wipe my brow with the back of my forearm. I flex my fingers and move forward.

I pick up the oil that has been warming in the hot water. Jesus, suddenly the smell of oil feels too musky and erotic. I gaze at his sinewy neck and feel the hair at the back of my own rise. He is like an animal, a big cat. Sleek and dangerous. I put the musky oil back down and pick up a random bottle.

I pour the warm, lemon scented golden oil on the plateau at the base of his spine. I watch it pool. Then I take a deep breath and open the massage with a long, slow stroke. He doesn't react. I shift my hands down to the two mounds of the gluteal muscles. They are firm, strong and tight ... and bulging insolently.

Make it hard. He likes it hard.

I dig down and get to work, careful not to make the mistakes that amateurs make – work too fast. My breathing rate increases, but the man does nothing. Just lies there silently. I move to the front of him, grab his shoulders and push down his back with my thumbs and finger pads.

Smooth and sensuous.

My hands roll back. It is almost hypnotic to feel my palms sliding down the tatted skin, and feel the strong muscles underneath move. By now sweat is running down my back. I am so caught up in the job I do not see his hands move, but they are, without warning, cupping my buttocks. I freeze, more in shock than anything else.

The inert body moved!

I jump back in horror. 'What the hell do you think you're doing?'

He lifts his head and looks at me with those wicked eyes. The light shines directly on his face. Vaguely, I register a white scar that starts at the edge of one eye and runs down the side of his face.

'I figured since you are not a real masseuse you were a hooker.'

'What gave you that crazy impression?' I demand, outraged. How dare he?

His eyes slide down to my breasts. I look down. The scarf is dislodged and my breasts are practically spilling out of my uniform. My ears burn as I pull the scarf upwards and clutch it against my chest.

'Well, I'm *not* a prostitute,' I deny hotly.

His reaction is swift and smooth. He rolls to his side and lands lightly on his feet like a cat, with grace and lightness unexpected for someone his size. Do Mafia kingpins receive some kind of stealth training? He straightens. His cock is massive and fully erect. Naked and utterly unashamed of his body, he takes a step towards me. Shocked and a little frightened I take a step back, but the wall pulls me up short. He stops a foot away from me, and leaning forward, his palms land on either side of me.

I gaze at him with wide eyes.

'Then why did you massage me like that?' he asks hoarsely.

The breath escapes me in a rush. 'Like what?' I whisper.

'Like you want to taste my cock.'

'I didn't. I don't,' I stutter.

'Then why are you fucking wet?' he asks softly. His eyes drop to my mouth.

'I'm not,' I say clearly.

His hands leave the wall and grab my hips. 'Do you want me to make a liar out of you?' he asks.

'Don't touch me,' I spit.

He pulls me towards his naked body until his rock hard cock twitches against my belly.

A strange languor overtakes me, and I am suddenly struck by the desire to submit. To let

him have his way. To let him fuck me hard. Because I know it will be a hard fuck. Yes, I'd be just a nameless fuck, and yes, there will be the walk of shame afterwards, but I can live with all of that. The thing that stops me is the thought of facing Stella.

'How dare you?' I gasp.

He laughs, a humorless, cold laugh. 'Is that a challenge or a fucking invitation?'

'It's a fucking warning,' I say furiously.

Ignoring my fury, he runs his fingers along my inner thigh.

I draw in a sharp breath. 'Let go of me or I'll scream.'

His eyes light up. They are like the underside of certain fish, silvery blue. He lets go of my hips. One of his hands comes up to my face. He drags his thumb along my lower lip while I stare up at him, mesmerized by the naked lust in his eyes. The fingers of his other hand arrive at the apex of my thighs.

'Don't,' I whisper.

He brushes his fingers along the crotch of my panties. There is no expression at all in his face when he finds them soaking wet. Without a word he pushes the material aside and inserts a long finger into me.

Holy fuck. My body starts trembling.

'Don't. I don't want you to,' I order, but even I can hear how weak my voice sounds. My brain is already thinking of his thick girth pounding mercilessly into me.

He withdraws the finger and jams it back in. 'Don't?' he taunts.

Blood rushes to my head and pounds so hard I can't even think.

'I … we … oh … ah … shouldn't.'

He doesn't even bother to answer me. Just keeps up the steady finger fucking. I am so excited I feel as if I'm already at the point of no return. To my utter shame and humiliation, my body shudders and I climax really hard all over his finger.

He smiles, a condescending, triumphant smile.

Suddenly I feel sick at what I've just allowed him to do to me. Jesus, I've behaved like a cheap slut. I swallow hard. I can't even look him in the eye. How could this have happened to me? He made me come with one finger! And that digit is still inside me and my muscles are contracting helplessly around it.

'Take your finger out of me now,' I say in a cold, hard voice.

'Why? Are you ready for me to replace it with my cock?' he mocks insolently.

I am so inflamed that it seems natural that he should bear the brunt of my fury. My right hand flies up towards his cheek. It never connects. Instead, a band of steel curls around my forearm.

'Don't ever do that again. I don't like it,' he says very softly.

I try to wrench my hand out of his grasp, but it's like someone has poured concrete around it. His impassive eyes watch my puny struggles almost curiously. Like a child watching an insect it has caught before it pulls its wings off.

I take a deep breath. 'Let me go,' I cry.

He curls his finger and starts stroking my inside walls, and I feel my body begin to respond to his manipulation. Oh no. I can't allow him to take total control of my body again. I stare into his eyes.

'Please,' I beg. My voice sounds strange and strangled.

One corner of his mouth lifts. It makes him look at once beautiful and cruel. He pulls his finger out of me and releases my hand. 'Fly away little bird,' he says dismissively.

I feel so ashamed tears start to burn my eyes. No man has ever reduced me to a feeling of such utter lack of worth. To him I am nothing but a sexual object. A thing. He thought I was offering myself, and he just helped himself even after I objected. Now he is just getting rid of me. My knees feel like jelly.

I press my lips together and take a sideways step. Some part of my brain tries to make sense of what has just happened. It's OK, you'll never see him again. No one will ever know what happened here today. It's just one of those inexplicable moments you have never experienced before. A powerful man totally floors an inexperienced idiot!

I straighten my spine. You know what, I can do the walk of shame. So what? I take one step in the direction of the door and another step and then another step. I put my hand on the handle and his voice, like warm honey, pours into my ears.

'Hey, if you ever need help or anything, anything at all, call me.'

I shouldn't have responded. It would have been better, more dignified, to walk out the door without even an acknowledgement that he has spoken. Instead, I whirl around.

'If you think I need more of what you just dished out you are very much mistaken. You can take your arrogant offer and stuff it up your ass.'

'The world is a dangerous place, *rybka*. You don't know when you need a helping hand. It is better to have a friend than an enemy.'

I look at him scornfully. A man like him could never be a friend of mine. He's the exact opposite of me. This man has ice water flowing in his veins. I nearly fainted once at a pearl farm when I found exactly how pearls are harvested. They cut through the flesh of the poor oyster and dig around in its flesh until they locate the pearl. Ugh! He is as unfeeling as those workmen.

'I wouldn't come to you if you were the last fucking man on earth.'

He shrugs. 'One day you will come to me again and you will be eager for what I dish out.'

'You'll die believing that.'

'I made you come harder than you've ever come using just one finger. You'll be back for more,' he says confidently.

I feel heat start climbing up my neck. 'You're a real bastard, aren't you?'

'Like you wouldn't believe.'

I shake my head with disgust. There is no way to win an argument with someone who cannot be made to feel ashamed of their rude and arrogant ways. I open the door and walk out.

Three

Zane

I watch her leave the room and hear the muffled sound of her footsteps go down the best of Italy's pink marble. I hit the button on the intercom. Noah replies almost instantly.

'Get Corrine to come up,' I tell him, and remove my finger from the button.

I open a drawer and take out a condom. I tear it open and fit it onto my dick. The door opens and Corrine slinks in with a seductive smile. She is blonde with long legs and a great pair of tits. She is wearing a semi transparent white blouse, no bra, an extremely short black skirt, and as I have stipulated, no panties.

I don't like wasting time.

I grab her by the wrist and throw her against the wall. She gasps as I rip her top open. Her pink-tipped breasts strain forward. I look at them without any feeling. I am dead inside.

'Suck my nipples, Zane, please,' she begs.

I'm not in the mood for that. If my mouth gets anywhere near those breasts, I'll bite hard enough to leave marks. I feel that vicious.

I hold my hand out and she immediately hooks her leg over it, giving me an uninterrupted view of her shaved, beautifully swollen and creaming sex. I never got to see the other one's pussy. It is her pussy I want to see open and dripping for me. I won't rest until I have her in this position of utter submission. Until the day I train her to hook her leg onto my hand and beg me to suck her nipples and slam hard into her, I won't be satisfied.

I ram my cock directly into Corrine's little hole and she makes a grunting sound. Today the sound irritates me. I place my palm over her mouth and twist her face to the side so that I don't have to look into her eyes, and carry on thrusting hard.

The room fills with the wet sound of my flesh slapping hers. I come in record time, so quickly, in fact, that Corrine moans and desperately rubs her unsatisfied sex against me in a submissive, almost animal like begging gesture. I stay still with my palm covering her mouth and her leg hooked over my hand, until she finds her own release.

Immediately I pull out of her clinging body and turn away, but not before I glimpse into her half-hooded eyes. At the desire and need still shining in them.

'Zane, I—' she whispers.

'Get out,' I say coldly.

I hear the sound of her clothes rustling, a small sulky sniff. It's nearly time to get rid of her. She leaves and I feel like punching the wall.

'Damn you,' I grate. 'Damn you to hell.'

Three months later...

Four

Dahlia Fury

www.youtube.com/watch?v=BxRQNO8vg2Y

'**Y**ou look beautiful tonight,' Mark says.

'Thank you,' I murmur sweetly.

Mark Sterling is gorgeous, and in the candlelight he seems even brooding and mysterious like a romantic figure from one of Byron's poems. So why, dammit, is there not even a tiny sliver of the seething desire and excitement I felt when I stood in front of the Russian? *Maybe because the Russian was hotter than the devil's dick.*

Shit! I'm at it again. I pull the handbrake on my runaway thoughts.

Zane, I remind myself firmly, is a cold-blooded criminal, a total jerk, and almost certainly, a dyed in the wool misogynist. He treated me shamefully. To be precise: like a piece of meat. Any smart person would have just chalked the experience up as the shittiest day of their lives and promptly put it behind them, but what do I do?

During the first week—and if I am honest for the two weeks that followed—I jumped like a demented frog every time the phone rang, and paced the living room carpet like a caged animal from the moment Stella left to go to her appointments with him until she came back. As soon as I heard her key in the door I would hop onto the couch and pretend I was watching TV. Then I would pathetically try to engage her in conversations designed to make her mention him. The end result of all my efforts was: no phone calls, no text messages, and apparently no change in his attitude towards Stella either.

There was no other conclusion to be had. He was an asshole and I was a moron. To my everlasting disgust I even used to dream of him. Some of my dreams should be classified as nightmares.

The worst one was when I dreamt I was lying in my bed and he entered my bedroom. He stood over my bed and calmly started peeling off that big-assed cobra tattoo, the one that started at his shoulder and curled itself all the way down his arm right down to his wrist. The skin-cobra suddenly became a real cobra in his hand, and the asshole threw it at me.

In order to be faster than the snake, I kicked at the wall like a Ninja boss and launched myself out of bed. The plan was essentially to land precisely and lightly the way a cat would on the floor, but I woke up on my back, shooting pains in my shoulders and hips. While I was still groaning in pain and trying to get off the floor, Stella opened the door and switched on the light.

'Fucking hell, what was that bloody noise?' she asked, blinking in the bright light.

'I fell.'

'Well, you must be a darn sight heavier than you look, then,' she grumbled before switching off the light and stumbling back to her room.

Inexplicably, months later, I still can't seem to stop myself from drooling over the Mafia don. He is like an ache ... an itch that hasn't been taken care of. I just don't know what to do about it.

'More wine?' Mark asks.

I am about to shake my head when the obvious occurs to me. Why the hell not? What am I waiting for? For my unhealthy obsession with the Russian to magically disappear? Why not be proactive? Why not get totally wasted and sleep with Mark tonight? It's only a freaking itch. Let him scratch it. It's high time I

move on, and Mark is actually the kind of guy any mother would kill, oh well, maybe not kill, but she'd maybe walk a few miles barefoot on hot coals, to have as her son-in-law. He is kind, well educated, good-looking (he might even be prettier than me), polite, strong, stable, to all intents and purposes, fairly loaded; and he treats me like a Princess.

'Sure,' I say, and watch him top up my glass. He does it, as he does everything, deftly with inborn elegance.

I pick up my glass, hold it out to him, and with a slow, sexy smile, say, 'To tonight.'

My meaning is not lost on him. His eyebrows shoot up into his hairline. One month I have kept him hanging on. Poor man can hardly believe that tonight he's getting lucky.

He puts his hand out and grasps mine. I feel his eyes on my body, admiring, caressing. I look down at our entwined fingers, then back up to his face. We share a look, and I am suddenly struck by the rightness of my decision. Mark's a good man. I should consider myself very fortunate. I smile again and he smiles back super slowly. His eyes are shining. Oh fuck! He's in love with me. My smile falters.

His grip on my hand tightens. His expression changes, and steely determination glimmers in his eyes. Apparently there's a lot more to solicitous Mark than meets the eye.

'I'm a patient man, Dahlia. I know what I want and I'm prepared to wait forever if I need to, so you just take it at your own pace, all right?'

'All right.'

I stare at him. Half of me pities him, and the other half admires his quiet resolve. I'd love to be that unshakeable. He focuses his gaze on me and I find my eyes sliding away. I reach out for my glass and hurriedly take a large gulp of wine. It goes down the wrong way and I end up in a coughing fit. Mark leaves his chair and comes over to me. He gets on his haunches by my side. My eyes are watering. Thank god for waterproof mascara.

'Are you all right,' he asks gently.

I take the napkin away from my mouth and dab under my eyes. 'Yeah, I'm all right,' I choke.

'Good,' he says softly. 'Because I'm *really* looking forward to the rest of the night.'

I smile shakily at him and realize that I don't even need to get drunk to sleep with him. It's the right thing to do. He'll help me forget the Russian prick.

'You can call for the check if you want to. I'm ready to go,' I tell him.

He grins. He cannot help the victorious look in his eyes. 'I love the way you Americans call the bill a check,' he teases.

'I love the way you English call the check a bill,' I tell him.

He throws his head back and laughs. It's a rich sound and I think, yes, maybe I can grow to love this man. He stands up, goes to his side of the table, settles the bill, and we leave.

It is a lovely autumn evening. The sky is filled with splashes of orange and red as we walk to his dark green BMW. He opens the passenger door for me and I thank him and slide in. Inside the car he switches on the music. G.R.L's *Ugly Heart* comes on. It is such a sassy, kick ass song about breaking free from a pretty boy with an ugly heart that I know what my sister would say. Take it as a sign from the universe that you've made the right decision. I turn to look at Mark's profile and smile to myself.

The other thing with ugly heart was purely a moment of madness. This, I lecture myself, is reality. This is what my parents had. This is what makes a successful relationship. Not that uncontrollable fire and lust. This is what is required to bring children into the world and nurture them. This is what a woman can grow old beside. This is the something warm and comfortable that I will be able to slip into on a cold, rainy English night. Yes, that's the right word. It will be comfortable. In time I'll forget the other's face. I'll forget those silvery-blue eyes that seemed to pierce my very soul.

Mark's apartment is in a really good part of St. John's Wood. It is tranquil and civilized. We go up to his apartment without speaking and he closes the door.

'I have an excellent bottle of Sancerre. 2009. Up for a glass?' he asks.

'Bring it on,' I say with a grin.

'Look who's so full of surprises tonight,' he says, tossing his keys onto a sideboard. 'Why don't you make yourself comfortable in there?' he suggests, nodding towards the living room.

'OK,' I say, and start moving towards it.

He has a nice flat. The décor is a bit dull with dark wood and paintings of fox hunting on the walls, but nothing I couldn't eventually fix. A sliding door leads to a balcony that has a great view of the park. I know because I have been here once before. The door to the master bedroom is open and I glance at the giant bed with its fluffy white throw. My first and instinctive reaction is to avert my eyes. The response irritates and annoys me. *Come on, Dahlia. This is simply the next step in your relationship. One that has been a long time coming.*

I hear him opening the fridge, the cork popping, and the clink of glasses. I am standing at the glass door looking down at the park when the lights in the room dim. I turn around and he advances holding a wine bottle by the neck in one hand and two glasses in the other.

'Awesome view.' Shit, I said that the last time too.

'Yes, I rather like it,' he says casually, and moves towards a long, chocolate leather couch. I follow him and sit beside him, quite close, but not touching. He hands me my drink. I take a sip and put it down on the glass table. He picks up one of the remote controls lying on the table and presses one of the buttons. Soft unrecognizable music fills the air.

I clear my throat.

'Just relax. There's no pressure to do anything,' he reassures gently.

I'm not actually nervous. I'm just not turned on. I take another sip of my wine.

He trails his finger along my wrist. Inside me nothing happens. There is no desire to do anything to him or with him. This is not a good sign, so I put the glass back on the coffee table, lean forward and lay my hand on his thigh.

'Oh Dahlia,' he mutters, and grabs me quite masterfully as he swoops down on my mouth.

Good start, Mark.

As it turns out he's a good kisser. Just enough of everything. He doesn't force his tongue into my mouth either. His hand slides under my top and goes around to my back looking for my bra's clasp. Finding none, he returns to the front where he defeats it in one efficient movement.

OK, he's done this before.

He breaks the kiss and looking deeply into my eyes starts unbuttoning my top. He pulls the material aside to expose my breasts.

'God, you have fabulous breasts,' he says thickly.

'Wait till you see my ass,' I quip, but he is in no mood for jokes.

He bends his head and takes a nipple in his mouth. It feels pretty good and I give him a small encouraging moan. He begins to suck harder, but not enough to cause pain. He has technique, I have to give him that. My brain doesn't feel like it is exploding in my head or anything like that, but I start to enjoy the sensation. Maybe people shouldn't knock comfortable sex so much.

My mobile rings suddenly. The sound is jarring and I freeze.

He lifts his head. His warm, brown eyes are dark with passion. 'Don't take it,' he orders throatily.

'Um … it could be an emergency. I'll just be two secs,' I say apologetically.

'All right. Go ahead,' he sighs.

I pull the edges of my top together and scratch around inside my bag. I can't imagine who could be calling me at this time of the night. I look at the screen and it is my mother. Mom never calls on my mobile. She thinks it's a waste of money. We communicate almost exclusively via Skype.

With a frown I accept the call.

Five

Dahlia Fury

She's my sister. Break her heart and I'll break
your face.

Dahlia Fury

'**D**ahlia,' my mother says urgently.

'What is it, Mom?' I shoot back, my
stomach contracting with dread.

'Has your sister been in contact?' she
demands anxiously without answering my
question.

Thrown by the unexpected question, I
blurt out, 'Daisy? No. Why?'

'When was the last time you spoke to
her?' she goes on.

'Uh ... four days ago. Mom, what are you
panicking about?'

'She hasn't called me, she hasn't updated
her Facebook, and her phone is switched off.'

The dread becomes a cold clamp of fear deep inside me. 'When did you speak to her last?'

'She hasn't called for two days.' My mother's voice has become high and screechy. 'You know how she promised me that she will call me every single day. Day before yesterday she stopped. I was a bit worried, but I let it go because she warned me that some of those remote places she was going to would have bad Internet connection. But nothing again today. That's two days, Dahlia. She'd never not call for two days.'

My mother holds back a distraught sob. 'I'm worried, Dahlia. I know something has happened to her. I've got this bad feeling in the pit of my stomach. I've had it for two days. Something's wrong. I know it. I shouldn't have let her go. Even at the airport I knew it.'

I clutch the phone hard. 'Calm down, Mom. There's bound to be a simple explanation. It's probably as she said, she's stuck in some little town where there is no Internet connectivity.'

'What about her phone? Why has that been switched off?' my mother fires back.

'Maybe her battery's run out.'

'And she never got a chance to charge it for *two* days?' she challenges. When my mother sounds more logical than me it usually means trouble.

I want to get my Mom off the phone and just think for two minutes. Obviously there is a reasonable explanation, but I can't think with her close to hysterical in my ear. 'Mom, can I call you back in half an hour? Let me see if I can contact Marie.'

'I already did. Her phone is switched off too.'

I feel goose pimples start crawling up my arms. 'What?'

'Why do you think I'm panicking?' my mother wails.

'Have you tried Marie's mother?'

'No, I don't have her number.'

I need to get my mom off the phone. 'OK, I do. I'll call her and call you back, OK?' I coax gently.

'Please hurry, Dahlia. I'm going out of my mind here. I'm so afraid. She's only nineteen. She's my baby,' my mom whispers and starts sobbing again.

'Mom, stop crying. Please. There's bound to be a reasonable explanation. I'll call you back in half an hour, or as soon as I know something.'

'Yes, please, Dahlia. I wish you were here. Oh God! I wish I'd never let her go. I warned her never to hitchhike and she promised not to. I only let her go because she promised and she's such a sensible girl. I don't know what could have happened to her.'

'Don't worry, Mom. Like I said there's probably a very simple explanation. I'll call you back in half an hour, or sooner if I get some news.'

'I'll be waiting here,' my mom cries tearfully.

My heart breaks to hear her little frightened voice. 'I love you, Mom,' I say, almost in tears myself.

'I love you too, Dahlia.'

I end the call.

'What's wrong?' Mark asks.

For a moment I don't answer. I can't. My mind is a big, empty blank. Then the words come to me.

'It's my sister.' I look at his concerned face. 'Daisy. She and her friend, Marie, went backpacking in Australia. My Mom hasn't been able to contact either of them for the last two days.' I am surprised to hear how calm my voice is. I think I don't, or just can't bring myself to believe anything bad has happened to my sister. Not to sunny Daisy. Who'd want to hurt her laughing, freckled sweet face?

Mark narrows his eyes. 'She's nineteen right?'

I nod.

'I don't get it. Is it really so unusual if a nineteen-year-old on a backpacking holiday doesn't call her mother for two days?'

I press my lips together and take a deep breath. 'Daisy promised my mom she would call every day. She knows very well if she doesn't call my mom will worry like crazy. I'm twenty-four and I've been living in this country for the last year. I still have to call my mother at least twice a week or she'll go out of her head with anxiety.'

I start biting my thumbnail, realize I'm doing it, and stop.

'Besides, my sister is not like other girls her age. She is incredibly responsible. She always keeps her word no matter what. If she hasn't called it is because she can't. I'm just praying that they've lost their phones in the desert, they've had their phones stolen, or something equally innocuous.'

Mark rubs his face thoughtfully. 'Don't get me wrong, but she's a teenager on holiday. Is it so unthinkable that she could have let her hair down in a place where no one knows her? In fact, it is usually teenagers who are the most responsible that feel the need to let off steam when they are far away from home. She could be trying to appear more of an adult by not reporting in to your mother daily, having fun, meeting people, partying and kicking up her heels a bit.'

I shake my head. 'Daisy doesn't drink. She's into clean living, healthy food and mystical things. She does yoga and chants mantras. The reason why she wanted to go to Alice Springs in the first place was because of the Aborigines. She thinks they are special and she wanted to go on a long 'dreaming' walkabout with them.'

'There you go then. She's on a walkabout.'

If only it was as simple as that. 'She would have told my mom then. Warned her that she would be out of touch for a few days.'

'Is there anything I can do to help?' Mark asks, frowning, finally getting the seriousness of the situation.

'Can you drive me home please?'

'Of course,' he says, and springs up instantly.

I get my bra on, quickly button up, and numbly follow him out of his apartment.

'Have the police been called?' Mark asks in the lift.

I can't think. All my thoughts are muddled. 'I don't know, but I don't think so.

There must be a simple explanation,' I insist. I realize I am desperately clutching at the idea that it is all a simple misunderstanding.

In the car I get onto Daisy's Facebook page. As my mother said, Daisy stopped posting two days back. Her last post was a picture of her and Marie standing outside Olive Pink Botanic Gardens in Alice Springs. I go into Marie's page. Her last post has a picture of her feeding a tame kangaroo. She is laughing, and I can see a little bit of Daisy in the photo too. I click out of Facebook and go into my email account. Daisy's last email to me is from five days ago. I read through it carefully. There is nothing in it but a great excitement and happiness to be out in the big wide world. I find Marie's mother's number in my address book and call her.

'Hello, Mrs. Reid. This is Daisy's sister, Dahlia,' I say calmly. If she is not worried I don't want to alarm her.

'Hello, dear. It's been a long time. You're in England now, aren't you?'

'Um ... yes.'

'Have you met the Queen yet?' she titters.

'Er ... no. I was actually calling to see if Marie had called you.'

She pauses. 'The last time I spoke to Marie was Thursday. They were going to go into the desert and I think she'll only call again when they get back to Adelaide.'

'Right.'

'Is anything the matter, child?' Worry has climbed into her voice.

'No. No, I just wanted to contact my sister. Her phone is off.'

'Oh yes, apparently there is no reception in the desert,' she says, relieved.

'Of course. I've got to go. Somebody's calling me. Thank you, Mrs. Reid.'

I end the call.

'You've got to call the police, or the American Embassy in Australia,' Mark says softly.

'I plan to,' I say quickly, but I don't want to call them yet. That would be acknowledging that she was truly missing. She can't be. I just want it to be a misunderstanding. I don't want Daisy to be missing. All kinds of horrible thoughts flash through my mind. They were going to the desert. What if they are lost there? What if they are lying somewhere, robbed and raped? Oh God!

I frown and try to think of where Daisy had told me she was going to stay in Alice Springs. I go back into her WhatsApp messages and find the name there. I Google the budget hotel and call them. A very sleepy man with a thick Australian accent answers the phone.

'Yeah, yeah, this is the bloody Traveler's Center. What do you bloody want?'

'I'm looking for my sister. She should have arrived yesterday.'

'Do you know what the bloody time is?'

I swing around to Mark. 'What time is it in Australia now?' I whisper.

'Day time,' he whispers back instantly.

I speak into the phone. 'I'm very sorry I woke you up, but please, I'm calling from England and I really need to find her. It's an emergency.'

'Go on. What's the Sheila's name, then?'

'Daisy Fury.'

'How you spelling that?'

'Daisy: D A I S Y Fury: F U R Y.'

'I got no one here by that name.'

My heart is racing in my chest. 'Can you check for one more name please?'

'Is that another sister of yours?' he asks sarcastically.

'No, it is the friend who was travelling with her.'

'What's her name then?' he grumbles bad-temperedly.

'Marie Reid.'

'How you spelling that?'

'Marie: M A R I E Reid: R E I D.'

'Sorry. No one here by that name.'

'Are you expecting anyone by that name?'

'Bookings are in a different book,' he says reluctantly.

'Please. Could you look? This is an emergency.'

He sighs elaborately. 'Hang on a minute.'

I hear him put the receiver down and move away. I even hear the thud of the book hit the surface of wherever he has thrown it on, then pages being turned. 'Yeah, it looks like they booked for five nights but were no shows.'

My heart is in my throat. Now I know without any doubt that it's not something simple. It's not innocent. 'OK. Thank you for your help,' I say and end the call.

'It's time to alert the police, Dahlia,' Mark says.

'Just one last call.' My last hope. I scroll up on my WhatsApp messages from Daisy. I know for sure she gave me the name. Bingo. Koala House. I Google Koala House. An aggressive sounding woman picks up.

'Hello, I am looking for my sister, Daisy Fury.'

'Yeah, I know her. She and her mate haven't settled their bill. All their stuff's still here. I'll keep it for two more days then I'm auctioning it off to the highest bidder.'

My stomach drops. My last hope is gone.

Mark parks outside my apartment. 'Do you want me to come in with you?'

'No. I'm sorry about tonight, Mark, and thanks for everything.'

'Are you sure you don't need me to go to the police station with you?'

I shake my head slowly. 'No, I need to speak to my mom first.'

'I'll call you in the morning. If you need me at all just call me. Doesn't matter what time of the night. Just call, OK?'

'OK,' I say distractedly. My mind is elsewhere. There must be some clue I'm overlooking. Something she told me. I refuse to believe that she is missing.

'I hope you get good news during the night.' He doesn't sound very hopeful.

I open the car door and let myself out.

'Goodnight, Dahlia.'

'Goodnight, Mark.'

I let myself into the apartment and find Stella stretched out on the sofa in front of the TV.

'You didn't put out again? The guy's going to end up with blue balls,' she says with a laugh.

I go and sit on the couch opposite her. I feel dazed and numb.

Her teasing expression changes. 'What's the matter?' she asks.

'I think my sister is missing somewhere in Australia.'

'What?' she screams dramatically, only for once it's not over the top melodrama. I'm screaming inside.

I cover my cheeks with both my hands. 'It looks as if she has vanished into thin air. Her phone is turned off or dead, her Facebook page hasn't been updated, and she never turned up at the bed and breakfast she had booked in to.'

Stella sits up and switches off the TV. 'Have you called the police?'

I shake my head in a daze. 'Not yet. I just found out and I can't bring myself to believe it is not all just a stupid mistake or misunderstanding.'

'Tell me everything,' she demands.

I pour out all I know so far. I can hardly believe the words that I am uttering, but to my

surprise, Stella doesn't scream or do the usual exaggerated theatrics.

'Let's think about this,' she says with a frown. 'If she had met with an accident, she would have been identified by now and your mother would have received a call. Best case scenario: she has gone on a walkabout and lost her phone. The other two options aren't so pretty. She's been taken by a serial killer, or she has been kidnapped by one of these gangs that sell women.'

I take a great gasping breath. 'Serial killer?'

'OK, I'll admit that that's more likely in America and not the outback, but she could have been taken by someone in the underworld!'

'Underworld?' I repeat stupidly.

She looks at me with big eyes. 'For the sex trade. I'm always watching movies about how they lure away young girls who are on vacation and sell them at these crazy auctions to super rich men.'

I cover my mouth with my hand. Silent tears escape from my eyes and roll down my face. I can't help it. I cannot imagine someone as gentle as Daisy kidnapped and held captive somewhere. It would destroy her.

Stella scoots forward and grasps my knee. 'I'm not saying she has, but if she has, the police might not be able to help. Even if we go to them right now, with the time difference, there might not be much they can or will do. We can go in the morning. Right now, we ask Zane for help!'

My eyes widen. 'Zane?'

'Not Zane personally, but Noah. I overheard him talking the other day. Zane has contacts in Australia, and if I am not mistaken he has some kind of office in Adelaide. If Daisy has been taken by anyone from the underworld, Zane is the best person to locate her.' She snatches her phone from the coffee table and dials it. While it is ringing she looks at me, and smiles encouragingly.

'Hey, Noah' she says. 'I need your help.' He says something and she nods even though he cannot see her. 'It's my roommate.' She glances at me. 'Yeah, that one. It was actually my uniform.' She takes a deep breath. 'Anyway, her sister's gone missing while backpacking with her friend in Alice Springs, Australia. Do you think you can put the word out and see if anyone knows or has heard of her?' She stops to listen. 'You have to ask Zane first? Right. OK.' She directs a look at me while talking to him. 'Can I send a photo of her to your phone?'

I nod vigorously and immediately send the photo to Stella's phone.

'Yes, I can do that right now. How long before you get back to me? OK, we'll be here. Thanks a lot, Noah. I really appreciate this.'

She kills the call and looks at me. 'He'll have to ask Zane first, but he thinks there should be no problem putting the word out.'

'How long before he asks Zane?'

'Zane's there now. He's doing it right away.' She sees my message and forwards the photo on to Noah.

I bite my lip. Part of me is utterly terrified for my sister and yet another part of me is suddenly wildly alive at the mention of Zane.

'I'm going to get you a brandy. You look as white as a sheet.'

She pours us each a large shot, and I chuck mine down my throat. It burns all the way to my belly. Nothing feels real.

'Thank you,' I whisper to Stella.

'You'd do the same for me,' she says, cracking a smile.

The phone rings and we both jump like startled cats. She picks up her phone, looks at the screen and announces, 'Noah.'

'Hello,' she says, listens, then says incredulously, 'He does?' She listens again while looking at me with a surprised expression.

'What?' I mouth silently.

She raises her palm to indicate I should wait until she finishes. 'OK, I'll bring her now.' She ends the call and looks at me, her eyes as big as dinner plates.

'Zane wants to see you, *now*.'

-I pick my poison ... and it is you-

Six

Dahlia Fury

We take a taxi to Zane's house. The trip is almost surreal, winding through the familiar streets, my heart filled with anxiety for my sister, and something totally inappropriate—throbbing excitement at the prospect of seeing the Russian again.

My hands are shaking so much I can't even separate and pull out the correct notes from my wallet. Stella takes my purse out of my useless hands and does it herself. We step onto the pavement and the taxi drives off. I look up at the impressive façade of Zane's home. There are three floors above ground and every one is lit up.

Stella looks sideways at me. 'Ready?' she asks.

It's not cold, but I shiver. 'As ready as I'll ever be.'

She straightens my collar and says in that English way of hers, 'Chin up. You'll be all right, duckie.'

We walk up the white stone steps and Stella rings the bell.

Noah opens the tall door and we enter the grand hallway with its black and white chequered floor, massive glittering three-tiered chandelier, and its curving double staircase. How different this place seemed to me on my first trip here. Then I went down the stairs, vaguely irritated to have been manipulated into the situation I found myself in, to that small, dim room, and learned how little I knew myself.

'He's through there,' Noah says to me, pointing to a door down a corridor.

Even he looks different. I had seen just a big goon the last time. Now he seems like a helpful figure that I want to envelop in a great hug and thank him profusely. 'Thank you for your help,' I say guiltily.

He nods gravely. 'No worries. When you're finished come and find us in the kitchen through there.' He points a stubby finger to another corridor in the opposite direction.

Stella squeezes my arm. 'Good luck,' she whispers, a deep longing swimming in her eyes. She wants to be the one going in to see Zane.

'Thank you, Stella,' I murmur gratefully. I know how much it must cost her.

I straighten my shoulders and walk down the corridor. Every step I take makes me feel more and more jittery. My back is rigid, my insides are all twisted into hard knots, and my heart is banging like it's about to burst. I stand in front of the door and turn my head around nervously. Stella and Noah are still standing where I left them. Stella nods encouragingly and mouths, go on.

I raise my hand and knock on the door.

'Enter,' the voice I have wet-dreamed about and longed to hear again, calls out.

I turn the knob and push the heavy door open. It is a large cavernous room, but I can only see Zane. My breath catches, and as soon as my eyes find his I feel myself exhale. Aching and weakness roll through my body. I feel as if I have not really been alive the last three months.

My eyes greedily drink him in. He is sitting behind a desk and is wearing a black shirt, the first two buttons distractingly undone, with a finely tailored dove grey jacket. His hair is slightly shorter than I remember. Although his hands are lying on the desk top, relaxed and loose, his face is expressionless, his eyes glittering like blue stars. Suddenly I think of him the way I last saw him. Naked and ferociously finger fucking me. What little control I have slips away and heat rushes up my neck and face.

He says nothing. Simply leans back in his chair and watches me. Palpable tension starts rising between us and he allows the feeling to build. It is feral and primal. I get lost in its hypnotic pull, and for a few seconds I forget why I am really here. I swallow hard. *Get a grip, Dahlia. You're here for Daisy. Laughing, freckle faced Daisy. Not to fall into the trap of his attraction.*

Closing the door I walk into the cage, OK, room. My knees are shaky. I feel quite unsteady. I stop a couple of yards away from him and watch his fingers, long and manicured, pluck at his collar.

'We meet again, *rybka,*' he says.

'You said you could help find my sister.' For some strange reason my voice sounds shrill and accusing.

His eyebrows rise. 'I said I'd try. I could put the word out, but no promises.'

'That's good enough for me,' I soothe quickly.

'Sit down and tell me what happened,' he invites politely.

I walk up to one of the chairs opposite him, sink gratefully into it before haltingly telling him the whole story. It's hard to focus. My thoughts keep recalling his touch and the words he said to me those months ago. He listens with narrowed eyes. Sometimes his eyes slip away to roam my body which makes me falter, and makes those luminous eyes return to my face.

'So do you think you can help?' I ask hopefully.

'If I can't find her nobody else can,' he says quietly.

'Oh, thank you. Thank you so much,' I gush, feeling like shit for all the horrid things I have repeatedly accused him of. Fortunately, it all happened in my head.

He keeps his eyes focused on me. 'I will help, but nothing is for free, rybka. If I give you something you want, then you must give me something I want.'

My mouth falls open. It is like looking at a beautiful butterfly and having it suddenly morph into a wasp and sting you in the ass.

'What do you want from me?' I ask, my voice, a whisper.

'You.'

His face is stoic. I stare at him blankly. This can't be real. Did I just hear him say, *you*?

As in me. Dahlia Fury. Am I even awake? 'What?'

'For one month I want you to be mine. Totally and utterly. Day and night. To submit to me and to do anything I ask of you.'

I prevent my jaw from hitting the ground. 'Just to clarify. You want me to be your slave?'

His lips curve into a wicked grin. 'Sexual slave. There is a big difference.'

Yeah, I'm awake. A misogynist through and through. And to think I felt guilty just now about my thoughts! 'Are you fucking with me?' I ask. My voice is pretty mild considering the murderous nature of my thoughts.

'No,' he says calmly.

'I have a boyfriend, OK?' I say.

He shrugs, casual and uncaring. 'Then I hope he is an understanding man,' he says.

I shake my head in disbelief. 'What is wrong with you? No man is going to understand something like this.'

'Then I'm afraid you'll have to choose.' He pauses. 'Boyfriend or sister?'

My anger deflates quickly and soundlessly. Daisy. Laughing, freckled little Daisy. 'What about my work?' I ask. I feel as if I have been anesthetized.

His jaw is as hard as granite. 'Take a month off.'

'They won't allow me to do that,' I protest uselessly.

'You decide. Work or sister?'

'You're a monster,' I accuse numbly.

He nods. 'Thank you.'

'That was *not* a compliment.'

He lifts one shoulder in an elegant shrug. 'Maybe not in your world, but it is in mine.'

I take a step back. 'You're mad.'

He seems genuinely surprised. 'Because I want you to be my sexual slave for a month?'

'Yes. What a horrendous idea. In this day and age.'

'Would it be so bad to submit to me?' he asks softly.

I feel my insides begin to tremble. I clasp my hands together so hard my nails dig into my flesh. 'I ... I could be with you for a month ... as an equal.'

He shakes his head. 'That would not be acceptable.'

I scowl. 'Why do I have to be in such a demeaning position?'

'Because that is what I want from you,' he says coolly.

I feel a rush of rage flood over me. It makes me feel giddy. If only I could stand up and walk out. How I ever wasted three months mooning over this unfeeling ass was beyond

me. He says nothing, just watches me silently. The silence grows. 'How can you be so evil? My sister has done nothing to you!' More silence.

I pause, then quietly sigh. 'I'm not into any kinky stuff.'

'How would you know what you're into? You've never tried anything but straight sex.'

'How do you know what I have and haven't tried?' I parry, although he is astonishingly spot on.

He laughs. 'Let's put it this way. If I do something to you and you even look for a second like you're not enjoying it, I'll stop immediately.'

'Thanks for offering to be so considerate, but I'm *not* going to be your sexual slave,' I say sarcastically.

'Then we have no deal,' he says abruptly.

I spring to my feet. I can no longer sit still. 'I don't believe this. You're just revolting. What kind of person are you?'

'I am an opportunist. I see an opportunity, I take it.'

I place my hands on the desk and lean forward. I thought looming over him would give me more power, but I am in for a shock. He tilts his chin upwards until his eyes are slits and locks gazes with me. Inside the piercing blue orbs, I see a bright, cold universe that goes on forever. It is so pitiless and ruthless that it makes me jerk back in horror.

I feel a slow panic shake me. How could I have imagined or fantasized that I could ever be anything but a temporary toy to a man like this? He lives a life exponentially faster than mine, in a kingdom of his making.

'You will be required to submit to a medical exam and be declared disease free first,' he says. It is the great sales trick. Don't ask the customer if he wants to buy it, ask him what color he wants it in or when he wants it delivered. Assume he has already agreed. Zane is talking about the details as if I have already agreed.

'And what happens if I am carrying some communicable disease?'

'Then I will have to protect myself.'

I draw a shaky breath. 'Will you take an exam too?'

One side of his mouth curves upwards. He is amused. 'No.'

'Why not?' I demand curiously.

'Partly because I am cleaner than a newborn baby, and partly because I fucking make the rules in this relationship. I tell you what to do and you do it.'

I shake my head, still unable to believe what has happened to my ordinary night out. Where did all this come from? It feels like I have fallen down a hole into a parallel universe where unthinkable, inconceivable things happen as if they are the most normal things ever.

'Are you on some form of contraception?' he asks.

See what I mean about unthinkable, inconceivable things. 'No,' I say curtly.

He nods easily. 'No problem. The doctor will prescribe it for you.'

'I can't believe you need to force a woman like this,' I say in a last ditch effort to shame him.

'If it makes you feel better to pretend I am forcing you then go ahead and think that.'

'You don't call this,' I wave my hand between us, '*blackmail* forcing me?'

'I'm not forcing you, *rybka*. You have a choice. You can always say no.' His voice is silky and full of slick charm.

'What the hell kind of choice is it if saying no means I may never see my sister again?' I ask bitterly.

'I admit, it's a difficult choice,' he concedes, 'but it's still a choice.' His expression is supremely indifferent and unaffected.

'You're sick,' I hiss.

He stands, his chair wheeling back noiselessly on the carpet, and I find myself backing away. I realize what I am doing and stop moving. Nervously I watch him walk towards me. God, he is so much bigger than Mark. I gulp down the rush of irrational fear when he towers over me. He is standing so close I feel the heat coming from his body and smell his lust for domination.

He lifts a hand and brushes a strand of hair away from my eyes. My skin immediately reacts to his touch. It starts to heat up, tingle and burn. I suppress the insane desire to clutch his shirtfront and jerk him towards me. It is disgusting and I'll never understand it, but I am filled with the burning need to taste him. With an iron will I force myself to stay still.

'What color are your eyes?' he murmurs.

'Hazel,' I say in a voice that sounds like I have been hypnotized.

'Hazel? No. They are like chameleons. They change shade according to what you wear and what you are feeling. They are the color of caramelized sugar when you are angry. They glow yellow like a wolf's eyes when you are turned on, and they are dragon green when you climax.'

I flush from head to toe.

He claws his hand in the hair at my nape and grasps a fistful. 'Why do you hesitate? You know you want it.'

'To be your sexual slave?' My voice is hoarse.

'To lose control. To have dirty animal sex. To come so hard you can't stop.'

He holds me firmly by my hair and lowers his face until his mouth is an inch away from mine. I stop breathing. He sniffs my cheek like a wild animal.

'He left you unsatisfied tonight,' he growls.

I jerk my face away. Away from the insidious warmth of his breath. My scalp stings, but the really scary thing is I want 'it'. I want everything he is talking about. I want it with a kind of mad desperation.

'My sister,' I gasp desperately.

'Do we have a deal, *rybka*?' he asks softly.

Seven

Dahlia Fury

I arrive at the doorway of a big and fabulously clean kitchen. Whoever cleans it deserves a medal. Stella is sitting at the island table staring into a generous glass of red wine. Noah is eating some open textured, black bread, probably Russian. A glass jar of artichokes in oil is open. As I watch he forks an artichoke, and still dripping, stuffs it into his mouth and chews slowly.

I cough politely and Stella turns around to look at me. God knows what I look like but she jumps off the chair and cries, 'What's the matter? Can't he help?'

'We have to go home, Stella,' I tell her. I feel empty inside.

'What's happened?' she asks again.

The phone on the wall rings. Noah swallows his food and rushes to pick up the receiver.

He listens. 'Right boss,' he says, returns the receiver to its cradle and turns to us.

'Boss wants me to give you girls a ride back.'

He takes his mobile out and calls someone. 'Got to go out on an errand. Can you take over?' He wipes his mouth on a paper napkin. Another man comes in through what looks like the back door. He is big and mean looking. His black eyes skim over us but he does not smile or offer any kind of greeting.

'How long will you be?' he asks Noah.

'As long as it takes to drop them off.' He turns towards Stella. 'Where do you girls live?'

'Victoria,' Stella says.

'You ready to go?' he asks me.

'Bye, Yuri,' Stella says.

'Yeah, bye,' Yuri says, sitting on the stool that Noah just vacated, and picking up the bread knife.

As soon as we get into our apartment, Stella turns to me. 'Are you going to tell me what happened or what?' she asks impatiently.

I sigh heavily. Oh God. What a horrible mess. The last thing I want to do right now is

hurt Stella. 'Come and sit down with me, Stella,' I say tiredly and walk towards the couch.

She follows, and instead of sitting on the sofa with me, she sits on the flowery armchair next to it. Perhaps subconsciously she already knows that I am going to wound her.

I don't beat about the bush. I take a deep breath and plow straight in.

'Zane will help to find Daisy, but if he does manage to locate and bring her back safely, he wants me to ... become his ...' (I tried, I really did, but I simply couldn't bring myself to say sexual slave), 'mistress for a month.'

'Sorry?' she gasps. Her eyes are wide and shocked. For a moment we stare at each other. Then her eyes widen with disbelief. 'You're not bloody serious?'

'I am.'

All kinds of thoughts flit across her expressive face. She can barely control her strong emotions. Unable to watch her suffering, I drop my eyes to the floor.

'What did you say to him?' Her voice is tight.

I raise my head. 'I said yes.'

She closes her eyes.

'I'm sorry, Stella.'

She opens her eyes and they are hard and probing. 'What really happened that time you replaced me, Dahlia?'

I wince inwardly. 'The way I was dressed and the unprofessional quality of my massage made him aware that I was no certified masseuse. He assumed I was a prostitute.'

'What a bloody cheek?' she explodes. 'Didn't you explain?'

'Of course I did.'

She shakes her head as if trying to clear it. 'So what ... did he make a pass?'

'Yes.' I don't tell her what really happened because that's nobody's business but mine.

'I knew it,' she cries suddenly. 'I knew something must have happened.'

'What? How?'

'Because you used to look at me with puppy dog eyes every time I came back from my appointments with him, and you were secretly cleaning the bathroom and toilet during the period of our agreement.'

'Yeah, I did that,' I admit guiltily.

'Why didn't you just tell me?' she asks plaintively.

I look at her pleadingly. 'I didn't want to hurt you, Stella.'

'What happened to us telling each other the straight-up truth?' she asks resentfully.

'I'm sorry I blew smoke up your ass. I was so confused.'

She draws a sharp breath and looks horrified. 'You were confused? That means *you* wanted him too,' she deduces.

My cheeks burn as I nod slowly.

She throws up her hands. 'Oh God! I don't believe this.'

'I'm sorry. Really I am. The last thing in the world I wanted to do was hurt you.'

She frowns. 'And now he wants you to be his mistress?'

'Only for a month,' I say, and I am shocked at how bitter my voice sounds.

She presses her lips together. She looks as if she is about to cry and my heart goes out to her. 'That was a low thing to do, Dahlia. I don't think we can be roommates anymore,' she says, her voice breaking, and turning on her heels, heads for her room.

I shoot my arm out and catch her. I look into her eyes. 'Just like you I couldn't help the way I felt. I wasn't expecting to feel like that. I don't want to feel the way I do,' I explain quietly.

'Yeah? If you were a real friend you would have told me.'

'Told you what, Stella? That I had the hots for the rude, arrogant man who had mistaken me for a prostitute? I wanted to forget that incident. I had rejected him and I thought I would never see him again. Anyway, what would it have mattered to you? You were not going out with him, and you yourself said you had zero chance of ever going out with him. You knew he had loads of ten feet tall girlfriends. What's the difference if he made a pass at me too?'

Her eyes sparkle with anger. 'The difference is you never told me. You made a fool of me. Call me old-fashioned, but friends don't do that to each other, Dahlia.'

'You were the one who forced me to go in the first place,' I cry out in frustration.

'And that's your excuse for being a lousy friend?' she asks sadly.

'I'm sorry I hurt your feelings,' I say beseechingly.

'Forget it, Dahlia. I don't need you to feel sorry for me,' she says with quiet dignity.

She pulls her arm out of my grasp and runs off to her room. I know she is really upset and hurt because she does not slam the door. I slump down on the couch and close my eyes. It's all way too much to deal with.

I think of Daisy. Where the hell are you, Daisy?

Suddenly tears are burning the backs of my eyes. I curl up on the couch, my mouth already opening to start crying when my phone rings. I look at it and it's my mom. I close my mouth, take a deep breath and accept the call.

'You didn't call me back,' my mom sobs.

'I'm sorry, Mom. I'm taking a flight back home tomorrow.'

'What about Daisy?' she asks frantically.

'Some people I know are looking for her, Mom,' I say with conviction.

There is a pause. 'Who are these people?'

'Powerful people, Mom.'

'Will we have to pay them?' she asks in a small worried voice.

'No, Mom. We won't. They're just doing it out of the goodness of their hearts.'

After my call, I go to my room. I don't allow myself the luxury of crying. I owe it to Daisy to be strong. I sit up the whole night and make a list of everything I can remember about Daisy's trip, going through all our phone conversations, our WhatsApp messages and emails, and note down anything at all that can be of help to the police or Zane. Then I make two copies. One I email to my mom to take to the police station with her, and the other I send to the number Zane asked me to send it to.

I buy my airline ticket and check in online.

Then I open my wardrobe and pack a small suitcase. When it is done I stand at the window looking down at the street. A couple pass. The woman laughs and the man grabs her around the waist and kisses her. I stare at them blankly. In truth, I still can't believe that something bad has happened to sweet Daisy.

No, it's not that I can't believe it. I *absolutely* refuse to believe it.

Eight

Dahlia Fury

Long before Stella wakes up I am ready. I go down into the street already filled with people and take the tube to work. I work at Fey Aspen Literary Agency as a reader. It's my job to read through the slush pile (that's trade speak for unsolicited submissions from would be authors) and pick up any raw talent that our agency would like to represent. I read chick-lit, fantasy, women's general fiction and comedy; Elizabeth does mystery, horror, thrillers, sci-fi and crime; and Miranda does YA and children's.

It is a Friday, and Friday mornings are market days, so I carefully pick my way through the lettuce leaves and bits of rubbish strewn on the pavement and turn into Eustace road. The agency is based in what used to be a two-story house with a basement. I usually take the outside steps down to the basement where I work with two other girls. Instead, I run up the four stone steps and enter the front door.

The door opens out to a narrow long hallway. To the right is the reception area of the agency. It is a nice sunny room with tall bay windows and cream sofas. The longest wall is lined with bookcases crammed with the books written by the authors we represent. Some of them are famous bestsellers. The back wall is covered with black and white photographs of our top authors inside glossy black frames. Wendy, the receptionist and Fey Aspen's secretary, is already at her desk. She has a very bright smile.

'Good morning,' she greets cheerfully.

'Good morning to you too,' I say very much less cheerfully.

'I'm just making a mug of coffee. You want one?' she offers.

I smile. 'No thanks. Er ... is Fey around yet? I'd like to see her for a few minutes.'

'She's in, but she's got an appointment in less than fifteen minutes,' she informs.

'Can I just see her for five minutes? It's really important.'

'Let me check,' she says, picks up the phone and calls Fey.

'Thanks,' I say gratefully.

'Can Dahlia have five minutes with you now.' She listens. 'Yes, I told her, but she says it's important. Sure. I'll ring through as soon as they get here.' She puts the receiver down and smiles. 'Go on up.'

I run up the stairs to the first floor and knock on the second door. The first door is the conference room and the third door is where Ellen and Ruby work. They run the TV and films rights department.

'Come in,' Fey calls briskly.

I turn the handle and enter Fey's office. The same books and photo theme downstairs is carried over into Fey's office. She is sitting at her desk looking absolutely immaculate. Every single strand of hair is in place and her makeup is flawless. Nobody really knows how old she is, but she must be in her fifties or perhaps even older if rumor is to be believed.

'Come and sit down,' she invites.

I take a seat and quickly tell her about my sister going missing.

'Oh dear, you poor thing,' she says worriedly, her intelligent grey eyes narrowing. 'How absolutely awful.'

'So basically,' I add quickly. Too much empathy could undo me. 'I need to take a week off and go home to be with my mother.'

'Of course,' she agrees immediately. 'Of course, you must go home. You will go quite out of your mind with worry if you stay here.'

Her phone rings. She picks it up. 'Yes, ask her to wait a while. I won't be too long,' she says into the phone.

I jump up. 'Thank you so much. I should be off. I'm leaving this afternoon.'

She stands. 'I hope they locate your sister fast.'

'So do I,' I say and feel as if I am about to burst into tears.

'Please keep me informed. If there is anything at all I can do to help don't hesitate to ask,' she offers kindly.

'I will keep you informed and thank you for offering to help.'

I stand and walk to the door. There I hesitate.

'What is it, Dahlia?' she asks.

'Would it be all right if I worked from home for one month the way Elizabeth does? It might not be necessary, but if I needed to?'

She scowls. 'You mean from your mother's house in the States?'

'No, I'll be in England. I'll come in two or three times a week to collect the manuscripts and I'll read them at home. There'll be no difference in my work output.'

 83

'Ah,' she says softly, and I can imagine her brain trying to process why I might need to do that. I hold my breath. If she says no, I'll have to leave my job and I really would hate that. I like this agency and my job.

'Well,' she says finally, 'as long as it is just for a month. I'm rather fond of the idea of a bustling office. If everybody starts working from home, I'll be rattling my old bones here all alone.'

'I promise it'll only be for a month,' I tell her with a thankful smile.

'All right,' she agrees. 'If it's just for one month.'

'It might not even happen, but if does it will just be for the one month.'

She smiles and I detect pity in that smile.

'Thank you again,' I call, and run down the stairs.

I wave at Wendy from the hallway and keep going down the stairs into the basement. None of the girls are in yet, and it is dark and cold. I switch on the lights, turn up the radiators and go to the back where my desk is. I stand for a moment looking at my work station with its view of the small walled garden, and feel a horrible sense of sadness. *You're just going away for a few days, girl.*

I quickly tidy up my desk and put away the pile of unread manuscripts in my drawer and leave a note for the girls. I will miss them, their laughter, our tea breaks, and our many forays into the biscuit tin. It was how the girls solve all their problems. 'Have a biscuit,' they'd say with a smile. I open the tin and even the smell makes me heave. I close the tin, bade Wendy goodbye and exit the front door.

Outside the agency I call Mark. He picks up on the first ring.

'Hey, Mark. Do you think I could see you sometime today, before lunch if at all possible? Maybe we can grab a quick coffee somewhere.'

'I'm free now,' he says immediately.

We agree to meet in Kensington high street Starbucks in twenty minutes as it is convenient for both of us. I am first to arrive and I take a seat at the back by the toilets where most people prefer not to sit. Mark arrives five minutes later.

'Sorry, I'm late,' he apologizes. 'Horrendous traffic.'

'It's OK,' I say letting my eyes rove over him. He is dressed for work in a white shirt, tie, black slacks, black shoes and a brown leather jacket.

He kisses me lightly and casually on the lips. 'Want anything other than the usual?' he asks.

I shake my head.

'Not even a muffin?' he tempts.

The thought of a muffin makes me feel ill. 'I couldn't eat a thing,' I tell him.

'You poor darling,' he croons and gently squeezes my hand.

'I'm all right,' I say hurriedly, looking away from his gentle, strong eyes.

'Right. I'll go get the drinks,' he says decisively, and walks away.

There is no queue and he comes back quite fast with my milky latte and his cappuccino.

'Thanks.' I tear two sachets of sugar and pour them into my coffee. I stir it with the long spoon and lick off the froth. When I look up and Mark is watching me intently. I flush and drop my gaze. Putting my hands in my lap I straighten my spine. The sooner I tell him the better.

'After you dropped me off last night, Stella and I went to see a Russian Mafia boss.'

'You did what?' Mark splutters incredulously.

I worry my lower lip. 'I know what it sounds like, but I would have gone to anyone who I thought could help.'

He looks at me in disbelief. 'You *know* a Russian mobster?'

'Well, he's one of Stella's client's really.'

He runs his hand through his hair agitatedly.

'Anyway,' I say quickly. 'He agreed to help.'

He looks at me with wary eyes. He already knows he is not going to like what I've got to say, but the poor guy has no idea how bad it is going to be. 'In exchange for what?' he asks quietly.

I take a deep breath. 'Me.'

His jaw drops and he stares at me speechlessly for a few seconds. 'Me? What the fuck does that mean?' he blasts out, and I am glad I chose this deserted corner.

'He wants me to be his ... well, mistress for a month.'

Mark's eyes widen. 'You can't be serious.'

I shift uncomfortably. He is starting to make me feel like I have sold my soul or something. 'I am. If he finds Daisy, then he wants me to be with him for a month.'

'Who the fuck is this guy?'

'Does it matter?'

'Yes. You're my girl and I'm not allowing you to be with some thug for a month.'

I look him in the eye. 'It's not up to you, Mark.' My voice is soft, but firm.

He stares at me as if he is seeing me for the first time. 'I cannot believe that you are seriously considering doing this. You can't get involved with this kind of people, babe. They are dangerous. You can't predict them. He may be a sadist for all you know.'

'I've said yes.'

He gazes at me with hurt eyes. 'Without talking to me about it?'

'What would you have done if it was your sister?'

He doesn't take his eyes off me. 'I wouldn't give you up for anyone.'

'I love my sister, Mark. I can give up one measly month of my life for her. It's just sex. It is so little to have my sister back. I don't expect you to understand and I don't expect you to wait for me. I've come here today to break up with you.'

He reaches out a hand. 'Absolutely not. We don't break up for anything. I'm not beat. Maybe he won't even find her.'

I snatch my hand out of his and gasp, 'Don't ever say that. He is my best hope of finding Daisy.'

'I didn't mean it like that. I meant maybe the police will find her first.'

'It didn't sound like it,' I say.

'Come on, Dahlia. You can't drop this bomb on me now and not expect me to blow a gasket. For crying out loud we were about to have sex yesterday.'

I look down at my untouched latte.

'I *love* you. I can't bear even the thought of another man's hands on you.' His frustration and complete helplessness throbs in his voice.

I cover my head with my hands. Suddenly I just feel sick. Why do I have to be made to feel guilty and bear the responsibility for other people's feelings? First my Mom, then Stella and now Mark. I have enough on my plate as it is.

I drop my head. 'If he finds Daisy and I go to him, I don't want you to wait. I think it is not fair on you, and it would make me feel terrible to think you are waiting for me. I just want a clean break. Maybe we were never meant to be.'

For a few seconds there are only the muted sounds of the coffee house, then he says, 'Look at me, Dahlia.'

I lift my head.

'You can no more tell the waves not to come to shore than you can tell me not to wait.

I told you last night and I meant it. I'll wait for you forever if I have to.'

I close my eyes. They feel as if they are burning from lack of sleep and the need to just fucking cry my heart out. I'm hanging on to my strength by the tips of my fingernails. I open my eyes and fix them on him.

'Please, Mark. Just let it go. I am being bombarded from all directions. I don't think I can take much more. What I really need right now is a friend. Someone who doesn't want anything at all from me.'

To my surprise he nods. 'You want a friend? You got it. I'll be the best friend you ever had. Tell me what I can do to help you.'

I smile sadly at him. I know what it must have taken for him to say that. 'Nothing. Just knowing you're a friend that I can turn to is enough. I'm going back to Michigan this afternoon. I'll text you if I have any news, OK?'

He looks suddenly miserable. 'You're leaving?'

'Yeah, my mom needs me.'

'When are you planning to come back?' he asks anxiously.

I shrug. 'I don't know. I bought a one-way ticket and I'm playing it by ear.'

He nods slowly. I have never seen him look so devastated. I resist the desire to reach out and stroke his hand. That would just be cruel. In the end it is clear I will never love him the way he loves me.

'I guess it is goodbye,' I say softly.

He looks at me fiercely. 'What's his name?'

'What does it matter?' I say gloomily.

'Tell me,' he insists urgently.

'Zane. His name is Zane.'

His expression doesn't change, but his eyes flash suddenly.

'Do you know him?' I ask immediately.

'I know of him. He is called Zane, but his real name is Aleksandr Malenkov and he is a very dangerous man. A ruthless killer,' he says slowly. 'Think very carefully, Dahlia. You could be making a very big mistake.'

I feel a shiver go through me at the quiet horror in his voice. Yet another voice in my head says, Yes, this is the name that suits him far better than Zane.

Aleksandr Malenkov.

Nine

Dahlia Fury

When I go back to the apartment Stella is awake. Her door is open, the radio in the kitchen is playing, and I can hear her moving about. I stand at the doorway. She is cutting fruit to make her breakfast smoothie. She looks up from peeling a banana then looks away without saying anything.

'I'm leaving for the States today,' I say.

'Good,' she says, and chucks the banana aggressively into the blender.

'I've paid my rent for this month, but I'll pack all my stuff and leave it in a corner of the room so you can start to show the room to prospective tenants. I'll also make sure everything is out before the end of the month.'

'Great,' she says, and viciously rips the stem off a strawberry.

'All right then. I ... I guess, I'll see you around.'

'Have a safe flight,' she says without looking at me.

'Thanks,' I say backing away as she cracks an egg on the side of a bowl with unnecessary force.

I hear her curse loudly when the shell smashes and the egg ends up on the counter. I can't believe that our friendship is going to end like this. I love this woman and in my heart I have never betrayed her, no matter what she thinks. That thing with Zane just happened. I go into my own room, close the door and lean against it. I press my palms tightly against my mouth.

'Oh God!' I cry into them. Then I straighten my shoulders. I didn't do anything wrong. No one is going to make me feel guilty for doing everything I can to save little Daisy. I pull my two suitcases out from under my bed and put them on top of the bed. I won't take very long. I don't have that much stuff and I will throw away what I don't need. My eyes fall on the string of flower fairy lights that Stella and I bought together when we went to that Christmas fair. It was the last one and we had tossed a coin to decide who would have it. I won. I have just taken it down from the mantelpiece when there is a timid knock on the door.

'Yes,' I say immediately.

Stella stands at the doorway.

'Do you want these stupid lights or shall I just bin them?' I ask her, not looking at her directly.

'I don't want you to move out,' she says.

I turn to look at her. Tears pouring down her cheeks. I start crying too. 'I don't want to move out either,' I bawl.

She comes into the room and we hug each other and cry.

'I'm sorry I didn't tell you. Really I am,' I sob.

'And I'm sorry I was such a bitch yesterday,' she wails.

'No you weren't,' I cry.

'Yes, I was.'

'We sound like two cats caterwauling,' I sniff.

'I'll have the lights if you don't want them,' she says.

'God, you're so greedy,' I say with a half-laugh.

'That's not true. The only thing I'm greedy for is shoes,' she says.

I laugh through my tears.

She pulls slightly away from me. We stand facing each other. 'When are you coming back?'

'I don't know yet. I just know that I need to be with my mom right now. She went to the police station last night and they didn't give her much hope so I pray that Zane finds her.'

'I'm not going to have Zane as my client anymore. You were right when you said I shouldn't keep massaging him. The sooner I cut him off and start to heal, the better for me.'

I smile at her. 'That's very brave of you.'

'It's not easy. I'm so jealous of you, Dahlia. Why couldn't he have wanted me?'

'Come here,' I say, and taking her hand, pull her towards my bed. We sit next to each other. 'I want to tell you something.'

'What?' she asks, a note of caution in her voice.

'Zane doesn't want me to be his mistress. He wants me to be his ... sexual slave.'

Her eyes widen. 'What does that mean?'

'During that one month I have to do anything he wants sexually.'

'What does *anything* mean?' she whispers making air quotes around the word anything. 'Is he allowed to hurt you?'

'He says if it appears I'm not enjoying something he won't do it.'

Stella turns beetroot red. She looks at me wishfully. 'If you thought telling me this was

95

going to make me less jealous of you, you have no idea about me. I am even more jealous.'

My mouth drops open. 'What?'

'Just think. It is the ultimate sexual fantasy for every strong woman. To be forced to submit to a big and powerful man. To be completely at his mercy.' She fans herself with her hand. 'Oh god! It makes me hot and bothered just thinking about it.'

I stare at her. 'Really?'

'Absolutely.'

'Don't you want to be an equal partner in a relationship?'

'Pfftt ... equal in bed? God, no. Where's the fun in that? I love a man who lets his animal instincts take over. Who just wants to fuck hard. I want someone hot to look me in the eyes and tell me "Turn over you fucking slut. Get on your fucking hands and knees and put your ass up." Yup, that's my kind of man.'

Slightly shocked, I giggle. 'OMG! I can't believe that's what you like!'

'That's me. A total slut,' Stella says airily.

'Oh, Stella. I'm going to miss you so much.'

'I'll miss you more, because you'll be off doing different things and I'll have to come back to this empty flat. I'm warning you now that I'll be using your perfume and your black dress while you are gone.'

I hug her. 'You have my permission to blast yourself with my perfume and wear any of my clothes.'

She grins. 'This might work out all right, after all.'

I laugh. 'You know I was so sad last night when I thought I'd hurt you and you were mad at me.'

'You did hurt me and I was mad at you, but it's OK now. It was my fault. I was being silly; carrying a candle for him all this time when I could clearly see that I was nothing to him. Besides, you thought you were protecting me. I know you didn't mean to hurt me.'

'No,' I say sincerely, 'I wouldn't willingly hurt you for the world.'

'Yeah. I know that. I was just jealous. I still am actually.'

'Are you going to be OK?'

'Of course. I just have to accept that he doesn't want me. Maybe it's all for the best. I should move on.' She smiles. 'Yes, I'll get over it. This is good for me. One day I'll look back and be glad this happened.'

Stella offers to cancel two of her appointments and come with me to the airport, but I refuse.

'Saying goodbye to me here will be exactly the same as at Heathrow. Anyway I will be back soon.'

So we say our goodbyes on the street. I turn around to watch her as the taxi moves on. She looks alone and miserable. When the taxi turns the corner I look out of the window blankly. It is a typical gray English afternoon and even though Stella and I complain about it all the time, I feel really sad to leave it. It is hard to sit still in the taxi. My mind is so full of unfamiliar images and thoughts.

It is easier at the airport when I am caught in the procedure of taking a flight, but once I am seated in the plane the anxiety starts again. I don't sleep during the entire flight. The woman next to me snores like a hog so I put in my earplugs, close my eyes, and think of Daisy. I remember back to our childhood days when she used to beg me to make daisy necklaces for her. They were so precious to her she would wear them even when they were shriveled, brown and ugly.

I guess even then she was already so different than me. 'Does the grass feel pain when we walk on them?' she asked my mother when she was three years old. My mother used to roll her eyes and call her Silly Billy every time she came up with one of her totally odd questions.

When she was six she announced that she was becoming a vegetarian. She was no longer going to eat anything with a face. That was until she found out about the experiment with the woman and the cabbage. It's the one where plants are hooked up to machines that record their electrical emissions. A woman is then told to go into the room and violently butcher a cabbage.

The scientists notice the plant responds by showing distress, by increased and frantic electrical activity. They conclude that plants have the ability to understand violence and exhibit fear. A week later the same woman is told to walk into the room with a knife and though she does nothing this time, the plants mark her arrival with increased activity.

After my sister read that she became a fruitarian. Sometimes she will sit for hours outside not reading or listening to music, or talking to someone on the phone, but in her lingo just 'being'. To think of such a gentle creature being abducted and harmed makes my blood boil, and I jump up suddenly waking the woman beside who mutters with irritation and goes right back to sleep.

I walk up and down the aisle restlessly until I have calmed myself by thinking that maybe they have already found her. Maybe by the time I get off the plane my mom will have good news for me.

My mother comes to pick me up from the airport. One look at her face and I know that she has nothing new to tell me. She looks pale and frightened. I hug her tightly.

'I'm so glad you've come, Dahlia,' she whispers into my hair. Her voice trembles with anguish.

'They'll find her, Mom. I know they will.'

'Do you really think so?' she asks earnestly.

'Of course they will,' I say firmly.

She nods eagerly.

We hang on to each other like the survivors of a war and walk to the truck. Suzie, our pit bull is in the back. She jumps out and goes crazy, launching herself at me as she whimpers and yelps with joy.

'She knows something has happened to Daisy. She's been acting strange for the last three days,' my mom says.

'Of course she hasn't, Mom. She's just picking up your fear,' I say while Suzie licks the hell out of my face.

I take the keys from my mother and get into the driver's seat. We don't speak in the car. I can see Suzie in the side mirrors holding her gorgeous diamond shaped head against the wind. Her top lip is pushed right back and all her sharp teeth are exposed. I feel a tug of sadness at the sight. It feels very strange to be back home with my mom and Suzie and no Daisy.

Just as I pull into our driveway a text message comes through for me. I park the car and look at it. I have to look again. I lift my head and look at my mother.

'Oh, Mom,' I cry.

'What is it?' my mother asks in a panicked voice. 'What is it?'

I can't talk. I just start sobbing uncontrollably. All that emotion and fear I had stored ever since I heard that Daisy might be missing gushed out of me.

I hold the phone out to her. She snatches it from me and looks at the screen.

It is just two words.

Found her.

My mom looks at me, her eyes wide and shining with crazy hope. 'Is this what I think it is?'

I nod, tears streaming down my eyes.

Suzie is whimpering and scratching pitifully at the grill because she thinks something horrible has happened to us. I get out of the car, let her out and hold her tight.

'Daisy's coming back, Suzie,' I say again and again, sobbing hard into her silky fur.

It seems like an eternity passes before Daisy is back home. The reunion is odd. My mother and I cry buckets of tears and young Daisy comforts us as if we are the ones who have been through an abduction ordeal. Later we sit on the porch just staring at her. She gazes back serenely, one hand absently stroking Suzie's head.

'So you never saw the men who took you?'

'Never. Like I said we were walking back from the restaurant to the little hotel when a dusty white van pulled up, two men got out, grabbed us, and bundled us into the van. There were four of them, but they wore Disney character masks. They immediately blindfolded, gagged and tied us up.'

'Didn't you and Marie struggle?'

'No. One of the men had a gun which he pointed at Marie's head. We were so shocked and they were extremely efficient and professional. All the while they never spoke a word, and when we arrived at that house they kept their interaction with us at an absolute minimum. We knew there were girls in the other rooms because we heard them crying in the night. Once we tried to talk to them, but the men banged on the wall and we shut up and so did the girls.'

'Did they ever … hurt you?' my mom asks cautiously.

Daisy shakes her head so vigorously her brown curls bounce about like something in a shampoo advert. 'No, never. In fact, they treated us quite well considering. We had food to eat, bottled water to drink, and when it was really hot they switched on some kind of fan that blew air through slats at the top of the walls.'

'So how were you rescued?' I ask.

'Well, one day the men started scurrying around and talking urgently in whispers. Then they came in, blindfolded us, tied our hands, and put us into a van. Then they drove us to the edge of a little aboriginal town, dropped us off at the side of the road and drove off in a rush.

We could see a town not far off so we just walked to it.'

'Were you very scared?' I ask.

She grins cheerfully. 'Actually I wasn't.'

That baffles me. I stare at her face, clean of all make up except for a good spray from some homemade aromatherapy concoction from a plastic spritzer bottle.

'Why not? I would have been terrified,' I tell her.

She looks at me calmly. 'It's called the universal law of action and reaction. When you live a life never hurting another being, you cannot be hurt yourself.'

My mom squeezes Daisy's hand and tells her how brave she is, but I just sit back in the chair and shake my head in wonder at my sister. Here we were sick with worry and frightened half to death about what had happened to her, and there she was abducted, held prisoner by human traffickers, and merrily floating about in fairyland.

For a moment I wonder what would have happened if Zane had not intervened, then just as quickly I shove the loathsome thought away. May my sister always remain so innocent and blissfully ignorant of all the horrible things that can and do happen to millions of blameless creatures every single day. Her action and reaction universal law sucks big time, but she doesn't need to know it.

I smile at her. 'A fairy was sitting on your shoulder, Daisy.'

She smiles back. 'A fairy truly was. That fairy's name is Dahlia. Mom told me that you asked a friend to help. It was because of him that they got scared and dropped us off, isn't it?'

I nod slowly. Yes, the law of action and reaction was truly at play. If only she knew how it all really worked in this big bad world.

'What's his name?'

'His name is Aleksandr Malenkov.'

'Thank him for me,' she says with the biggest, sweetest, most adorable smile.

That night an email arrives from Aleksandr Malenkov's solicitors. The attachment is a twelve page Non Disclosure Agreement. I sign it without reading it and the next day a courier comes to pick it up. That afternoon I keep my appointment at the clinic for the necessary blood tests, and since my period came early thanks to all the stress I also go on the pill.

The test results arrive in a week and I send them on to Zane. The next day I say a tearful goodbye to Mom and Daisy and catch a flight back to England.

Stella is happy to see me. She sits on the bed and provides me with a bossy but entertaining running commentary as I pack a small suitcase to take to Zane's.

'No, don't take that. That makes your legs look like sausages. You have to take the red dress. That makes your boobs look twice the size they really are. Oh God, not that. It looks like you stole a tablecloth from a French bistro and stuck a belt on it. I was hoping you'd leave that behind for me, but all right, take that and the black ankle boots to go with it, etc. etc. etc.'

When the appointed time comes for me to leave, she kisses me on both cheeks. 'I can't believe you're leaving me to go live with a boy,' she wails in a baby voice, but her eyes are actually wretched.

'One month will fly by in no time,' I tell her.

'It will for you. It won't for me,' she replies.

Yeah, reckless behavior...

Ten

Dahlia Fury

It is not Noah, but Yuri who opens the door for me. 'I'll take your bags up to your room,' he says wearing a funeral director's expression.

'Thanks.' I hand them over to him.

'The boss is on the lowest floor, minus 3. You can take the stairs.' He jerks his head towards the stairs, 'Or the lift down that corridor.' He nods in the direction of the study where I met Zane the last time.

'I'll take the stairs,' I say.

'Keep going down until you reach the bottom.'

'OK. Thanks.'

A hefty, florid-faced woman in a black skirt and white blouse passes us on her way to the kitchen. She smiles politely at me and I smile back.

I take the stairs and start walking down into the lower floors. I go past the two flights of stairs I descended the last time to go to the massage room and down the last one. It opens up to another black and white chequered landing with a plinth holding an antique headless and armless statue, and under it a large arrangement of white flowers. Beyond it is a grand set of white and black doors. I grasp the intricately carved metal handles, push them open, and gasp with surprise.

The whole floor is a fabulous open plan, mosaic-covered, steamy bathhouse held up by a forest of pillars. Steam rising from a large raised pool mists the space, making it seem magical or from a different time. A time when powerful rulers of great empires lay in similar pools and scantily clad slave girls came to wash them. I breathe in the fragrance that has been poured into the water. Jasmine. Deliciously Oriental and exotic.

I walk towards the pool and stop when I am about twenty feet away from it. Inside the marble tub capable of fitting at least ten people, Zane is lying back facing me. His powerful shoulders and arms are out of the bubbling water and resting along the edge of the tub. His skin gleams like polished metal in the humid air.

His eyes are open and he is gazing at me. There is something very relaxed about his pose, but something frighteningly alert about his eyes. I think about that time when I looked into his eyes and saw that cold, pitiless universe they held within them. I let my gaze slide away from that barren wasteland.

I don't want to be afraid of him. He has done me a great favor. I want to show him my appreciation, my deep gratitude. I watch the ink on his body. Somehow it seems even more beautiful in this setting. I want to stand here a little while longer and simply soak in the decadent sight of this marvelous man in his luxurious pool.

'Won't you join me?' His voice is silky and caressing. Still, it is clearly not an invitation, but an order.

I lean against a pillar and take my shoes off. Then I unbuckle my watch and leave it next to my shoes. Barefoot, I advance on the smooth damp marble. I stand at the edge of the pool, my blood hot and thirsty for him.

'Is a sexual slave expected to wash her master?' I ask softly.

He remains very still. 'Take your clothes off.'

My heart starts pumping faster. I unzip my dress and let it slip down. I take off my bra, and though the expression on his face doesn't change in the slightest, his eyes flash when my breasts pop out. Letting the bra fall from my hand, I hook my fingers into the waistband of my panties and pull them down my legs. He doesn't say anything, just watches me expressionlessly as if I am an art exhibit that he is not sure he actually likes. I straighten, completely naked but for the layer of mist on my skin.

'Thank you for finding my sister,' I say, my voice a hoarse whisper.

His eyes gleam through the rising steam, black pupils fixed on me. 'Good. Show me how grateful you are,' he says.

There is a black lacquer container by the edge of the pool. It has loofahs, sponges, cloths, and soaps in it. I walk to it, pick up a cloth and a bar of soap, and go behind him. Getting on my knees I take his hand between mine and turning it palm up begin to meticulously wash his fingers. One by one. They are long and elegant, the pads firm and fleshy, the nails beautifully manicured. A pianist's hand, full of hidden strength. Like a sleek racehorse.

He turns his head and watches me, but I don't look at him. I keep my head bowed as I raise his hand. He smells of something wild, storm rain perhaps. With infinite gentleness I kiss the inside of his wrist, right on the tip of that cobra tattoo. His body freezes. My heart jumps sideways. My gaze flies to his face. Locks on his eyes.

Both of us are startled, me by the sudden shift in him, and him by something I cannot know. A shadow passes in his eyes. For a shocking microsecond he reminds me of a wounded animal, of the way Suzie looked at Mom and me when we went to pick her up from the animal shelter. Fear, pain, distrust, hope and a profound longing for love. But like a trick of light it is gone, and whatever scary secrets he hides remain in the dark. I am reminded of a little used word I learned a long time ago: bloodthirsty. He yanks his hand out of my grasp suddenly and curls it around my wrist in a steely grip.

'Squat.' The word is like a gunshot. It slams against the hard surfaces in that space, reverberates up my spine, and hurts my teeth.

I stare at him in horror. I can't breathe. He wants me to assume the most demeaning position possible! I draw in the thick, humid air in a rush and it escapes in a hiss through my clenched teeth.

'No.' My tongue glides pleadingly over my lips. 'Please.'

His eyes watch my tongue. 'I'm not in the habit of repeating myself,' he says coldly.

My stomach twists dangerously, but I force myself not to react with anger. I won't give him the satisfaction. It is an ordeal but I shall triumph. I recognize what he is doing. He is establishing the terms of our arrangement. There is to be no tenderness, no kindness ... not even the simplest loving gesture is to be allowed. It is going to be just sex. The kind of impersonal interaction men have with prostitutes. A transaction between two uninvolved parties. He mistook me for a prostitute once, and he has been determined ever since to treat me as one.

'Fuck you,' I whisper, my flesh sweaty.

His eyes glitter like ice chips on a freezing morning.

As I look into those cold, electric eyes, a strange sensation of invincibility overtakes me. I feel like Cleopatra or Delilah. A temptress full of rage and lust. Then too, the men thought they were the ones with the power. Little did they know. I will show him. I'll show him I can be naked and proud and fierce even in this wet heat. The air between us is syrupy, flecked with water drops. These are the last few moments before the battle.

I sit back into a squat and expose my slick and ready entrance. He reaches out a hand, drags his fingers along my slit, and watches me shudder violently. I force myself not to avert my eyes from his taunting ones even though I can hardly bear for him to see the flush of lust on my face.

Still staring into my defiant eyes, he parts the wet folds and spreads the moisture pouring from within. With deliberate carelessness he inserts a long finger into me. Goddamn, it feels like it's molten hot. I want to scream. My muscles contract helplessly around the intrusion. There is nothing I can do but take it. Take his finger. Take his cock. Take his dominance.

'Having fun, Dahlia?' he mocks.

'Gloating, Zane?' I retort, but my voice is choked and unsteady.

He chuckles. 'I'm going to enjoy taming you, little spitfire,' he says, moving his finger in and out of me.

With a great deal of effort, I pass the words through my lips. 'You are despicable.'

'I know,' the son of a bitch agrees arrogantly, as he puts his thumbs where my thighs join my body and curves his large hands around my buttocks. With a smirk on his wicked lips he eases his head between my legs and begins to lap at my swollen sex. With each little movement of his tongue, I suppress the desire to whine and whimper with pleasure.

I have been on edge for this for so freaking long. Pushing back the lips of my pussy, Zane plunges his tongue into me, and suddenly it is no longer possible to hold back. No longer possible to pretend to be fierce or proud. I grasp his shoulders and cry out with abandon and ecstasy.

His hands dig into my flesh as he holds me in place while the torrent of pleasure makes my world erupt into hot white light. My muscles spasm and I arch my back, my spine jerking uncontrollably. I am only vaguely aware of screaming. The orgasm is long and strong, and I think I lose track of time.

When he lets go of me I slowly lean forward, and lay curled on my side, panting and utterly drained. My muscles quiver as if I have run a long race. I turn my face in his direction and I see a dark predatory glint in his eyes. He is hungry for me! Instantly my body responds to the hunger with an insistent aching between my legs.

I watch him place his palms on the edge of the pool, haul himself up into a crouched position and stand. Again, as I thought the first time I saw him move, I have the definite impression he is trained in stealthy combat maneuvers. Water sluices off his tightly muscled, naked body. Angled out from his sleek body, his cock is red, thick and massive. Underneath it hangs a heavy sack with purple and green veins. I look up at him almost in awe.

He is truly splendid.

He takes a step towards me, slips his hands under my neck and my knees and lifts me up into his arms. I make a small mewling sound. I have never heard that sound come from me before. When I am with him I don't recognize myself. My hands curl around his neck.

He carries me past the forest of pillars towards a large round green divan covered with many pillows, and throws me onto it as if I am no more than a rag doll. He stands over the bed and watches my breasts jiggling as I bounce. I stare up at him as he crouches down and spreads my supine body out. Pulling my legs apart he impales me, his hard shaft ramming into me so suddenly that there isn't time for me to adjust to his size. It shocks me into a long whimper of submission.

That drags a rumbling animal growl from his throat.

Every inch of me feels like I am on fire. My hips thrash upwards as my hands grab the firm, strong buttocks and shove him towards me, our bodies crash together and he is in, balls deep. I scratch my nails down his spine like a wildcat and wrap him so tightly to me it feels as if we are melded together. I know exactly what I want. I want every last inch of him inside me. I need to feel him in the depths of my belly.

'Make yourself come,' he orders.

His voice fucks my ear. I stare up at him angrily. His cock swells and jerks inside me.

'Do it,' he growls.

I arch my back, press into him, and grind myself against him until I feel a knot forming in my stomach. At that moment he slips his hands under me, lifts me up and, for his pleasure begins to slam into me. He fucks me like a feral beast, the veins in his throat bulging. The burn inside me turns into raging flames.

'Zane,' I cry lustily, my whole body jerking under his.

I claw at the sheets, the cushions, his skin. It feels as if my body is shattering into a million pieces. I thrash. I cry. I scream. His hot seed spills deep inside me.

I watch his face, contorted and transformed, his eyes darkened. For the first time since I have known him he is reachable. He catches me watching him and the switch back to the cold, unreadable man totally in control of himself is instantaneous and effortless.

Breathing hard I stare up at him. He is still lodged inside me. There is a whole frozen world hidden behind those eyes. Another woman might have thought she could thaw that world and live in it. I don't.

'Come to my study in an hour's time. I will require you again then,' he says and withdraws from my body.

My heart goes cold. I watch him stand, his cock still half erect and shining with our juices. He turns from me and begins to walk away. He stops at a low stool and picks up a dressing gown. He shrugs into it and leaves without ever looking back.

Eleven

Dahlia Fury

I listen to the doors click shut before I sit up on my elbows and look at the steam rising from the pool. It beckons to me. I have never been in such a pool. His milk flows out of me and stains my thighs as I get off the divan and walk to the water.

I lower myself into its silkiness, lie back where I had found him, and let my limbs sway in the water.

Ah ...

He has declared war.

I duck underwater. Even the bottom of the pool is gorgeous. A naked Adonis type hero wearing laurel leaves is fighting mythical snake-like monsters. It is made of thousands of tiny pieces of mosaic.

I emerge a few seconds later and slick my hair back away from my face. I swim back to the side and notice what I had been too strung up to see before; a bucket of ice with an

 119

unopened bottle of champagne inside it, two flute glasses, a shallow dish full of ice, and two silver bowls, one smaller and covered, and the other much bigger and uncovered There are large strawberries inside the uncovered bowl. I lift the lid of the smaller bowl and find a mound of shiny black caviar.

I grasp the neck of the bottle, fish it out of the bucket and look at the label. My eyebrows rise. Well, well, Dom Perignon. Never had that before. I pop its cork and pour myself a glass. I raise the glass of fizzing liquid in a silent toast to me. *Here's to me.* I take a sip.

'Mmmm. Lovely.'

I eye the caviar, but reach for a strawberry and bite into it. It is so ripe and ready sweet juice runs down my fingers. For some strange reason it reminds me of the time I was four maybe five years old and I found a half-eaten bright pink lollipop in our garden. I remember watching my mom yelling at me from the window not to eat it, and me defiantly licking the dirt encrusted sweet anyway, finding it rough and delicious on my tongue. By the time my mom ran out I had not only chewed it up, but swallowed it all, so there was no chance she would put her finger in my mouth and hook it out. She smacked the backs of my legs, but I refused to cry. I didn't think I had done anything wrong.

I take another delicious sip of champagne, lie back and close my eyes.

How the fuck am I going to survive one month of this? Will I really go to him again in an hour and be treated as a complete sex object? I should be disgusted, but the contrary is true. Even the thought of going to him merely to slake his lust makes me feel all hot and tingly. It seems totally crazy that I could feel addicted to his body when he deliberately treats me like a prostitute, but I am.

I take another strawberry and wash it down with champagne. I wish Stella was here with me. What a laugh it would be. She'd be reaching for the caviar for sure. I down the glass and pour myself another. No point wasting good champagne. Besides, I *love* champagne.

Four, oh all right, maybe five glasses of champagne later I gingerly climb out and get dressed. My movements are quite sloppy. The zip won't go all the way up on my dress. I have to conclude that I am slightly tipsy. I sit on the floor to put on my shoes and my head swims. Jesus, I am more pissed than I thought. A giggle escapes. It was fun though.

He said one hour, but it can't have been more than half an hour. I could get myself some coffee. Sober up before I go to him. I'll lose the next battle too if I go like this. Besides it's bad form. I push myself upright and, swaying on my feet, head towards the door.

'Whoa, this floor is a proper tragedy,' I say. My voice is worryingly slurred and very loud in the empty space.

I push open the doors and contemplate the curving stairs. They seem to go on forever. I grasp the cool banister and, holding on to it, take the first step. I lift my other foot and put it on the next step. *Derived from patience*. I shall triumph.

'The prisoner shall be free,' I mutter to myself as I ascend to the surface of the earth.

As my feet touch the ground floor a woman dressed in a white skirt and black blouse crosses my path.

'Hello,' I greet brightly. She may be another captive sexual slave. I giggle to myself.

She nods and runs off like a frightened rabbit. I watch her disappear down the corridor and I wonder how many people are held in the house. I sway towards the kitchen. As I get closer I can hear people talking. I push open the door. Noah is sitting at the kitchen counter drinking a cup of coffee, and the matronly woman I had seen earlier is preparing food.

'Hey,' I say very carefully. I don't want them to know I am a bit high.

'Come in and meet Olga. She is the chef,' Noah says.

'Hello, Olga,' I enunciate clearly.

Olga smiles, but doesn't offer any greeting.

Noah looks at his watch. 'Boss wants you in the study in twenty minutes.'

'I'd rather die than submit,' I declare grandly.

Noah's eyes narrow and Olga's widen with surprise. I might have crossed a line back there, but damn, I hate the idea that every person in this house knows I am here just to service Zane's sexual needs. 'Can I please have a cup of coffee?' I ask gloomily.

Noah stands up and goes to the machine. 'Cappuccino, espresso, latte, American?' His tone is an interesting paradox. At once respectful and disapproving.

'Give me an American.' A little slur happens on American, but fortunately no one notices ... I don't think.

He brings me a cup. 'After you have been to the study I will show you around the house and take you to your room. You will then be

free until dinner is served at seven. Boss has a dinner engagement so you will eat alone tonight.'

'Sounds like a plan,' I say slowly. I feel even more wasted now than I did while I was walking up the stairs.

I reach for the teaspoon sticking out of the sugar bowl and miss. I watch it fly out of the bowl into the air and sugar grains scatter on the immaculate surface.

'Ooops,' I say apologetically.

'Are you drunk?' Noah asks suspiciously.

I grin at him and both he and the cook exchange glances.

'You've fifteen minutes to sober up,' Noah says worriedly.

'Why? What's he going to do to me if he finds me hammered, hmmm? Kill me?' I find the thought very funny. Laughing, I lean forward. 'I mean, he does kill people, doesn't he?'

Noah says something in a foreign language, Russian presumably, and the cook moves towards a covered tray. She puts it in front of me and uncovers it.

'Eat,' Noah instructs.

'Ooo … little buns?' I exclaim looking at the golden mounds covered in caraway seeds.

'Piroshki,' Olga corrects automatically.

'Not that it makes a blind bit of difference but, OK,' I say loudly. 'Piroshki.' My pronunciation is not bad and I feel pleased with myself. I repeat the word. 'Piroshki.'

'Eat it. It's bread stuffed with Swiss cheese and roasted onions,' Noah says.

'Thanks, but I'll pass.' My stomach doesn't feel so good.

'You must sober up,' Noah says sternly.

Both of them stand over me watching me expectantly.

I shake my head and the sudden movement makes me feel quite sick. 'No. I'm full. I've just eaten a bowl full of strawberries.'

Noah frowns. 'Look Dahlia. This is your first day. You don't want to make the boss angry. It's not a good idea.'

'Shame on you, Noah. A big guy like you afraid of Zane.' I look at him sideways, slyly. 'I bet you could take him.'

Olga gasps.

Noah looks again at his watch worriedly. 'You have ten minutes left.'

'You worry too much, Noah. Of course I'll make it. I'm not afraid of him, you know. He ...' I trail off as I feel my elbow start sliding on the marble surface. Oh Jesus. I'm trashed as shit. I lean my face against my forearm and with a long sigh I go off to sleep.

I am vaguely aware that Noah and Olga try very hard to wake me up, but I have not slept properly for days, and after the long flight back I am also jet-lagged so they have no success. I just snuggle up against Noah's strong warm body and go off to sleep. 'You're like a bear, Noah,' I mumble. At least I think it is Noah. Unless it's Olga and in that case she has a surprisingly muscular body ...

Zane

She didn't present herself in my study as she had been instructed to do. Instead she got drunk on three-quarters of a bottle of champagne and passed out in the kitchen. I should be annoyed, but I am not. I'm excited by that streak of rebellion in her.

I walk into the cool darkness of her bedroom, switch on the bedside lamp, and watch her. In the pool of golden light her skin glows softly. Her lashes lie like sooty fans against her downy cheeks. Her mouth is reddened and slightly open. Her dark-chocolate hair fans out across the pillow. Her dress has not been properly zipped and one side of it has slipped off her shoulders exposing the soft swell of one luscious breast. Her right hand is softly curled and lying beside her cheek, the nails are painted creamy blue. They exactly match her dress. The whole effect somehow seems staged. Too beautiful. Like a carefully planned fashion shoot. For a moment I wonder if Noah did it.

Nah! Noah doesn't have a dramatic bone in his body.

I stare transfixed at the smooth curve of her neck. How delicate and vulnerable it is. So easy to snap. Something inside me moves. I've had other women as equally beautiful as her, yet only she calls to me like a fucking siren. Even now I'm as horny as fuck. My cock is so hard and painful I'll have to relieve myself.

Sure she's fucking hot, but I won't let any woman get to me like this.

I have exactly one month to use her and exorcise this obsession completely from my system. I know the immutable rule of supply and demand. The more you have of something the less you want it. Even the most delicious will become stale when you have overindulged, so I will over indulge.

I will have her at every turn.

Until I want her no more.

Then I will discard her. As I have done with every other woman I have ever been with.

Things were good before her. They will be good again when she is gone.

I don't need one woman. I never have and I never will. Not for me: weakness and dependence. I reach out a hand and touch her face. Her skin is like silk. Like a fucking dream. One day her face will blend into the endless line of faces and bodies I have fucked and dropped. She is just a sickness. Her poison will eventually lose its potency and be expelled out of my bloodstream. She will become a distant memory and I will be free.

I won't feel this emptiness every time I look at her.

Twelve

Dahlia Fury

I wake up in a strange bed and for a bewildering moment I don't know where I am. Sunlight is filtering in through the gaps in the curtains. My mouth feels sour and there is a dull throbbing in my head.

Then it comes back to me. I am in Zane's house. I got very drunk yesterday evening. I remember drinking coffee in the kitchen. Noah must have brought me up here. I look down and thank God, I am still wearing my clothes. My watch tells me it is nearly seven o'clock.

I look around curiously.

The room is feminine, and yet impersonal the way an expensive hotel room is. It is large with cream walls and three lots of tall dusty pink curtains on one side, which means there are three windows. Beside the middle curtain there is a round table covered with a soft pink tablecloth. A vase of fresh flowers sits on it. Two white armchairs face it. It is obviously a place to have breakfast, but I am immediately happy about the table as it means I can work in this room. The headboard is an elaborate padded thing with pink velour upholstery and gilded wood.

Stretching and yawning noisily, I notice a plastic tab with two pills in it and a bottle of water. Excellent idea, Noah. I take the pills and drink half the bottle of water. I must be really dehydrated. I flip the duvet and swing my legs out of the bed. There is a pair of pink bedroom slippers waiting below. They obviously have a pink theme going on.

I pad over to the first window and draw open the curtains. With the curtains open the room seems light and bright. A perfect place for me to work in. I look outside the window and realize that the room is on the third floor. It faces a formal garden with mature trees and topiary that looks pretty spectacular in the morning sun.

Still yawning I pad over to the bathroom. The bathroom makes me smile. If I had not believed Zane was a Mafia boss, the bathroom would have convinced me. It is entirely done up in pink marble and is, I suppose, very impressive. The taps and fittings are all gleaming gold. Brand new toothbrushes, combs, hairbrushes, soaps, and moisturizing lotions have been put out next to the basin. I use what I need in the shower and wrap myself in a fluffy white bathrobe hanging behind the door.

Back into the room and feeling more human, I notice that Yuri or somebody else has neatly tucked away my battered suitcase with its Michigan Girl sticker, my rucksack, and my cheap shoes next to the wardrobe. They look out of place in these opulent surroundings. I open my suitcase, get dressed in a simple blouse and skirt, and put the rest of my stuff away in the wardrobe.

My headache is nearly gone. I open the door and step into a circular landing. There are two other doors around the curving central staircase, but they are both closed, and since I have zero desire to explore, I go down the three flights of stairs to the ground floor. There is no one about in the hallway so I veer into the corridor that leads to the kitchen. Olga is in it. She is sitting at the counter, her hands curled around a mug. She stands and smiles politely when she sees me.

'Good morning,' I greet.

She nods. She mimes the act of carrying her right hand up to her mouth.

'Breakfast. OK.' I bite my lip. 'No English?' I ask shaking my head.

She shakes her head.

'Not even a word?' I ask hopefully.

She looks at me blankly.

I sigh. Great.

She indicates that I should follow her, which I do, into a sunny breakfast room. The sun is streaming in and the table is already set and loaded with food.

'Wow,' I say. I look at her and point at my chest. 'All for me?'

She nods and makes a motion for me to sit.

I sit and look at the selection of food. Pancakes. She points to the jars of jam and honey and a pitcher of some thick and whitish liquid. It doesn't look like cream.

'What's that?' I ask, pointing to it.

She indicates I should wait, goes out of the room, and comes back with a can that she puts into my hand.

'Ah, condensed milk.' Ugh. 'I eat this with the pancake?' I ask politely.

She nods, smiles and gives me the thumbs up signal.

Over my dead body. 'OK. Thanks.'

She lifts a little dish and exposes a slimy, whitish pudding that shivers like jelly and looks like it has been set in a gelatin mould. She picks up a jar of runny raspberry jam and pours a generous amount on top of the little mound.

She looks at me encouragingly. I take a spoon and try a little. It is semolina. I hate semolina. She looks at me expectantly. I smile, swallow, rub my belly, and make an 'mmmm,' sound.

She smiles happily and points to some open sandwiches. Buttered bread slices topped with pink sausage meat or slices of cheese.

'Kolbasa,' she says pointing at the meat, and gives me another thumbs up signal.

'Right, Russian sausage.'

She points to a cold omelet sprinkled with dill, and I make a mental note to stock up on cereal.

I make a sign of drinking and say. 'Coffee?'

She nods and leaves the room. I push the semolina away and reach for a pancake. I've seen these in the supermarket, but never bought them. Blinis. I butter it and add some honey. It is good. Olga comes in with a mug of black tea. I shake my head. 'Coffee,' I say slowly, as if saying it slower will help her understand.

'Oh,' she says, and rushes out of the room.

I take another bite of my blinis and stare out of the window. It is so beautiful and peaceful. As I watch, a thickset man in a black leather jacket crosses the garden and disappears behind some bushes. I glance at my watch. Stella is probably still asleep. My other life seems a world away. It feels as if I am not even in the same country. Olga comes in with my coffee. I hold my finger up to her and, taking my phone, Google thank you in Russian.

'Spasibo,' I say haltingly.

'Pazhalooysta,' she replies.

'She's telling you "That's all right",' Noah says from the doorway.

'Good morning,' I greet.

Olga says something to him in Russian and leaves.

'Are you going to join me?' I ask.

He looks at me strangely. 'No.'

'There's so much food here,' I say.

'I eat in the kitchen,' he says briefly.

'OK.' I put two teaspoons of sugar into my coffee.

'After you eat I will show you around the house,' he says.

I stir my coffee. 'Thanks.'

'I'll be in the kitchen. Enjoy your breakfast,' he says and leaves.

After I have finished my meal I wander back into the kitchen where Noah and Olga are laughing about something. They stop when they notice me.

'I'm finished,' I say to Noah.

He pushes off the counter and passes me. 'You've already been to the study, the breakfast room, and the bathhouse. So we'll leave those out.'

The tour of the house is accomplished quite quickly. Underground there is a gym, a temperature controlled cellar, a sauna, a steam room, a cinema room, a swimming pool, a large room on the floor Noah calls minus 2 for throwing parties. Above ground there are the usual rooms that any London mansion would have, dining room, multiple living rooms, eight bedrooms which we don't explore, and surprisingly a music room with a glossy grand piano.

'Who plays the piano?' I ask.

'Nobody,' he says stiffly.

'Just for show, huh?'

Noah shrugs and refuses to be drawn into conversation. So far he has been polite but distant, which makes me feel he doesn't like me. Especially since I saw him affectionately rub Stella's head in the kitchen. I suddenly remember how very rude I was to him on my first visit. I stop in the middle of the corridor.

'Look, I'm sorry if I was rude the first time I was here. I didn't want to come so I was in a bad mood, and you kind of pissed me off too.'

'No worries,' he dismisses casually.

'So we're cool?' I insist, because I really am grateful to him.

A ghost of a smile flits across his face. 'We're … cool.'

I grin at him. 'Oh and thanks for hauling me all the way to the top floor.'

'There's a lift in this house,' he reminds.

'Otherwise you would have left me on the kitchen floor.'

'Maybe.'

I smile. 'So what's the plan for today?'

'Boss wants to see you in the study at 10.00am. He hates to be kept waiting. Please don't be late.' Then he strides off in the direction of the front door.

I glance at my watch. It is only nine o'clock. Maybe I can get an hour's work in before I face the tiger. I head back to the kitchen. There is no one there so I make myself a mug of coffee and go back up to my room.

I pull out my rucksack crammed full with a fraction of the submissions from the slush pile. I take it out, place it on the table, and pull out a white armchair. Well, it certainly is a peaceful place to read.

The first submission is terrible. If I had a cent for every submission that begins with the female protagonist checking out her face in the mirror, I'd be rich. Fifty Shades has a lot to answer for. I put the neatly stapled three chapters down, dip my finger in the coffee, smear it on the rim of my mug and place the mug on the manuscript. Then I thumb the edges to give the impression that someone has read it while drinking coffee.

It is a charade, but unfortunately it is necessary. In the past when I used to return bad manuscripts to their owners, they would write back accusing the agency of not having read their work. With this technique I don't get such letters anymore.

I pick up the next envelope. The first thing I see is a professionally taken photo of a pretty woman. Her letter says she would like to use that photo on the back jacket of the book. Not a good sign. Usually the worst bits of writing come with glamorous photos attached. I start reading it and sigh. I can barely get past the second page.

I put on the coffee stain, dog ear the manuscript and slip it with our agency's polite rejection slip into its self-addressed envelope, and stare out of the window. I will do no more this morning. I am not myself. I look at the time.

Ten minutes to ten. Time to go down.

I'm gonna love ya, until you hate me.

Thirteen

Dahlia Fury

I rap my knuckles smartly on the study door. I no longer feel nervous and frightened like I did the first time I timidly knocked on this door. Daisy is all right and I already know all the steps to this dance. *Maybe even with my eyes closed.*

'Enter,' Zane calls.

Keeping my shoulders straight I push open the door, and hot damn, the undigested blinis in my stomach do little somersaults. His hair is damp, and he is wearing a crisp cream shirt that exposes his strong throat. The raw power and masculinity takes my breath away. I steel myself not to react.

'Good morning,' I greet. Outwardly, I'm as cool as a cucumber, inwardly, an irrational, hot mess.

He doesn't waste time with pleasantries. 'Is your pussy naked under that dress?' he asks.

Damn him. If it was his intention to pull the rug out from under my feet he has succeeded with flying colors. My breathing is definitely faster and more audible.

Sarcastically he raises one eyebrow.

'Er ... no.'

'Take your pants off. You are never to wear any again while you are in this house, or when you are out with me.'

My eyes widen. The fuck? The arrogance! 'What about when I have my period?' I ask caustically. 'Do I just bleed all over your furniture?'

'I don't remember forbidding the use of tampons.'

My only defense is to look contemptuous and dismissive as I take my panties off and scrunch them up in my fist. 'Well, if it's all the same to you, it makes me feel safer to use panties during that time.'

'It's not all the same to me,' he states proudly.

Overbearing bastard. 'Why should you care? It's not like we'll be having sex then?' I challenge.

'Whatever gave you the impression we won't be having sex then?' he oozes.

I recoil. 'What?'

He smiles fiendishly. 'Why Dahlia *moy*, don't tell me you have never had sex while you are bleeding.'

'Of course not,' I say haughtily.

'Then you have missed something special. Even a dog knows when a woman is about to come on her period because her hormones are going crazy. She's like a piece of tinder. One little spark and she will burn like a fucking bonfire.'

My heart kicks. This is so far removed from what I am used to in a man.

'Come here,' he instructs quietly.

I walk up to his desk and look down at him. My heart is racing and I can already feel my body responding. It's truly incredible how my body starts reacting as soon as I come into his vicinity. It is as if his fingertips are already on my spine and moving downwards. Every moment spent in his company is rich with excitement and pleasure or throbbing with anticipation. I would never have believed such a wild and crazy experience would open up for little ole me a few months ago.

He tilts his head. 'Over here,' he invites coolly.

However, I have to admit I really don't care to be treated like a whore. *Come here.*

Squat. Open your legs. I grit my teeth, but obey his command and walk around the desk.

He rolls his chair back so a space between him and his desk opens up. 'Sit in front of me,' he instructs.

I glance at his desk, lick my lower lip and ask, 'Don't you want to move those papers out of the way first?'

He doesn't miss a beat. 'No.'

'Do you want me to move them out of the way?'

'No. I want you to follow my instruction,' he says with elaborate politeness.

Ugh. He deserves to perish horribly. I get between him and the desk and hop onto the surface, my legs dangling down. Unconsciously my eyes stray down to his crotch and he is hard and bulging under the expensive fabric of his slacks. I avert my gaze quickly and he laughs. A taunting cold sound.

'You didn't come to me yesterday,' he says softly.

'I ... er ... I ... got drunk.'

'So I heard.' His eyes seem to glow with promises and danger, and I like that hint of the deadly and the unknowable. Does that make me a bad girl?

My pulse starts throbbing hard. 'Well, you did leave the champagne in a very accessible place,' I reason.

'That's true,' he concedes generously.

'I could make it up to you,' I suggest.

He takes my right ankle in his warm hand. It's like a molten spike of sensation, but I don't fidget or react. I keep my palms firmly glued to the surface of the desk on either side of me. With a mocking smile he removes my shoe and lets it drop to the floor. A half-grin tugs at his mouth. 'Oh yeah?'

That half grin turns my insides to mush. My face feels flushed. His hand on my ankle is doing things to me, making me tingle. 'Yeah,' I whisper, my voice husky.

He takes off the other shoe. 'How?' he purrs.

Jesus! My brain feels completely addled. 'I don't know. I do give an incredible blowjob.'

Something flashes in his eyes. He drops the shoe. 'That's good to know, but I'm afraid, we Russians, we're big on honoring debts and keeping our word. If we say we'll be somewhere in an hour, we make sure we're there.'

I think for a moment. 'We Americans are too. And that is why I am sitting on your fucking table without my panties.'

He eyes me hungrily as if I'm food or prey. 'It warms my heart to hear that Americans honor their word.'

I smile seductively. 'Hmmm … but I heard somewhere that you ate your own heart.' Let him know that I'm not backing down.

Laughter pours out of him like oil from a jar. Smooth, golden, dazzling. 'You shouldn't listen to gossip, Dahlia *moy*. Now be a good girl and open your legs. I want to fuck you.'

I lick my dry lips. 'Just like that?'

'Uh … huh.'

'And it's always going to be like this?'

He raises his eyebrows. 'Like what?'

'So emotionless.'

He considers the question. 'I guess so.'

'Why? Why does it have to be so cold and impersonal?'

A smooth shrug. 'Because I like it so.'

I swallow hard. 'Or maybe because you are afraid?' I whisper.

Dizzying seconds pass. His eyes glitter dangerously, and I see the helldamned shadow inside him, but then, he laughs. 'Afraid of what, little one?' he queries softly.

'Of feeling something.'

'Something for you?' he mocks.

I don't let my expression show my embarrassment. 'For any woman,' I bite back.

He looks at me curiously, intrigued. 'What would make it less ... cold for you?'

'Maybe if we kissed?'

His expression does not change. 'Go ahead. Kiss me.'

I lean forward and instantly his scent envelops me. Heady. I let my hands drift up to his wide shoulders and settle on those lean muscles. I start moving towards him. His lips come closer and closer to mine. *Hell, must he be so gorgeous?*

My heart is beating so loud he probably hears it. Breathlessly, I let my mouth dust the side of his neck, and he becomes completely rigid. Under my fingers his muscles are hard and tense. Not exactly the reaction I am looking for, but at least he's not immune. I nuzzle at a madly throbbing pulse and treat it to delicate little kisses. Soft, innocent butterfly whispers.

Leaving that fiercely beating pulse I rest my forehead against his. My hands rise up to capture his face. His skin feels like raw silk against the palms of my hands. His warmth seeps through. My lips part and so do his. Our breaths mingle.

As bold as a lamb approaching a lion, I let our lips touch.

His mouth is soft and full. He tastes of coffee and something magical. Savoring the taste I move my mouth over his, gently and suggestively ... deepening the kiss. My whole body flushes with heat and euphoria. From the roots of my hair to the tips of my toes. Warmth spills out of my heart. Oh God! How long has it been since I felt like this? Smoldering heat uncurls deep inside me.

Then I realize.

He is *not* kissing me back.

I draw back slightly, the lovely heat inside me evaporating like mist in the morning sunlight. He remains still and unresponsive. I lift my eyes and look into his. They stare back at me like beautiful, lifeless stones.

'Now can we do it my way?' he asks.

It is like being slapped. He deliberately trapped me into humiliating myself. I let my hands drop away from his face and lean away from him. Inside, my pride and something else are fatally wounded, outside, I show only fury.

'I think I'm going to end up hating you,' I spit venomously.

'There you go. Emotion,' he taunts.

I glare at him. God, I have never met such an infuriating man. I want to rake my fingernails down his smug, arrogant face, and add another scar to go with the one that's already there.

Calmly he reaches forward, grabs the front of my blouse, and rips it open suddenly. Buttons fly in all directions.

'What the hell are you doing?' I protest angrily, my hands automatically covering my chest, even though he has already seen my breasts bare.

'What I always want to do when I'm around you. Ravish you.'

'What, the great Zane needs to force himself on an unwilling woman?' I taunt.

His eyes glint with genuine amusement. 'I think we both know that you are not unwilling.'

'I was willing, but I've changed my mind. You're a cold, unfeeling brute. I don't know what I ever saw in you. I am no longer willing. So there.'

He laughs. A hard mocking sound. So different from the earlier laugh. 'Lust and passion don't come from a tap, American fox. You can't just turn it off.'

'Well, I just did,' I tell him coldly.

He smiles wickedly. 'So you don't mind if I put it to a test?'

I look at him suspiciously. 'What are you planning to do?'

'If you don't completely lose your head in the next two minutes you can walk out of this house and never return.'

My eyes widen with shock. 'What?'

'You heard,' he growls.

Two minutes. I can do two minutes. I'm not that desperate. Forewarned is forarmed. I'll do the same thing he did to me. No matter what I feel inside, I will remain cold and unresponsive. I glance at my watch. 'Your time starts now.'

He looks at his own watch. 'It's not that I don't trust you. It's just that—'

'Of course not,' I interrupt acidly.

'Mine has seconds,' he finishes.

My jaw juts out. 'So does mine.'

With unhurried movements he unfastens the front clasp of my bra. My breasts burst free, and unfortunately for me, my nipples are already hard. I take a deep breath and sneak a look at my watch. Seven seconds have passed. He takes the globes in his hands and kneads them gently.

I smile tightly at him and he laughs confidently.

Casually, I let my eyes slide towards my wrist. Twenty seconds. His dark head moves downwards towards my chest. He captures a nipple and suckles it, and hot velvet alert! His mouth is so hot and cunning I feel a jolt go right down to my sex.

Shit. You need to find a way to distract yourself.

I close my eyes and try to think of a particularly bad manuscript that I once read. It started off with a sex scene that was so unintentionally funny it deserved some sort of turkey award. The girls and I laughed for …

Oh God! Zane has captured a nipple between his teeth. I turn the moan that rises up my throat into a kind of throat clearing cough. At chest level the slick bastard stops and chuckles. He thinks he is so badass. Someone should tell him, he who laughs last, laughs longest.

His hand starts moving up my thigh and, what the hell? My legs, as if separate from me, part sluttishly to give him access. I lean back on the palms of my hands and close my eyes. *Take deep breaths. If he can resist you, you can resist him. You're not a Fury for nothing.*

One finger enters me. Oh. My. God. It has to be at least one minute by now. He slips another finger in. Then his thumb gets in on the act. It starts circling my clit like some sort of killer shark. Damn, if that doesn't feel good.

My head starts feeling light. Against my will my hips rise up, a little, but it is definitely a rise. My belly feels like it's starting to melt. Oh, hell. The throbbing in my sex becomes ferocious. It's all getting to be too much. No. No. No. I'm not going to … come. Fuck it. I'm not. I'm just not. Oh no …

'About to lose it, little fox?' he mocks.

'Don't … Fucking … Call … meee … litt … Ahhhhh.'

The world begins to spin and spiral. Sparks of heat land on my skin. My head drops back and blood explodes in my brain. I lose all control and climax, screaming ferociously at him. Reality returns slowly. The fire inside me dims and I'm faced with reality. The ceiling is sky blue. Nice actually. I straighten my head and meet his sharp eyes.

He raises a condescending eyebrow.

'A bit of humility would be an attractive quality to nurture,' I say unsteadily.

'I wonder how you would have crowed if you had won.'

'I wouldn't have.'

'Well, we'll never know,' he says carelessly, and pushes me down on my back.

A sheaf of papers and a pen press into my flesh. I close my eyes and hear the metal rasp of his zipper. Fresh desire tightens my belly. I want his flesh inside me, and he knows it too. He grips my bare ass with hot, rough hands and pulls my hips towards him. He forces his cock between my thighs and he rams it home, stretching me. I gasp. So full.

'You're so fucking tight,' he growls, his breath rough and ragged, and his fierce eyes kindling like live coals.

He begins to thrust. Hard and slow, then faster and faster. The force makes me breathless, and my body arches and jerks on the desk. Hell, the man's a demon. With a great roar and his whole body shuddering, he comes. His fluid mingles with mine, hot and sweet.

For a few seconds longer he remains inside me. Then he withdraws and I lift myself up. As he pulls up his trousers and zips up, I hop off the table, do up my bra and pick up my shoes. Wordlessly I start walking towards the door.

'By the way I don't like the way you dress.'

The cheek of the man. My temperature shoots up. I turn around and look at him with a withering expression.

'Noah has arranged for a personal dresser he knows to come and point you in the right direction. Tell her you need an entire wardrobe. Evening dresses, beachwear, casual wear. The whole works.'

'Yes, sir.'

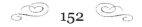

'Get something for tonight. I'm taking you to dinner.'

I don't respond. Let that be my little rebellion.

Zane

I shake out a cigarette, tap it, light it and take a deep draw. Nicotine fills my lungs. I turn my chair around to face the window. The vista beyond is my favorite part of the garden. No one ever goes in it except my Japanese gardener, Akio. Most people who stand at my window and look out will see a bunch of rock, some shrubbery and some stones, but if they looked, really looked, they'd see its real beauty.

They'd see a waterfall.

They'd see that the rocks and the stones have been composed to look like water cascading through shrubbery. Sometimes I watch Akio working, meticulously and lovingly raking his plot of small white stones as if he is combing his lover's hair. The teeth marks left by his rake are faultlessly straight. There is never a moment when he falters, hesitates or dithers.

His dedication to detail is impressive. He is bent over with age, but even the smallest

stone rolling away does not escape his beady eyes. It is picked up and returned to its exact place.

A place for everything and everything in its place.

I take a few more puffs and grind out my cigarette. Fuck it. She's just a stone that has rolled away from its proper place. I need to get her back to where she belongs.

She's just a bit of pussy. Nothing more. The hunger will pass and the sooner I get that through my thick head the better.

Fourteen

Dahlia Fury

Back in my room I clean up, don a baggy T-shirt, and notice that Stella has left a text message.

U won't believe. Crazy Richmond bitch finally came through with her rich and famous contacts. Got me an appt. with Andre Rieu next week!!!! :) xxxxxx

I have no idea who Andre Rieu is and quickly Google him. Turns out he is a famous Dutch violinist and conductor. I call her immediately.

'Congratulations, babe,' I shriek. 'You've arrived. I'm so impressed. Your dainty fingers will soon be dancing over the A-List!'

'Nobody is more impressed than me,' she says bashfully.

'Soon all kinds of celebrities will be flying you all over the world as part of their entourage,' I tease.

'If they know what's good for them,' she jokes.

I laugh and sit on the bed. 'So what are you up to today?'

'Nothing much. I've a dance class in an hour and three sessions this evening. What about you? How's sexual domination working out for you?'

'It's ...'

'Actually don't tell me. I'm not ready to hear.' There is an awkward pause. 'How's Noah?'

'He's fine. I don't think—'

At that moment I hear a sharp buzzing sound. 'What the hell? Hang on a minute. Can you hear that noise? Do you know where it's coming from?'

'It sounds like the intercom system. Go pick up the phone by the door.'

I look towards the door and notice a wall phone next to it. 'Don't go away. I haven't finished talking to you yet,' I tell Stella and pick up the phone.

Noah says, 'Lunch will be served at 1 p.m. and your appointment with your personal shopper is at 2 p.m. Her name is Molly Street.

Wait for her in the living room. The one with the big painting of fish.'

'OK. Thanks.'

'See you later,' he says and rings off.

I return the receiver to the wall and put my mobile back to my ear.

'What's going on?' Stella asks.

'I've got a woman coming at 2 o'clock to help me revamp my wardrobe. Apparently Zane doesn't think much of my fashion choices,' I explain sourly.

She giggles. 'Did you wear your striped blouse and grey skirt?'

'Yes,' I admit reluctantly.

'They're truly awful. I warned you not to take them,' she scolds.

'I know, but they are so comfortable.' Well the blouse was until Zane tore it.

'You get to keep the new wardrobe, right?'

'I don't know, but I guess so.'

'Get some sexy stuff and get something in my size too.'

I laugh. Then she has to go because the postman is at the door, so I end the call and work until lunchtime. Lunch is roast duck with apples, vegetables, roast potatoes, and some kind of creamy salad. I eat alone. I leave the door open so I can hear the staff in the kitchen eating and talking animatedly, but I don't attempt to join them. They're all talking in Russian, and if I go in there they will be forced to start speaking in English, when it's clear they are more comfortable speaking in their mother tongue. Besides, I'm just a temporary installation. No point in getting too close.

After lunch I go into the living room with the painting of the fish and wait for Molly Street. There's a glossy racing magazine on the coffee table and I flip through it without any real interest.

I don't hear the doorbell, but the living room door opens and Noah shows in a pretty lady with shoulder-length strawberry blonde hair, bright blue eyes, and a cute button nose. She is dressed in jeans, a pink sweater and a darling pair of pointy, two-inch high ankle boots in black suede.

'Thanks Noah,' she says.

He nods and closes the door. She turns towards me and smiles broadly. 'Hello. So you're Dahlia Fury. Sensational name,' she says chattily.

I smile back. 'I think your name's rather special too.'

'Well, it's not really my name. I made it up,' she confesses with a wide grin.

I laugh. I think I'm going to get along just fine with Molly Street. She looks around her. 'God. Isn't this house gorgeous?'

'Yeah. I guess it is.'

There is a knock on the door and the woman I had met coming up the stairs yesterday comes in. She offers us refreshments. I shake my head, but Molly asks for tea. After the woman goes out Molly comes towards me.

'Right, let's have a little look at you,' she says and walks around me quickly casting a professional eye over me. She stops in front of me.

'Here's how I normally work. You tell me what you want to achieve: three inches taller, three inches slimmer, impress a new boss, seduce an old boyfriend, seduce a new boyfriend,' she smiles, 'then, I'll run around tomorrow, find the clothes and accessories that I think will suit your needs best, and bring them over to you. You'll try them on and if you like them you keep them and I'll bill you, in your case, Noah for the clothes and my time. Is that OK with you?'

'Yeah, great.'

'So, what look are we going for today, sophisticated, smart, sexy, casual ...?'

'I'd like to look more ...'

She waits expectantly.

'Glamorous and sexy,' I finish.

'With a smoking body like yours, piece of cake,' she assures confidently.

I blush to the tips of my ears.

'Believe me, sometimes I have my work cut out for me. Having said that though, I haven't had a single client who hasn't been left standing in front of a mirror admiring the change in her appearance.'

'With that kind of job satisfaction you must really love what you do,' I say, thinking what a lovely job that must be. So much better, I think, than leaving coffee ring stains on manuscripts and sending out sterile rejection letters all day long.

'Well,' Molly says with a sunny smile. 'I love finding beautiful things, sometimes rare things, and putting them all together with the right accessories. I love making my clients look the way they always dreamed of. I also come across a lot of snooty cows that I want to bitch slap even as I am saying, "And what about this lovely coat Madam? It's so this season."'

I laugh.

Her phone rings. She looks at me. 'Do you mind? It's my fiancé Mark. He needs some information. I'll only be a second.'

'No. It's fine. Go ahead.'

I walk away from her towards the windows thinking of my Mark. Since I told him that Daisy has been found by Zane, I have not spoken to him again. He's a nice guy. I wonder how he is now. I should call and thank him for all his support. Then again, perhaps it's better I leave it alone. I never felt a fraction of what I feel for Zane. It would never have worked.

'Yeah, OK. See you there tonight,' Molly says.

I turn back to face her with a smile. 'Going anywhere nice tonight?'

She crinkles her nose. 'His mother's place. She hates me.'

'I can't imagine why. Any man would be lucky to have you,' I say.

'Oh bless you. What a sweetie you are. No, she thinks her son can do better. Where were we?'

'She's dead wrong.'

She smiles gratefully at me, then claps her hands decisively. 'Now for the most difficult part,' she says.

I grin. 'There's a difficult part?'

She reaches into her back pocket, snaps out a tape measure and says, 'I'm afraid most women hate this part.'

I scrunch up my face. 'I'm not too hot on it either.'

'You have a stunning figure. I know a lot of women who gladly suffer weeks of pain and suffering and bandages to achieve the kind of figure you have.' She sets about measuring me and recording the information into her phone.

'What's your shoe size?' she asks as she measures the thickest part of my calf, presumably as a guide to shop for boots.

'UK 6,' I tell her.

'Now a quick photograph. This is for my color reference. Smile.'

I smile awkwardly.

'Looks like we're all done here for today.' She looks up. 'I'll come around tomorrow with a whole load of things for you to choose from.'

'What if I need something for tonight?' I ask.

'What's the occasion?' she asks, flipping her phone closed.

'Dinner.'

'Where?'

I bite my lip. 'I have no idea.'

She flicks her phone open again, scrolls down it and calls a number. 'Hey Noah,' she says. 'Where is Dahlia being taken to tonight?' She listens then thanks Noah and ends the call.

'You are going to Uncle Ho,' she announces and smiles mysteriously. 'You won't believe this, but I have just the thing outside.

Come on,' she says, and starts walking towards the door.

'What's Uncle Ho like?' I ask as I hurry after her.

'Very smart and very in. It has a wonderful Vodka Bar, and some of the tables in the restaurant have this new-fangled Le Petit Chef thing.'

'What's that?' I ask curiously.

'If I tell you I'll spoil it. It is much better if you simply go and enjoy it,' she advises.

We go out of the front door to where her white van is parked. She opens the back doors and it's like Aladdin's cave in there. She hops onto the steps and goes in.

'You've got a mini shop in here,' I say in an awed voice.

'It's what I've collected over the years. Some of it is from second hand shops, some are things designers have handed down to me, and some I've wheedled from customers who simply didn't have the figure for them.'

I watch her professionally running her hands through two rails displaying a beautiful variety of clothes. There are hangers of chunky jewel-colored knitwear, camel coats, silk dresses in a rainbow of colors, leather jackets, velvet wraps in a selection of rich colors, luscious cream woolen trousers, tweeds in salmon and purple, a racy red miniskirt. There are boxes crammed full of belts and scarves, a glass case with hundreds of pieces of costume jewelry, and shelves filled with shoes. Stella would think she had died and gone to heaven.

Molly pulls out a long silver-grey cashmere coat that looks like it must have cost the earth. She comes to where I'm standing and holds it out to me. 'This will go perfectly with your hair and the dress I have in mind for you.'

'Oh it's lovely,' I breathe.

The label says, Lolita Lempika. I stroke it and it's deliciously smooth and luxurious as the velvety tummy of a puppy.

'It will be perfectly cozy in this weather,' she says with her back turned to me. At the end of the second rail she finds the dress she is looking for and pulls it out triumphantly.

I shriek. For the first time in my life I actually shriek.

She beams like a girl. 'I know,' she gushes. 'I've been saving this one for ages. I knew it was special, but I never found the right customer for it. It's vintage Valentino. It's even got a bra built into it. I found it in a carboot sale in Weybridge. Can you believe it? Weybridge!'

I stare in amazement at the black silk, art deco confection. It has short spaghetti straps covered with narrow, delicate frills, and filled in with a panel of sheer organza material to form the illusion of a boat neckline. An enormous flower bow fashioned of thin strips of velvet sits over the top of the right breast. The dress is form fitting until just below the waist then flares out into an A-line skirt.

I don't know where the hell Weybridge is, but it is truly unbelievable that anyone would ever want to part with such a glamorous dress, let alone take it to a carboot sale.

'It had a small tear near the hem, but I had it taken up by half an inch and voila,' Molly explains.

I take a step towards the dress and touch the panel of transparent material.

'That's the sheerest organza you can find,' Molly says quietly.

'Is it my size?' I can't believe how much I want to hear her say yes.

'Down to the last half-inch.'

'It's mind-blowingly sexy, isn't it?' I whisper back.

She waggles her eyebrows. 'It is, but just in case anybody thinks you haven't got morals, we have these.' She dips her hands into a plastic drawer and comes up with great handfuls of pearl ropes and necklaces.

I laugh. 'Molly Street you are brilliant.'

She throws her left hand in an arc in front of her face and snaps her fingers. 'Tell me something new,' she sings with a grin. She pulls out a pearl choker and a matching pearl bracelet and puts them aside. 'You will be putting your hair up, won't you?'

'Well ...'

'Here. This will make it easy for you.' She passes me a pearl pin. 'Put your hair into a simple bun at the nape of your neck and stick this in anywhere. Can't go wrong.'

'Thanks,' I say taking the pin from her.

'Now shoes. The thing about vintage dresses is never to pair them with vintage style shoes. You'll look like you're going to a fancy dress party. What's the time now?'

I look at my watch. 'Nearly three.'

'I know the perfect pair. They are to die for. Very, very high, in pewter with silver heels and a velvet trim all the way around. The curving straps in the front are held by tiny silver buttons. They're a work of art. I'll go pick them up now and drop them off before four. How's that?'

'Awesome.'

Then she helps me carry the coat, dress, and the accessories to the house before she leaves.

Fifteen

Dahlia Fury

-Ask for money and get advice-

As I glide down the stairs in the most beautiful dress I have ever worn, my pearls, my expensive coat over my arm, and my fantastically fabulous new shoes (I've already ordered a pair in Stella's size), Noah appears at the bottom. His black eyes run down my body quickly and professionally, as if I'm a room he's checking out for trouble.

He frowns. 'You're early. Wait in the White Room for Boss. He'll be about fifteen minutes.'

'OK,' I say easily.

He nods and disappears down the corridor towards the kitchen.

I head towards the living room, open the door and peek inside. It's empty. I close the door and move towards the music station. I press play and classical music fills the room. I have never really listened to classical music, but this piece is really beautiful and I'm standing there listening to it when the door opens and a man enters. He's quite tall, very pale and probably in his forties. He is wearing a sharp suit.

'Oh,' he says when he sees me. He seems surprised. 'I'm sorry. I'm looking for Zane. I was told he'd be here.' His accent is from the rough end of London and there is something mean in his lean face, but his tone is polite.

'He'll be down soon,' I say.

He shifts uncomfortably. 'Maybe I should wait outside.'

'It's OK. You can wait here,' I say. I'm not one to quickly judge people, although I have to be honest, I don't like him one bit. There is something about him that makes my skin crawl.

He grins suddenly, a smarmy, sly lift to his lips. 'Are you Zane's new ... girl?'

There are a multitude of insults in that slight pause. I straighten my spine. God, sometimes you try to be nice to someone and they fucking stab you in the head.

I'm saved from answering by the door being thrown open. Zane is standing in the doorway. He seems massive compared to his guest and his body language is like nothing I have ever seen. His eyes are like sparks in his thunderous face and his scar looks livid. He is not looking at me. His entire attention is on the man who entered the room.

'What the fuck are you doing here, Lenny?' he rasps.

The man seems to have been caught off guard. For a few seconds he stares silently at Zane then the man who seemed so sly and knowing only moments ago goes on the defensive. At that moment I know who the lion in this jungle is.

'Noah asked me to come in here and wait for you,' he blurts out.

Zane strides into the room. 'Next time you come into a room and you see her, you turn around immediately and fucking walk out, do you understand?'

'I understand. I'm really sorry. I'm out of line, but it was an honest mistake. I didn't do nothing, anyway. I just said hello, you know, to be polite to your lady. I'm sorry, OK,' Lenny says, slippery and so obviously disingenuous.

I know I've gone completely still with shock at the pure aggression in Zane, but I am also aware that Lenny is not to blame. Even though I don't like him, and right now he looks like a wriggling, slimy worm, it is not his fault. I asked him to stay. Besides, it occurs to me too that I'm probably in the wrong room. I assumed this was the white room because I met Molly here and I'd been told to wait in the same room.

'It's my fault,' I say, hoping to change the air of menace in the room. 'I told him he could wait for you here.'

Zane turns his eyes on me and they are blazing with fury. 'Who the fuck gave you permission to talk?' he snarls.

I take an involuntary step back. I have never been spoken to like that by anybody. My first reaction is one of pure fury. A kind I have never experienced before. I am so livid with him I start trembling.

'I'll come back tomorrow,' Lenny mumbles, and slips out of the door as fast as his legs will carry him.

As soon as we are alone I lose my shit. This, as far as I am concerned, is the last straw. I'm out of here. I've had enough. I didn't sign up for this bullshit. The deal was he doesn't do anything I don't like, or the deal is off. He just did something I detest. I absolutely will not allow him or any other man to talk to me like that. No matter how hungry my body is for him, I simply won't allow such abuse. Maybe I'm not built to be someone's sex toy. I'm too

171

independent and free-spirited to be anybody else's sidekick. He can go find himself another pliable sex toy to bully.

'You're an arrogant bastard, Zane. How dare you speak to me like that in front of other people?' I fume, striding towards the door.

He stands in my way, magnificent and menacing. 'I'll speak to you how I like. I own you.'

I gasp. 'Well, I've got news for you. You *don't* own me.'

'Yes, I fucking do,' he snarls. His arm shoots out and he yanks me to him.

My new shoes lift off the ground and my body slams into his, knocking all the wind from my lungs. Stunned, I stare up into his furious face. There is a muscle ticking at the side of his jaw. His eyes are impenetrable as his head swoops down, and his lips crush mine in an angry kiss.

His mouth is hot and wild.

Intoxicated, I open my mouth and emit a low moan. His tongue forces its way in instantly. The kiss is my salvation and my torment. It's more than anything I could have imagined. It's magic; like when I sat on a hill right in the middle of a summer storm and saw lightning crash through the sky and felt it in my veins.

He draws my tongue into his mouth and sucks on it. I feel as if I'm floating on air. No matter what happens after this, I know I will carry the memory of this first kiss for the rest of my life. I will die with it still on my lips.

Like an addict, my arms reach up and tangle helplessly around his strong neck. I feel the hardness of his shaft press into my belly.

He pulls away. My head swims as I lean away to take in his face, contorted with lust, hunger, possession and feral ownership. We stare at each other, both of us breathing hard. For that time his mouth was on mine the world itself ceased to turn on its axis, or even exist. Never in a billion years did I expect it to be like this between us. It is absolutely, unquestionably awesome. Every fiber of my being just aches for him.

'You wanted to see me lose control? Now you've seen it,' he says tightly.

I shake my head. My anger in shreds. I have no words.

A bitter half-smile crosses his face. 'Not a pretty picture, huh?'

I stare up at him with wide eyes, exploring and learning. There is so much to know and so little time. A deep angry flush colors his face and his eyes are molten with angry emotions, but it only makes him even more impossibly sexy and attractive. 'You shouldn't talk to me like that in front of people,' I whisper.

His face is hard and unapologetic. 'You shouldn't disrespect me in front of my business associates.'

'I didn't.'

'My world is a ruthless one, Dahlia. Let someone think you're soft for a bit of pussy, and you're signing your own death warrant.'

The thought makes my blood curdle. 'I didn't think of it like that.'

'You have nothing to do with my businesses. The less you know the better. Don't make yourself valuable to my enemies. I wouldn't trade your innocent life for my worthless one.'

Still dazed, I nod. He called his life worthless!

'Good,' he says softly.

He walks me backwards in a hard, rough tango, and twirling me around, bends me face down on a sofa back. My elbows are pressed into the cushion of the seat and the hard wooden frame of the sofa digs into my midriff. I can smell the sprays the cleaners have used on the upholstery. He flips my dress over my back and I feel his eyes on my naked ass and splayed legs.

I hear him draw his breath in harshly. He lays his palm on one cheek and strokes it gently. God, I'm *so* wet. In the silence of the room I hear the sound of a zip tearing open in a hurry, and the whisper of his clothes being roughly pushed aside.

I shiver as he grasps my hair and pulls my head up. I pant as he leans down and drags his fiery mouth from the base of my ear all the way down to my collarbone. He even licks the pearl choker.

'What does it feel like to be so beautiful, so fucking tempting that men are helpless to resist you?' he mutters.

I don't answer him and he yanks at my hair. 'Tell me, my little cock tease, what does it feel like to swan around knowing your hot, little pussy is driving me crazy?' he asks.

My mouth hangs open, my breaths come so fast and hard they sound louder than his voice. 'I don't believe for a minute that you are helpless to resist me,' I pant.

'No? Then tell me why I've been dying to lick your pussy all day.'

'You have?' I ask incredulously.

'All fucking day.' His hand pulls my zip down to my waist and slips into my dress to roll my nipple between his fingers. The sensation is immediate and electric.

He pinches my nipple. I whimper with the mixture of pain and pleasure and feel that undeniable aching, festering insistence between my legs. My thighs tremble with excitement and anticipation.

'P ... please,' I groan, almost in tears with need. 'Don't tease me.'

'Have you been thinking of my cock inside you, little fox? In your mouth, in your tight pussy and your hot ass.'

I make an incoherent sound.

'Tell me what you want,' he urges, his breath steamy.

'I want you to fuck me. Hard.'

His erection rubs my naked ass, hard and angry. 'Where?' he asks.

'Every fucking where,' I cry in frustration.

He slips a finger into me. A strangled sound escapes my throat. I feel like I am gasoline about to combust.

'And why do you want that?' he asks softly.

'Because you own me,' I groan.

'That's right. Every. Fucking. Inch. Tell me all this is mine.'

'It's all yours. Every last inch.'

He strokes my ass.

I'm not proud of it, but I swear at him with frustration.

'Fuck it, Zane. Take me *now*.'

I feel like an animal. An animal in heat. He hefts my hips and rubs the head of his cock up and down my slick folds, coating it in my juices. Goosebumps rise along my skin as I feel his cock force itself between my swollen lips, stretching me tight around his thickness. My hands dig into the sofa. Jesus, his erection feels as hard as stone.

'Oh, God, yes,' I groan as that smooth shaft slowly spears my body until he jams his full length deep into my pussy. 'Yes. Just like that,' I moan, gripping the hell out of his massive dick. 'Exactly like that.'

No longer gentle, he becomes exactly what I've always wanted. A rough god. He rams into me, his need overpowering, irresistible, savage, driving his cock deeper and deeper. With every thrust my juices spurt around his cock and soak my thighs. My muscles feel like beaten butter. My sobs and moans echo through the room and my body thrashes over the sofa as his entire cock goes in and out of me.

He reaches around so his fingers can play with my clit while he drives into me. Furiously. Relentlessly. All pretenses at civilization gone. We are just two animals fucking. Oblivious to the world around us.

My body starts to spiral out of control. 'I'm coming,' I shudder as the waves of contractions start. Vaguely I am aware of calling out his name again and again as I become a creature of ecstasy. I hear a roar. Then his cock jerks inside me and he shoots hot sperm into my body. He did it hard. As if he can't help himself. As if this thing we have is a madness and this is the only cure.

Our bodies become still.

He rests his forehead against my back. Both of us are still breathing hard when he pulls out of me. I try to get up, but he lays his hand on my back. His cream trickles out of me. I twist my head to look at him. He returns his cock into his boxers and zips up. With a lush smile he slips a finger into me. More of his cream gushes out of me. He smears it all over my sex, thighs, and behind my ears. Then he pulls my dress down over my ass, his hand lingering on my flushed curves. He zips up my dress and pulls me off the sofa.

'Shall we go?' he asks.

'Steady on,' I say with a wobbly, crazy, impractical, fucked-up smile. 'I'd like to wash and freshen up a little first.'

'No, you smell and look exactly the way I want you to. I want every man who looks at you to know you're mine.'

My knees go weak. *Oh my! You are in so much trouble, Dahlia.* 'You sound like a dog marking its territory.'

'That's exactly right. I've left my scent on what I own.'

'But there'll be a wet spot on my dress.'

He smiles. 'And so there will be.'

Sixteen

Dahlia Fury

https://www.youtube.com/watch?v=1cQh1ccqu8M

A quick look at the big mirror over the fireplace shows me a woman with two spots of high color on her cheeks, swollen lips, and glittering eyes. Her hairdo is most definitely lopsided. There is no freaking way I am going anywhere without repairing that, at least. I pull the pearl pin out, comb my hair out with my fingers, and leave it loose. I turn around to look at Zane. He is standing very still in the middle of the room just watching me. I was so angry before it did not hit me how darkly handsome he looks in a faultlessly cut black suit and a midnight-blue shirt. Like a fallen angel, actually.

'Have I told you that you look ravishing tonight?' he asks.

Wow! First compliment. Butterflies are going mad in my tummy, but I affect an air of sophistication. 'Not in so many words.'

'Well, you do.'

'Thank you.' Then more softly, 'You look kick ass hot yourself.'

He smiles slowly, sexily. 'If you keep looking at me like that I'm going to have to bend you over the sofa again.'

How crazy, I actually want him inside me again, but my stomach rumbles. I walk towards him, my hips swaying, my eyes fixed on his. I stop in front of him. 'Feed me first.'

'Good idea,' he murmurs. 'Let's fatten you up before the great feast.'

I look at him through my lashes. 'You speak as if I'm on the menu tonight.'

His fingers tease the nape of my neck. 'You're the special for all of this month,' he says, with the dark smile of a predator.

That reminder hurt. A lot. I suck in a quick breath and avert my eyes. He doesn't know how his words affect me.

Zane helps me into my coat and opens the door. We find Noah cooling his heels in the hallway. As soon as he spots us he goes into full security mood, nodding at Zane and simultaneously talking in Russian into his earpiece as he starts moving towards the front door. He opens it and goes out before us, his head turning from side to side, his big body moving quickly down the steps. He opens the back doors of a long Mercedes with blacked out windows and waits for us.

Yuri is already in the street and two other men I do not know are getting into the two cars parked in front of and at the back of the Mercedes. The faultless precision of all their movements surprises me. It's like watching something from a movie.

Slightly awed by the seriousness of the procedure, I slide into the backseat of the Mercedes and Noah closes the door with a firm click. Zane walks around and gets in on the other side. I have never been in a car with tinted, presumably, judging by the elaborate security measure I have just witnessed, bullet proof glass windows. Bizarrely it feels cozy and expensive. I turn to look at Zane.

'Wow,' I stage whisper.

He looks at me with his smoldering eyes. 'What?'

'What are you scared of?' I tease.

'I'm scared of how much I want your pussy.'

My smile dies away.

He slides his hand under my dress and lets it move along my inner thighs. 'Open,' he says.

'No, I really don't want to arrive at the restaurant with a massive wet patch on the back of my dress,' I protest with an unsteady laugh.

'Open,' he repeats sternly.

I bite my lip and part my legs. His fingers engage with my clit while he watches me.

'I really don't want to come right now,' I gasp.

'Too bad,' he says callously.

He carries on until my body buckles and I'm on the verge of coming, when he suddenly stops.

'You're not going to finish what you started?' I blurt out.

'We are nearly there,' he says casually, and pulling out a fresh white linen handkerchief, wipes his fingers.

I stare at him dumbfounded, my clit throbbing madly. 'You could have finished. We're not there yet,' I complain.

'I know, but I enjoy seeing you frustrated,' he says cruelly.

My jaw drops. 'That's not nice.'

'I'm not... nice.'

I turn my face away from him and fuming quietly, stare out of the dark windows. No more is said until we reach the restaurant, which, in fact, is only a few streets away from my workplace.

Uncle Ho has an awning made of bamboo and lots of bamboo plants in large round clay planters. The same elaborate security measures are taken before we can get out. Noah comes to open my door and Yuri opens the door for Zane. I snuggle deeper into my lovely coat. I feel a hand on the small of my back and Zane guides me to the doorway.

We are shown to a lift where a large man is already waiting with the door open. We get in and it takes us all the way to the top floor. The lift door opens and, wow! The entire rooftop has been turned into a giant conservatory with a vaulted ceiling. Through the glass ceiling I can see the inky night sky full of stars.

A wiry, white-haired man in an immaculate cream suit and a thin, pink tie comes up to welcome us. He has a deep tan. He could be European. His eyes are sharp and they keep darting around the restaurant as he speaks to us.

'Would you care for an aperitif at the bar?' he asks, smiling, his head tilted in a half-bow. His accent is pure French.

'Yes,' Zane says without consulting me.

I should have been irritated by the imperious way he had decided for me, but I am too awed and fascinated by my surroundings to make any kind of issue. The décor is a meticulous and impressively successful attempt at recreating a lush Asian garden. There is a profusion of exotic plants and flowers. Beautiful, colorful orchids sprout out of halved coconut husks and the bark of trees. There are giant ferns, hanging creepers and a rocky pond full of large koi.

We have to cross a sweet wooden bridge built over a stream to get to the bar area. I notice the bar is made entirely from frosted glass, and looks like a massive ice sculpture. All the chairs are over-the-top thrones, with flamboyantly rich and colorful upholstery.

We are shown to a glass-topped table. *How You Remind Me* by Nickelback is playing in the background as I slip into one of the marvelous chairs ... and holy cow, it is easily the most comfortable chair I have ever rested my ass on.

'We have to find a way to take one of these chairs back with us,' I joke, leaning back and feeling like a Queen. I haven't forgotten that he left me high and dry at the back of the car, but I plan to bide my time and take my revenge when the opportunity presents itself.

'Take it if you want,' he replies with an offhand shrug.

'What?'

'If you want the chair I'll have it sent over to your apartment.'

I stare. The idea was kind of gross. Like a big kid stealing candy from the smaller children. 'Are you able to just walk into any restaurant and demand their furniture?'

Zane looks at me strangely. 'This is my restaurant, Dahlia.'

My eyebrows fly upwards. 'This is yours?'

'Hmmm ... what's so surprising about that?'

'Well. I never expected you to have an Asian themed restaurant called Uncle Ho. I mean. You're so ... Russian. Russian breakfast. Russian staff. Russian artwork.'

An exotically beautiful woman in a red and white pants suit brings us both food and drinks menus. I open the drinks menu and there are at least fifty different vodka cocktails to choose from. I dither between Agent Orange and White Russian, but eventually decide on the latter. Zane has the Moscow Mule.

'Well,' I prompt after the woman leaves us. 'What made you open such a restaurant?'

'It's actually inspired by Ho Chi Minh,' Zane explains.

I frown. I'm sure I've heard of him before. 'Isn't he some kind of Vietnamese Communist?' I ask.

'I'm glad to see they teach you world history in America,' he observes mockingly.

'Why? Don't they teach world history in Russia?' I retort.

'Yes, but we probably learn a different ... um ... version than you do.'

'Why's that?'

'You recognize him as some kind of Vietnamese Communist, I know him as a great revolutionary figure.'

I look at Zane, curious and intrigued. 'There are so many great revolutionary figures. Why him particularly?'

His eyes glint and his lips seem very red and erotic. 'I admired his ferocity. He took on the French Union and won.'

'So you admire ferocity in a man?'

'Ferocity gets you what you want.' His gaze hasn't unlocked from mine. I feel mesmerized by his raw beauty, but the subject we are talking about is important.

'Maybe in your world, but not in mine,' I whisper fiercely.

'You don't think ferocity rules your world?' he asks with deceptive softness.

I look deep into his icy, dispassionate eyes. Yes, he is strong, and rich with power and wealth, however I saw something in his eyes once. Just once, but it was enough for me to know ghosts blew through the deserted corridors of his soul like gusts of cold wind.

'I know it doesn't,' I say clearly.

He says nothing, just smiles, calm and cool.

The waitress comes with our drinks. My White Russian is not what I expected. It is not the color of milky-coffee I am used to. Instead it comes in two layers, the Kahlua in a rich brown bottom layer, and the cream and vodka as a glossy-white top layer. There are little rectangles of Kahlua jelly resting on the surface of the concoction. I use the two little black straws to stir the drink and watch the Kahlua swirl into the white layer.

He lifts his glass in my direction. 'To ferocity.'

I copy the action, but not the words. 'To kindness.'

Seventeen

Dahlia Fury

Over the rim of his glass he watches as I remove the straws and sip the fragrant cocktail. It is like a liquid dessert.

'Good?'

'Poetry in a glass.'

A reluctant smile tugs at his lips. 'That good?'

'This is Oh-My-God good.'

The waitress comes back to check if we have decided what we want to eat.

'What's good to eat here?' I ask Zane.

'Do you like prawns?'

'Yes.'

'Then the flaming prawns dish is exceptional.'

'OK,' I agree. 'I'll have that. Any suggestions for the main course?'

'I'm having pork with broken rice.'

'Sounds suitably exotic. Why not?' I say.

Zane gives our order to the girl.

189

A young woman with a long luxurious plait down her back comes and puts prawn crackers on the table. She gives a lingering sideways look at Zane and I feel a tightening in my belly. I can't be jealous! It's the last thing I need. I shift my gaze to Zane and realize that he doesn't even notice her, and I feel an enormous sense of relief, and my body relaxes. *Oh boy, you're in so much trouble.*

'By the way,' I throw in casually. 'I need to go to work tomorrow afternoon. I'll just be an hour.'

Zane nods. 'Sure. Let Noah drive you there.'

'Uh. No. That won't be necessary. I'll be quicker if I just take the tube.'

'I'm afraid you can't take public transport while you are with me.'

'Why not?'

'There is always the risk of kidnap and harm.'

'Surely no one with half a brain is going to kidnap the new toy of the great Russian Mafia boss.' My voice is heavily laced with sarcasm.

'This is true, but there are people with less than half a brain and I have to be very wary of them. They will be unbelievably sorry afterwards, but the damage would have been done. While you are my property you are my responsibility.'

I raise my palm up. 'OK, you've made your point, but I don't want Noah to take me. Can't I just take a taxi? They'll send someone to come right to the front door, wait at the destination, and bring me back.'

His eyes narrow. 'Are there men in your agency?'

'Men? No, there are no men there except for Mr. Hawthorne, the bookkeeper who comes in on Tuesdays, but he's at least a hundred and twenty years old.'

'Then why don't you want Noah to take you? Has he done something to upset you?'

'No,' I deny immediately, 'of course not.' I sigh. 'It's not him. It's just that I have not told anyone at work about our ... arrangement and I don't want to arrive in a blacked out Mercedes.'

He finishes his drink in a single gulp. 'Then Noah will take you and park in the next street and walk up the road with you.'

'What? No way. Noah looks so dangerous.'

'He can wait across the road,' he says haughtily.

I sigh again. 'Fine. But he can't be seen with me.'

'I will tell him.'

'Good. Thank you. I appreciate that.'

A waiter arrives to escort us to our table and we follow him to a round table spread with a snowy white tablecloth and, unusually, set with two pure white serving plates. There is no pattern or the restaurant's monogram on it. Once we are settled in and glasses of champagne have been placed in front of us, Zane resumes our conversation.

'So what is it that you do at this literary agency of yours?'

I take a mouth full of bubbles. 'Well, it's my job to help read the massive pile of manuscripts that come in the post every day and try to find raw talent that our agency would like to represent.'

'Do you find many?'

'No. Unfortunately, everybody thinks that just because they can craft a sentence they can write a book.'

He leans forward. 'How many have you found since you have been at the agency?'

'I've found three, but two were vetoed out by the other girls as not good enough. So I guess I found one, but she was a really good one. Fey, the owner of the agency, put her book to auction with the big four publishers and she got a £250,000 advance.' I grin. 'And that's just for her UK rights. She got a similar amount for her American rights. Cool stuff, huh?'

He nods slowly. 'Not bad. How many manuscripts did you have to read to find this gem?'

'I don't know, sometimes it feels like a million. But to give you an idea of the statistics we deal with, the agency gets in the region of 200 to 250 submissions per week, but we only signed up four authors last year.'

He leans back in his chair, surprised. 'That's almost like winning the lottery.'

'Exactly what I say,' I agreed.

He drags a finger down the condensation on the flute glass thoughtfully. 'Have you never wanted to write a book yourself?'

'I don't consider myself a writer. I guess I never have. I do scribble down my thoughts when my mind gets so overwhelmed that I feel I have to empty the box. Since they are all random often they make no sense at all, but occasionally I sound like a wizard or Einstein. Those pieces I've stashed away and maybe one day I'll read them to my kids. Something for them to remember their mom by when I am gone.'

Zane stares at me as if he is seeing a ghost.

'What?' I ask defensively.

'Nothing,' he says quickly.

Embarrassed that I carelessly shared something so personal with him, I pick up a prawn cracker, nibble on it as if I don't have a care in the world and say, 'So tell me about your job.'

He smiles. 'Are you asking me to incriminate myself?'

'I won't tell a soul. Girl Scout's honor.'

He takes a sip of champagne. 'Maybe you won't, but the walls have ears.'

I put the remainder of the prawn cracker into my mouth and let it melt on my tongue. 'Someone told me your real name is Aleksandr Malenkov.'

'Is he the one who told you I ate my own heart?'

I pierce him with my eyes. 'Actually, he told me you are a very dangerous man.'

He raises an eyebrow. 'Yeah?'

I lick my dry lips. 'He told me you're a killer.'

His face remains watchful, but he is now also guarded. 'You have a wonderful amendment in your country's constitution that I'm rather fond of. The Fourth, I believe.'

'You're very casual about it,' I murmur.

'Is it cruel when a cheetah outruns an impala and kills it?'

'The cheetah does it because it's hungry.'

'There are many kinds of hunger,'

My senses flash like the warning light on a car's dashboard. Not dazzling. Just insistent. *Beware, your little heart. Beware, your little heart.* 'So you feel nothing for your victims. Not even a tiny twinge of guilt.'

'Be assured, little fox, anyone who *might have* perished at my hands will have richly deserved it. I don't knock on the doors of ordinary people. Everyone in my world understands the rules on the day they enter it.'

'Why did you enter this world?'

'Because I knew it was the fastest way to get everything I wanted, and I knew I could be more ferocious than anyone else.'

'And it never occurred to you to do something legitimate?'

'I have legitimate businesses. You are sitting in one.'

'Is it really worth it to have to guard yourself day and night?'

'I never think about it. You have greenish-gold eyes. I have bodyguards.' He shrugs lightly.

'Will you ever walk away from it?' I realize I am holding my breath.

'The chances are I will be gunned down long before I get a chance to leave it.'

My mouth opens in a gasp. 'Knowing that you still stay?'

'If I die in the gutter so be it, but I will not live in it like a rat.'

'Are you trying to say that my life equates to living in the gutter like a rat?'

He smiles lopsidedly. 'My choices were slightly more ... stark than yours.'

'What about the people who love you? Don't you care that they must be worried sick all the time?'

His eyes flicker. 'There is not a single person on this earth who cares if I live or die, and that is exactly how I like it.'

I open my mouth to reply to such an epic statement and, to my shock, I see a tiny hole about two inches in diameter suddenly appear on the tablecloth close to my plate. I blink in astonishment. Hell, how much champagne have I had? Out of that tiny hole a little chef, the size of Thumbelina, emerges and bows to me as if he is about to start a performance. Other than his size he is completely lifelike.

Oh my God! Have I been drugged? Or am I just hallucinating because I'm going crazy?

'What the hell?' I exclaim.

The little chef is now opening a bag. I reach out a hand and try to touch him, but only catch thin air. The chef goes on about his business opening the bag and taking out a tiny fishing net.

I look up at Zane. 'What's going on?'

He grins like a schoolboy. The seriousness of our earlier conversation feels as if it belongs in a different lifetime.

'It's a hologram.' He points to the ceiling and I look up. Two projectors are mounted over the table. 'It's called 3D projection mapping. Le Petit Chef is preparing your dinner for you.'

A hologram! So this is the new fangled thing Molly was talking about. The illusion is so real I had to try and catch the digital chef with my fingers. Completely awed by the technology, I watch the tiny Chef use an electric saw to cut a hole into the tablecloth and start fishing for my prawns in the water below. As he catches them he flings the giant prawns still wriggling and struggling onto the tablecloth. They land twitching and twisting realistically.

The little chef then reaches under my plate and starts cranking a lever. It causes my plate to become a sliding surface. A metal dish shaped like champagne coupes rises from beneath.

With comic difficulty he drags the prawns one by one onto a spoon, and expertly slings them so they end up curled over the lip of a metal dish. He starts up his chainsaw again and cuts down a red chili from a chili tree. Cursing and swearing to himself like a real chef, he pulls the other ingredients out of the tablecloth and catapults them all into the metal dish.

He then finds a bottle of alcohol and squirts it in an arc; like water from the hosepipe onto the prawns. Muttering to himself he conjures up a firecracker and directs it to the prawns. The prawns start flaming, he falls backwards, a spark catches on his clothes, and he runs, hands flapping back into the hole he originally emerged from.

I laugh, delighted by the little show. As if rehearsed, the waitresses arrive with our flaming prawns. The dish looks exactly like the one the little chef had so amusingly prepared.

'How am I going to eat this?' I ask looking at the marvelous creation.

'When the flames die down, with your hands.'

I follow his lead, peeling the skins and biting into the succulent flesh. They are absolutely delicious and so juicy I have to constantly lick and suck my fingers. OK, I'll admit I might have overdone it, but how am I supposed to help it when I catch his eyes on me, attentive, mysterious, and full of lust every time I do it? It is only a little revenge compared to what he did to me in the back of his car.

Then I eat the last prawn and lick the last drop of juice from my fingers, and suddenly my idea of revenge doesn't seem so sweet anymore.

Eighteen

Dahlia Fury

'**C**ome,' he says, standing suddenly.

I am still staring at him in surprise when he takes my wrist in his hand and tugs me upright. Conscious that my fingers are still stained with prawn juices, I quickly grab a linen napkin just as he pulls me away. I lengthen my stride to match his. The reaction of the other diners to us moving quickly through the restaurant is standard. They stare openly at him.

Why wouldn't they? Tall, built, menacing.

He shoves me into the Ladies, quickly checks the toilet stalls, and when he finds them all empty, he jams the door with a fancy pink chair. He turns around and fixes his gaze on me. His eyes scorching.

'What happened to that wild, lustful look in your eyes, my little cocktease?'

'I ...' The napkin falls from my suddenly nerveless fingers.

He starts advancing on me. 'You enjoyed tormenting me, didn't you? Sending all the blood from my brain into my dick?' he glowers.

I batten down the hatches, cross my arms over my chest, and do what my mother says is one of my greatest talents since I was two years old. I lie with a straight and brazen face.

'I assure you,' I say imperiously. 'It wasn't intentional. What am I supposed to do if a perfectly ordinary action like eating turns you on?'

'Either one of the toilets is badly blocked or that statement is a steaming pile of *bullshit*.' He shoots the word bullshit at me like a bullet.

My eyes dart to his crotch. There is definitely 'bulge' going on. A very big one at that.

'Do you know how hard I am?' he growls. Grasping my left wrist, he pulls my arm out of its crossed position and places my hand on his crotch.

Oh yeah, hard as a damn rock.

'Oops,' I say softly.

'Oops? You think you should be able to tease me like that and not get punished?' he purrs.

'Well, you started it first. You left me high and dry in the car.'

'I'm allowed. You're not,' he mutters. Before I can query the hell out of that lordly statement he goes off on a totally different tangent. 'What shampoo are you using?' he asks hoarsely.

'I don't know. I found it in the bathroom compliments of your housekeeping staff.'

'It's fucking epic,' he breathes in my ear and I can't stop a smug smile happening.

He rubs my hand along his thick shaft as he moves his face in front of mine and stares into my eyes. Then he takes my stained right hand and brings it up until it's between our faces and starts licking and sucking my fingers one by one, slowly, deeply.

I find myself holding my breath. My mouth opens as he grabs a fistful of my hair. I claw at his jacket as a pathetic animal-like moan escapes my lips. Bending his head he takes my lower lip between his teeth and nips it.

'Ouch.'

'Awww ... did that hurt baby?' he growls.

'What's the matter with you?' I gasp, running my tongue over my lower lip. It stings but I can't taste blood.

'I'm frustrated,' he replies.

'Do you want me to suck you off?' I offer, my hand moving over his trouser-clad erection.

He takes my hand away from his crotch. 'Yes, but not here.'

I scrunch my eyebrows. 'Then what?'

'I want you to feel what I feel.'

'Don't forget I was frustrated too.'

He licks my earlobe. 'Not like me.'

'What's the difference between your frustration and mine?' I ask.

He sucks the fleshiest part of my ear. 'You want to know?'

'Yes,' I whisper, my hips inching closer to his body until his hardness digs into my belly. The sensation is downright erotic and I feel my pussy start to cream.

'Are you sure?' he asks.

I nod and grind my mound against the muscles of his thighs.

He places his hands under my ass cheeks and hefts me up to the polished granite countertop where there is a selection of perfume bottles and some glass containers of hand lotion. He spreads my legs and looks down at my dripping sex, then brings his gaze back to my eyes.

'I told you, you're not the only one who's gagging for it,' I say shakily.

Someone knocks on the door and I jump and close my legs in a rush.

'It's occupied,' Zane snarls without breaking eye contact with me.

'You can't take over the whole Ladies. I'm going to complain to the staff,' a woman yells back.

'They'll be here soon,' I warn.

'They won't if they know what's good for them,' he says brutally.

'Wow, all this macho shit is turning me on,' I tease.

'Then you'll fucking love this,' he says. Reaching into his jacket pocket, he fetches out something that looks like bits of straps attached to a blue jelly-like object.

'What the hell is that?' I ask curiously.

'You're going to wear this for the rest of the night,' he says untangling the straps. 'It's a butterfly vibrator.'

'What happens if I come while I'm eating my pork and broken rice?'

'That dish will achieve a cult status,' he says, unconcerned.

I giggle as he slips the larger strap around both my feet and the smaller straps around each foot. He pulls them up until the larger strap is around the widest part of my hips, and the other two snugly circle each thigh. The butterfly, complete with little wings, is made from some sort of pliable material, maybe rubber or silicone. It fits over my sex and even has a little curving tail that juts inside me.

'Now what?' I ask.

He takes a little blue gadget out of his other pocket. 'There are nine settings and three speeds and we'll find out what you like best.'

Someone pounds at the door. 'Excuse me, Sir, but you can't jam these doors. Open them immediately, or I'll have to call the police,' a man shouts.

I grin at Zane. 'I'm ready if you are!'

The man bangs on the door again and rattles the handle. 'Open it right now,' he demands.

I jump off the counter and we walk towards the door. Zane opens it and the man who was shouting insults so aggressively deflates in the most spectacular manner possible. His eyes widen, he gulps audibly, and actually takes a long step back.

'Oh! Sorry, Sir. I ... I had no idea it was you,' he stammers.

'Good job,' Zane says coolly and palms some money into the man's surprised hand. As he escorts me to our table, the thought that I have given total control of my sexual pleasure to him is actually much hotter than I would ever have dreamed.

Hmmm ... the butterfly vibrator.

Well, it starts off with a gentle hum that causes havoc to my ability to enjoy my pork and broken rice. Then it goes up a notch and does such a splendid job of totally turning me on. Desperate to come, I start to think that really it is only fair that I should share the blessing.

I lick my lips lasciviously and tell Zane that even though I'm sitting there with a vibrator strapped to my clit, I can't think of anything else but wrapping my lips around his big dirty cock.

When his eyes widen with surprise I get even more filthy.

'Just thinking about having your dick in my mouth is making me sooooo fucking wet. God, I want to be on my knees for you right now.' I rub my neck suggestively and croon, 'I'm all yours, baby. You've just got to come and get it.'

He retaliates by taking the butterfly from level one to four in a vicious rush. Oh, sweet baby Jesus. More vibrations race through me than I have ever thought possible. They cause fireworks of sensations. A very familiar

pressure starts to mount, and I become terrified I'm going to climax and scream out right here in front of all these snooty people.

'Oh My God! I can't take it anymore. You have to stop it,' I hiss at Zane.

'Relax, you're not there yet, *rybka*. Take a deep breath. I'm just building up the tension,' he says unconcerned, but he does dial down the intensity to almost nothing.

Needless to say I refuse dessert.

The car journey is, as Stella would call it, a bit fraught. I just about make it out of the car and walk calmly up the steps. In the hallway Zane grabs me and pulls me to his study.

'A whole mansion and you bring me here?' I ask.

'My biggest fantasy is of taking you here.'

'Oh yeah? What was I doing in your fantasy?'

'Lying across my table.'

I put a finger on his mouth. 'Say no more.'

His eyes gleam.

I turn around and present my back to him. 'Unzip me, please?'

I feel the warmth of his fingers down my back. The dress pools around my fabulous shoes. I step out of it and turn around. I am naked but for the butterfly vibrator that is barely humming. My thighs are glistening, my nipples are like little pebbles. His hand reaches out to grasp my naked flesh and I evade it easily.

'Tsk, tsk,' I tut, shaking my head sternly.

He grabs my chin. 'I want to fuck your mouth.' Still holding me he starts unbuckling his belt. I use both my hands to stop him. He is at the edge. His hold tenuous.

Feeling a bit like a porn star, I whisper huskily, 'Let me.'

He stands there all golden and fiercely sexy while I unzip his trousers and out pops his thick, hard length. I get on my knees in front of his cock, and holding the smooth base, look at it. It is a warm, silky, beautiful thing. It could be a work of art. Pale as a cobweb, straight, and perfectly unblemished. Like a Dorian Gray portrait in reverse. The more he sins the more beautiful his cock becomes.

Then his hand is in my hair, and he forces my mouth to swallow all that beauty.

'Take it, memorize it, the taste, the feel, the smell, because it's going to be keeping your mouth busy daily now,' he promises.

Looking up into his eyes I begin to suck him earnestly. I feel drunk off his taste.

'Fuck, what a great mouth,' he grunts.

He has no idea that I got dragged off by Stella to a Blowjob Attitude class where a woman with frizzy red hair started the class off by saying, 'There are only two things you need for a mind-blowing blowjob.' She ticked off her fingers. ''One: a mouth in working condition. Two: enthusiasm in spades. Of the two, enthusiasm in spades is by far more important. All the other little tricks of the trade I will provide.'

I unleash blowjob trade secret number one on Zane. I grab his hips and, leaving only about three inches of him in my mouth, simply roll my tongue. Round and round his cock, as if it is the most delicious thing I've ever tasted.

'Fuck,' he swears.

I don't want him to ejaculate just yet, so I slow things down a bit and start super-slowly licking the whole shaft from base right to the tip, always paying a bit more attention to the rim and slit at the tip. When he is least expecting it: I unleash secret number three. I impale my mouth on his shaft all the way into my throat until my nose is in that dark nest of hair. I stare up at him hungrily.

He looks down at me with such possessiveness that it makes his face look dark and wild. 'You clearly love sucking cock,' he growls. 'Let's see how good you really are. Lie on the desk and hang your head over the edge so I have full access to your throat.'

He pulls me to my feet and guides me to his desk. I quickly position myself across it and hang my neck and head off the edge.

'Open your legs,' he instructs in a super-crazy hot voice.

I do as I'm told, aware of just how obscene I must look, but reveling in his total dominance. Looking down at my nakedness, his face full of lust, he takes his jacket off and from one of its pockets removes the remote to my vibrator. He throws it on the desk.

'Open your mouth,' he orders, and when I do he grasps my breasts and pumps his cock directly into my throat.

'Look at you,' he says almost proudly. 'My cock is balls deep in your mouth.' He pushes his hips in and starts fucking my mouth in earnest.

'Suck me. I'm going to fill your stomach with my cum.'

His hands leave my breasts. Suddenly the vibrator goes on full.

'Ahhhhh ... fuck'

He starts thrusting into my mouth even faster.

'That's it, baby. Suck me. Milk my dick and swallow it all down,' he roars, his cock throbbing and jerking in my throat as he begins to deposit his cum directly into my stomach.

He takes my head in his hands and with total control withdraws his dick out of my throat so the last spurts happen in my mouth. Secret number two to giving an awesome blowjob: swallow his semen as if you are desperate for it, as if you haven't had a drop of water to drink for days.

I swallow Zane's cum while sucking for more.

I start to swallow the warm, salty liquid filling my mouth, but in fact that reaction is an automatic one because I am shuddering towards an orgasm that feels as if it is more important than breathing. The spasms are so fast and intense they overwhelm me. Beyond pleasure or pain they make my body arch off the table and my mouth open in a strangled uncontrollable scream. His seed runs out of the sides of my gasping mouth and down my cheeks.

'Cum suits you. You'd make a good slut,' he murmurs when the convulsions die down. Gently he rubs his cream into my cheeks.

Secret number three: show how much you love the taste of his semen. I grin up at him. 'When can I have some more?'

'You really are a dirty girl, aren't you?' he says, a tender and probably unintended inflection in his voice.

'Mmmm,' I moan sweetly, but already I can feel him mentally withdrawing from me.

He moves away and comes back with my dress, then helps me up and even zips me into my dress.

'That really was fucking something, but I've got work to do,' he says, picking his pants up from the floor and zipping them up. 'So I'll say goodnight now.'

'Good night, Zane,' I say politely, but I don't think I've ever felt so knotted up with hurt.

'Sleep well.'

We are like two strangers. I walk out of his study and vow there and then that I will never trust him again. No matter how nice he is, or how desperate he seems to have sex with me. It is just that. Sex. Did I make a mistake? I behaved like a slut and he treated me like a slut.

When all is said and done, there is nothing left.

Nineteen

Dahlia Fury

Unless I fall into bed in a drunken stupor I am usually a very light sleeper, and the least noise will wake me. I don't know what, but a noise filters through my sleep.

My eyes fly open.

The room is lit only by the bluish glow from the nightlight that I plugged into the wall just outside the bathroom. I listen intently and I hear it again. Footsteps. Someone is coming up the stairs. Someone is standing outside my door. For a few seconds whoever it is just stands there. Then the door opens.

It's him!

I quickly shut my eyes and pretend to be in a deep sleep. From the slits of my eyes I see him advance towards the bed. He stands over me and looks down. It's extremely difficult to fake sleep and breathe evenly and deeply when every damn cell and nerve in my body is screaming for me to switch on the light and

invite him into my bed, but the memory of how coldly he dismissed me earlier is still raw and bleeding.

What seems like forever passes before he bends down and quietly leaves something on the bedside table. He turns and walks back to the door. He is more than halfway across the room when something makes him stop and come back.

For a few heart stopping moments he does nothing, just stands there barely breathing. Then he grasps the duvet and gently pulls it up over my chest and lets it fall softly down on my body. He straightens, walks to the door and closes it soundlessly behind him.

Hell! What was that all about?

I am so shocked I don't move even after I hear his footsteps go back down to the lower floor. Eventually, I switch on the bedside lamp. There is an envelope on the bedside table. I tear it open and out falls a gold card with my name on it, a letter with my new pin number, and another letter advising me of my credit limit.

My eyes nearly pop out of their sockets. £10,000.00!!

Well, well. You want me to spend your money so you feel better about your behavior?

Consider it done.

I skip breakfast the next morning because I really can't face the cold omelet, the pink, raw-looking sausages, or the semolina pudding again. I just go down for a cup of coffee and work steadily until lunch.

By then I am starving. I eat a lot of rye bread with a man-size plate of beef stroganoff, and wash it all down with Russian apple pie. More stodgy than the American version, but good nevertheless.

At two o'clock Noah and I come down the steps and a grey Audi drives up and stops in front of us. Noah opens the back door for me and I get in. He closes the door and sits in the front passenger seat.

'Can we stop at Harvey Nichols for like an hour? I need to buy something,' I tell Noah.

He nods and gives the driver his instructions in Russian. Twenty minutes later the driver drops us off outside the department store and Noah and I enter it. We take the lift to the men's department. When we get there I ask a sales assistant where I can find leather jackets to fit Noah.

Noah frowns. 'What are you doing?'

'We're getting you a brown leather jacket.'

'Me?' he asks, jerking his head back in surprise.

'Yeah, you.'

He narrows his eyes suspiciously. 'Why?'

'I know you're part of Zane's bodyguard/security personnel, but you don't have to look like one all the time.'

Noah scratches the back of his neck in a touchingly bewildered way, and I take the opportunity to grab his huge forearm and start walking him towards the area the woman pointed out to us. Once there I ask another assistant to show us some brown leather jackets for Noah. While she runs a practiced eye over him he clears his throat uncomfortably.

While she goes to find a selection of jackets, I receive a text. It's a blast from the past.

How's it going? xx

For a fraction of an instant I hesitate. Then I text him a reply back. One that tells him exactly where he is in my life.

Great. Thanks for a being my friend. I really appreciate it. X

Mark's reply is instant and a bit intriguing.

I'm the best friend you have at the moment. Don't forget that. No matter what happens you can rely on me. xx

But the sales lady comes back with four different styles for Noah to try on so I just send Mark some kisses and a hug.

'Go on, then. Try them on,' I urge, putting my mobile back into my bag.

Noah takes the jackets from her, looks at the price tag of the first one, and recoils so drastically it is comical. 'Fucking hell,' he says with a horrified expression. 'This *thing* is nearly two thousand pounds. Who's going to pay for it?'

'I am.' I watch his eyes bulge with surprise and amend my statement. 'Well, Zane is. He gave me a credit card and presumably that means I can buy whatever I want with it, right?'

He rubs his jaw. 'Yes, but … you're supposed to buy pretty things for yourself.'

'I don't remember him making any such stipulation.'

'I'll have to check this with the boss first,' he says holding the jacket at arms length.

I fold my hands. 'I don't care what you do, but you're not coming with me to my workplace unless you are wearing something other than that thuggish black leather jacket you've got on.'

'All right. I'll take my jacket off and stand in my shirt.'

'Absolutely not. I'm not standing here arguing with you. You're buying a jacket or you're not coming with me.'

For a few seconds he looks at me with a stunned and confused face, then he takes off his jacket and tries on the first one.

'There's a mirror there,' I say nodding to the wall behind him.

I trail behind as he walks to it and stop when he does. I look at his reflection. 'You like?'

'I don't know,' he says shyly. 'What do you think?'

'I kinda like it, but it's very similar to the one you already have. Let's see what the other three look like before we decide, huh?'

Meekly he takes it off and tries the next one.

We hit eureka with the third jacket. Both the sales assistant and I agree, Noah looks gorgeous.

'How is it possible you haven't got a girlfriend, Noah?' I tease.

Big, strong, stoic Noah who wanted to body search me the first time he met me, flushes a deep shade of red.

I give the sales assistant Noah's old jacket to put into a carrier bag, and pay for the new jacket.

'Thank you,' he says gruffly.

I smile at him. 'Thank you for ... protecting me.'

'It's my job.'

Then we pop upstairs to the Food Hall for a box of cereal before we go back down to the ground floor where I wander into the handbag department. As I pick out a smart, black leather handbag, I see Noah checking his reflection out in a mirror. Smiling, I slip the bag into the crook of my elbow and look at Noah.

'Do you think Olga will like this?'

'Olga?' he asks with surprise. 'You're buying that for Olga?'

'Mmmm.'

He looks at me with narrowed eyes. 'Why?'

'Why not? She's always cooking for me and getting me coffee and stuff, and I'd like to get her something to say thank you.'

'Oh,' he says, looking at me as if I have just grown a second head.

'So? Do you think she'll like it?'

He shrugs. 'I'm not a woman. I wouldn't know.'

He looks so out of place in the perfumed, feminine environment that it makes me cheeky. 'But would you fancy a woman who carried a bag like this though?' I insist.

At first he stares at me as if I am mental, but then he grins, his first real grin. 'Are all American people like you?'

'Some,' I say, and sail towards the cashier.

As I am paying I see Noah talking on his mobile. It must have been with the driver because by the time we get out of the doors the driver is already waiting. We get in and he drives us to my workplace.

Noah waits at the corner where he can still see me go into the building but not close enough to be seen by anybody from my office.

The girls are happy to see me and offer to make a pot of tea and open the biscuit tin. I know they want to have a little gossip, but conscious of Noah waiting outside, I tell them I am in a hurry. I drop off the read manuscripts and pick another massive pile of submissions and go back out to Noah.

While we are in the car Molly calls to tell me that she will be around at about seven with new clothes for me. I look at Noah.

'Is it OK for Molly to come around at seven today?'

'As long as she is gone by ten. Boss wants you to be at the Matrix at eleven o'clock.'

'That's great. I'll see you then,' I say, and end the call.

'What is the Matrix?' I ask Noah.

'A club,' Noah says shortly.

I suppress a sigh. 'Does it belong to Zane?'

'Yeah.'

When we get back to the house Noah and I go into the kitchen. Olga is sitting flipping through the pages of a magazine and listening to Russian pop music playing in the background. She grins at us and makes the hand sign of drinking to me to ask if I want a coffee.

I nod.

Noah says something in Russian and she turns towards me with her eyebrows raised and an enquiring look in her eyes. I walk towards her and give her the Harvey Nichols carrier bag.

'For you,' I say, my finger wagging at her.

She points at her own chest with her eyebrows raised.

I nod and smile.

She takes the shopping bag from me and opens it, looks inside then looks again in disbelief.

'Go on take it out.'

She takes the protective white cloth cover off, gasps at the handbag and looks up at Noah. He just raises his eyebrows as if to say, Don't look at me. This has *nada* to do with me.

I see her eyes drop to his jacket and she fires something to him in Russian and nods. She turns towards me. Her eyes are misty as she reaches out and rubs her rough palm on my forearm.

I take my coffee and leave them. As soon as the door closes I hear Olga grilling Noah in earnest.

Twenty

Dahlia Fury

Noah goes out into the street to help Molly bring in two rails of clothes on wheels and three cardboard boxes full of shoes, belts and handbags. For nearly two hours Molly stays with me while I try on all the stuff. I learn a lot from her.

She encourages me into styles and shapes and colors that I have spent a lifetime saying no to. She puts me in stripes and matches it with polka dots. She teams orange with red and green with blue. She has even brought me that racy red miniskirt I saw at the back of the van to be worn with knee-high, black wedge boots.

Talking of shoes I suddenly find I have ten fabulous pairs to add to my collection. There are ankle cuff pumps, ink blue leather boots, ballerina flats in geranium-pink glitter material; slip-on calf-skin sneakers, leopard print loafers, white lace-up sandals; pearlescent snakeskin, caged, peep-toe sandals;

and strappy leather and raffia sling back platforms. Then Molly reaches into the cardboard box for the last item. With a great sense of drama she opens the shoebox while her hands are inside the cardboard box and slowly lifts her pièce de résistance dangling from her fingers into sight.

'Oh. My. God!' I shriek, my hands flying to my cheeks.

It's a pair of black crystal mesh stiletto Jimmy Choos. Not even in my wildest dreams have I ever dreamt of owning Jimmy Choos!

She puts them on the floor in front of me. 'These are from their private stock. I only got them because I know someone who knows someone.'

I pick a shoe up and kiss it. 'It's so gorgeous. Was it very expensive?' I whisper.

'Could have paid off my mortgage with it,' she whispers back, smiling.

'Well, I might need you to get me another pair.'

'One size smaller?'

'Exactly,' I agree with a grin that threatens to split my face.

'Can I become your best friend too?' she jokes.

'Honey, I'll demote my sister to best friend status and you can take her place.'

We giggle like little girls.

https://www.youtube.com/watch?v=ouLI6BnVh6w

After Molly leaves I dress in a black fitted satin mini dress with a high halter neck, illusion-netting diamond cut-out front, and a low scoop back. I wear sheer black thigh-high stockings with lace elastic tops, and my brand new Jimmy Choos. My hair is loose and full of waves, my eyes are extra smoky, and my lips scarlet. Then I slip into a glamorous hooded cream coat with faux fur trim and silky lining. The feel of the silky lining on my bare arms makes a shiver go through me.

Downstairs Noah raises his eyebrows but makes no comment. I'm used to it by now. He escorts me outside, opens the car door, and I slip in. Before he closes it he says suddenly, 'The boss will like your outfit.'

Before I can thank him, he's closed the door and gone to sit in the front passenger seat. The Matrix is actually in the same building as Uncle Ho. There is a queue of people to the side of the building and they seem to be entering

the club from a different place. The driver parks outside the restaurant entrance, Noah jumps out, opens the door for me, and escorts me towards the door. Yuri stands near it smoking a cigarette. He nods at us and says something to Noah in Russian.

Noah answers and we get into the lift. He presses the necessary buttons and stands quietly with his hands clasped in front of him until we reach our destination, one floor below the restaurant. The doors open to a bustling kitchen. We walk through it, go through a swinging door, and enter the club.

The club is very dark and futuristic. The walls are black with downward flowing digital green rain-like graphics featured in the Matrix movie series. We skirt the edges of a dance floor with a similar green code flashing under it and get to a sectioned off area marked VIP.

I see Zane sitting at a round black banquette. His legs are spread wide and he looks relaxed and totally in control of his environment. No matter how much I don't want it to, my heart does a little excited flip at the sight of him. He is on the phone. He raises a finger and Noah makes a stopping gesture with his palm to me. We wait until he gets off the phone and I am seething with resentment before Noah tells me to move forward. I do, until I'm standing in front of Zane.

'There you are,' I say coldly.

In the darkness of that club Zane's eyes glow as they move down my body. He slides his arms along the back of the banquette and says, 'Take off your coat.'

I shrug out of my coat casually as if I wanted to and was not responding to his instruction. He smiles, slow, sexy, possessive, admiring, tigerish.

'Have a seat,' he invites, tipping his head slightly to the right of him. I sit where he has indicated.

'Want a White Russian?' he asks, brushing his finger on the bare skin of my back.

I feel goose pimples rise up on my skin. Here our worlds meet. Always. 'No, thanks. I think I had my fill of White Russian yesterday,' I say coldly.

His eyes flash. 'So what'll it be today?'

'Perhaps a cosmopolitan.'

He makes a quick fan-like gesture with his fingers and a black clad waiter with a round silver tray materializes before us.

'Same again and one cosmopolitan,' he says to him before turning to me. 'I heard you spent the afternoon bribing my staff.'

'I wasn't bribing them. I was showing my appreciation for their services,' I explain serenely.

He smiles. 'How strange. When I start buying people expensive presents it's always deemed as bribery and corruption.'

'Well, not knowing all the facts I can't comment on your situation.' My tone is even and nonchalant. If I can just keep this up.

'I've increased the limit on your card by the way.'

My eyebrows rise. 'Does this mean every time I spend more you're just going to keep increasing my limit?'

'When it gets outrageous I'll let you know.'

'What do you consider outrageous?'

'Get there and I'll tell you.'

'No, seriously. I've never been someone's sex toy before so I have no idea what would be considered going over the top. What's a sex toy worth in today's market?'

He has been indulgent and amused until now. Now, I see a tightening of his lips. 'You should learn to quit while you're ahead, rybka,' he advises.

'*Rybka*? You keep calling me that. What does it mean?'

He lets his hand brush my nape. His fingers are warm and distracting. 'It's a Russian endearment. It means little fish.'

I crinkle my nose. 'Calling someone a smelly old fish is an endearment in Russia?'

'I said little fish. Not dead fish.'

Our drinks arrive and he lifts his glass. 'To my *rybka*,' he says.

'Hang on one second.' I take out my phone and Google Russian translations. I find the word I am looking for, put my phone down, and raise my glass. 'To my *zaika*,' I say.

He half grins. 'That means bunny.'

'I know,' I say coolly. 'It was a toss up between bunny and little mouse.'

'In that case I will wear my endearment with pride.'

I take a sip of my drink. Nice cosmo. Just then a souped up, club version of Elle King's *Ex's & Oh's* comes on. I put my glass down and look at him. 'I *love* this song. Do you want to dance?'

'I don't dance,' he says staring at me, his body language watchful.

'Oh, that's a shame.'

'Why?'

I shrug. 'Because it's fun.'

I'm so involved in my conversation with him I don't notice the couple who are standing next to us until Zane lifts his head and smiles. I look up at a stunningly beautiful couple. The man is without doubt the most handsome man I have ever seen. He looks like he's a three dimensional photo of one of those impossibly good looking models after they've been through a three hour make-up session and been airbrushed for another three hours. As for the woman, she is exotically and extraordinarily beautiful, with blue-black hair and very pale skin. Her eyes are enormous and as green as grass.

Zane stands up and shakes the man's hand and, to my great surprise, introduces them to me. The man's name is Shane. Apparently he owns a club nearby called Eden. The woman is his wife and her name is Snow.

Shane sits down next to Zane, but his wife excuses herself to go to the Ladies.

'You know what. I'll join you,' I say jumping up.

She smiles warmly at me and though we walk together we don't try to talk until we get to the girl's room. The music is so loud there's no way we can hear each other talk. Once we've both used the facilities, we meet in front of the mirrors.

'I love your dress,' she tells me, stroking her lips with a lip gloss wand.

'Thank you. I love everything about you.'

She smiles and puts the top back on her lip gloss. 'So you're American?'

'Yup. That's me. American. That's not a British accent you've got going there.'

'I'm half Indian,' she explains, putting her lip gloss back into her purse and shutting it.

'Um … how long have you known Zane?' I know I sound desperate, but honestly I might never get another chance to speak to anyone else who knows Zane.

Her eyes catch mine in the mirror. She knows I'm fishing for information. 'Not long.'

'I see.' Looks like she's not going to play ball.

Then she changes her mind and turns to look at me. 'However, my husband has known him for a lot longer, and once when we were going through a very bad period he told me the only person I must turn to if anything ever happened to him was Zane. That I could completely trust him. Even with my life.'

My eyes widen. 'He said that?'

'Mmmm … and my husband is not given to exaggeration. Now. Shall we go back and see what the men have got up to while the cats were away?'

I grin. 'Yeah. Let's do that.'

But as soon as we get out of the Ladies we find her cat is waiting outside.

'Sorry, Dahlia,' he says. 'Something's come up and I'm afraid we have to leave.'

'We must do dinner soon,' Snow says.

'Yes, that would be nice,' I say, but I know it will most likely never happen.

I make my way back to the VIP lounge and see one of those stunningly beautiful ten feet tall creatures that Stella told me Zane usually hooks up with almost lying on my cat's lap. One of her long legs is slowly rubbing against his and she is staring into his eyes. I stand there frozen.

As if in slow motion, Zane turns his face away from hers and looks directly into my eyes. His expression is still. His eyes are veiled. Casually he pats the empty seat next to him. He wants me to share him with this Amazonian woman?

It's just a test, Dahlia. He just wants to see how you'll react.

Fucking sick bastard. I'll show him how I react.

I force myself to smile sweetly before I turn around and walk away from them. I have money in my purse. I'll take a taxi to Stella's, and he can have that woman tonight. Actually, he can have her for the rest of the month. I'll move out tomorrow. I am so angry my blood is bubbling and my heart is racing.

A hand curls around my upper arm.

'You're not going, are you, babe? You haven't danced with me yet.'

I look up at the owner of the hand. He's just one of those creeps who hangs around the dance floors of clubs making nuisances of themselves. Ordinarily, I would have brushed him off and not even politely, but it occurred to me that fuck it, I should have a dance. I deserve a dance. I haven't had a dance since I hooked up with the Russian monster.

'Yeah, I'll dance with you,' I say, and watch his eyes light up like twinkling fairy lights.

He pulls me towards the dance floor and immediately starts gyrating close to me. It hits me instantly that this has not been one of my better ideas. The guy is just such a creep his idea of a dance is to keep bumping into me and grabbing my buttocks in the guise of a dance move.

It happens so fast it's like one moment I'm dancing with a hairy octopus and the next the octopus is lying flat on his back, out stone cold, on the green rain flashing floor. The women around me are screaming, and the crowd has parted like a scene from Moses. There is only

Zane and me. Everything else is just noise and shapes. He stands there looking at me, looking like he is carved out of ice, his face motionless and completely expressionless.

He holds out his hand.

'You don't dance,' I whisper, shocked by the casual violence.

'There's always a first time for everything.'

There is no anger left inside me. Only an inexplicable excitement fizzling through my veins and making me tremble. My voice when I speak is shaky. 'See, if it was me, I wouldn't have engineered a captive audience for my first time.'

'I'm not you,' he says.

I take his hand. It's hard, sure and warm, and he twirls me around and catches me expertly.

I gasp in surprise. 'You lied.'

'I said I didn't dance. I didn't say I couldn't dance.'

I glance down at the inert man. 'Do you think he's all right?'

'Nah. He'll always be an asshole,' he says in my ear.

I laugh. 'Where did you learn to dance?'

He pulls me so close to his body I feel it throbbing with vitality and masculine energy.

'We were taught to,' he says.

'Who is 'we'?'

He runs his lips along my jawbone. 'Curious little thing, aren't you?' he murmurs in my hair.

'Is it a secret?'

Something flashes in his eyes. 'The door is closed and you don't have permission to enter.'

'Who has permission?'

'No one.'

'Isn't it lonely in your golden castle, Zane?'

'It's safe. Anyway, why do you want my secrets? You'll be gone in a month.'

'Why does it have to end in a month? What if it's good? Can't we carry on and find something that suits us both?'

'That door is closed Dahlia. Just enjoy this moment. That's all we have. There is nothing beyond this.'

My body trembles with pain. I feel as if I'm standing in a boat that's slowly sinking. Soon the water will swallow it all.

'Nothing?' I hear my voice ask.

'*Nichego.*' There is a wistful sadness in his voice.

'Is that Russian for nothing?' I ask looking up into his face, searching for that corresponding sign of emotion.

He nods.

I press my face into his chest so that I can't see his eyes. So that he can't see mine and see

235

how hurt I am. 'OK. If we truly have nothing after this then why can't you tell me your secrets? You have nothing to lose.'

'Ahhhhh, Little fox. Don't you know, the king is never killed by his enemies, but by his courtiers? By the people he trusted with his secrets.'

'You think I would betray you?'

'I don't know. What do you think, little one? If someone was pulling out your fingernails one by one can I still trust you?'

I shake my head slowly. 'Probably not.'

'I'm glad you were honest. I prefer an honest coward to a lying hero.'

We dance, while a man lies inert on the floor. It is the strangest dance I have ever had. A hushed crowd. His minders looking like they are ready for any kind of action. Then the security guards come and pick up the guy on the floor and couples start moving back to dance.

When we get back to the house, I start to move towards his study and he grasps my wrist in his hands. I look up at him.

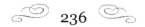

'I have other fantasies of you,' he says.

'Like what?'

'Like having you in my bed.'

He takes me upstairs to his room. It's just like the rest of the house. Beautiful, faultlessly tasteful, and cold. He undresses me and we have sex for hours. He makes me come over and over. Eventually, we both end up on our backs, totally drained.

'Just give me a minute and I'll go,' I whisper.

He turns his head to look at me. 'I want you to stay.'

Shocked, I stare at him wordlessly.

'Tell me why you really bought the handbag for Olga?'

I frown. 'Why do you find it so extraordinary that I bought a handbag for her?'

'No other woman I know would have done something like that.'

Twenty-one

Dahlia Fury

Your naked body should belong only to those
who fall in love with your naked soul.
                                    - Charlie Chaplin

The next day I meet Stella for lunch at our
favorite steakhouse. Noah, who has come
along, grins in a very friendly fashion at her. In
a way that he has never done with me.

'How's it going?' he asks her.

'Not bad,' she replies with a laugh and,
going on tip-toes, kisses him soundly on both
cheeks.

'How's the new masseuse working out?'
she asks with a sly smile.

Noah gives a rough shrug. 'She's not as
easy on the eyes as you, but no complaints from
the boss.'

'Oh, you big flatterer you,' she giggles.

They exchange some more small talk then Noah moves and sits a few tables away from us.

I sit down opposite Stella and put the box of shoes on the table, but deliberately put it to one side. I watch her eyes stray towards it. I don't say anything.

'Is that for me?' she asks finally.

'Yes,' I say with a grin, and she squeals with delight and pulls it towards her. She opens the lid and, oblivious to all the other diners who turn to stare, screams, 'Oh my God! Oh my God! They're so gorgeous.'

I smile to think what her reaction will be when I give her the Jimmy Choos. She takes them out of the box, and kicking off her shoes immediately tries them on.

'Oh wow!' she says, standing up. She turns her foot this way and that to admire the shoes. Then she walks up and down the restaurant before coming back to our table and sitting down.

'Thank you,' she gushes. 'They look really expensive though.'

'Well,' I say. 'Remember that personal dresser I told you about. She sources them all from Hong Kong for a fraction of the price you would pay in Britain.'

Her eyes nearly pop out of her face. 'Did you get the name of her source?' she gasps.

I grin at her. 'Do you think I'm stupid? Of course, I did.'

She leans forward. 'Do they have a website?'

'Not yet. I think at the moment she's just doing it on the sly without the tax authorities knowing about it. I've got her phone number though.'

'Well, go on then,' she says.

I text the number to her phone.

When her phone pings with my message, she says, 'I miss you a lot, you know, D. Even more than I thought I would.'

'Me too,' I say immediately because I do. I really do miss Stella's warmth and laughter and easy chatter.

She looks at me as if she is about to cry.

'I'll be home soon, you'll see,' I promise blithely. It never even occurs to me then that I could be wrong. That I might never live with her again. That my life could dive into chaos and total darkness of a kind I could never imagine.

We order our food and she drops her little bombshell.

'I'm going on a date tomorrow night.'

'Wow! Who with?' I ask.

She shrugs. 'Just some guy. I'm not really that interested, but I figure I'll have to start somewhere.'

I reach out a hand and squeeze her forearm. 'I'm proud of you. You told yourself you were going to get over Zane and you went out and started the process.'

'Yeah,' she says unenthusiastically.

'Look, it's almost certain that this is not the guy for you, but the main thing is you've told yourself mentally that you're available again and that's like a taxi driver putting his taxi light on. Now someone can flag you.'

She bends her head, chews on her lower lip, then looks up at me pitifully. 'So how is Zane?'

I want to tell her how sorry I am that it all worked out so bad for her, but I know she doesn't want to be pitied. Besides, very soon it will be me in her shoes when Zane moves on to his new flavor of the month.

'He's all right,' I say softly.

'How's it going between the two of you?' she asks, in a voice that tells me she desperately wants to know and yet she hates herself for being weak enough to ask.

I decide to be truthful. The last time I didn't tell her because I thought I was protecting her we nearly fell out. 'The sex is like nothing I've known, really out of this world, but to be honest I don't know what to think, babe. He kind of blows hot and cold on me. Every time I think we're making progress he goes and pulls the rug out from under my feet.'

'Why?'

'I think it's because he is determined to keep our arrangement as impersonal as possible.'

She frowns and nods. 'I see.'

'Yeah,' I sigh.

She stares at me incredulously. 'Oh fuck! You're falling in love with him, aren't you?'

I look at her sadly. 'I can't help it, Stel. I'm pretending I'm fine, but I'm shit scared of what is going to happen when my month is up. It feels as if I'm in a lift where the cables have snapped and I just can't stop myself from falling.'

That evening I take a long time over my make-up and hair. Then I zip up my red, high necked, floor-length gown and look at myself in the mirror. My hair is up and I have glamorous drop earrings on. Molly did a fine job.

I do look good.

Zane is taking me to see Yo-Yo Ma live in concert. I don't know if I will enjoy the performance because I'm not really into classical music. In fact, the only reason I even know Yo-Yo Ma exists is because I once had a pretentious boyfriend who had the Bach Cello Suite No. I Prelude as his phone's ring tone. At first it seemed boring but after a while I started to like it.

I come down the stairs and Zane is waiting at the end of them. He is sexy and incredibly handsome in a black tux. His eyes lock on mine and never let go. I reach the second last step and am standing six inches away from him.

'Every day you grow more and more beautiful,' he says quietly.

I can feel myself trembling with pleasure even as I quip, 'I was going to say that.'

He smiles.

'Actually,' I confess, 'I really don't know much about classical music. In fact, I'm not sure I'm going to enjoy tonight.'

He strokes my cheek with the back of his hand. 'All music is beautiful and good, but classical music alone is food for the soul, Dahlia.'

My eyes widen. There is nothing I can think to say to such a profound statement from a man who takes great pains to reveal as little as possible about himself.

https://www.youtube.com/watch?v=cWuoj3rUO88

The hall is very grand and lofty, and it is full of men and women dressed to the nines. We follow Noah up curving stairs. Noah opens a door and I enter a balcony box. There are only two chairs in it.

'Would you like to have a drink before the concert starts?' Zane asks.

I shake my head and sit down on the seat that Noah is holding out for me.

After we are both seated Noah goes out, presumably to wait outside the door.

I look around curiously. At the people down below, at those in the other balconies, and at the crowd where I would have sat if I had come on my own, the peanut gallery. The stage is empty and the background matt black.

Then a hush falls over the people. The lights dim in the theater and the orchestra pit

begins to gently glow. The musicians are now faintly visible. Finally, Yo-Yo Ma himself arrives on stage. He is a small, bespectacled, nondescript Japanese man who carries a cello that is almost as big as himself. He bows politely towards the audience. The audience claps enthusiastically and the orchestra stands in reverence.

Yo-Yo Ma takes a seat.

There are a few seconds of silence as the musicians prepare to begin. In that expectant silence the conductor begins to move his hands and the first haunting notes fill the air. I realize immediately that I not only know that piece of music, I actually love it. It is Sayuri's Theme from the movie, *Memoires of a Geisha*. I turn to tell Zane that and freeze in surprise.

Zane is leaning forward, his expression rapt as if he is not just listening to the music, but absorbing it in through his very pores. Feeling it inside him. *Classical music is food for the soul.*

I turn back to the stage and try to emulate him. Try to see if I can enjoy this kind of music with that kind of intensity. After a while I realize that indeed classical music does something to me that other music does not. Other music makes me want to move my body, but this kind of music makes my spirit soar. So much so I feel almost high as we leave the concert hall.

Zane takes me to a quiet restaurant. They know him well there and a table in a secluded corner has been reserved for us.

'That was beautiful,' I say to Zane.

'Good. I'm glad you enjoyed it,' he says, but something about him feels off and distant. The rest of our conversation is equally stilted and strange.

'Is everything ok?' I ask.

'Yes, I'm preoccupied with some work. If you've finished we should go,' he says.

We hardly speak in the car, and when we get back Zane turns to me in the hallway. 'Go to bed and don't wait up for me. I've a lot of work to catch up on.'

'OK, goodnight,' I say.

Before I can even kiss him goodnight he has turned away and is striding towards his study. I go up the stairs feeling dejected and confused. Once upstairs I change into my nightclothes and go down to his bedroom on the first floor. The bedside lamps are on and the maid has turned down the sheets for the night. I go to my side of the bed and lie down and stare at the ceiling. For at least an hour I lie there until eventually, I fall asleep.

I wake up suddenly, feeling cold and uneasy. It must have been a dream, but I cannot remember it. Immediately I turn my head and Zane isn't there. He never came to bed.

I sit up and listen to the quiet house. Nothing. I get out of bed, pull my dressing gown around myself and go to the door. I open it and listen. Nothing. I walk down the corridor to the top of the stairs. I stand at the balustrade and look down into the hallway. It is in darkness, but I can hear the faint sounds of music.

My slippers are silent on the marble as I go down the stairs and walk towards the music. It's coming from the small reception room that no one ever seems to use. The one with the grand piano.

The music is louder now. Someone is playing the piano.

I go closer to the door and put my hand on the handle, but for some bizarre reason I am afraid to open the door. I feel like Bluebeard's wife. It's as if there is some great secret hidden behind the door. I snatch my hand away and step back. My hand has found its way to my chest where my heart is beating so fast I can feel it thudding against my ribcage. I don't have to go in. *You have to Dahlia. Everything you want to know is in there.*

With shaking fingers I reach for the handle, turn it very quietly, and swing the door open slowly ... and my breath is whisked away.

The entire room is vibrating with music. It is crashing against the thick walls and hitting me in waves. Zane is still in his tux and playing the piano. Rooted to the spot, I stare at him in shock. His back is to me and I can see by the tension in his powerful neck and shoulders how completely lost he is in his music. His whole body is swaying and alive with vibrant energy. It is as if the beauty of his own music has possessed him. That's exactly it. He's like a man possessed!

I am frozen.

I know this man so little. So little.

I thought he was cold and unfeeling. Look at him now. I have never heard anyone play music like this. Like it's pouring out of his soul. I had no idea he is so incredibly talented. I don't make a sound. I don't even think I breathe, and yet ...

He stops mid-note.

The silence is deafening. I hear my own heart.

Slowly, he turns his head and looks at me. Our eyes meet. His are so hostile, so unwelcoming, and so furious, I take a step back in shock.

'What do you want?' he asks quietly, his voice dripping with such cold menace that I feel my blood chill.

'Nothing,' I whisper, backing away, tears coming to my eyes.

Somewhere deep within me I understand. I have seen something I shouldn't have. I turn and begin to run. I race up the stairs and into our bedroom. I close the door and stand with my back to it, panting. Then I take my dressing gown off and go to sit on the bed. Suddenly the door slams open and Zane is there. Startled out of my skin I jump up. I want to apologize, but I don't know what for. He says nothing.

He just comes up to me and, grasping the material of my nightgown at my cleavage, he rips it in two. He cups my breasts and swoops down on my neck. He starts sucking my neck, hard. He does it with such prolonged intensity and in so many places I know I'll be covered in love bites tomorrow. He sucks my nipples. He sucks my breasts. Then he falls on his knees and sucks my stomach.

I'm so wet and so turned on my thighs are trembling. He sucks my belly. He sucks my hips. He sucks my mound. He gives my clit a miss and sucks the insides of my thighs. Then he stands up and turns me around and sucks my back.

He pushes me on the bed so I am face down, then he spreads my legs and plunges in. I grab the edges of the mattress and bite back the scream. He withdraws, slams back in, and explodes inside me with an angry roar.

He moves away from my body and switches on the bedside lamp. 'Sit on the pillow, open your legs and play with yourself.'

'No,' I protest.

'Do it.'

He is like an angry stranger, but I'm not afraid of him. I am afraid *for* him. 'All right,' I say, and reach for the bedside lamp.

His hand shoots out and catches mine. 'No. I want to see you come.'

So I look at a spot on the wall and rub myself. As I hover at the brink of coming, he swoops down and, holding my hips, pushes his tongue deep into me so that I am writhing, shaking and clenching uncontrollably around his tongue.

I'm breathing hard and my muscles are still quivering when he says, 'Don't you ever come to look for me when I am in that room again.'

I nod.

We fall asleep with his arms wrapped around me. In the early morning hours I wake to find him standing over me, the duvet lifted. He is staring at the marks on my body. My first instinct is to cover myself, but I don't. I let him look at the bluish maroon marks. Unashamed of what he has done, he gets into bed and takes me again, laughing with haughty triumph when I climax with a scream.

Twenty-two

Dahlia Fury

You are the knife I turn inside myself; that is love. That, my dear, is love"
                    - Franz Kafka, Letters to Milena

After that episode the walls that guard his heart become impenetrable and I don't try to scale them anymore. My days settle into a routine. I wake up, have breakfast, sometimes with Olga and the boys, sometimes in my room on the top floor where I still go to work. I swim and use the sauna before lunch. After that I work more.

As for our relationship, it has settled into one of mutual sexual desperation, the kind that makes us claw at each other. We meet in his study, or wherever he calls me to, and we fuck as if it's the last time we will see each other. And every time we have sex in that reckless, hopeless, crazy way it feels as if a little part of me dies. A week passes like that until the morning Daisy Skypes me.

'Where are you?' she asks, not recognizing the room I'm sitting in.

'Um ... I'm at a friend's place.'

'Oh. Um ... OK. Dahlia, I ... er ... have a bit of bad news.'

I feel my insides constrict with fear. 'What is it? Is it Mom?'

'No, no. It's not Mom. She's fine.'

'Then what?'

'Suzie passed away last night.'

'Ohhh,' I utter slowly, thinking of sweet Suzie's face. I don't know why but I never expected that. Suzie has been in the family since I was eleven years old. I just saw her a couple of weeks ago and she looked so healthy.

'She didn't suffer or anything,' my sister consoles. 'Also you've got to remember she was very, very old.'

'Yes,' I say faintly.

'She knew she was dying. She went into the bushes and refused to come out when we called to her. And when I gave her water to drink she just turned her face away and looked at me with so much love. I was holding her when she took her last breath.' Daisy's voice catches. 'I took some photos of her and if you want I can send them to you.'

I stare at my sister's face on the screen. She looks normal. In the smaller rectangle at the bottom right hand corner, I just look white and stunned.

'She was nearly fourteen years old, Dahlia. That's really good for dogs. And she had a fantastic life,' my sister says reasonably.

I take a deep gasping breath. 'How's mum taking it?'

'Oh, you know her. She cried herself to sleep last night, but she's a bit better this morning. I'm driving her to the pet crematorium. It's a special place. I found it on the Internet. They burn the pets separately and give us the ashes in an urn. I'll keep her ashes at home for you, OK? Mum says we won't do anything with it until you get home. We can scatter them in the garden, or at sea, or whatever you want.'

'Oh, Daisy,' I cry suddenly.

'Now I don't want you to be sad. Suzie never harmed a fly in her lifetime and so she's off to a good place. We'll see her again. I'm sending the photos to your email address right now. At the end of the day she had a really good death. Really good.'

'OK, thanks,' I choke.

'Oh, Dahlia, please don't be sad. We'll see her again,' Daisy tries to comfort me.

'I've got to go, but I'll call you later,' I say and click into my email account. All the photos are already there. I go through them one by one with tears pouring down my face. I should have been home. I should have been there. Daisy has even sent the photos of Suzie after she died with her poor tongue twisted between her teeth. Feeling devastated and wishing I had never seen it, I delete that photo immediately. I hear the wall phone ringing. For a moment I think of ignoring it then I get up and answer it.

'Boss wants you,' Noah says.

'Tell him I can't come right now,' I sob, and put the receiver back on the cradle.

I go back to the bed and, sitting with my legs crossed, I think of Suzie and say a little prayer.

'Wherever you are now, little sunshine, just remember I love you and I'll love you always,' I say tearfully. I'm so consumed with trying to pray and send her my love I don't hear footsteps come up the stairs. I nearly have a heart attack when the door crashes open and Zane appears in the doorway.

'What's wrong?' he asks.

For a moment I can't speak.

He strides into the room. 'What's the matter?'

'Suzie died,' I sob.

He frowns. 'Who's Suzie?'

'Our family dog.'

He comes and stands over me, his face is curious and surprised. 'Your dog? You're crying over a dog?' he asks as if to confirm the situation because it sounds so implausible to him.

'Yes, I'm crying over my dog. We've had her for thirteen years.'

'Oh,' he says and sits next to me. 'I suppose you can get another one.'

'Would you say that to someone who has just lost their child or a member of their family?'

'No.'

'Then don't say it to me. Suzie was family,' I say tearfully.

For a while there is an awkward silence and then he puts his hand on my knee.

I look up at him, surprised. This is his way of comforting me.

'I'm sorry,' he says quietly.

'That's OK,' I whisper, shocked that we are communicating on this level.

He stands. 'I'll be downstairs if you need me.'

'Thanks,' I say again.

He nods gravely, walks away, and shuts the door quietly behind him.

I don't see him again until late. I'm already in bed watching a You Tube music video when he leans against the doorframe staring at me. He is dressed completely in black, black polo sweater and black jeans, and his eyes are half-closed. I feel that something about him is different. It's even possible that he's a little drunk.

'How do you feel?' he asks.

'I'm OK,' I say warily.

'Is this working?'

I scowl. 'Is what working?'

He pushes away from the doorframe and comes into the room. 'This thing we have. Is it working for you?'

'Not really,' I say truthfully.

'Why not?' he asks, taking his jacket off.

'Do you really want the truth?'

'Why not? Hit me with it,' he says with a wicked grin, and I know. He has been drinking.

'Maybe because I care for you and you're always pushing me away.'

He tilts his head. 'You care for me?'

'Yes.'

'How can you care for me? You don't know shit about me.'

'Maybe I can care without knowing everything.'

He smiles, but his eyes are strange. 'You know what your problem is? You're too uptight.'

'I'm uptight.'

He nods slowly. 'You're uptight. You should take up yoga or meditation like your sister. That'll help calm you down.'

For an instant it doesn't hit me. And then it does and it's like a kick to the gut. I stare at him and he stares back. I take a deep gasping breath.

'How do you know my sister meditates?'

He doesn't say anything.

'It's you,' I accuse, my voice trembling. 'You planned it all. You had her kidnapped, didn't you?' The ice in my voice shocks me.

He simply looks at me.

'Didn't you?' I scream at him.

'I did,' he admits, utterly indifferent to the magnitude of his crime.

I stare at him open-mouthed with horror.

'Do you still care for me, *rybka*?' he mocks.

Rage slams into my brain and it feels as if my head is on fire, ready to explode. I see red. With a shriek of pain and fury I jump out of bed and fly at him. My fingers clawed and aiming for his face. At that moment I *hate* him. My nails don't connect. He catches me easily and holds my hands high up in the air, looking down at me with a curl of contempt to his lips. I start kicking his legs and he suddenly, in a quicksilver move, turns me around so my back is pressed up against him and I am completely immobilized.

'Let me go, you bastard,' I yell in a mad frenzy.

'When you stop trying to hurt yourself,' he says serenely.

'I'm not trying to hurt myself, I'm trying to hurt you, you stupid prick,' I curse.

'If you hurt me I will have to hurt you, and I don't want to do that,' he says.

'You've already hurt me,' I sob.

'You are a child who is crying because she has stubbed her toe on a piece of hard furniture, but by tomorrow you will forget and you will be laughing again.' He lets go of me.

I put some distance between us and look at him blankly. I am beyond anger or pain. Look at us. There is a chasm between us. It has always been there. Who knows how many wonders it holds, but I can never reach him, and I don't want to anymore. I'm not sure how long I stand there frozen, simply looking at him. One minute, five, or perhaps even ten. All I know is that it is over. There is nothing left.

Then my senses come swimming back to me and I feel the first shaft of pain, and oh sweet Jesus, such loss. Such terrible loss. And anger. And betrayal. And sadness. Everything is jumbled up and bewildering, but I know only one thing. I have to get away from this house, this man, these feelings I have for him.

I run past him.

He doesn't even attempt to stop me. I sprint up the stairs and into my room. Once there, I haphazardly throw a few things into my suitcase and stuff my manuscripts into my rucksack. I know I'm leaving my stuff, the stuff that I came here with, but I don't care. I just need to get out of his house. I hook the rucksack into the crook of my elbow and, carrying the other bag, I exit the room.

I run down the stairs and as I pass the first floor I see that he has closed his door. Suddenly tears start pouring down my face. He can hear me running down the stairs. He knows I am leaving, but he doesn't come out of his room. Just lets me go.

On the last flight I can see that there is no one at the landing. All I have to do is open the door and run out into the night. There are always taxis around and I can just hail one and go back to Stella, but in my mad dash I miss a step and tumble down the last few steps, my hands flailing, trying to grab the banister, and missing. I land sprawled and in pain on the floor.

I make a ruckus with my involuntary scream, and the clattering noise of my fall carries all through the house, but Zane doesn't come out of his room to see if I am OK.

Fresh tears of pain and hurt run down my face.

'Son of a bitch,' I swear, and get up onto my hands and knees. I'm sore, but fairly unhurt. I hear footsteps coming from the kitchen.

Twenty-three

Dahlia Fury

I look up and Olga is standing there. She walks up to me and helps me up to my feet.

'Are you all right?' she asks.

For a moment I forget to be hurt and wounded and furious. 'You don't speak English.' I say stupidly.

'Of course, I do,' she says briskly.

'What? Then why?'

'Oh, child. Every time a new woman comes in here, it's the same damn thing. They fall in love with him and expect me to listen to their pathetic stories. I got sick of it, and unless it was a Russian girl, I just pretended I could speak nothing but Russian.'

This house is full of liars. 'I don't believe this,' I say shaking my head.

'Well,' she says dryly. 'Try listening to the same idiotic story again and again.'

'I'm leaving,' I tell her.

She glances at the bag that is lying on the first step of the stairs. 'No, you're not.'

I sniff pitifully. 'Yes, I am.'

'Well, come and have a cup of coffee first.'

'No, I don't want to stay under his roof for another minute.'

She points to a little red light blinking in a corner of the hallway that I have not noticed before. 'See that.'

'Yeah.'

'That's a camera. Yuri is watching you right now from that small room there. The moment you try to open the door he will come out and quickly escort you back to your room. That is his job. No one gets in or out without Aleksandr's say-so.'

'I'm a prisoner?' I ask incredulously.

'Not exactly, but you cannot run out in the middle of the night. If I was Aleksandr I would not allow it either. It is not safe for a young woman to be wandering about alone at this time of the night. Why don't you come into the kitchen for a cup of coffee and a little chat?'

I sniff. 'Coffee and a chat?' Everything seems so surreal.

She goes over to my bags and picks them up. 'Can you walk or do you need help?' she asks.

I cough. 'I can walk,' I say, and begin to limp towards the kitchen. She holds the door open.

The kitchen is fragrant with the smell of baking.

'Are you cooking at this time of the night?' I ask, my mind latching onto meaningless inconsistencies around me in my moment of shock and betrayal.

'Yes. I don't like waking up early in the morning. I prefer to work at night and have an extra hour in bed in the morning.'

I hobble over to a stool and sit on it. She puts my bags on the floor next to me, and slides a box of tissues towards me. 'Now, let's get you some coffee.'

I pull out a couple of tissues, wipe my eyes and blow my nose.

She puts a mug of coffee in front of me. 'I've already put the right amount of sugar in it.'

'You know how many sugars I have in my coffee?' I ask, weirdly and helplessly exploring more meaningless inconsistencies.

'Of course.'

I wrap my hands around the hot mug. 'Did you know that he kidnapped my sister too?'

She nods. 'I might have heard something to that effect.'

'And Noah? Does he knows too?'

'Of course. It doesn't take a genius to work it out.'

'What do you mean by that?'

'You come to this house in a tight dress—'

'It was a uniform,' I correct automatically.

'OK, a tight uniform and run out like a bear was on your tail and three months later your sister gets kidnapped. In Aleksandr's world, glaring coincidences like that don't happen unless they are made to happen.'

I stare at her unperturbed face. 'But you don't think he has done a terrible thing?'

She shakes her head. 'No. I don't think it was so bad. It is an English saying no, "all is fair in love and war"?'

I throw my hands up. 'This is unbelievable. Do you know how upset my mom was? We didn't know what to think. She could have been dead.'

She shrugs. 'We are Russian. We are not so emotional. We are more, how do you call it, stoic. No one was hurt. Sometimes it is only when something bad happens to the people you love that you come to see just how much you love them. It teaches you to appreciate them more.'

I hold my head. 'You can't seriously think what he did was not wrong?'

'Wrong? What is wrong? One hundred years ago it was not wrong to buy a man and use him as a slave. In Aleksandr's world it was not wrong to take your sister to have you. In his world she was bait he put on a hook to catch a fish he wanted.'

My God. How he must have laughed at me. Calling me *rybka* and letting me think it was a Russian endearment. 'That's so fucked up,' I say, my voice quivering with anger. Little fish, my ass!

'Aleksandr makes his own rules.'

'And that makes it OK?' I demand angrily.

She looks directly into my eyes. 'Aleksandr makes his bed and he lies on it. You think it was an accident that you found out what he did today?'

'What do you mean?'

'Aleksandr has many secrets buried inside him that he will carry to his grave. You will never know them even if you spend a lifetime with him. If you have found out something it was only because he wanted you to know.'

Then I remember his eyes, the way he watched me while he told me to take up yoga and meditation like my sister. There had been something there. He knew how I would react.

He wanted me gone.

I gasp and cover my mouth with my hand. 'Oh my God! He doesn't want me anymore and that is his way of getting rid of me.' My heart aches with this new knowledge. It was better when I thought I was the one leaving him.

She shakes her head and sighs deeply. 'You are too young to understand a man like him. He does not want you gone.'

'What do you mean?' I ask instantly.

'Have you ever thought it may be the opposite of what you think? Perhaps he wants you too much, and he is afraid of being hurt by you.'

'Hurt by me? I'll never hurt him,' I deny hotly.

'Look at you. At the first sign of trouble you've packed your bags and are running away with your tail between your legs. What good are you for a man like him? He needs a strong woman. A woman he can trust.'

'Why, because he's an asshole and a criminal?' I retort, stung by her criticism.

She smiles a secret smile. 'Have you seen him play the piano?'

I still with the memory. 'Yes,' I whisper.

'Then you have seen the real man. The criminal is just the mask he puts on to survive. That man playing the piano.' She drops her voice to a whisper. 'That's the real him. That's the man who needs a good woman he can trust because he has wounds that only she can heal.'

'Why are you telling me this?'

She opens a drawer near her and takes out a thick, hardcover book and shows me the title. *The Big Book of American Recipes*. 'They won't give me the money back and it will be a useless buy if you don't stay.'

I try to smile but I can't.

She opens the book and looks at the random page she has opened it to. 'I can make you fried pickle. You like that? Remind you of your home. Hmmm?'

I smile through my tears. 'That's Southern food. I'm not from the South.'

She raises her hands into the air dramatically and says impatiently, 'So. I will make you Northern food.' She taps the book and nods. 'Recipes from all of America are in here.'

I rest my chin on my fists. God, what a mess I've gotten myself into.

She looks at me seriously. 'Both Noah and I want you to stay.'

'Noah? He doesn't even like me.'

She laughs. 'Ah, child! Sometimes you are like an American tourist. You need a map for everything.'

'Those are Japanese tourists you're talking about,' I tell her.

'Japanese, American, what's the difference?' she dismisses roundly. 'Noah has always been on your side. He told me he arranged you on your bed in such a way that when Aleksandr came into your room later, he would see not a drunk slut, but a sleeping angel.'

I stare at her dumbfounded. 'Noah did that?'

She nods.

'Then why is he so cold and distant with me?'

'Noah works for Aleksandr. There is a phrase, what is it, way of conduct—'

'Code of conduct,' I correct.

'Yes, that is right. Code of conduct. He cannot be too friendly with you.'

'Why do you want me to stay and not any of the other girls?'

'Because you are not like all the others. You alone can find a way to his heart.'

I look at the table sadly. 'I don't know if I want to. I'm not Russian. I was brought up in a different way. I can't forgive him just like that for what he has done to my family.'

'The path of love is a thorny one. Fight for your love.'

I smile wistfully. 'He doesn't love me.'

She fixes me with her dark eyes. 'You do.'

I bite my lip. 'What good is that? He won't even let me close to him. When he caught me watching him playing the piano you wouldn't believe how furious he was. He ordered me never to enter that room when he's in it again.'

Olga walks away from me and switches off the oven. She dons oven mitts, pulls open the door, and takes out a tray of little buns.

'Learn from the national symbol of your country. The eagle does not fight the snake on the ground. It picks it up into the sky and changes the battlefield. The snake has no balance, power or strength in the air. Take the fight into the air where you are strong and he is vulnerable.'

'But I don't know how to fly,' I say.

She takes the mitts off her hands and looks at me, and quite seriously says, 'Then you must learn how to.'

Oh God! How the fuck do I learn to fly?

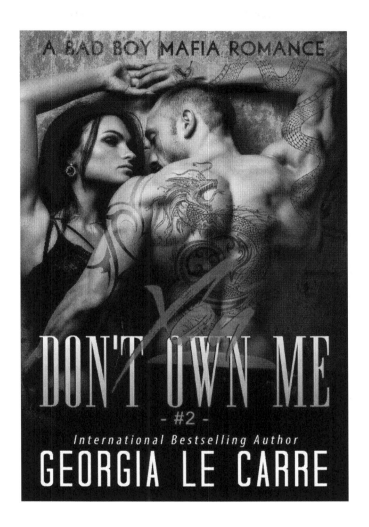

A BAD BOY MAFIA ROMANCE

DON'T OWN ME

- #2 -

International Bestselling Author

GEORGIA LE CARRE

You Don't Own Me #2

One

Aleksandr Malenkov
(Training)

https://www.youtube.com/watch?v=4zLfCnGVeL4

I let their names fall away a long time ago.

They are still here in the graveyard of my soul,
dragging their dismembered bodies, cursing and
swearing at me, but I don't hear them. I have
mastered the art of pretending the blood
dripping from my hair is my crown, my liquid
crown. But she came, and like a spade slicing
into the earth she is turning up forgotten thing,
buried things. I have started to hear their voices.
Faintly, but getting closer ...

'Aleksandr,' my father calls from his tall
leather armchair that is as big as a throne.

I leave my toy soldiers in their battle
formations on the floor of my room and run to
stand next to his knees.

'Yes, papa.'

I am in awe of papa. He is tall and strong with forearms as meaty as ham shanks. He can lift mama with just one hand as if she weighs nothing more than a bottle of vodka. Not taking his shiny black eyes off me, he brings his large hairy wrist up to his right ear and listens to his watch.

'Looks like my watch has stopped working again.' He takes his hand away from his ear and puts on his thinking face. 'Hmmm ... I can hear mama making a cake in the kitchen, but it's not my birthday, and I don't think it's hers either.' He raises his bushy eyebrows. 'Is it yours?'

'Yes, papa. Yes,' I cry excitedly.

'Well then, how old are you today, my son?' he asks.

'Seven. I am seven today,' I tell him, standing as straight and tall as I can.

There is a hint of a smile playing about his lips. There is something familiar about that smile. I don't know why, but the apartment suddenly becomes strangely quiet. Even the noises of mama cooking in the kitchen stop. It is so quiet I can hear papa's watch ticking. Tick. Tick. Tick. I start to remember something from long ago. Something horrible. *Mama is bleeding and I am hiding under the bed.* How could I have forgotten such a thing?

Frightened, I take a step back.

Then my papa grins at me, and it is the happy grin from before his accident. From when I was still a small boy and we used to huddle up together in his big chair and drink sweet black tea from the same mug. I realize it must have been just another bad dream. Mama was not bleeding and I was not hiding under the bed. I grin back at papa. I love my papa. I'd do anything for him. I wish we could drink tea from the same mug again.

Papa leans forward. 'Shall we try on the gloves?' he whispers.

I nod happily. When I was born papa bought me a pair of boxing gloves and every birthday since I can remember we try them on to see if they fit. Until now they have not.

'Go fetch the boxing gloves.'

I run to papa and mama's room and open the drawer where they are kept. The battered ones that are bigger than my face belong to papa, and the small, bright red ones, shiny with newness are mine. I run back to papa with them.

'Take your T-shirt off,' Papa says.

I quickly pull it over my head and the winter air makes me shiver.

'Brrrr ...' I say, purposely making my teeth chatter and my body shiver.

Mama would have laughed and called me a clown, but papa doesn't. I stop chattering my teeth and shivering and stand still while papa puts my gloves on my hands and binds them securely around my wrists.

'Papa, they fit,' I tell him with a whoop with joy. Finally papa is going to teach me to fight. He has been waiting patiently for this day to begin my training.

'Yes, they do. You are a man now, Aleksandr,' he says.

'I'm a man now,' I echo as I look at my gloved hands. Papa says if I train everyday I will become as big and strong as him.

'And what do men do?'

'They fight,' I shout proudly.

'That's my boy,' papa says with a big, happy smile.

I am so happy my heart feels as if it will burst in my chest.

'I hope you ready to begin your training.'

'Yes, papa,'

While papa puts on his gloves I hold my fists in front of my face and start dancing on the spot the way the boxers on TV do. Feeling powerful and happy-I'm a man now-I even throw a few jabs in the air with my right hand.

'Are you ready?' papa asks.

I stop moving my legs. 'Yes.'

'Hold your hands up over your head.'

Immediately I raise both hands.

'The first lesson is learning how to take a punch like a man,' he says and punches me in the ribs.

The blow hurts, but I am able to keep my hands up.

Papa looks me in the eye and nods with approval. I feel a flash of pride. I truly have become a man.

I take a deep breath and he punches me again. I breathe in sharply. That one was more painful.

'Good,' he encourages before hitting me again, harder still. Then, before I can recover properly he gets the fourth one in. It knocks the wind out of me and I double over, my hands automatically going around my belly to protect myself.

'Hands up,' he orders.

I stare up at him, shocked. I don't recognize the man glaring at me angrily. This is not my papa.

'Hands up,' he says sternly. 'I'm doing this is for your own good.'

Slowly I straighten my body and raise my hands up.

'Let's see if I have a son or a daughter,' he says.

Then his arm shoots out. Wham. So hard hot tears fill my eyes. I don't want to cry. I'm a man now.

'If you can't take this how are you going to be the greatest fighter in the world?'

Wham.

'For God's sake, stop sniveling like a little girl, I'm not even using half my strength.'

Wham.

He laughs. 'You think it's so easy to be the best fighter in the world, huh?'

Wham.

This time I fall to the ground, unable to breathe.

My father flies out of his chair. 'Get up, you pathetic little sissy,' he spits furiously.

He grabs a handful of my hair and pulls me up to my knees. I start crying. He brings his face so close to mine I see the little holes in his skin and the mad light in his shining eyes.

My mother appears at the doorway. Her face is white. 'That's enough now,' she pleads. 'Please Igor. That's enough for today. He's just a child.'

My father carries on staring at me, at the tears rolling down my stunned face, at the snot running from my nose, at my shivering body.

'You disgust me,' he says and lets go of my hair.

I fall back to the floor, but he is not finished.

'Stand up,' he orders.

'Please Igor,' my mother begs. Her voice is shaking with fear.

'I said stand up,' my father shouts.

I get on my hands and knees and stand unsteadily. My head feels dizzy, my knees are like jelly, and my stomach and ribs are so full of pain I am sure that I am dying.

'Now fucking put your hands up.'

I am trying my best not to cry, but my entire body is shuddering with agony as I lift my hands up.

My father throws a punch. It is so vicious my body goes flying backwards, crashes into a chair, and both the chair and I slide along the floor and slam into the wall.

'Get up and fight,' papa screams.

Whimpering, and twisted into a heap, I stare bewildered at my mother. She is running towards me, but she never reaches me. My father grabs her by the hair and jerks her back. I see her mouth open, but no sound come out. He throws her and she goes hurtling backwards and slams into the wall with the most awful thud. Winded and shocked she lays propped up against the wall. Mama legs are open wide and I can see her underwear.

Papa hisses at mama like a snake and calls her a bad word. 'Stay out of this you, witch. This is for his own good.'

Then he turns towards me. I can see mama beginning to crawl on the floor.

'Don't hurt him, Igor,' she snarls.

Papa freezes, his face twisted and ugly. He turns around, goes back to her, picks her up as if she is a doll, and smashes her face against the floor. Blood gushes out of her nose. I can't breathe. I can't say single word. Gasping sounds come from my mouth.

'Don't interfere,' Papa says as he kicks mama again and again in her poor belly. She curls up into a ball and doesn't make a single sound.

'Mama!' I scream again and again, but nobody pays any attention to me.

I get up even though my whole body feels the way my finger felt when it was crushed under a rock, and rush screaming towards my mama. 'Stop, papa. Stop. You killing mama.'

Papa grabs me as I lunge towards him.

'Scream will you?' he bellows, and kaboom, punches me in the side of head. My whole body sails backwards. Then there is no more pain. Just blackness...

What you want baby, I got.

Two

Dahlia Fury

Supreme excellence consists in breaking
the enemy's resistance without fighting

Sun Tzu

I turn the handle and open the door without knocking. Only one lamp is lit and the room is full of long, still shadows. I can make him out sitting fully clothed on the armchair by the window. His legs are crossed at the ankles and resting on the low glass table in front of him.

Our eyes meet.

His are luminous, like that of a wolf. My heart lurches and suddenly my knees feel weak. I close the door and stand leaning against it.

'You shouldn't have kidnapped my sister. It was a despicable thing to do,' I say, my voice making ripples in the heavy silence.

He doesn't move. 'How else would I have made you come to me?'

'What you did was wrong. My sister had nothing to do with us and you made her suffer.'

'If only all the suffering in the world could be that mild,' he says callously.

'My mother went out of her mind with worry. She is old and she didn't deserve that.'

'Yeah? I didn't deserve to feel the way I did either.'

I sigh. We'll be going in circles. 'Anybody else would have just asked me out.'

'I didn't want to ask you out. I wanted to steal you away and own you; do whatever I wanted with you.'

'Why?'

He leans his head back against the back of the chair. 'I don't know why. I just knew I had to have you. From the moment I laid eyes on you.'

'That's no excuse for what you did.'

'It is you who is trying to find an acceptable excuse for me. I don't need one. I don't wait for anybody to give me what I want. I just take it. I wanted you and I took you. Now you are mine until I say otherwise and heaven help anybody or anything that comes between you and me.'

'You talk of me as if I am your possession.'

'You are.'

'I'm not. I'm a person,' I say, but my voice has neither strength nor conviction because I am drawn to something sad and lost in him. He is like a big, still lake. Full of secrets. Underneath the surface I can see things floating around in the darkness. They are as pale as corpses and they frighten me. I want this man so much it hurts to imagine even for a second that I might not be able to call him mine. That I'll just be another body he used for a month.

He closes his eyes tiredly. 'Have you not enjoyed being my woman, little fish?'

I purse my lips. God, I am so conflicted, so confused. No man has ever made me feel this way. 'Yes,' I say truthfully, 'but I hate that you made my sister and mother suffer.'

'Deep in your gut have you not known that it was I who took your sister?'

A chill runs up my spine and I freeze. The very idea is revolting, shocking, ugly, but it is not unfamiliar. We are two wolves. Neither can hide from the other. In the wind, hidden to all but me, I have already sensed it. Yes, oh God, yes, I've always known, but I hid it from myself so I'd have an excuse to do the thing I was dying to do: submit to him.

Now that he has opened the door I never wanted to open there is something else to face up to before I can go forth. Something else I need to know. I have pretended to myself all this while, but no more. I can't be an ostrich, my head buried in the sand if I am take control of my situation. I have to know the truth, and if it is what I suspect it may be, and he refuses to change then I can't stay. No matter how much it hurts I will walk away. Clearing my throat I fumble for the words and will myself to say them. 'Are you ... involved in ... people trafficking?'

'No.'

I feel myself sag with relief.

'But Daisy said that there were other girls there. They heard their voices.'

'They came from a tape recorder. So it'd look real to authorities.'

'I see.' *One more thing, Dahlia. Just one more last thing*. 'Are you in any way involved with child porn?' I ask.

He looks disgusted. 'Never. Not in a million years.'

I blink away the tears of pure joy that want to pour down my face. I could never be in a relationship with someone who could abuse children, or is in anyway involved in such a barbaric activity. That's a deal breaker, a hard limit for me. Everything else I can work around.

My voice is soft. 'I would have been yours if you had just asked me?'

He turns his head. 'Be that now then.'

'What do you mean?' I whisper, watching him with hypnotized eyes.

A cruel glint comes into his eyes. 'Show me that I own you ... *yield*.' His voice is soft and suggestive.

My heart starts beating hard. 'How?'

His eyes begin to smolder and his voice is a sensual caress. 'I want you to take off your clothes, sit in front of me, and brush your hair.'

I stare at him surprised and curious. Definitely curious. 'Why?'

He remains deathly still. 'Because I asked you to.'

My throat is so tight the words stick. 'And after I have brushed my hair?'

'What do you think comes after that?'

'We fuck?'

His eyes are fierce and penetrating but his voice is so light it is almost playful. 'Tsk, tsk, why so crude, *rybka*?'

There are so many ways I can do this. I can do it angrily, flirtations, carelessly, sexily, coldly, or even reluctantly, but I decide to own it. Why not? I love the thought of taking off my clothes and brushing my hair for him, then watching the lust come into his eyes, seeing his erection grow right before my eyes. I want to feel beautiful, desired, needed by him.

Why pretend he is forcing me when I desperately want to do it?

I kick off my shoes, grasp the edges of my sweatshirt, lift it upwards, and tug it over my head. Shivering in the chill of cold air touching my skin I let the sweatshirt fall to the ground. His eyes roam my exposed skin hungrily. The chill I felt goes away and a familiar warmth

I unzip my jeans, push them down my legs, and take off my socks. There are sock marks around my ankles, but he doesn't seem to notice. I undo the clasp on my bra and let my breasts pop out of them. Unconsciously, I sigh with relief that the restrains are gone. I feel the lace scrape my skin as it travels down my arm. With a whisper it touches the ground.

I hook my fingers into the waistband of my panties and drag them down my legs. Then I am standing there naked, my back straight, my bare toes gripping the carpet and my breasts aching for him.

He takes his feet away from the table he has been resting them on.

'Sit,' he invites softly.

I draw in a shuddering breath and walk to the table. Going around it I sit facing him, my palms flat on either side of me, my knees close together. The glass is cold under my bottom and thighs and goose bumps scatter my skin.

I lift my head and look at him.

Without saying a word he gets up, goes to the bathroom, and comes back with a hairbrush. He holds it out to me. I take it and he resumes his position on the sofa. I turn my head to the side and looking at a point on the curtain, drag the brush through my hair, the downward sweep slow and rhythmic. When all my hair swings straight and shiny I put the brush down on the table beside me and look up at him.

His eyes are veiled, but something raw throbs between us. His eyes slide down to the tips of my breasts. I feel his gaze like fingers, full of warmth and texture. The invisible fingers slide lower.

'Spread your legs,' he says, his voice thick.

I open my legs and expose my swollen wet sex to him.

'Do you know your pussy is … quivering. It's all soft and pink and ripe and quivering for me?'

I draw in a sharp breath as he reaches out a hand and lets his fingers slip into the opening between my legs. A finger rubs my swollen clit and I gasp.

'Lean forward,' he whispers.

I take a shuddering breath. I know what he wants me to do. He wants me to spread my sex on the glass.

'Why do you want me to do these humiliating acts?'

'I want to know that I have total control over you. If you can say no, then I am still not your master.'

To hunt the snake the eagle must fly into the undergrowth. I spread my legs and press my bare sex on the cold glass. My breasts hang forward.

He gets off the sofa and lies down under the table so he right under my spread open, slick flesh.

'Now rub that naughty pussy until she comes,' he says.

I close my eyes. Some part of me wants to obey. Wants to do these degrading things while he watches. So I allow him to lie under me while I shamelessly angle my dripping sex on the glass and rub myself on it until I climax. Even after I climax I don't get up and walk away. I know its not over until his cock is buried deep inside me ... and I am waiting for that.

He gets up off the floor and comes to stand in front of me. He doesn't say a word, but his eyes are full of lust and triumph. My deviant hands immediately start unbuckling his belt. His cock is so hard it jumps out into my hand. He stuffs it into my mouth and I suck until an animal sound emanates from his throat and he explodes deep inside my throat.

I keep him inside my mouth. I don't know what he will do next. Is he going to turn away again? For a moment we are both frozen in an act of master and sexual slave. Can he never love me back? Will my love remain forever hopeless and unreciprocated? Then he does this one thing. It's an unconscious thing, and it is only a tiny thing and perhaps it will mean nothing to anybody else, but it is a big thing to me.

He strokes my hair.

Just once.

But it is enough for me. He cares. Maybe just a little, but he cares. My grandmother used to say, everyman, even the most hardened criminal, has a soft spot in his heart. Maybe, just maybe I can be that soft spot in this man's heart.

I lift my feet up on the table and get into a crouching position. Reeking of sex I drag my breasts up along his body until my erect nipples brush his face and I am standing a head taller than him. Bracing my hands on the planes of his hard chest our faces loom, dangerously close, separately only by the cast iron bars of mutual distrust. His eyes, so radiant they are azure, stare back into mine.

Unnerving. Beautiful. What is he seeing, I wonder.

Feverishly, I cup his cheeks between my palms and press my mouth against his. A long trapped moan escapes. We kiss. Kiss? No, He opens his mouth, our tongues entangle and we hold on tight, and fucking drink. So deeply it is as if we are desert nomads who have travelled for weeks to find a vein of cold water in the ground. Succulent. Succulent. He is.

We flood our senses with each other and the room disappears. The whole world stops spinning. Raw desire courses through every fiber in my body. It is madness. It is obsession. We fuse irrevocably and indisputably. Time passes in our singular state. Eventually, I raise my head breathing hard, and look into his eyes. They are impossibly dilated. My breath hitches.

'Have you ever heard the story of the scorpion that asked a frog to help him across a river?' he asks, his voice low and strange.

I stare into the crystalline eyes. They are inscrutable crystal worlds. Fabulously beautiful but inhospitable to carbon based creatures. Slowly, I shake my head and feel the strands of my hair brushing my bare shoulders.

'The frog said, 'No. You could sting me while we are halfway across the river and I will die." The scorpion said, "If I sting you I will die too." That logic made sense to the frog so it said, "All right. Climb on my back and I'll give you a ride." Halfway across the river, the scorpion stung the frog. The frog cried out in mortal pain. "You stupid scorpion, now we are both going to die. Why did you do it?" And the scorpion replied, "What do you expect I'm a scorpion. That's what I do."'

I feel an eerie sense of calm permeate my whole body, perhaps even my soul. He doesn't know it is too late to turn back.

'The frog should have learned to fly. He should have taken the battle to the air where the scorpion would have been disorientated,' I whisper, my jaw tight.

He smiles sadly. 'You'd have made a good mafia general,' he says.

'Actually I got the idea from Olga,' I say.

'I take it back. You're far too truthful to be one.'

'I've told my share of lies. Ask my mother,' I say lightly.

'I'm a ruffian and a murderer, Dahlia.'

'Difficult to tame, I know,' I say softly, 'but not impossible.'

He stands immobile and as tense and sprung as a fully stretched catapult, 'I don't want to break you.'

'Don't worry. I'll bend.'

He lifts me off the table. I curl my thighs around his hips and he carries me to the bed and lays me on it. I lie on my back and look at him shedding his clothes and think, *you are mine. You don't know it yet, but you are mine. For ours is not a monkey love. It's pure and beautiful. One day he will realize that jut having animal sex with me is not enough.*

He lies down beside me.

'I own you, Dahlia. I own every inch of you,' he states possessively.

'How can you say that if you are planning to give me away in less than a month's time?'

'I'm not giving you away, *rybka.*'

I squash the urge to grin like an idiot. I open my mouth to reply and he places a finger across my lips.

'Don't speak,' he says, and his eyes are so desolate I feel frightened for him. What is it that this man hides? Why does he suffer so?

I stare up him mutely. He says nothing more and eventually I fall asleep inside the tight circle of his arm.

Three

Dahlia Fury

I wake up the next morning alone, touch the indent in the pillow, and sigh. I have no idea where he is or when I will see him again. My relationship with Zane reminds me of a falconer training a wild falcon. He brings the bird to 'flying weight'. It is a euphemism for keeping the bird hungry. Only through small gifts of food will it recognize the falconer as a benevolent master and hunt for him. Like a falcon in training I feel underfed for his attention.

I get out of bed, use the bathroom, and going up to my own room get dressed before I go downstairs to the kitchen. Yuri is sitting at the counter. When he sees me he nods in acknowledgement, but his eyes slide away quickly.

'Good morning,' I say with as much dignity as I can muster. He saw me fall down the last few stairs yesterday. I turn towards

Olga. She is standing on tiptoe putting something away in a top cupboard. She pops her head out from behind the door of the cupboard and smiles cheerfully. 'Good morning.'

'Can I please have a word with you, Olga?'

Yuri stands up and brushes crumbs off his clothes. 'Right I'm off.'

I watch him leave and take the seat next to the one he just vacated. Olga closes the cupboard, goes to the coffee machine comes back with a mug of coffee that she puts in front of me.

'Thanks Olga,' I say and take a sip.

She sits opposite me. 'So ... how can Olga help?'

'I wanted to ask you something.'

'Hmmm ...'

'Last night you said that I have a chance of finding a way to Zane ... well, Aleksandr's heart.'

'Yes, I said that.'

'What made you say that?'

She tilts her head and regards me speculatively. 'Because he looks at you as if he can't believe his eyes. Like a boy looking into a shop window full of the toy he wants most in the world, but can't have.'

I shake my head. 'I'm starting to feel like a Japanese tourist here. Give me a map please.'

She smiles. 'With all the others he was doing basically the same thing. Different positions with different bodies to vary the boredom. But what he does with you. This is beyond what he ever dreamed of.'

I blush. 'Oh, you mean the sex.'

'I'm sure that is very good but no, not that. How can I explain to you? It's like you woke him up from a deep sleep.'

I think of the way the gentle stroke on my hair that escaped out of his iron mask last night.

'You're the only one he wants, little fish,' Olga says softly.

After a breakfast ruined with confusing thoughts I step out through the French doors into the garden. There is no one about and it is so quiet and tranquil I can't even hear the faint sound of traffic from here. I take a deep lungful of the fresh, cold morning air and it kinda starts to clear the cobwebs in my head. Maybe I should spend a little time alone in nature.

I drift around the side of the house. My destination is the Japanese garden that I saw from Zane's study window. Leaving the springy grass I step onto a stony path and follow it until it opens out to a secluded stone garden.

I stand by a rock and look at the meticulously exact garden. There is no grass just a rectangular plot full of stones that have been so carefully raked the lines are as straight as a ruler. I guess it is beautiful the way a brand new chrome coffee machine is beautiful. In a cold, modern, flawless and functional way.

Me, I like a garden with flowers, weeds, bees, birds, worms, the occasional frog, a messy dog running through my flower beds, digging things up, barking, and the sound of children playing.

I rub my cold face with my hands.

Still, I guess this is Zane. This is the world he is trying to create inside and outside him. A flawless, exact, cold world where cascading water is represented by carefully placed stones. Something moves in my peripheral vision and I half-turn in that direction. It is in the window of Zane's study.

Sunlight makes the glass glint so I have to lift my hand to shade my eyes in order to see into it. To my surprise I see him standing there watching me. For a few seconds we simply look at each other. Static starts up on my skin and I feel as if I am drowning in his gaze and all these crazy emotions swirling inside me.

As if pulled by a magnet I start walking towards him.

I reach the window and place my palm on the glass. The glass is freezing. Slowly, like a man in a dream he lifts his hand and places it on the other side of glass facing my hand. I smile at him and a ghost of a smile tugs the corners of his mouth. Behind him, I see the door open and slimy Lenny enters the room and waits by the door. I bring my gaze back to Zane and watch him change right before my eyes.

First his smile dissolves.

A distant and wholly professional smile takes its place. Then his eyes become cold and forbidding. Fascinated and transfixed I watch his chest lift and fall heavily before he takes his hand away from the glass. Then he turns away from me and faces the world with his mask firmly in its place. I retract my hand and walk back in the direction I came from, my mind's eye replaying his transformation.

As I reach the swing, my phone rings. I hit accept and Stella starts shrieking into my ear. It is a long and melodramatic screech and I begin to laugh. When she runs out of breath, she takes a quick snatch of air, and carries on all full speed.

I sit on the swing. 'Stop it,' I tell her with a laugh.

'I want to, but I can't,' she says and keeps up the shrill sound.

It is so infectious I almost want to join her. We've done it before. Both of us shrieking away. It's actually quite fun, but if I start I'll probably have all Zane's staff out here in a second. 'So you like them then?' I ask instead.

'Like them? Like them?' she screams in my ear. 'I'm fucking in love with them. I couldn't believe my eyes. I thought I was seeing things.' She pauses suddenly and in a far more, by far more, sober voice asks, 'They're not knock-offs from China, are they?'

'No, they're real,' I say reassuringly and put the swing into motion.

'Oh Jesus! I nearly gave myself a small heart attack there!' she exhales with relief. Then she is back into gush mode. 'Oh my God, Dahlia. They are fabulous. It's the best freaking present ever. I couldn't believe it when I opened the door and postman goes, 'Been shopping have ya? I was half-asleep and I thought you had sent me the shoes from that woman with the Hong Kong connection, which of course, I would have been over the moon with, but bloody hell! Jimmy fucking Choos! I thought I'd died and gone to heaven.'

'Have you got them on now?' I ask with a smile.

'Don't be daft. I've made an altar in my bedroom and placed them there.'

I laugh, feeling the cold wind in my face as the swing rocks me. 'Do they fit?'

'Of course, they fit. If they didn't I'd have cut my feet to fit,' she declares intensely.

'You're so mad, Stel.'

'That's no insult. That's a gift. Haven't you heard we throw the best parties. Talking of parties, we have to go out and celebrate my new shoes.'

'Oh yes, lets, but hang on. Didn't you go out on a date last night?'

'Oh, screw him,' she dismisses in a disgusted voice.

'Why what happened?'

'I'll tell you everything when I see you,' she says cheerfully, 'I've got loads of exciting things to tell you. Shall we meet tonight?'

'Tonight is good.'

'Let's go to Jamie's. We'll get drunk on something completely vile.'

'Jamies! I can already taste the hangover.' She can't see me but I am nodding happily. I really miss Stella. She's as irresistible as a laughing child.

'I'm on a diet by the way,' she says, 'so can we meet early? That way I can just drink my dinner.'

'You mean to say we're not going to end up at Taki's afterwards?'

'I said I was missing dinner not supper.'

I laugh.

'Seven OK with you.'

'Yup.'

'Oh, and I might be wearing my new shoes.'

'You're wearing them now, aren't you?' I ask.

She laughs. 'You know me too well.'

We say goodbye and I get off the swing and go in search of Noah. As I get to the doors I turn back to look at the garden. At the bottom of it I can see Nico, a young shy boy, filling the bird feeders with seeds. I stand for a minute watching how quickly the blue tits come to feed. As I watch a robin comes and chases the smaller bird away.

That surprises me. I know from watching the birds from my window that the pigeons can be belligerent and antagonistic to each other, but it has never crossed my mind that the pretty Robin could be so aggressive. It reminds

me of Zane's assertion that the world is run by
ferocity. Even the thought he could be right
makes me sad.

With a sigh I open the door and enter the
house. I tell Noah that I am meeting up with
Stella at Jamie's at seven o'clock and he doesn't
bat an eyelid.

'I'll check with boss and let you know if
it's OK,' he says.

'You can check with him all you like, but
I'm going to see Stella tomorrow no matter
what,' I say coolly and walk out of the kitchen
door.

My morning is mapped out. I'll work for a
bit, then I'll work out in the gym and use the
steam room.

Four

Dahlia Fury

Humidity's rising, barometer's getting low ...

The steam room is made entirely from some highly polished black stone. There is a bench carved out of the same material pushed up against the opposite wall. I close the door and go to sit on it. The seat is full of cool water droplets. I lean back against the wet wall, close my eyes, and breathe in the hot damp air.

Minutes pass and my body begins to bead with sweat.

My eyes fly open when I hear a sound. I see a hulking shape through the frosted glass door. Someone is outside hanging up his towel. It can only be Zane. I straighten my spine and touch my hair self-consciously. It is impossible to look good in a steam room. The door opens and Zane walks in.

For a few seconds he towers over me, naked, his thick cock standing proud between his thighs. Then he walks over and kneels in front of me. Tiny droplets of steam billow between us. His black hair is plastered to his head and for some inexplicable reason he seems ... dangerous.

Heart in mouth, I stare at him. I can't look away or speak. I feel like a freaking rabbit, huddled, small and helpless. From the very first night he has had this ability to completely immobilize me purely by his presence. My lips feel hot and swollen, and I lick them nervously.

Without saying a word he unclasps my bikini top, and when it falls off, he bends forwards and takes a nipple in his mouth.

'I'm all sweaty,' I protest.

He sucks.

A warm gush of excitement spreads through my veins. My body arches. My hands rise up to curl on the hard, shiny muscles of his shoulders. His skin is feverishly hot, but my hands are so wet they slip on his skin. I look down at him and his piercing eyes are watching me intently. He holds my nipple between his teeth and not taking his eyes off me me bites down. The deliberate cruelty sends a jolt of sensation right down to my groin.

I cry out.

'Real lust is like this,' he whispers thickly, and licks the throbbing tip. Soothing it. Coaxing it into arching again into his mouth. He rewards it by sucking it gently. I fidget and moan restlessly.

He moves to the other nipple and I snuggle closer to his powerful body, my hips rocking, rubbing, wanting. Wrapping his arm around my waist, he lifts me off the bench, and lays me on the damp floor. My mouth parts in invitation as he drags my bikini bottom down my legs and flings it behind him.

'Yes,' I whimper.

He crouches like wolf over my naked body and hungrily sucks and licks every inch of me. Finally he eases my swollen lips apart and slips a finger into me. I gasp loudly and arch my back, involuntarily making his hand shove deeper into my wet heat.

'Your pussy is so fucking hot and tight,' he says and finger fucks me roughly while I writhe and twist on the floor.

I almost scream when I feel his warm mouth suddenly latch on my distended clit. He sucks it hard and my body starts shaking uncontrollably. Waves of pleasure explode out of my core and ricochet inside me as I come hard and long. He laps at my folds, greedily drinking my juices.

'Your turn,' I whisper, my body still tingling.

'My turn,' he agrees, and reaches under the bench for a little black object. About five inches long and smooth, it has the thickness of a frankfurter sausage, but narrows down to a blunt tip no bigger than my little finger. The other end looks like a plunger.

'What is that?' I ask intrigued.

He smiles slowly. 'It's to hold you in place.'

I rise up to my elbows. 'What do you mean?'

'Let me teach you how to use this,' he says, uncoiling to his feet. He strides to the door and opens it, and marvelously cool air flows into the room. I stay on my elbows and watch him take bottle from one of the metal shelves and pump a good dose of gel onto his palm. He comes back into the steam room and coats the black object liberally with it. The sweet scent of strawberries hits my nostrils. He holds out his hand, I slip mine into it, and he pulls me upright.

Zane slaps the object, plunger first on the wall, and with a sucking sound it sticks to the smooth stone.

'Wha-' I say, but I am cut short.

Zane pushes me up against the wet tiles and I look up at him with startled eyes. Water runs down his face in rivulets and drips from his eyebrows and nose. He pushes his hips into my flesh so I feel the wood of his cock press into me. My mouth parts with invitation.

'My sweetness and my hope,' he mutters.

Then our tongues touch and searing heat fills me. Dizzily, I reach between our bodies, wrap my palm around his hard shaft, and tug on it vigorously. Without breaking the kiss he curls his large powerful hands around the backs of my thighs and lifts me clean off the floor. I wrap my legs securely around him and he immediately reaches under me and jams his thumb into my pussy.

I am so wet his entry makes a squelching sound. Distracted by his thumb thrusting in and out of me I don't realize he has hoisted me to the black object stuck to the wall. The tip presses into my back.

'Zane,' I breathe looking into his lust glazed eyes.

'What?' he asks.

'I've never had anything up my ass,' I whisper anxiously.

'A virgin ass. How sweet?' His eyes glitter with satisfaction.

Unwrapping my legs from around his hips I stand.

'Ready?' he asks huskily.

I nod.

'Bend your knees,' he instructs and guides me so the tip of the plug touches the puckered entrance of my ass.

'Now push up against it,' he commands and watches as I slowly push myself onto the lubed up plug. The tip is rounded and fine so it eases past the initial resistance easily and quite suddenly it is inside my ass. And I am like a butterfly pinned to a board.

'Look at you,' he says, staring at my open and exposed pussy. 'You're dripping like a leaking faucet.'

He is not lying. This is a new pleasure for me and I am so turned on I can feel my own juices gushing onto my thighs as the plug traveling deeper into me sends intense shivers of pleasure running up and down my spine. I hang my head and take several deep breaths before I push it in a little more. Once it is about three or four inches deep he caresses my back and says, 'Relax.'

'Take me hard, Zane. Make me scream.'

'I fucking plan to,' he growls.

Taking a step forward he slams his hard cock so forcefully into me, I become so deeply impaled on the plug that I feel the cone of the plunger spreading my ass cheeks.

God, this is amazing,' I gasp, my mouth open with surprise.

I never thought I would, but I love the sensation of being double penetrated. It is amazing to have his giant cock stretching my pussy and the slippery black plug in my ass.

'You wanted it hard,' he says as he pulls me away from the wall and thrusts hard into me. Both his dick and the plug jam into me at the same time.

'Yes, give it to me,' I pant.

Again his cock and plug are withdrawing from my body. 'Tell me you're my little bitch.'

'I'm your little bitch,' I breathe unsteadily, as I take both him and the plug again.

'Who's your daddy?' he asks on the next withdrawal.

'You. You're my daddy,' I groan.

And so it went. Thrust. Thrust. Thrust. Until I am sweaty mess, my thighs are trembling, and my cunt is gripping him like a vise. Hot and excited and shivering like someone who has a fever I teeter wildly on the brink of coming.

'I can't hold on much longer,' I cry.

'Scream for me,' he orders and sinks himself to the hilt.

I come apart, shuddering violently, animal grunts tearing from my throat, as he roars and shoots his load deep inside me. Covered in sweat and panting hard we stare at each other.

'You liked that?'

I nod breathlessly.

He exhales deeply and withdraws out of me and watches his seed leaking out of me. Then he pulls me away from the plug on the wall, lifts me into his arms, and carries me out of the steam room.

'No. No. Don't do it-,' I scream as he chucks me into the swimming pool. I emerge spluttering, push hair out of my eyes, and look for him. He is in the water a few feet away watching me. His eyes are mocking.

The water is wonderfully cool on my flushed skin.

'Fuck you,' I say, and turning on my back lazily swim in the opposite direction. I'll get my own back eventually. A few strokes later he pops up next to me. We do two laps languidly, with him keeping to my idle pace.

Then he stops, curls his hands around my waist, and pulls me upright. He encircles my waist and draws me closer to him. Our naked bodies touch and I sling my arm around his strong neck.

'I'm meeting Stella for drinks tonight.'

His body stills but expression doesn't change. 'Want me to get a table for you at the Matrix?'

'Nah, we're just going to go to Jamies.'

He raises a soaked eyebrow. 'Jamies?'

'You won't have heard of it. It's very low rent and a bit of a dive really, but it's our local and we like it. They play the kind of music we dig.'

He nods. 'Right. What time will you be home?'

My stomach flutters. We sound like a real couple. 'I guess around midnight.'

'Midnight? All right, I'll be waiting for you.'

The thought comes unbidden. *I'm so in love with you, Zane.* I hurriedly drop my gaze so he does not see anything he shouldn't in my

 311

eyes. I let my fingers trace the crevice of the scar on his face. 'How did you get this?'

'He had a knife and I did not,' he says simply.

'What happened then?' I prompt.

'I got a scar and he lost his life.' His voice and face are devoid of any emotion.

Oh God! How can I possibly live in his world? Yet I cannot walk away. Not yet.

'Do these stars mean anything?' I ask softly, tracing the blue star tattoos on the front of his shoulders with my fingers.

For a few seconds I think he is not going to answer then he gives a slight shrug. 'Since you ask I will tell you. They denote the highest distinction that can be reached in *Vor v Zokone*'

'What is that?' I am very curious about his past, but I keep my tone light. This is the first time he has ever offered any information about his past and I don't want to scare him off by being too insistent or intense.

'A rough translation would be Thieves in Law.'

I look at him levelly. 'Thieves in Law?'

'*Vor v Zokone* is the elite of Russian organized crime and operates under a very strict code of ethics. Breaking the code is punishable by death. When I got these stars

they meant something. Nowadays, a lot of young men have them without belonging to the organization.'

'Why do you have the same design on your knees?'

'The stars are worn to declaring an intention never, no matter what the circumstances, to kneel or co-operate with what we call *musor* or pigs. but you probably know them as the police or government officials.'

'So you are a member of this elite organization?' I ask cautiously.

'I did. A long time ago.'

I stare into his eyes, so luxuriously fringed by thick, wet lashes. 'You are no longer part of it?'

'When the Soviet Union collapsed the character of the Russian mob changed. The stupid ones quickly ended up behind bars, the highly connected ones bought up state resources for a song and became billionaires, others looked for new homes far from the motherland to run their often ingenious smuggling operations.'

'Ingenious?'

He shrugs, the movement careless, elegant and foreign. 'They were clever scams.'

'Yeah. Like what?'

'Like dyeing wood grain alcohol blue, labeling it windshield washer liquid, shipping tanker loads of it back to Russia, un-dyeing it, and selling the stuff as vodka. The goal was to avoid paying alcohol taxes.'

'I see.' I say softly. 'So you were one of those who came to England?'

'Uh .... hmm.'

'Did you run the alcohol scam too?'

'Nope.'

'Drug dealing?'

'I used to. I still have good contacts and I can arrange a major deal.'

'Drugs kill people,' I whisper.

He looks at me completely unrepentant or ashamed. 'Drugs are not produced in Russia. I was just the middle-man. Find out who guards the opium fields in Afghanistan and South America then come and lecture me.'

I bite my lower lip. 'So what did you do? Prostitution?'

'That's a great money making model, but it's not for me. Too messy. I don't like dealing with people and all their dependences, obsessions and compulsions. I like clean operations.'

I nod. Relieved. 'What else did you do?'

'Arms dealing.'

I suppress the frown that wants to knit my forehead. 'Gun running?'

'Not just guns. After the fall of communism there was a lot of government arsenal for sale. Long range missiles, tanks, submarines, everything.'

'Did you sell to the terrorists?'

'Does the butcher care who buys his meat? I sold to the highest bidder, but I'll tell you this: the greatest terrorists are governments since I mostly I sold to government-funded terrorists.'

'If all this is in the past what do you do now?'

'I specialize in cyber crime.'

'What kind?'

'We use sophisticated software to get around the security of banks and the credit card companies, take over their systems, and transfer money into thousands of different accounts that we control. We then move the money so fast and zigzag it through so many different continents it becomes impossible to track.'

I look at him doubtfully. 'Really? Hackers get caught all the time.'

He shakes his head. 'The media make a huge fuss over the handfuls of small time hackers operating from their parent's basement that the authorities catch because they know they can never touch the real criminals. Banks will never reveal how much they are losing because if you knew how many billions are stolen every year by organized crime you would never keep your money in the bank.'

I clear my throat. 'Is that what you are doing with Lenny?'

His face becomes suddenly stony. 'I warned you before. Don't get involved in my business, Dahlia. The less you know the safer I can keep you.'

A sudden fear drops into my stomach. I think of the elaborate security measures that are in place around him. 'Even you're not completely safe are you?'

'It comes with the territory,' he dismisses. 'There is also someone who is ready to betray you, who wants what you have.'

'Why did you chose this life? Constantly being on guard for your life and the threat of prison looming in the horizon.'

'I didn't have much of a choice.'

'You told me once that ultimately everything is a choice. Some are more difficult than others to make, but it's a choice nevertheless.

'I had as little choice as you had when I used your sister as my bargaining chip,' he says quietly.

I feel light headed. 'What happened to you, Zane?'

Something flashes into his eyes and for an unguarded instant he looks haunted. 'I don't want to talk about the past,' he mutters, and starts swimming away from me.

'Why won't you let me in, Aleksandr Malenkov?'

Five

Aleksandr Malenkov
(Mama)

https://www.youtube.com/watch?v=KmzFDEu2R0A

When I wake up my whole body is in so much pain I just want to huddle up and cry, but I force myself not to because Mama is lying next to me and watching. My mama is purer than a white swan. She has black hair and blue eyes like me. She is perfect except for one dark tooth and a broken jaw, which makes her mouth look ever so lightly lop-sided.

She broke her jaw when a door hit her in the face before I was born, and the tooth went dark when she fell down some steps and banged it. She told me it happened one night when she was pregnant with me. Mama said she was very lucky she did not lose the tooth or me. She said I could have fallen right out of her stomach that night. I have put my finger in mama's mouth and I know that the dark tooth is loose. It rocks in her jaw the way my front tooth did before I pulled it out.

'You're alive,' I say in wonder and reach out to touch her swollen face.

'Of course, I am,' she smiles.

'Mama your tooth!' I gasp. There is a hole in her smile.

'It's gone,' she says cheerfully. 'I'm glad. It was rotten.' She pushes her tongue through the gap. 'It's saved me a trip to the dentist.'

'Does it hurt?' I ask worriedly.

'No. Not even a bit.'

I touch her broken lip. 'Does this hurt?'

'No. Some things look worse than they are.'

'Shall we put a bandage on it, mama?'

'No,' mama says with a small laugh.

I stare at her. 'Are you sure? It looks painful.'

'Yes, I'm sure. You know I would never lie to you.'

I nod. That's true. Mama never lies. 'Where is papa?' I whisper.

Her blue eyes look sad. 'He's gone out.'

'Has he gone to work?' My papa works odd hours. Before his accident, when he hurt his head and the doctors had to put metal plates in back of his head, he used to go away for days. Mama says he works for the government. She says what he does is secret, like James Bond, so we can never ever know where he goes. All my friends are frightened of my father. Their parents smile at me a lot, but they always look nervous when I am in their house.

'Yes, I think so,' mama says softly.

'Is he still very angry with me, mama?'

'Oh my dear, dear Aleksandr, he is not angry with you at all.'

'Yes, he is. He thinks I'm a coward, because I cried. I tried not to cry, but I couldn't help it, mama.' The tears are trying to come, but I blink them away.

'You're not a coward, my little star. You are braver than most people I know.'

'Really?'

'Yes, that is the absolute truth.'

'But papa doesn't think so.'

'Papa loves you and just wants you to be a great fighter like him, but sometimes he can't control his temper. He is not himself. It was accident. It changed him. Remember I told you about it.'

'Yes, I remember.'

'One day he will get better. You'll see,' she says.

'I hope so.'

'I know so,' she says fiercely.

'I'm sorry he hurt you, mama. It was my fault.'

'He did not hurt me and it was not your fault. Never say that again.' Mama smiles softly.

I nod. 'Mama,'

'Yes, my love.'

'Maybe I shouldn't start my training yet. Maybe we should wait until papa is better.'

Tears fill mama's eyes. 'I'm sorry, my darling, but you will have to train. You are a man now. Papa will expect it. It will only be once a week, maybe twice. It will get better. I promise.'

She lays a gentle hand on my ribs and I gasp with the terrible pain.

She pulls her hand away quickly. 'Did I hurt you, *lyubov moya*?'

I shake my head. 'No, mama. You've never ever hurt me.

Mama presses her lips together and her eyes are so sad I want to wrap her up in cotton wool and hide her in a place no one can ever find her.

'Come we will play the piano together,' she chokes out.

Slowly, very slowly, because I am in so much pain, I get out of bed and together we stand. She holds out her hand and I put mine in it. It is hard to take big breaths. We begin to walk out of the room and I see that she is limping.

I stop and look up at her anxiously. 'Is your leg hurt, mama?'

'No, *lybo moya*. I have a lazy leg. It just went to sleep. I feel no pain.'

'Me too, mama. I feel no pain either.'

We sit at the piano together and mama looks at me. 'What shall we play?'

'You choose, mama.'

'Shall we play something happy?'

'Yes, let's.'

'How about Chopin's Spring Waltz?' she suggests brightly.

'That's a good idea, mama.'

'Ready?'

'Ready.'

We begin to play and music fills the air and enters my body. It is so beautiful tears roll down both our cheeks. This is the only time mama ever cries. We play happy songs and we cry and cry. We are allowed to because the music mama and I make together is so beautiful. So very beautiful. We can escape into it and say to each other what our lips dare not say.

Listen ...

Six

Dahlia Fury

I am first to arrive at Jamie's. Someone is having a birthday party and it is hot, crowded, and very noisy. Fortunately, a couple stand to leave just as we arrive and Noah immediately swoops down on their table even though they are still in the process of getting into their coats. The woman gives us a dirty look, but her man says nothing and avoids any eye contact with Noah.

'Want me to get you something to drink?' Noah offers when they are gone and I am seated.

'Nah, I'll wait until Stella gets here. Thanks,' I say with a smile.

'No problem. I'll be over there at the bar,' he says jerking his chin at one corner of the bar.

'OK,' I say.

Stella and I love coming here. It's a bit of a dive but the booze is cheap, the atmosphere is great, it's close to our apartment, we know the staff, they always play a fantastic selection of songs, and there is a small dance floor at the back that we always dance the night away on.

I am dressed in jeans, a pair of brown boots, and a emerald sweater, but Stella swans in dressed in a stripped black and white mini dress, a short white faux fur jacket, her new Jimmy Choos and her hair cut short and dyed Little Mermaid red. She looks stunning and heads are turning all over the place.

'Jesus, Stel. Your hair,' I squeal, standing up to greet her.

She strikes a pose and tosses her head this way and that so I get to see her new hairstyle from all angles.

'You look like a freaking star,' I tell her.

'Don't I just?' she mouths, grinning cockily.

'And what have you done with your face?' I ask. 'Your skin is glowing.'

'Honey, baking soda, and lime juice mask,' she throws nonchalantly as she air-kisses my cheeks. I watch her put her purse on the table, slide into her seat, and fix me with stern, narrowed eyes. 'You don't look so hot though. What's with you?'

'Tell you in a minute. First, what are we drinking?'

'Who's paying?'

I grin. 'Not us.'

Her eyes shine. 'Bubbles have no calories, have they?' she asks impishly.

'Absolutely not. They are just round bits of clean air covered with a negligible film of champagne,' I say virtuously.

'In that case,' she says with matching virtuousness, 'we really should be good and stick to bubbles.'

'Excellent choice, Miss Spencer. I'll nip over to the bar and get it, and in the meantime you can go say hello to Noah. He's over there.' I nod towards the edge of the bar where Noah is nursing a bottle of beer.

Stella jumps up and practically skips over to him. I watch her throw her arms around his neck like a big kid and wonder what to make of this new fun and full of joie de vivre version of Stella. It is like the girl I met for lunch the other day is a totally different person. Then I suddenly remember that she used to be like this when I first met her, before she started crushing on Zane and going about with a long, depressed face.

Andy, the barman looks surprised when I order champagne. 'Celebrating?' he asks.

'Just treating ourselves,' I reply.

He finds a bottle at the back of a fridge, plunks it into a narrow plastic bucket, and pushes it and two glasses towards me. I pay him and carrying my loot, I go over to where Noah and Stella are standing. Stella has one hip pushed out provocatively and Noah's eyes are roaming her body as he talks to her.

'Want to join us, Noah?' I ask.

'No, I'm all right. You girls go ahead and have fun.'

'You sure, big boy?' Stella pouts.

He looks her up and down, his eyes assessing in the way only a man's can be. 'Don't play with fire, babe.'

Stella takes my wrist in her hand. 'Ooooo, promises, promises,' she taunts cheekily and starts walking backwards away from him.

He just shakes his head and turns back to his beer.

'Why are you flirting with Noah like that?' I ask when we get back to our table.

Stella shrugs. 'Just something to do, I guess.'

'What?'

'Well he's hotter than a brick shit house, but he's always so controlled and professional I kind of like provoking him to see how far I can

go before he snaps,' she says giving a sly sideways glance in his direction.

'But wouldn't you like to date him though?' I persist hopefully.

'I never really thought about it, but I don't think I'm his type.'

I look at her curiously. 'How do you know you're not?'

'Come on. When a man really wants you it oozes out of his pores.'

'I don't know. From what I saw he seems to like you well enough,' I say, tearing the foil on the champagne bottle.

'Enough is the key clue. I don't want enough. I want desperately, can't live without, dying for, madly, deeply, etc. etc. You know, the kind of stuff you have with Zane.'

I ease the cork out with a quiet pop. 'What should we drink to?' I ask.

'Hot men,' she says with an impish grin.

I fill our glasses and we clink glasses.

'Hot men,' we say in unison and giggling like two naughty schoolgirls let the bubbles slide down our throats.

'Oh God, yes. Mmmm ... Heaven,' Stella moans and rapidly flutters her eyelashes to indicate just how blissed she is with the taste.

'Come on tell me how your date went.'

She pulls a face. 'Ugh ... he was an insufferable idiot.'

'Really? What did he do?'

She leans in. 'He asked me out to a restaurant and proceeded to gobble up everything in sight including my leftovers. I swear he was like a bloody turkey. When he was not eating he was boasting about himself. Brag, brag, brag. How much money he had. How good he was at his job. How much property he owned. God, you should have heard him. Anyone would have thought I was sitting with Warren Buffet.'

I smile at her.

'Honestly, I've come to the conclusion every father should tell his son what my granddad told my brother. When a man starts bragging he's compensating for something small between his legs. The consequence of that small heart to heart between my granddad and brother is: my brother never brags.'

She pauses to take a sip.

'Then, when this turkey had just about talked my head off he called for the bill and started tapping and fumbling about in every pocket he could find on himself.

So I was sitting there watching him and,' she taps her hair, 'you know the brain underneath all this pretty, was going, oooo this guy must think I fell off an Irish turnip truck.'

I start giggling. I can almost picture the scene.

'After he had tapped the shit of all his pockets he looked at me all innocent and astonished and told me he must have left his wallet in the side pocket of his car door. Then came the big ask: would I be so kind as to get the meal first and he would see me all right later? Mind you, it wasn't like it was an expensive place or anything.'

'What did you do?' I ask her.

'I looked him in the eye smiled really seductively and said, "You run along and get your wallet and I'll wait right for you, honey."'

'Wow, you're really brave to call him out like that. If someone did that to me, I'd just pay for the meal and never take his calls again.'

'No way. I'm a pretty laid back person, somebody calls me a bitch and I'm like, true, but I'm not down with what he did. Paying for that meal would have been encouraging him to go out and do that to another poor girl. It was a matter of principle,' she says firmly.

'And just in case he was planning on doing a runner, I scratched the inside of his thigh and told him I had something super special planned for him when we got back to my place. To seal the deal I looked at him as if he was going to get the best damn sex of his life.'

'Stop, you're killing me,' I say.

'What a blinking idiot. He actually thought he could stiff *me* with the bill. I mean, I'm all for women's lib and everything.'

She takes a sip of champagne.

'I hate a man opening a door for me as much as the next girl. Not. But for fucks sake don't invite me out for dinner and then pretend you've left your wallet in the car.'

'So did he come back with his wallet?'

'Of course he did. He was out of that restaurant like a bat out o hell and back in six minutes.' She toggles her eyebrows meaningfully. You have no idea how powerful my thigh scratch is.'

'So he drove you home ...'

'At breakneck speed.'

'And then?'

'And then ... I got out of the car and told him the next time he decides to be such a cheapskate he should just suck his own dick.'

Seven

Dahlia Fury

https://www.youtube.com/watch?v=XZGwHt
GBZJU

'**W**ell, you must teach me that thigh scratch of yours,' I tell Stella when I stop laughing.

She looks at me with bright, inquisitive eyes. 'Why? It doesn't look like you need me to teach you anything.'

To my surprise I flush bright red.

Scenting good gossip, she leans forward eagerly. 'Oh my God! Look at you. You're redder than my hair. I want to know *everything* that's going on with you.'

'It's just hot in here,' I say taking a gulp of champagne.

'Oh no, you don't get off so easy,' she threatens. 'I'll be needing details. You know, stuff like measurements, girth, frequency of emissions. The lot!'

'I thought you didn't want to know.'

'Well that was before I quit making a fool of myself.'

'Huh?'

'Yeah. I suddenly realized that Zane and you hooking up was the best thing that happened to me. You were right all along when you told me to let it go and move on. I can't believe I let myself get so down over him. For fucks sake the guy didn't even know I existed and there I was wasting my life away waiting for him to notice me. Me? Super duper delicious me. It was almost as if I was under a spell. And now when I look back I'm like ...' she pulls back as if in horror. 'I did that.' She jerks even further back. 'I said that.' Then she slaps herself comically. 'God, I was such a sad bitch I want to send myself a sympathy card.'

I can't stop grinning. 'Oh Stella, I'm so happy you've moved on. You can't imagine how bad I felt about Zane and me.'

She winks. 'Yes, I realized you must have been *really* sorry: the bathroom never looked so clean during that period.'

I look shamefaced. 'So you forgive me?'

She reaches out and grasps my hand. 'There's nothing to forgive, babe. It's not like

you broke up my happy meal, or anything. I was so miserable when I thought I was in love. Now when I look back I only see how completely stupid it all was. Why would anyone do that to themselves unless they were masochistic? And everybody knows I'm not. I love myself.'

'I am actually really proud of you. I like this new and shiny Stella,' I say smiling happily at her. In truth I am very relieved and impressed by how fast she has turned the corner on her infatuation.

She beams back. 'Well, join the club. I'm really proud of myself too. Now, enough about me. How big is Zane, really? Every queen needs a king size and I'm not talking about no bed.'

I laugh.

'Give me details, woman,' she demands.

'OK, are you ready for this?'

'Shoot.'

'I got to practice what we learned at the blowjob course.'

Her jaw drops. 'You swallowed?' she splutters.

I nod calmly.

She slaps her thigh. 'What happened to discreetly spitting while pretending to swallow?'

I shrug. 'I couldn't help it. It was rather delicious.'

She gasps. 'Never. You fucking liar. Spunk is *not* delicious.'

I grin. 'Actually it was.'

'Forget it. Nobody, not even you, is ever going to convince me that sperm is delicious.'

I chuckle at Stella's expression. 'I think I wanted to because I'm so crazy about him.'

Stella leans forward, fascinated. 'Yeah?'

'Yeah,' I say.

'Wow! You're really falling for him, aren't you?'

'I'm not falling for him. I think I've already fallen.'

Stella is staring at me in astonishment. I know now would be a good time to drop the bombshell about Daisy. I've never been any good at keeping secrets, and anyway, I want her to know. Before Zane came into our lives we always told each other everything and I don't want that to change. However, I already know exactly how she will react and I feel a little nervous flutter in my stomach.

'I want to tell you something, but I don't want to you overreact,' I tell her.

'Me overreact. When have I ever overreacted?'

I raise my eyebrows and look at her with a come-on-it's-me-you're-talking-to expression.

'Don't worry I won't.'

I look at her warningly.

'All right. All right. I promise not to. Go on, spit it out.'

'OK, remember that you have promised. No hysterics.'

'Go on,' she urges impatiently.

I take a deep breath and plunge in. 'Zane is the one who kidnapped Daisy.'

'What?' she explodes so loudly a lot of heads turn.

I look around us and notice that even Noah has turned to watch us. 'Remember you promised,' I hiss at her.

She picks up her glass of champagne, drains it dry and carefully puts the empty glass back down. 'Whoa, Dahlia. You're not surely going to hold me to my promise. This is so mind-blowing. How can you sit there and tell me something like this so calmly? What is wrong with you? I'm fucking freaking out here.'

'I reacted the same way when I first found out, but I've had time to assimilate.'

'Time to assimilate? Fuck! When did you find out?'

'Last night.'

'Jesus, Dahlia am I going crazy, or are you still with him?'

I pick up the bottle of champagne and fill Stella's glass. 'You're not going crazy and I'm still with him.'

'Oh my God. Oh my God! I don't believe this. While I was not watching you've gone and morphed into one of these weird women who thinks it's OK to write romantic letters to serial killers on death row, haven't you?'

'Stop being so dramatic.'

'Dramatic? If I can't be dramatic now, when the hell am I ever going to be dramatic?' she demands intensely.

I sigh. 'Olga explained it all to me.'

Stella's eyes become dinner plates. 'Olga? She's the fucking cook! How on earth did she explain it all away?'

'I don't know. She made sense.'

'He kidnapped your sister, Dahlia!'

'Do you want to calm down and listen, or do you just want to rant for the next hour?'

'I'm torn. I want to rant, but I'd really like to hear how his cook explained away a kidnapping too,' she says sarcastically

'Basically, she believes that Zane has suffered some horrendous trauma and that is why he is the way he is. He's like a tortured soul,' I pause, 'and she thinks I'm the person to save him.'

She folds her arms. 'It'll be interesting to hear how you plan to do that?'

'Well, I don't know yet, but I'm working on it.'

She shakes her head in disbelief. 'So you've forgiven him and all is hunky dory in your world.'

I look at Stella's understandably horrified face and I realize don't know how to explain what Zane and I have. How can I tell her that I am so connected to Zane it feels as if I don't derive my real nourishment from food and drink but him? Sometimes it is impossible for someone outside a relationship between a man and woman to appreciate or even comprehend the nature of the bonds that hold the couple. The bonds that hold me to Zane are like tempered steel. I want him. I need him and I cannot even imagine my life without him in it anymore. He holds my wellbeing in the palm of his hand.

'It's not that I've forgiven him,' I explain, 'it's just that I'm trying hard to understand him. I come from a loving, close knit family so I have no right to judge someone who might not have had the things I take for granted.'

I shrug.

'I don't know anything about Zane's past. He won't talk about it, but I can tell that he is the product of something unhappy. He exists in a violent world with brutal rules and has to abide by them just to survive, but underneath the cold exterior that he projects to everyone, I've seen glimpses of a beautiful but wounded and suffering man.'

For a few seconds she simply stares at me blankly then she grabs the neck of the champagne bottle and pours herself another glass. I know she is trying her best to grasp what I am telling her, but it is hard for her. She takes a big gulp.

'Did he know?' she asks, jerking her head in Noah's direction.

'Apparently they had all guessed.'

'Bloody cheek. Pretending to be all nice and helpful to me. I've a good mind to go there now and tell him off.'

I reach out and grab her hand. 'Don't you dare do any such thing, Stel. It's not his fault. This is between Zane and me. They didn't know for sure. They just guessed.'

'I'm surprised that you are not more angry.'

I look down at my hands. 'I guess it's because I understand what it feel like to want

someone so bad you're willing to do almost anything to get that person.'

She looks at me curiously. 'Do you feel that way about him?'

I bite my lower lip and nod slowly.

'Oh no,' she gasps in horror. 'What a mistake it was to let you go in my place that night.'

I shake my head. 'Don't say that. I wasn't even truly alive until I met him, Stel. Even if it all falls apart tomorrow I'll never regret what I've had with him.'

'Oh Dahlia. I hope and pray things work out for you,' she cries softly, but her voice is full of doubt and worry.

I smile. 'Look no matter what happens I'll survive, but here's the thing, we didn't come out tonight to be depressed. Remember we're getting irretrievably wasted. Let's just do that. Come what may.'

She smiles back. 'OK, bottoms up.'

We empty our glasses and Gloria Gaynor's *I Will Survive* comes on the music system. We both look at each other with widened, disbelieving eyes.

'Is that the universe talking to us?' Stella asks.

'If it is what're we waiting for?' I ask, jumping up.

Together we race to the tiny little dance floor at the back of the wine bar. No one else is dancing, so we have the whole floor to ourselves. We've danced to this track is so many times.

'Go. Walk out the door,' Stella and I scream as we strut our stuff.

It is just like old times, Stella and I kicking it on the dance floor. Well, all right, making a total fool of ourselves on the dance floor.

In the background Noah stands watching us. We call him over to join us, but he shakes his head and gives us a thumbs-up signal. Laughing we dance and down our drinks and dance some more and drink some more.

Eight

Dahlia Fury

'**I** am positively drunk,' Stella slurs.

'Me too,' I agree, my voice no less wobbly.

'Kebab?' she asks.

I shake my head.

She grimaces. 'It's all right for you. You'll be settling down to a super size sausage with lashings of sperm?'

I pull a face. 'Stop being so rude you.'

'Come on. I'm hungry,' she cries plaintively.

'All right. Let's get your ass to Taki's. I suppose, I could eat a bag of fries.'

'Panties are kinckers, and fries are chips in England,' Stella corrects fuzzily.

'Right. Bag of chips,' I say.

We stand up, stumble into each other, and start giggling uncontrollably.

Noah comes to us. 'Ready to go?'

'We're off to get some food from Taki,' Stella says, still laughing.

Noah scowls. 'Taki?'

'The kebab joint down the road,' I explain.

'Fine. Get in the car and we'll drive down.' Noah glances at his watch then back to me. 'We don't have that much time. You have to be back before 12.00.

That perks Stella up. She turns to me and wags her finger. 'What? You have curfew,' she exclaims and nearly falls backwards on her Jimmy Choos.

I grab her waist and hold her upright. 'No, I don't. I just told Zane I'd be back before twelve.'

'For tonight's helping of sausage and gravy?' she slurs.

I glance at Noah, and his eyebrows are as high as I have ever seen them. It's obvious he has no idea how to deal with two falling-down-drunk women.

'We'll have to take Stella home first,' I tell him.

'No need. The driver will take her back and make sure she is safely through her front door, and I'll take you back in my car.'

'God, you're very efficient,' I say, swaying slightly because Stella is swaying like mad.

'Here let me take her,' he offers and swings her easily into the crook of his elbow.

With his great arm around Stella's tottering body, and with her heckling and calling out friendship overtures to all kinds of strangers on the road, we make our way to Taki's. There is a queue of people waiting to be served, but Taki throws half a chicken on the grill, calls something out in Greek to the other man manning the shop, goes to the vacant end of counter, and beckons us over.

He slings a tea towel over his shoulder and leaning with his forearms on the glass counter cries out expansively, 'Aiiiii, it's my favorite Kouklas.' The word, he explained to us a year ago, means beautiful dolls in Greek. Not in pervy way Taki is old enough to be our grandfather. It is usually used to describe pretty young girls or babies.

'Hey Taki,' both Stella and I say in unison.

'Long time you no eat Taki's food? Where you been?'

'It's her,' Stella complains. 'She's gone and found herself a man and now she won't come out with me.'

Taki raises both his veined, wrinkled hands and shakes them in front of his mustached face and says. 'You find a man. So what? You still have to eat.'

I grin and he looks over at Noah standing by the door. 'Is that him over there?'

'No, he just a friend,' I say.

'He's big,' he says puffing out his shoulders and widening his old eyes.

'Do you think he is big where it counts?' Stella whispers.

'Stella?' I whisper.

'Go have a feel,' Taki urges with an evil grin.

Stella turns to do just that, but I catch her by the waist. 'Stella,' I say warningly.

'What? He'll never know. I'll be discreet' she says innocently.

'Don't do it. You'll regret it in the morning,' I whisper under my breath.

'Just one quick feel,' she wheedles.

'Remember the last time you were this drunk and you didn't listen to me.'

'When I set fire to that bouncer, you mean,' she says with a little giggle.

'And what happened to us after that?' I prompt.

'We got banned from ever going there again,' she says sulkily.

I turn to Taki. 'She's been drinking on an empty stomach so please don't encourage her.'

He raises his hands in surrender.

'What's there to eat then?' Stella asks Taki, and emits a huge hiccup. She covers her mouth. 'Ooops. Sorry.'

Taki waves towards all the raw meat inside the glass case.

While Stella leans against the glass counter and looks at the food on display, I order a bag of chips, and turn to Noah to ask if he wants something to eat. He shakes his head quickly and turns his attention back to a group of young guys outside who've had a lot of drink and are obviously spoiling for a fight.

'What's the lowest calorie thing you have here?' Stella asks.

Taki picks out a lemon slice decorating the edges of a plate full of skewered meat and, grinning widely, holds it up to Stella.

'Ha, ha. Very funny,' Stella says and leans her cheek into her palm. 'You know what. Fuck it. I'll break my diet for tonight. Give me a large lamb kebab with salad and lots and lots of garlic sauce since I won't be kissing anyone tonight.'

'Oki-doki,' Taki says and goes off to shave some meat from the rotisserie.

We stand by glass window and wolf down our food between sips from cans of coke.

Afterwards, we walk back towards the place where the driver's car is parked. Noah stuffs Stella into the backseat of the car and shuts the door.

'Wait here,' he says to me. 'I'll bring my car around.'

The back window winds down and Stella pops her head out.

'Where's he gone?' she whines.

'To get his car.'

She grabs my hands. 'I know I'm drunk and raving, but you do know that I love you with all my heart, don't ya?'

I feel such a great love for Stella at that moment I want to hold and protect her from every man that could ever try to hurt her. 'You know I really love you too, right,' I choke.

For a second Stella looks like she is about to burst into tears and I bend down and kiss her cheek.

She grabs me tightly. 'I can't wait for you to come back. You don't have to clean the bathroom anymore. I'll do it,' she says in my hair, her voice wobbly and I feel my heart clench with sadness. I truly am going to miss this girl. I know I will have to tell her soon that I don't know when I will be coming back, but I have no heart to say it then. Another day. I'll say it another day.

At that moment Noah's car roars into the street and both Stella and I turn to stare at the massive black machine with surprise. It is like something from a superhero comic book.

'Wow. Is that a bat mobile?' Stella asks.

'I don't think so, but it sure has one heck of an angry engine.'

Stella hiccups. 'My brother calls them go-home-in-a-neck-brace cars.'

'Your brother better not be right. I have to get into it.'

Stella laughs uproariously.

Noah stops next to a car behind us and signals the driver to go. The car starts to move and Stella emerges out of the window waist high and waves her arms at us.

'Nite, nite, my babes,' she shouts, her voice sloppy and happier than I have heard in a long time.

'Get back in,' I shout.

She quickly gets back into the car and a couple of seconds later I hear her scream in a high-pitched voice 'weeeeee,' and see a pair of long legs waving slowly out of the window in a slow scissoring motion. Just like a Folies Bergère dancer. Laughing, I pull my phone out and take a video of her legs. I'll post it on Facebook in the morning. I bet she won't remember.

'Let's go,' Noah calls.

As I am about to turn away one of her shoes comes off her foot and falls to the side of the road. Before I can do anything the traffic lights change, Stella retracts her legs, and the car speeds off. Stella is so plastered she doesn't even realize she has lost a shoe.

'Come on, Dahlia' Noah urges again.

'Just hang on one sec,' I say, and run the few yards to pick up her precious shoe, but as I get to it a man who was coming from a different direction bends down and takes it in his hand. He straightens and my mouth drops open.

'Mark,' I whisper.

'Hello Dahlia,' he says softly, and holds the shoe out to me.

I take it from him. 'What are you doing here?' A gust of wind blows hair into my face. I push it back and stare at him.

'I was in the neighborhood,' he says.

Even in my intoxicated state the statement doesn't make sense. 'Look Mark, I-' I begin when I feel Noah step next to me. I turn my head and look up at him and his face is like granite. His eyes are cold and hostile and his mouth is an intimidatingly straight line.

'All right, Dahlia?' he asks, his eyes never leaving Mark.

'It's all right, Noah. This is my friend, Mark,' I explain hurriedly.

Mark immediately holds out his hand, but Noah rudely ignores it. 'We should go,' he says still staring at Mark.

Mark lets his hand drop to his side.

'Nice to see you again, Mark,' I say awkwardly.

For an instant it looks as if Mark is going to say something, then he flashes a lop-sided smile and says, 'Yeah, it was great to see you again. You look beautiful.'

Next to me Noah stiffens even more.

To diffuse the situation I trust Stella's shoe into Mark's hand. 'Give this to Stella for me, will you?' I say.

He grasps the shoe and nods.

I smile and follow Noah to his car. When we get to it I turn around and Mark is still standing there clutching the shoe. I wave and he waves back. I feel something strange inside me, like a warning, or an instinct that something bad is going to happen, but I am too tipsy to make any sense of it.

I slide into the passenger seat, Noah closes the door, and the feeling evaporates. I turn around in my seat to look at Mark, but he is gone. I crane my neck looking for him, but he has completely disappeared. Maybe he went down one of the side streets.

Noah gets in and starts the car. I quickly text Stella and tell her that Mark has her shoe before turning to Noah.

'What kind of car is this?' I ask. The interior smells of leather, glue, resin, and polished metal. A truly masculine smell.

'It's a TVR Sagaris.'

'Hmm ... it's a gorgeous car.'

'Thank you.'

'How fast can it go?'

'Zero to 60mph in 3.9 seconds.'

'Wow, and the top speed?'

'185mph,' he says instantly and there is quiet pride in his voice.

'I bet you get a lot of speeding tickets.'

He grins. 'I don't get speeding tickets.'

I turn to look at his profile. 'How come?'

He winks. 'Trade secret.'

I lift my hands up as if in surrender. 'OK.' There is a pause.

'Have you worked for Zane for long?' I ask and I don't imagine the wariness that enters his body.

'Not really.'

'Have you lived in London all your life?'

'No,' he says shortly.

'What about Zane?'

'You'll have to ask him that yourself.'

Just to see his reaction I ask, 'What's Zane favorite color?'

He scowls. 'I have no idea.'

Jesus, getting information from him is like getting blood from stone. I throw my hands up. 'Is there anything at all you can tell about Zane?'

He glances at me. 'Not really.'

I reach forward and switch on the stereo and a Russian pop song comes on.

'Who's singing?' I ask.

'Pussy Riot.'

I stare at him. 'Are you kidding me?'

'Nope. I'm a big fan.'

I shake my head. 'Of a band called Pussy Riot?'

He gives me a cocky look. 'With a name like that what's not to like?'

Nine

Dahlia Fury

https://www.youtube.com/watch?v=37FGwDMMZEg

Yuri opens the door for us and says something to Noah in rapid Russian who looks at his watch and immediately starts walking towards the study. I guess we didn't make the twelve o'clock curfew.

'Thanks for bringing me home, Noah,' I call to his retreating back.

He lifts his hand in acknowledgement but doesn't break his stride.

'Goodnight,' Yuri says.

'Yeah, same to you,' I reply and run up the stairs.

I actually feel a bit queasy. Getting into such a low swung fast car after drinking so much and eating a whole bag of greasy fries is not exactly a good idea.

I quickly clean my make up off, brush my teeth, use the toilet, change into my nightgown and go down to Zane's bedroom. I open the door and he is already there. I have the impression that he is full of leashed energy, that he was pacing the floor impatiently, even though he is standing with his legs shoulder-width apart and looking at me with a deliberately blank expression. Sexy as hell, actually.

'Hi,' I greet.

'Noah says a man was waiting for you,' he says neutrally.

'Mark was not waiting for me,' I scoff. 'We just ran into each other outside the bar.' I shake my head. 'I can't believe Noah is such an old woman. Imagine running to you with that bit of gossip.'

'It's not a bit of gossip. It is Noah's job to notice even the smallest inconsistencies. You didn't just run into him. He was waiting for you and only approached you when you were alone.'

I frown. I guess he is right. Mark was waiting for me. I shrug. 'It doesn't matter. We're just friends now.'

'Is he the boyfriend that you talked about?' His voice is very quiet, his eyes intense.

'Yes, but I ended it before I came here and our relationship had not become physical.'

'Are you still in contact with him?'

'Yes. He's a nice guy.'

'I don't want you to see him again.'

'Why? We're just friends. I feel nothing for him but friendship.'

He walks up to me, swirls my hair in his fist, and pulls my face upwards. From every pore of his body seeps raw masculinity, neither manufactured no harnessed, just a true force of nature. An Alpha in the truest sense of the word.

'You might feel just friendship,' he murmurs, 'but he lusts for you, Dahlia. A man who waits on the street for a woman is crying out for her.'

I lick my lips.

His head swoops down. He takes my bottom lip between his teeth and sucks it. 'You can tell him this. If I catch him within ten feet of you I'll stuff his dick into his ass.'

I stare into his searingly bright eyes. 'His dick in his ass? How Neanderthal of you,' I say to lighten the mood.

'Call it what you want, but do not make the mistake of thinking it's an idle threat because it isn't,' he says softly, and nibbles my earlobes. He raises his head and looks down

possessively at my breasts, but his voice is cold and businesslike. 'I don't take kindly to other men sniffing around my woman.'

'OK, I'll tell Mark.'

His eyes become less guarded.

'What did you do tonight?' I ask.

He bends his head and brushes his mouth against my cheek. I close my eyes and revel in the sensation of his warm lips against my skin. 'I waited for you,' he whispers.

Something inside me starts melting like butter in a hot pan. I'm going to blow it. I've had a bit to drink and I can't be trusted not to throw my arms around him and admit that I'm in love with him. *Activity. I should engage in activity.*

Silently, I start unbuttoning his shirt. He helps me by unzipping his pants and pulling them down his legs. He kicks them away and I get onto my knees. When I am mouth-level with his boxers, I lean in and catch the waistband with my teeth. I tug it outward and over his turgid cock and pull it down his legs. When I rise up the long thick shaft is millimeters away from my lips.

I extend my tongue and delicately lick his cockhead. It is satiny smooth.

'Your cock is so fucking beautiful,' I say.

Zane kneads his fingers into my hair and groans, as I swallow the tip and bob my head up and down the shaft. I look up at him and he is staring down at the sight of his cock disappearing into my face. It is sexy and I hungrily take him even deeper, but when he touches the back of my throat I get a sudden uneasy sensation in my stomach. My eyes widen with shock.

Oh my God, no. No fucking way. No, this can't be happening to me.

I pull away abruptly, but it is already too late. Vomit is hurling out of my mouth and landing directly on to his crotch and thighs. Bits of fries are hanging from his balls. Ugh. Yuck. And the smell.

Until that moment I have never known what it is like to wish for the ground to open up and swallow me, or for lighting bolts to blitz the room I was in. Totally mortified I cover my mouth with both my hands and look up at Zane's face. I'm pretty sure vomiting while giving a blowjob is a major passion killer, but I don't know what I expected. Probably him staring down at the mess I have made of him with revulsion, shock and maybe even irritation, but what I see is a man who doesn't seem to care that I have been sick all over him.

Instead he stares down at me with deep concern etched in every line of his face.

He reaches down and pulls me up by my upper-arms. As I am pulled upwards I see his cock is already at half-mast. Shit. How embarrassing. All I can think of at that moment is: thank God I didn't have a kebab or a burger. Bits of undigested meat will look so much more disgusting.

'What's wrong? Are you ill?' he asks, frowning.

I am so horrified I can hardly bear to meet his eyes. 'I think I'm not used to being in a sports car after drinking so much. I'm so sorry,' I mutter, awkwardly using the backs of my hands to wipe my chin.

He lets go of my arms, picks up his shirt, and roughly wipes his groin and legs. Then he takes me by the hand and leads me to the bathroom. I follow him like a lamb. He switches the shower on and helps me undress.

'I'm so sorry,' I apologize again. 'I bet nothing like this has ever happened to you.'

'No,' he admits.

'Oh God, I groan.

'Hey,' he says suddenly. 'It's only the contents of your stomach? I'm planning on putting my tongue in your ass!'

Struck dumb, my face reddening, I stare at him.

'It was nothing. A bit of vomit,' he says kindly.

'I ... er ... should brush my teeth,' I say and move to basin. I squeeze some toothpaste on my toothbrush and quickly clean my teeth. Our eyes meet in the mirror.

'You should have seen your face though,' he says, his eyes full of mischief.

'You should have seen yours,' I retort.

He smiles and so do I. We are like two kids trying to make friends for the first time. He stops smiling and so do I. He bites his lower lip in such an unconsciously seductive gesture I feel something inside me contract and can only hope it is not my stomach. I quickly look away, spit, rinse my mouth, and put my brush back into its holder. I look up and he is still looking at me.

'I'll clean up the mess. The smell ...,' I trail away embarrassed.

'It's OK,' he murmurs. 'We'll sleep in your room tonight.'

By now the shower stall has filled with steam. He opens the door and we step into it. Deliciously warm water sprays down on us and washes away my sick. Zane pours liquid soap into his palm and rubs it on my chest, my breast and down my body.

I squirt some onto my hand and rub it on his abs, his flat stomach, and lower still. I notice that his cock is no longer at half-mast but hard as fucking steel. I pour more soap and languorously stroke his cock. My slippery hands pull at it and he groans. I cup his balls and massage them gently while my other hand carries on tugging firmly at his cock.

He pivots me around and my palms slap against the tiles. I exhale as he grabs my hips and tilts them upwards. Warm water beats down on my head and back with sensuous insistence as the blunt head of his cock starts to part then slide into my pussy. I push eagerly towards it taking him deeper into my body until I feel his balls on my pussy lips. I wriggle my ass and it sends tremors of pleasure shooting into my veins.

'Don't stop,' he growls and I hear the thick hot lust in his voice.

I press my legs together to make my sex tighter and grind myself into his groin.

'Oh fuck. You're so fucking tight,' he groans.

My pussy throbbing with pleasure I attain greater and greater heights of pleasure. My eyes turn half-shut. My pussy wants to feel him explode inside, feel his hot cum shooting deep into it. I start bouncing on his shaft, harder and harder, but it's not enough. The craving for him is like fingers inside my belly. I want him to thrust like the wild beast he is.

'Take me harder than you've ever done,' I cry harshly.

He doesn't need a second invitation. He grabs my hips and pounds me so hard and so damn deep my feet come off the floor and I am suspended in the air. He keeps going like that, his hard cock punishing my wet and hungry sex until a shuddering, pulsing climax overtakes us. For a while we remain joined and breathing heavily, the soft rain sluicing down our heaving bodies, then he withdraws and the water washes away all history of our coupling.

In a rare moment of tenderness he wraps me in a towel and gently pats me dry. I stare at his dark head. If only it could always be like this.

If only.

Ten

Aleksandr Malenkov

https://www.youtube.com/watch?v=jWFb5z3kUSQ

I am ten years old tomorrow. I can punch and I can take a punch. There is no school tomorrow. I hang my uniform in my cupboard and hear my father roar at my mother from the living room. There is something wrong with his tea. It may be too sweet or not sweet enough. The walls are thin and I hear my mother walking into the living room.

I close the cupboard. It is one of those old ones with a beveled mirror on the door. I look at my reflection. The first thing everyone sees when they first meet me is my eyes. I look into them and it is like looking into a stranger's eyes. I hear my mother reply, her voice is muffled, placating, frightened. Then come the inevitable flat, dull sound of her flesh being hit.

I turn away from the mirror and walk to my door. I open it and go into the living room.

'Papa,' I say.

My father turns his murderous gaze my way and starts advancing on me. He is drunk. My mother grabs his arm and tries to pull him back.

'Leave him alone,' she pleads.

He elbows her in the neck and she falls to the floor choking.

My fists clench. God, I hate my father.

Blood pulses through my ears, the world becomes silent. There is only me and him. He comes up to me and swings his fist. I evade it easily. With a roar of anger he swings again. This time more wildly. I duck. He misses. His fist crashes into the wall. His eyes almost pop with pain and he bellows with fury.

I don't say anything. My heart feels cold. I know I will eventually have to let him hit me, but it is better if I tire him out first. Once he banged his head on the wall and knocked himself out. That is the best case scenario. When he woke up he was livid but it would be worth it.

Cursing, he nurses his injured knuckles in his hand for a few seconds. Then he flexes them and clenches his hand into a lethal fist. He looks up at me, his face twisted with hate.

'If you don't stand still boy I swear I'll kill your mother with my bare hands,' he snarls

This is it. The fight is over. I lock eyes with him and stop moving. He comes towards me and punches me in the gut. I don't see it in slow motion like in the movies. His hand flashes through the air and suddenly it is in my stomach. Kaboom.

My mother screams.

I love you, mama.

Forever and ever.

Eleven

Dahlia Fury

For my birthday, buy me a politician.

https://www.youtube.com/watch?v=-4kTeioXrCs

'**H**ey Molly,' I say into the phone.

'How's it going, doll?' Molly's cheerful voice comes through my cellphone.

'Great. How are you?'

She sighs. 'I've got a client who insists on wearing leopard and tiger prints at the same time. If it gets out that she consulted me, my reputation will be in tatters.'

I laugh. 'You'll make it work.'

'I do hope you're right. So what can I do for you today?'

'I need something to wear to the races.'

'At this time of the year you're presumably going to Cheltenham?'

'Yes, I am.'

'It's less high fashion than Ascot, but it can be lots of fun and very romantic if it rains.'

'*What*? English rain is just wet and cold.'

'The object is not to go into the rain, but snuggle up to each other in the bleachers.'

'Sorry, I'm not going to hope for rain.'

She chuckles. 'Coming back to your outfit. I think I have exactly the thing for you. I just saw it like three minutes ago at my friend's boutique. It's very, very French. A two piece skirt suit.'

'Brilliant.'

'Do you want to wear a hat?'

'A hat? I haven't worn a hat since I was a kid.'

'Then you must wear one. The races is one of the last few places left that one can wear a hat to anymore.'

'You have successfully convinced me,' I say with a laugh.

'When are you going?'

'Day after tomorrow.'

'Oh, that soon.' She pauses. 'I have your measurements so I'll see if I can get a milliner to make one to match your outfit. Marney should be able to do it, but I'll call you back and let you know if she can't, and I have to find something readymade instead.'

'OK,' I say, impressed by Molly's list of contacts and her ability to rustle up the perfect outfit at moment's notice.

'Right see you tomorrow night,' she says crisply.

'Thanks, Molly.'

I slip into nude block heels (Molly says high heels will simply mean I'll spend my day balancing on the balls of my feet on grass) and stand in front of the mirror looking like a character from Beverley Hills Housewives. My dress is immaculately tailored, lush pink, knee-length number. It comes with a coat in the same material an inch longer than the dress. The hat is a side sweep felt concoction in a delicate shade of blush, and decorated with three silk camellias dyed to match my outfit.

'Go knock him dead, Dahlia,' I whisper to my reflection, and go down the stairs to Zane's room.

As I open the door he is getting into a dusty-black single-breasted jacket. His shirt is bottle green and his tie mustard brown. Wow! He looks precious yes, but complicated.

Somehow astonishing. Like coming across an extinct saber-toothed tiger and knowing that loving him or bringing him into your world can only mean loss. But he is real and I love him. The visceral desire to protect him is so strong I feel it like something the size of a fist in my throat.

He stops mid-shrug and stares at me.

Don't address him seriously or carefully. This is a light occasion. I clear my throat and I twirl around. 'Well, what do you think?' My voice is light and easy.

He pulls the lapels of his jacket together and walks up to me. 'I think,' he says brushing the back of his hand on my cheek, 'it is cruel that one woman should have been given so much beauty.'

I grin. 'And I think it is cruel that one man should have been given so much charm.'

He smiles. 'That is one adjective I've never heard used on me before.'

'That's probably because you didn't decide to lay it on thick before.'

His eyes glow. 'There was no one worth laying it on thick for.'

I place my hand gently on his chest and look up into his gorgeous eyes. 'Good. I'm glad.'

He smiles. 'Have you got your betting money ready?'

I lift up my pink purse. 'Yup.'

He smiles. 'It's going to be very difficult for me to keep my hands from sliding up your dress today.'

I laugh.

We go outside and there is a spanking new, astoundingly beautiful Aston Martin DB11 waiting outside. Noah opens the passenger door for me and I slip into it feeling like a movie star. The seat is snug, deep and form fitting. It doesn't smell of masculinity like Noah's car, this one just smells like something very, very expensive. Practically every surface – including the headliner and rear deck has been finished in luxurious leather or some other exotic material.

I touch the smooth leather as Zane slides into the driver's seat.

'That's handcrafted raccoon,' he says.

'You shouldn't have told me that. I like raccoons.'

'Yeah, well, when I die Aston Martin is welcome to my skin if it's going to end up in a car like this.'

'You're one crazy Russian,' I tell him.

Zane grins and guns the car. Raucous doesn't describe the full glory of a V12 engine's menacing roar. There is no point screaming over the noise so Zane switches on a Bang and Olufsen stereo system that is powerful enough to counteract the thunder of the engine, and the car fills with lively violin music. An hour and a half later and we are at Cheltenham Racecourse.

As Zane drives up I see Noah and another member of Zane's security team, I think his name is Boris, are already there. We get out of the car, and Boris gets into it and goes off to park it.

I look around us in wonder. Everyone is colorfully dressed, which is rather unusual in Britain, and there is an air of festivity and excitement about them as they mill about talking and laughing.

The three of us make our way to one of the private boxes. Zane's friends and acquaintances are already there. Rose champagne and canapés are served by smiling staff. For the first time I get to see Zane interact with other people and I am shocked to see how different he is with other people. He hardly speaks and allows the other person to make most of the conversation while he inclines his head politely and listens and gives the occasional nod. There is almost an invisible force field around him that discourages anybody to get too familiar or close.

After about fifteen minutes Shane and Snow arrive and I smile happily at them. They are such a beautiful couple everyone turns to watch them. They come up to us.

'Hey Dahlia,' Shane says.

Snow kisses me on my cheek. 'You look absolutely wonderful,' she says with a lovely smile.

'So do you,' I say, sincerely looking at her long sleeved powder blue dress. It has little birds embroidered on it.

As we are making plans to have dinner together, Lenny comes through the door, and Snow pales. Shane puts his arm around her waist and she looks up at him. He smiles down at her and in that look he gives her there's everything I would love to see in Zane's face. There's love, there's protection, there's reassurance, there's lust, and there's permanence. *I'm here forever.*

My eyes slide to Zane and he is looking at Lenny. Lenny is talking to some other people.

'Don't worry. I won't leave your side and he will never approach us,' Shane tells his wife.

'It's OK. I'm prepared. It's not like I didn't know he'd be here,' she says with a shaky laugh.

'We're going down to the paddock. Want to come with us?' Zane invites them.

'Shall we go see the horses,' Shane asks Snow.

'No, I want to do this. I want him to know I'm not afraid of him,' Snow says.

'OK, sweetheart.'

'We'll see you guys later then,' Zane says, and leads me away. I look sideways up at Zane. 'What was that all about?'

'Snow used to be with Lenny.'

'What?' Even the idea that someone as beautiful as Snow could be with a man as repulsive and slimy as Lenny is unthinkable.

'It's a long story.'

'I don't like Lenny.'

He frowns at me. 'I told you to stay out of it.'

'I'm not interfering. I'm just stating my opinion.'

'Just stay as far away from him as you can, Dahlia,' he says softly.

'Don't worry I plan to.'

Here we are. This is where one comes to see how a horse is behaving before the race starts.

I have never been to a racecourse before and Zane explains me that horses are like people. They have good days and bad days and the paddock was the place to see if they are nervous and sweating a lot (the ones with big dark splotches on their coat) or even ill if the sweat patch is near its kidneys. He shows me the difference between a preppy horse eager to race, and a jittery one, biting, rearing and turning in circles. That horse he tells me has spunk but is wasting its energy before the race and should be avoided.

'Do you go to the races often?' I ask.

'Yes. There's not much to beat spending the whole afternoon and evening watching horses racing and performing at their peak ability.'

'Is that a good horse to pick?' I ask pointing to a beautiful black stud with a white star on his forehead.

'I wouldn't,' he replies.

'No? Do you have a recommendation then?' I ask curiously. Stella has asked me to place a bet for her too.

'Last Arabian.,' he says pointing to a gleaming brown horse tossing its head proudly.

'How much should I put on it?' I ask.

'Everything you've got,' he says seriously.

My mouth drops open in astonishment. I lean forward and whisper. 'Are you saying the races are fixed?'

'Not all, but that one is.'

I stare at him in disbelief. He is so beautiful yet so spectacularly foreign to me. 'How do you fix a match in this day and age?'

'Pay the other jockeys to throw the race.'

'Oh my God,' I gasp. I have never met anyone who was so relaxed and casual after doing such a criminal thing.

He looks at me curiously. 'Why are you so shocked?'

'Of course, I'm shocked,' I whisper fiercely.

He seems surprised. 'Why? The most important things in this world are fixed. From gold prices (twice a day) to mortgage rates, to which country gets to host the Olympics. Even the results you see on Google are completely manipulated. It's all corrupt, but so well hidden that you never know about it.'

'Why isn't what you already have enough, Zane? Why do you need more money?' I ask sadly.

He reaches out a hand and brushes a stray lock of hair away from my cheek. 'To enter the mafia,' he says, 'is to become a shark. The shark must perpetually swim if it is to breathe and therefore exist. We must constantly expand. We must take more than we give, even to the extent of eating our own young.

'If the mighty empire has to eat its young to expand then it's not sustainable and must die an agonizingly long and horrible death.'

'To the contrary in my profession death is usually brutal but quick.'

'This life you have chosen is so dangerous. I am so afraid for you,' I whisper, my voice full of dread.

'I really meant it when I said I'd rather die a violent death as a lion then live forever as a rat in a sewer.

'I know you said you didn't have a choice to enter this brutal world, but you have a choice now. You can stop. You can walk away from this life.'

'This the only life I know, *rybka*.'

Last Arabian wins his race in the last few seconds. It looks so real. No one could have suspected. I look at Zane and his face is no different than any other gambler there. Shane and Snow don't stay. Lenny keeps away from me.

We go into the restaurant and eat a five-course delicious meal with an international twist to it. I talk and laugh and put on my happy face. Stella calls and is disappointed that I did not put any money on a horse. I will tell her later about Last Arabian. I know she will understand that I have put, but a foot in Zane's world and only because it is the only way I know to stay in there long enough to try and pull him out of it.

Twelve

Dahlia Fury

'**Y**ou know it is Aleksandr's birthday tomorrow,' Olga says when I go downstairs for breakfast.

I look at her in amazement. 'Oh? He never said anything.'

'He never does. That is why I am telling you. In case you wanted to celebrate it in some way ...' She lets her voice trail off as she packs the cavity of a duck with herbs and sausage meat and orange slices.

I frown. 'What usually happens on his birthday?'

She glances at me. 'Absolutely nothing.'

'What? Not even a cake with some candles on it?'

'I've been working for Aleksandr for nearly ten years and not once has he celebrated his birthday. I've never so much as seen a birthday card arrive.'

I look at her curiously. 'Why will nobody even send a card?'

She shrugs. 'Probably because he doesn't tell anyone it's his birthday so no one knows to do anything.'

'How do you know it's his birthday then?'

'Well, I saw his passport sitting on his desk one day and peeked into it,' she confesses.

'Olga,' I shout and burst into laughter. Honestly, she is so cute.

She makes a face. 'It's not like I harmed anyone. I just wanted to know how old he was.'

'So how old is he?'

'He is thirty-four tomorrow.'

I think for a moment. 'Should I plan something for him, Olga, or is that just going to make him angry that I have been putting my nose where he obviously doesn't want anybody's?'

'It's up to you, but I could bake a cake if you asked me to,' she says, looking at me hopefully, willing me to pick up the gauntlet and run with it.

For a few seconds I hesitate. What if he is one of those sour people who don't like anyone to make a fuss over their birthdays? Stella's grandfather is like that. He goes mad if

 378

anybody even wishes him happy birthday, let alone buys him a present. He grumbles that presents are a total waste of money. Then I think: what the heck? I should throw a little surprise party. It'll be fun. This house is way too dead.

'Yes, bake a cake, Olga. We'll surprise him with a party. Nothing grand or too intrusive, just the staff.'

Olga smiles and nods with approval.

'I think we're going out for dinner, and when we get back I'll bring him into the living room. It has to be dark and when he switches on the light everyone can pop up from their hiding places and scream surprise. Then you can bring in the cake with lighted candles. We'll all sing happy birthday and maybe have a toast.'

Olga smiles happily. 'That sounds like a wonderful idea. I'll make strawberry cake. It's his favorite.'

I smile back excited by the idea of throwing a surprise party for Zane. 'Thank you for telling me, Olga. He should have a proper birthday.'

'Yes, he should,' she says softly.

'I'll go out today and buy him a present.'

That afternoon I go out with Noah. First we pass by my workplace to drop off read manuscripts and pick up more. Then we go shopping.

It's hard to know what to get for a man who already has everything. Of course, Noah is no help. Just for fun I get him a set of 4 Star Wars flash drives. They are really cute and they should make him smile. I chose Darth Vader, Yoda, Chewbacca and C-3PO.

With my flash drives safely in my bag I get the driver to take me to Coco De Mer. Neither the driver nor Noah show any reaction. Noah waits outside while I go in and buy an A10 Cyclone hands free Male Masturbator and the lubricant that goes with it.

Outside, Noah's eyes drift to my package. 'Done?'

'Nearly. I just need to quickly pop into Non Stop Party in Kensington to pick up some stuff.

At Non Stop Party I buy loads of silver and black balloons, streamers, banners, wrapping paper and a funny card with a grinning monkey with the words:

Don't panic. You've still got it.

For my last item I walk into Dune and buy every scented candle they have in stock. It comes up to just over a hundred.

'All done,' I tell Noah.

'If you think of something else you need let me know. I'm around anytime,' he says.

'Why thank you, Noah,' I say.

A small smile tugs at the corners of his mouth. 'Glad to be able to help,' he says gruffly.

Once we get home he helps me carry all my purchases up to my room. After he has gone, I sit down on the bed and begin to wrap them up. A part of me can't wait for tomorrow. To see Zane's reaction. Halfway through wrapping Yoda, my sister calls me on Skype.

'Hey you,' I say cheerily.

She doesn't even say hello. 'Are you still at your friend's house?' she asks.

Shit, she has recognized the background. 'Yeah. I'm kind of staying here. I know I said it was a friend's house, but actually it's my ... er ... boyfriend's house.'

She frowns, her eyes narrowed and suspicious. 'What? Why would you hide that from me?'

'Ummm ... it's kind of complicated, but basically, I wasn't sure if it was going to come to anything so there was no point in saying anything if it was going to be a non event.'

She rolls onto her front on the bed and lays her chin in her folded hands. 'You haven't told mom either, have you?'

'And have her quiz me about it all the time? No thanks!'

She grins. 'So come on, who is he?'

'Uh ... his name is Zane, well, that's like a nickname. His real name is Aleksandr Malenkov.'

'That's not an English name,' she notes.

'No. He's Russian.'

Her eyes widen. 'You're going out with a Russian guy?'

'Yup.'

'Is he nice?'

'Here let me send you a pic of him,' I say and send a pic over to her.

'OMG!' she exhales. 'He looks so big and fierce. What's he like, a wrestler or something?

'No.'

'So what does he do?'

'Umm ... he's a businessman.'

'Oh, what kind of business?'

'Er ... something to do with credit cards,' I say vaguely.

My sister is on to me straight away. 'Are you hiding something, Dahlia?'

'No, why?'

'I don't know. You sound sort of evasive. Is everything OK?'

'Of course. It's his birthday tomorrow and I'm just sitting here wrapping some presents for him.'

'Oh yeah. How old is he tomorrow?'

'Thirty-four.'

'God, that's old.'

'No, it's not,' I say immediately.

What did you get him anyway?'

I pick up the unwrapped Star Wars flash drives and show them to her.

'Cool,' she says.

'So what about you then? Everything OK with you?' I ask.

'Yeah. I think I might get promoted soon.'

I beam at her. 'Really? That's fantastic.'

'Yeah, Mr. Stevens said I was doing a fine job and that he might have some really good news for me next month.

'That's awesome, honey. You always give your best and you sooooo deserve it.'

Daisy looks pleased.

'Daisy?'

'What?'

'Um … you know when you were kidnapped?'

'Yeah.'

'You don't have any lasting ill effects from it do you?'

Her forehead creases. 'What do you mean?'

'I mean like flashbacks or bad dreams … or any phobias?'

'Nah,' she says immediately and I feel a great sense of relief. 'Now it feels more like a dream. It's so surreal. But I'm more careful now though. I wouldn't trust strangers as easily as before.'

'Do you hate the people who kidnapped you?'

'No, but I feel guilty.'

'Guilty? Why?'

'Sometimes I think about those other girls. What has happened to them? Where are they now? Are they still even alive?'

It makes me feel really bad that I can't tell her there were no other girls. It was just a tape recorder. 'Girls are abducted every day, Daisy. It just never directly touches us so we never think about it, but even if we did what can we do about it? In that respect we are as helpless as they are.'

'I guess you're right,' she says slowly.

'Just don't think about them, OK. You can't help them and you'll just end up being less grateful for all the blessings you have.

'Dahlia, can I ask you something?'

'Of course.'

'Is this man you're going out with the one that helped to find me?'

My heart feels heavy. I've never deliberately kept a secret from my sister, but how can I ever tell her this? 'Yes,' I say. In a way it is not a lie. He had a hand in her release.

'Maybe one day I can thank him myself,' she says.

'OK,' I say with a smile.

'Yeah, I'd like to. I feel really grateful to him. Give me your address and I'll send him a card.'

I text the address to her and we end the conversation. For a long time I stare at the Chewbacca flash drive feeling guilty and confused. It is such a big secret to keep forever, but maybe I won't have to. Maybe one day when I have learned how to fly, when I have pulled Zane out of this life, I will sit Daisy down and tell her everything.

I wrap the flash drives and go downstairs to see how Olga is coming along with her preparations for the party.

Thirteen

Dahlia Fury

http://mp32016.xyz/play/happy-birthday-russian-song

As it turns out, Zane is busy in the early evening and asks me to meet him at the restaurant at eight o'clock. This works out brilliantly as it means I can help prepare the living room and the bedroom. Olga and I fill the living room with balloons and streamers, hang up Happy Birthday banners, then I go upstairs to the bedroom and fill it with the hundred candles. I make a path that leads to the bed. Olga says she will get Noah to call her when we are ten minutes away from the house.

Then I have a long soak in the bath and think about the night ahead. My crafty plan is to don a very simple, sleeveless black dress with a high neck. Boring as hell and suitable for funerals, but it is the perfect cover story for what I plan to wear underneath. A halter neck chemise dress with horizontal slashes from the neckline to hem, and a lace-up back that basically leaves my bare bottom peeking out of the crisscross of the laces. With it I will team black thigh highs and scarily high heels. Naturally, I won't wear any panties. Evil grin. He won't know what hit him.

Nun outside and slut inside, I go with Noah to meet Zane at Parma. We proceed to have a lovely dinner, but it kind of shocks me how utterly secretive he is. At no time during dinner does he ever mention that it is his birthday. His demeanor is so normal that I begin to doubt that it's his birthday. Who completely ignores their birthday? What if Olga got it wrong? But it is too late to change my plans and so what if it is not his birthday? A party is a party, so I smile, laugh, eat, drink and tremble inside with suppressed excitement at the thought of what I have planned for him.

It's nearly ten thirty by the time we leave the restaurant, and I have to marvel at how fantastic these Russian men are at keeping secrets. There is nothing in Noah's face to indicate he's in on the plan. No secret wink, knowing smile, or tap on the nose. God, with all these stoic people around I pray my party doesn't fall flat on its little face. Where is Stella when I need her?

We walk in through the front door and from the corner of my eyes I can see Noah holding back.

'I'm so sleepy today,' I say, affecting a huge yawn.

'It's 10.30,' Zane says.

'Maybe one drink,' I say, and start walking towards the living room where everyone is hiding. I open the door and suddenly Zane grabs me by my upper arm and jerks me back so I tumble against his body. A yelp of shock exits my mouth. What the hell? With lightning speed Zane closes the door and with his hand still gripping my arm turns towards Noah.

'Why are there no lights in that room?' Zane asks urgently. His face is wary, and his voice is low and tense.

I look at Noah and very nearly laugh. For a second his face is a classic picture of shit-what-the-fuck-do-I-do-now? But I have to hand it to these Russians. They really are closed books, by closed what I mean is super-glued shut.

With a totally straight face Noah says, 'It's my fault. We had a short circuit earlier, the electrics tripped, and I forgot to switch the lights back on.'

'I'll go and turn them back on,' he offers.

Zane visibly relaxes. His hand uncurls around my arm. 'No, it's OK. You can leave now. Thanks.'

Even though he has been reassured, he does not let me go in first. 'Wait here,' he says and opens the door. He goes in, switches on the light, and in a flash all his staff jump out from the hiding places and scream 'Happy Birthday.'

Zane freezes, frowns, shakes his head as if in disbelief, then looks at me with a confused expression. 'You did this?'

'*S-DYNOM va-RYEN'-ya!*' I yell. Olga taught it to me: Happy birthday in playful Russian. Russian is apparently not like English. There is also the serious version. I hope I pronounced it right.

Zane lips curve with amusement, which means I obviously didn't.

Then Olga brings the cake with all the candles towards us. It has intricate black candy melt mesh and is decorated with lots of fresh strawberries on top. Music starts and everybody sings the Russian birthday song. It has the kind of beat that I associate with Zorba the Greek. Zane just stares at everybody with a slightly dazed expression. I can see that he is totally floored at being ambushed in this way. The song stops and everybody claps.

'*Za-ga-DAT-zhi-LA-nee-ya,*' Olga says. I know she is telling him to make a wish.

His eyes dart towards me. I smile widely at him. He takes a deep breath and blows out the candles in one puff. Everybody cheers and claps. Glasses of vodka are produced and passed around. One quickly finds its way into my hand.

Noah shouts out a strange thing, 'Ah, the cake is bitter.'

I look at him in surprise. What the hell is he talking about? The cake has not even been cut. Zane turns to look at me.

'What?' I ask looking around because everybody is looking at me with a teasing expression.

'It's an ancient Russian custom. Your guests are asking you to make it sweeter with a long sweet kiss.'

I pass my glass to Nico, the boy who feeds the birds, and smile cheekily at him. 'I'm game if you are.'

Zane sweeps me into his arms in a grand and dramatic gesture dips me back over his arm. 'Don't drop me,' I laugh.

Then he starts kissing me. I imagined it would be a quick peck or a little comedy kiss to entertain the crowd, but our lips lock, and to my surprise everybody starts counting the seconds off.

One, Two, Three …

After the count of five I stop hearing their voices. My mouth opens. The kiss becomes magical, like a kiss from a fantasy. I've never been kissed so passionately in front of so many people. There is so much emotion in the kiss, the world around me becomes an indistinct blur and finally ceases to exist all together. There is no one else but Zane and I.

I could have remained in that beautiful fantasyland forever, but Zane lifts his head and rights me. Everybody stops counting and raises their glasses in a toast. For a few seconds Zane's eyes are dark with passion then he takes a deep breath, his nostrils flaring, and straightening me, turns to face everybody. My knees feel like jelly. *Oh, God, please don't let that kiss and that look be only a stolen moment.*

'*Osvezhit*,' Noah says.

'That means refresh,' Zane translates for me.

Our glasses are quickly refilled.

The next toast is by Yuri and literally translates as no long breaks between the first and second toasts.

'Because we Russians don't allow long breaks between toasts,' Zane explains and everyone downs the second lot of alcohol.

More vodka is poured. Olga is already starting to look red-cheeked.

'*Nu, poneslis,*' everyone yells, and down the hatch the vodka goes.

'Here we go again,' Zane translates for me.

'How many more toasts are there going to be?' I ask, feeling the burn in my veins.

'We cut the cake now,' Olga says. She cuts the cake and puts the slice on a little plate and offers it to me.

'First one is for the birthday boy,' she says.

I break off a piece and put it into his mouth. He catches my fingers and licks them. Around us the staff are milling about eating cake and helping themselves to all the delicious goodies Olga has made. I look into Zane's eyes and all I want to do is tell him I love him, but I can't. I know it's too soon.

More glasses of vodka are passed around. 'To the beautiful women in this room,' Zane says looking into my eyes.

I know that it is probably just another Russian custom because all the men are echoing it in Russian, but for some crazy reason I blush with pure pleasure. The vodka is going to my head and I really should stop or I'll ruin all my plans.

I fork a bit of crabmeat salad into my mouth and watch Zane surrounded by his staff. They treat him the way people who have suddenly discovered a lion is tame do. They try to touch it, but carefully, and with great caution. There are many birthday cards for Zane, but I notice that nobody has bought him anything. I guess they had the same problem as me, but can't buy him a masturbator like I did. After about an hour Zane calls the last toast.

'*Na pososhok*,' he says, and everybody drinks the last drink.

He takes my hand and we leave them to carry on drinking. When the door closes he looks down at me. 'So you threw me a surprise party, huh? How very American of you?'

I grin. 'An American party with vodka, Russian toasts, and strawberry cake?'

'So ... who told you it was my birthday?'

'Er ... I'm not really at liberty to say.'

'Olga then.'

'I'm not saying.'

He grins. 'I might want to give her a raise.'

'Do you really?'

He shrugs. 'Maybe.'

 393

'You'll have to promise that you will before I consent to reveal my source,' I say sternly.

'You've already revealed your source, silly dove.' He musses my hair. 'Thank you. I haven't had a birthday party since I was twelve.'

'Wow! Why?'

A cloud passes across his face. 'That's a story for another day,' he says.

I don't let that cloud rain on my parade. I smile seductively. 'I've got one more surprise for you.'

'Oh yeah?' he asks cockily.

Fourteen

Dahlia Fury

Have some candy.
                    -King Candy

'**O**h yeah,' I say, and take him upstairs to his room. I open the door and find the two girls have had time to slip upstairs after the cake was cut and light more than a hundred candles. The flames are flickering and dancing all over the floor, on the bedside table, the dresser, the windowsill. The candles on the floor are arranged to make a clear path towards the bed. I turn around to look at him and he is gazing around the room with a bemused expression. I lead him to the bed and placing both my hands on his chest push him. He falls back on the bed and looks up at me.

In the yellow flickering light of the candles he is as beautiful as a fallen angel or a wonderful marble statue. The aquiline nose and strong jaw are like something a Renaissance stonecutter might have spent years sculpting in his drafty studio.

'I come bearing gifts,' I say to him.

His eyebrows rise. 'You're the gift, babe.'

I giggle. 'No, you'll like this one, and I want you to know that I didn't use your credit card to get these, OK?'

'OK,' he says almost warily, and sits up.

I reach out and take the two packages covered in silver wrapping paper. I sit on the bed and give them to him. He shakes it and the little Star Wars flash drives rattle in their box.

'Go on open it,' I urge.

He tears the wrapping paper and opens the box. 'You got me toys?' he asks incredulously.

'They're not toys. They're flash drives.' I take Chewbacca from the box. 'See, pull it apart and there you go.'

'Right. Great. Thanks,' he says.

That didn't go down too well. Maybe Star Wars flash drives are really a Star Wars fans sort of thing. Never mind. Luckily I got the male masturbator. 'Now open the other one,' I say, holding that out to him.

He takes it, opens the packaging, and looks up at me with even more incredulity than he had shown when he thought I had given him toys. 'You got me a male masturbator?'

'Yeah, and the lubricant that goes with it. You insert your dick in here,' I say pointing to the hole in the gadget.

'Of course,' he says dryly.

His lack of enthusiasm is perplexing. I think it's a great present. 'Don't tell me you already own one?'

'No,' he denies quickly.

I switch it on. It makes a gentle whirling sound as all the little fingers in the hole start their massaging movements. 'Don't you think it is fun?'

He switches it off firmly. 'Sure, but I'd rather insert my dick into you.'

'This is for when I'm not around,' I say softly.

He turns away, puts the presents on the bedside cabinet, and leans back against the pillows. 'Since you're around now. Give me my real present.'

My mouth goes dry with the sexual heat in his eyes. Our bodies seem to pull at each other. He wants me so bad I can feel it like an invisible, powerful magnet. In that moment I feel powerful and strong. Smiling provocatively, I stand and slowly and deliberately start unzipping my dress. It pools around my high heels and I am standing in my chemise with its horizontal slashes all the way down the middle. His eyes drift from the slit exposing the round fullness of my breasts down to the one that reveals my pussy.

'Jesus, Dahlia!' he mouths. 'You're pure woman. Every inch of you is just such a fucking turn on.'

I snake my hands above my head, whirl slowly around, and pushing my butt out gyrate my hip sensuously. I can feel my bare ass rubbing against the laces running across it. I swivel my head back to look at him. His eyes are entranced, lost, staring at the soft, wet flesh between the diamond-shaped gap at the top of my thighs. He lifts his gaze up to meet mine.

'Tell me what you want, Aleksandr Malenkov?' I ask softly. 'The spirits I have consumed have made me daring, so tonight I'll do anything you want me to.'

His eyebrows rise. 'Anything?'

I turn around. 'Any ... fucking ... thing.'

'I'll have to take a rain check on any ... fucking ... thing, cause tonight I only want your tight, wet cunt fucking my cock in that dress.'

Crouching down, I take off his shoes and socks, and drop them on the floor before climbing on the bed and crawling in my stripper shoes over to him. Holding his eyes I unbuckle his belt, undo his trouser button, and pull down the zip. His cock is so hard it pokes out of his underpants. Urgently he lifts his hips so I can slide his pants out from under him. I peel his briefs down his hips and his dick springs free. I pull the material down his legs and sit on his thighs, inches away from his throbbing cock. Unhurriedly I unbutton his shirt. He lifts off the bed and, rising to my knees, I take off his shirt to reveal his nudity.

I can't take my eyes away from his glorious body.

It's not that I want to stare. I simply can't stop myself. No matter how many times I look at him, the sight makes me want to lick him all over. His inked chest moves up and down with the rhythm of his breath. It makes me crazy for him. I want to crawl into his skin. I move my wet pussy over his cock, grazing it.

'Touch yourself,' he says thickly.

I spread my legs wider and stroke my swollen clit. I plunge a finger in and moan, 'I want you inside me.'

He reaches forward and pulls my dress so it is bunched up around my waist.

'Sit on my cock. I want to see my cock disappear into your body.'

I grasp the thick shaft, point his cock at my slick opening and thrust down. The sensation of being so suddenly penetrated and stretched so full makes my body arch. His cock jumps inside me.

'All the way,' he commands.

I slide down that thick shaft until I feel the hard muscle of his thighs. Then I lean forward so my throbbing clit is touching his pubic bone and grind my pussy on it. The sensation is amazing. I love it. I move faster and faster, sliding up and down that glorious shaft of hard meat.

When I feel the ecstasy begin, I ride him as hard as I can, my thighs quivering, juices squirting out of me. There is no stopping me now. My pussy clenches, my skin starts tingling. Let him fuck me until he understands that I am his. Mind, body and soul.

But without warning he grabs my waist and pulls me clear off his cock.

'Nooooo,' I protest, but he lifts me off his body.

'I want you to sit on my face and move your wet cunt all over it. I want to eat you out until you come,' he growls, and holding my pussy suspended over his face, he inhales my aroma as if it is heady perfume.

I drip onto his tongue.

 400

'This pussy is mine,' he mutters and lowers me onto his mouth. First he swipes his silky tongue along the entire pulsing crack to lick up all my juices, and then he starts lapping at my pussy just like a thirsty dog. My head is thrown back and my body arches and twists against his mouth. Gripping my hips he fucks me with his tongue. Then he-oh fuck-sucks my clit into his mouth until I am screaming. Just screaming.

I ride out my orgasm grinding into his face and yelling out his name. My juices gushing into his mouth, and running down his face and neck. He grabs my ass cheeks and keeps on sucking, fucking, and licking my pussy, forcing me to come again. And again. My muscles are still shaking and convulsing, and his face and hair are soaked and glistening in the candlelight when he moves abruptly. He rolls me to my side, gets on top of me and, opening my legs wide, plunges into my hot flesh.

'Oh yes,' I cry. 'Take me hard, Zane.'

'Like this?' He grabs my wrists and, holding them high over my head, slams even harder into me.

'Fuck yes,' I whimper.

'And this?' he says thrusting savagely into me. To my astonishment I can feel myself starting to climax again.

My mouth opens in a gasp. 'I can't control myself,' I burst. 'I'm going to come all over your cock.'

'No,' he says, slowing his movement down. 'You'll come when I tell you to come.'

My body jerks spasmodically and my head turns from side to side in desperation. 'I'm gonna come, Zane. Sorry. I just can't hold on.'

He pulls his cockhead clear out of me, waits for a second, then rams back inside. Burying himself to the hilt. Like a greedy thing my pussy pushes upwards to meet the thrust.

'Fuck, baby. I've got to come. You gotta let me come,' I beg.

'Not yet. This is my pussy. Mine. I'll decide when she comes.'

He bends his head and bites my nipple. The pain brings me back from the edge. He licks the throbbing tip rapidly and a gloriously warm sensation spreads out from that nipple into the rest of my body.

I grip his erection tightly.

'You're so damn tight,' he shudders, as he starts slamming and pounding into me with a real frenzy, grunting, chasing his release. Every time his body touches my clit, I squirm, coil and writhe like a cut snake underneath him. I am holding on to my own release by my fingernails, waiting for him to say, 'yes, let go.'

He rides me until the muscles of his shoulders and neck begin to strain, and there it is, the permission to come.

'Come now,' he orders ... and instantly I come. Excruciatingly. Laid bare. Raw. Wild. Naked. Exposed. My heart wide open.

He is still exploding inside me when I whisper, 'I love you.'

He gazes down at me as my shuddering pussy milks the last drops, the very last seed out of his cock.

Something in his eyes. They can't look into mine. He heard me.

I capture his chin and wait until his gaze meets mine. 'It's OK. You don't have to say it back.'

He stares at me and I wonder what horror has brought such sorrow into his eyes. Then he bends his head and takes my lips. The kiss is so full of soul and tenderness that suddenly I know.

His body is telling me what his tongue cannot say.

Fifteen

Aleksandr Malenkov

Mama comes to help me stand up.

'I'm all right,' I tell her.

'Shall I get you some tea?' she asks.

'No, I'm fine.'

I look at her. Her face is white. How the years have changed her. She has become more and more silent. Her spirit is broken. He broke her spirit.

'Mama, why don't we run away?'

Her lips tremble. She presses them together. 'There is nowhere to go. I have no money,' she says.

'I can work. I'm old enough.'

'You're twelve.'

'I can fight for money. I can beat grown men.'

She grasps both my hands together and shakes her head vigorously and fixes me with a desperate stare. 'No. You will not fight. You will go to school. You will study and you will become something special. I'm all right. If only you wouldn't interfere when we argue, my precious son.'

'I'll never let him hurt you,' I say angrily.

'He doesn't hurt me. A few punches. Nothing serious. These things happen between adults.'

'I hate him,' I mutter.

'Hush. Don't ever say that,' she says sadly.

'Why not? He is horrible.'

'I will always be grateful to him.'

I stare at her in disbelief. 'Why?'

'Because he gave me you.'

I close my eyes in despair.

'And because he has no one else. When he was well, before that trauma to his brain, before that bullet lodged in his head he was a good man. A really good man and I promised to stay with him through sickness and health. So now that he is ill, and he is ill, Aleksandr, it is an illness, I can't abandon him just like that. I made a promise to be loyal to him and I can't break it.' She smooths my hair away from my forehead and kisses me gently.

'One day you will fall deeply in love with someone and you will understand that no matter what the other person does you will be unable to kill the love you have for them.'

'I will never fall in love with anyone,' I swear bitterly. 'Never.'

Sixteen

Dahlia Fury

I wake up two mornings later and Zane says to me, 'We're going to Rome.'

'What? When?' I ask with a big stupid grin plastered all over my sleepy face.

'Today.'

'Huh? Why?'

He shrugs casually. 'Weekend break.'

'But why didn't you warn me?'

'It's a surprise. A bit like your surprise party.'

'OK, great.'

'We'll be travelling incognito though.'

My grin dies away. 'What do you mean?'

'We'll be travelling as Mr. and Mrs. Zhivanecskaya.'

I stare at him stunned. 'You mean we'll be using *fake* passports?'

He reaches to the bedside cabinet drawer and extracts two passports. He looks into the first, then passes me the second one. I look at it and there it is. The photograph of me that Yuri took for security purposes teamed with the name Dahlia Zhivanescskaya. Age 24.

'I can't even pronounce my last name,' I whisper.

He says it slowly.

My eyes narrow suspiciously. 'Why do we need fake passports? Are we going to be smuggling drugs, or some kind of contraband?'

'Not drugs. You'll be carrying 15 million Euros worth of diamonds.'

The passport falls from my hand. 'What?' I splutter.

He actually looks at me sheepishly, as if asking someone to illegally carry 15 million Euros worth of diamonds is a sheepish matter. 'Don't worry,' he adds in a conciliatory tone, 'there is no chance of us getting caught. We'll be flying private and I know the people at the airport.'

I shake my head in disbelief. Us? He means me! 'You want *me* to be a diamond mule?' I'm not sure if that is what the idiot carrying the diamonds is called, but this conversation is so out there my brain can't compute. Then I become absolutely livid. 'How dare you even ask me to do such a thing?'

He seems surprised by my reaction. 'Do you have a problem with it?'

'Yes, I fucking have a big problem with it.'

'The others didn't,' he says mildly.

I glare at him. 'I don't know what kind of women you've been dating, but *yes*, I *do* mind very much. I'm not carrying diamonds for you. You must be out of your head to think I would do something like that.' Then another thought occurs to me. 'And how am I supposed to be transporting these diamonds?'

'Inside your vagina,' he says slowly.

My mouth drops open. 'Oh my God. I don't believe this. You think it is OK to ask me to stuff a bunch of diamonds up my vagina and take them across borders for you? I really thought better of you.'

'Will you at least think about it?' he asks in a wheedling voice.

That fucking makes me explode. 'Fuck no,' I yell.

'Damn. Does this mean I'll have to take someone else instead?' he ponders, staring away from me.

Then it hits me. 'You bastard!' I cry and, pulling up a pillow, smack his head as hard as I can. He goes down laughing.

'I really thought you were serious,' I say, and continue hitting him.

He grabs a pillow and swings it into my body. Immediately I slam my pillow back at him really hard and feathers start flying around us. I get on my knees to take my attack to the next level but he tackles me and brings me down. Pinning me down with his body he grins at me.

'You're an asshole, you know?' I pant.

'You deserve it for assuming I'd ask you to do a low thing like that,' he says with a laugh.

'I don't know you well enough for you to play those kinds of jokes on me,' I say primly.

He raises his eyebrows. 'You don't know me well enough? How well do you have to know me? I suck your pussy!'

'Nevertheless it was a horrid prank,' I say, pretending to be angry.

He smiles at me. 'Sorry. I couldn't help it. You're delicious when you are outraged.'

I crack a smile. He is so gorgeous it is impossible to even pretend to be angry with him. I want to kiss his throat. 'So why are we really going?'

'Because the oppressive heat of summer is gone, Italy is an explosion of color. Autumn is also harvest season for truffles, chestnuts, and pumpkins so it is the best time to eat pasta *al tartufo* or pumpkin risotto.'

I look at him curiously. 'I got all that, but why are we travelling incognito?'

'Because I love it. Incognito means there is no need for security. We will go to a villa that Boris has rented and paid for in cash. Nobody will know where we are. We will be completely free to go anywhere we want and do anything we want.'

'Just the two of us?'

He nods.

'No one is coming with us?' I ask because it is such a novel idea.

He shakes his head.

'No Noah?'

He shakes his head again.

'No Yuri or Boris?'

He repeats the movement of his head.

'Not even the driver?'

'Just you and me, *rybka*.'

'Actually it sounds awesome.'

'I think so too,' he says softly. He reaches into the drawer again. I lift my head up to look. 'What's that?' I ask curiously.

Taking my finger he slips a platinum ring with a massive stone on it.

'That's a diamond by the way,' he says casually. Then he adds a plain band on top of the first ring.

My lips part with a strange emotion, but neither the gesture nor the moment has any real significance to him.

'There, it fits perfectly,' he says.

'Yes,' I whisper. I take a deep breath. I have to act normally. I have to be cool. Maybe a little humor. 'You do realize that you won't be getting these babies back after the vacation, don't you?'

'They're yours,' he says, an odd inflection in his voice.

I swallow hard. Does he even realize what he is saying? *Quick change the subject, Dahlia.* 'Are you sure travelling with fake passports is safe? What if we get caught?'

'These are real passports. The owners died in a car crash and their families sold them on to forgers. These here are exactly the same type of documents used by Mossad agents. There is absolutely no way anyone can tell the difference unless they investigate deeply, but nobody's going to investigate us deeply. We're just going to spend the weekend in Rome.'

'OK, but if we end up in prison ...' I warn.

He drops his voice to a whisper. 'It's an adventure, little fish.'

His hands start spreading my thighs. I glare at him. 'I'm still angry with you.'

He slips a finger inside me. Of course I have to be soaking wet. 'No, you're not,' he says with a chuckle.

Ah, what the heck. It's hard to pretend to be angry when you're having such fun, anyway.

Seventeen

Dahlia Fury

https://www.youtube.com/watch?v=QowZQ
bK938Y&nohtml5
(Happiness)

I've been to Venice before, but never to Rome
so it is all, as Stella would say it in a fake post
accent, 'terribly exciting'. We are just like two
tourists. I really get into character. I catch
myself wondering what Dahlia Zhivanescskaya
would do right then. Even in my wildest
dreams I never imagined travelling on a fake
passport with a Russian mob boss.

I must admit my heart races like a bullet
train when we are asked to show our passports,
but Zane doesn't even bat an eyelid, and quite
right he was to be so chilled about it all. We
were waved through after a cursory
examination of our passports. The adrenaline

spike dies down and at this point I am beginning to really appreciate the adventure I'm on. I've just broken God knows how many international laws and you know what? It feels absolutely brilliant.

Maybe even a bit Bonnie and Clydeish.

Like any other tourists we go pick up our luggage like everyone else and walk to Customs. We don't hold hands. That would be silly at this stage of the relationship ... until that is, he takes my hand and then it's panic stations ... Oh my God: we are holding hands!

The weather outside is beautiful. Bright and pleasantly warm. We get into a taxi and Zane gives him the address. Twenty minutes later we're in fabulous Rome. Wow! What an amazing city. I stare at all the wonderful buildings full of history and beauty. We pass the Coliseum and I crane my neck out of the taxi to stare at it.

'We'll see it tomorrow,' Zane says.

I turn to him. 'Great. I've always wanted to see it.'

'It is one of the most fascinating places on the earth,' he says quietly.

The villa is located in Formello about twenty kilometers from Rome, and is surrounded by lush trees and greenery. The wrought iron gates are opened by a small, white-haired man who nods at us formally as we drive through to a gorgeous house painted in burnt orange. It has a white stone balustrade and slated wooden shutters painted duck-egg blue on the windows. There is an ancient green Mazda parked by the side of the house.

We step out onto the dusty road and a tiny woman comes out of the large wooden door and smiles in greeting. The man who opened the gates comes up the driveway as the taxi driver is taking our bags out of the boot.

'Benevenuto Senor e Senora Zhivanecskaya,' the woman says. Her face is full of wrinkles and her eyes are brown and rheumy, but her smile is real and full of spirit.

'Grazia, Senora Rossi,' Zane says.

I smile at her.

By now the sprightly old man is upon us and his weathered face is split into a large welcoming grin. He reaches forward and grasps Zane's hand in both of his. To my surprise Zane starts talking to him in fluent Italian. After a while the man lifts his hand and bids us both goodbye. The woman, presumably his wife, nods at us, and they both get into the rickety car and drive off.

'It's just you and me now, *rybka*,' Zane says with a wink.

'I didn't know you could speak Italian.'

'Many Russians can speak German, French, and Spanish too.'

'Wow! Impressive.'

Zane hauls up our luggage and we go into the villa. It is cool inside with terrazzo flooring and cold white walls. The hallway leads to a very large lounge with exposed beams, a massive fireplace, and a graceful rusted-iron chandelier. It is sparsely filled with reproduction rococo style Italian furniture and an upright piano in one corner of the room.

The lounge opens up to a dining room with a long, highly polished table and eight tall chairs. At the back of the house there is a large country style kitchen with a much smaller farmhouse table and wooden chairs with straw seats. All the rooms wrap around an oriental style courtyard in the middle of the house.

Up a flight of stone stairs there are three spotless double bedrooms with en-suites. We put our bags in the master bedroom. It is a beautiful room with a king-size bed covered in a damask bedcover, a large tapestry on the wall, and a velvet daybed. I go over to the window and see that there is a swimming pool right underneath the window. To my delight there is also a lemon grove in the grounds.

It is nearly five by now and I turn to Zane with a happy smile. 'What do you want to do, Mr. Zhivanescskaya?'

'Guess, Mrs. Zhivanescskaya?' he says, coming towards me.

'Oooo, but Mr. Zhivanescskaya I—' The rest of my words are cut out by his mouth swooping down on mine.

I lie on the softly scented pillow and I think that though all our other sex sessions have been awesome this one has been undoubtedly the best. Why? Because Zane is a different man. His body is without that strung-wire tension and his eyes don't house that peculiar wariness that I always associate with him. He even looks younger.

A gust of wind redolent of the smell of lemons and fallen leaves comes in from the open window and blows over our heated skin. Outside it's still light, but it is a kind of translucent light never found in England. I turn my head and look at Zane. A lock of his hair has fallen on his forehead. I push it away with my hand. He opens his eyes and looks at me.

'Do you think it will rain?' I ask.

'No,' he says softly.

'I really like it here,' I say, yawning and stretching lazily.

He takes the opportunity to slip his finger into me. It makes my body arch and his finger crooks in me and starts stroking the delicate tissues inside me.

'Oh, Zane,' I whisper.

'I love watching you come,' he says and continues playing with me.

Eighteen

Dahlia Fury

We shower and get dressed. Zane wears a charcoal suit with a silk, oyster shirt and I slip into a white dress with a full skirt and knot a pale blue sweater around my neck. Doing my make up I watch him in the mirror. His hair is still damp and he looks virile and full of vigor.

'I'll wait for you outside,' he says.

'I'll come out when I finish putting on my face,' I say.

I keep my make up very light and, wearing blue pumps with espadrille heels, I go outside. The air is beginning to cool. I find him smoking a cigarette on the terrace. The last embers of the sun are in the sky, giving his hair a reddish hue. When he hears me he turns around and looks at me. I shiver, intoxicated by the magic of that moment.

His eyes light up as if from within and he smiles slowly. 'Oh fuck, I'm going to be fighting off men all night, aren't I?'

I blush and twist my pretend wedding band around my finger. 'And I'm going to be scratching out women's eyes all night, aren't I?'

'You really think so?' he asks cockily.

'I know so,' I tease, feeling shy. He is so, so, so different, so out of character. I love this warm, cheeky, gorgeous man.

He takes a last drag of his cigarette and kills it in an ashtray on the wrought iron table, then comes towards me. 'How hungry are you?'

'Starving,' I admit.

He puts his hand on the small of my back. 'Good. Let's go.'

There is a bright yellow Fiat Cinquecento waiting outside.

'Where did that come from?' I ask.

'It was in the garage,' he says looking at me closely. 'Don't you like it?

'Yeah, it's cute, but I didn't expect you to hire one.'

'When in Rome ...' he trails away, and opens the passenger door for me.

I get in and it smells of new leather and the sickly sweet smell of air freshener. I turn around to watch Zane get into the driver's seat.

The sight of him folded inside the interior of such a small car makes me giggle.

'Rome is not made for big cars,' he explains.

I soon see why. The streets are narrow and full of parked cars. There is hardly any parking space, and when Zane parks in a minute space with only an inch front and back to spare, I see the wisdom of the tiny car.

He locks the car and we walk down a narrow Roman street with only a little sliver of sky above us. There is no sidewalk and cars and mopeds whizz by right past us. Laundry hangs out of first floor windows and in tiny balconies filled with flowerpots.

Street musicians are playing outside the restaurant. There are tables outside and people are sitting at them. They have the air of locals and look at us curiously. A balding man in a white shirt and black apron rushes out to greet Zane.

'Ahhh Aleksandr,' he calls loudly. 'Che meravigliosa sorpresa.'

'He's telling me what a marvelous surprise,' Zane translates for me.

The man's dark eyes slide towards me. 'E chi è questa bellezza?' he asks.

Zane looks down at me and winks mischievously. 'This beauty, Luca, is my wife, Dahlia.'

Intense heat creeps up my neck and into my face. How casually he had called me his wife. How awesome if we were not pretending. If we were really married. If I was really his wife.

Luca makes a circle with his thumb and forefinger. 'Bellezza,' he cries dramatically. 'But of course a beautiful man catches a beautiful woman for his bride,' he says switching to English.

'Hello,' I say.

He tilts his head. 'English?' he asks with a frown.

'American,' I confirm with a smile.

He holds up a knowing finger. 'Ah, I knew it.'

'Come, come,' he invites warmly, and gestures us towards a table covered with a black and white striped table cloth. As we are being seated, he says, 'Let Luca make something,' he brings together his thumb, index and middle fingers together and kisses them with a loud smacking noise, 'for you.'

'OK.' I grin at him appreciatively.

He looks at Zane. '*Cacio e Pepe con Tartufi?*'

Zane looks at me. 'Would you like to try a handmade egg pasta with Pecorino Romano cheese, black pepper, and black truffles?'

'Sounds great.'

Zane looks to Luca. 'What would you suggest for the main?'

'*Saltimboca*.'

'That's Roman dialect for 'jump in your mouth,' Zane tells me. 'It's a fry up of tender veal wrapped in Parma ham and sage and marinated in white wine.'

'Yeah, sure. I'm game,' I say.

'*Va bene*,' Luca approves, and goes away, head held high and humming to himself, oblivious to all the people in the restaurant.

'What a character he is,' I whisper to Zane.

Zane smiles. 'It's all a charade. He's as sharp as nails. He counts the parmesan shavings he drops on his customers' plates.'

I laugh.

The waiter arrives with aperitifs for us.

'What's this?' I ask.

'It's Luca's sense of humor,' Zane says. 'He made you an Americano.'

'An Americano for an American. Nice one.' I try it. 'Hmmm ... not bad. What's in it?'

'It's a twist on the Negroni. Campari, *Martini Rosso* vermouth and soda.'

The diamond on my finger catches the light and sparkles. I resist the impulse to stare at it.

'I know so little about you,' I say.

'There's not much to know.'

'Zane, I don't even know what your favorite color is.'

'Magenta.'

I tear open a packet of breadsticks and take one out. 'That's not a very masculine color. Why do you like it?'

'I don't know why. Maybe because it's so rich and strong. What about you? What's your favorite color?'

I break the breadstick in half. 'I love baby blue best, but I also love black and pink and green, and orange, and most shades of yellow.'

He smiles and looks at me the way one does a child. Indulgently.

'What's your favorite food? Like if you had to live on it for the rest of your life,' I ask, putting the breadstick into my mouth.

'Hmmm ... Probably Argentinian steak and Hong Kong style French toast.'

'What the heck is a Hong Kong style French toast?

'Two pieces of toast slathered with peanut butter, soaked in egg batter then fried in butter and served with more butter and syrup.'

'Jesus, that sounds like it would give a whale high cholesterol.'

He takes a sip of his drink and looks at me over the rim of his glass. 'It's very, very good though.'

'Maybe I'll try it one day.'

'Maybe you will,' he says softly.

Nineteen

Dahlia Fury

Whoa. That brings me out in goose bumps.

'Ok, my turn now' I say quickly. 'My rest-of-my-life food is chocolate, pizza, warm brownie and ice cream, fried chicken, Peking duck, melted cheese on tacos, baked potatoes with cheese and beans—'

He starts laughing. 'That's cheating. You're supposed to pick your favorites.'

'Sorry. It is impossible to choose between them,' I tell him.

'Right.'

'Favorite alcoholic drink?'

'Vodka I suppose. Yours?'

'I love champagne and ... Margaritas and ... Boozy Bubbly Sherbet Punch ... and also ... Baileys.'

He makes a face. 'Do I want to know what a Boozy Bubbly Sherbet Punch is?'

'Oh yes, you do. It's frozen raspberries, ice-cream, vodka, ginger ale and pink lemonade, and all of that goodness is topped with champagne.'

He smiles. 'I seem to remember you are partial to White Russians too.'

I grin. 'That's true, I have to admit a weakness for those.' I pause. 'Now favorite movie.'

'Matrix.'

'Really? Is that why you named your restaurant Matrix?'

'Yeah. What about yours?'

'Pretty Woman.'

He stares at me blankly.

'Have you never seen it?'

'Nooo,' he says slowly.

'Well, it's a romantic comedy.'

'That'll be why I haven't seen it.'

'OK. Let's get to serious stuff. Name a leader you admire.'

'Putin,' he answers promptly.

My eyes widen. 'Putin? As in the Vladimir Putin? The President of Russia?'

He nods. 'Uh ... huh.'

I lean forward and wave my breadstick at him. 'Are you kidding me?'

He shrugs. 'He's a strategic leader.'

'You can't be serious!'

429

'Why not? He's good for Russia.'

'He's a criminal,' I exclaim passionately.

'I really don't think we should talk politics,' he says mildly.

As Stella would say: 'Why ever not?'

He grins lasciviously. 'Unless you want to end up fighting and having rough make-up sex.'

I look at him with raised eyebrows. 'Aren't you able to have a civilized discussion about politics without fighting, then?'

He looks amused. 'It's not me I'm worried about, little fox. It's you who won't be able to control yourself.'

'Whoa! I think I am perfectly capable of controlling myself. Perhaps you are afraid that I might destroy your untenable position that Putin is as pure as the driven snow.'

His amusement deepens. 'I didn't say that, but out of curiosity, how much do you know about him?'

'Enough,' I say confidently. 'I read the newspapers and I catch the news on TV.'

'Yes, I thought so.'

'What the heck is that supposed to mean?'

'It means you are not qualified to talk about the issue at hand.'

I jerk my head back. 'Why not?'

'All right, I'll enter into a discussion about him with you if you can tell me one positive thing about him.'

'Well, I ... um, I don't—'

'See what I mean. Nothing in this world is either totally bad or totally good, *rybka*.' He grins. 'Yet all the material you seem to have read and heard about him is negative. It means you're getting all your information from biased sources. That makes you unfit for a rational discussion of the subject at hand.'

I don't know what I could have said to that, but thank God, divine smelling plates of food arrive. I'll have to think about what he said later when my adventure as Zane's wife is over. Now there is the matter of a food to deal with.

Luca himself comes over with a mini grater and a small truffle the size of a pigeon's egg. He handles the truffle with the care and deference a jeweler might employ to show a rare and precious stone to a customer. He actually waves it slowly under my nose to let me have a whiff of the mushroom.

To be honest it doesn't exactly endear me to it. Musky, earthy and kind of garlicky. Maybe even reminiscent of the faint odor of old sweat, or dare I say it, urine. With theatrical flourish he shaves a tiny amount of paper-thin flakes on the top of our pasta.

'*Bon appetito,*' he cries gaily.

We thank him and he moves away looking extremely pleased with himself.

'Have you had truffles before?' Zane asks.

'Only chocolate truffles.'

'In that case,' he says and lifts a fine shaving on his fork and moves it towards my mouth. Not wanting to let the side down I obligingly part my mouth. It lands on my tongue. The taste is well, strong and unique, but surely this is not what the fuss is all about. I move it between my teeth.

'Well?' Zane asks.

'Unusual,' I say vaguely.

'Now try it with the pasta,' he suggests.

I roll a bit of pasta on the tines of my fork making sure a few flecks of truffles get caught in the pasta, slip it between my lips and let it settle on my tongue. Suddenly my eyes widen with surprise.

He grins. 'Good, huh?'

'Fuuuuuck yeah,' I say rolling the food around my tongue.

He laughs, as carefree and happy as I have ever seen him.

We leave the restaurant and walk down the street. The temperature is lovely and cool and stars stud the sky.

'Where are we going?' I ask.

'Nowhere, but we might see some beautiful sights along the way.'

He is right. There is beauty everywhere; in the stone fountains, the cobblestones streets, the beautiful squares full of stylish Italian youth, the illuminated ruined buildings.

We stop to buy chestnuts from an elderly man roasting them in a huge round pan. His face is rosy from the fire and his hands are blackened with soot. He fills a paper cone with hot, sweet smelling nuts, and holds it out to us. Zane hands him two euros and we walk to a stone bench to eat the nuts.

'You remind me of my grandmother,' I tell him, peeling a nut and slipping it into my mouth.

'Whoa! Don't go overboard with the compliments, will you?' he says.

I grin. 'No, I mean the way you eat. Simple. Enjoying the taste of the ingredients fully. You know, not smothering things in ketchup and barbeque sauce. My grandmother

used to eat from small plastic trays like what they use on airplanes, so she could enjoy each taste separately.'

'That sounds more like OCD,' he says.

I jostle him with my shoulder. 'It wasn't. She was a connoisseur of food.'

He gazes at me, a sudden softness in his eyes that makes my throat tighten. 'The only thing I am a connoisseur of is your sweet pussy.'

I lift my face and kiss his mouth. 'You've got me so wet I could do you right here,' I whisper into his mouth.

His grin flashes in the night light, dazzling and dangerous. 'What did we learn today?'

'You like pussy and I'm wet?'

'Drop 'like' and try 'crazy for' and you'd be there.'

I widen my eyes flirtatiously. 'Prove it.'

'Can you wait until I get you home and naked?'

'Is this place too public for you?' I taunt.

'You just got me hard,' he mutters, and shifts uncomfortably.

I bite the inside of my cheek to keep from laughing, but he catches the laughter in my eyes.

'It won't be so funny young lady when you are at the end of my dick,' he growls, his expression hot and sexy.

I snuggle up to the warmth of his big body. 'Oh, Zane. I want you so damn much it's not funny at all, and I'm terrified of losing you.'

I hear the sharp intake of his breath as his arm tightens protectively around me. 'Let's go back,' he says gruffly.

When we get back to the car there is another vehicle double-parked and blocking us in.

'I can't believe someone did that,' I say. 'What do we do now?'

'What the Romans do,' he says, and opening his side of the door leans on the horn. Almost immediately a man sticks his head out of a first floor window and says something in Italian.

'He'll be down in a minute,' Zane translates.

The man rushes out in less than a minute and, with an apologetic smile and a wave, gets into his car and drives off.

'You sure know this city, don't you?'

'Like the back of my hand.'

You eat, and you eat well. What does it matter that that the world is bleeding and dying at your feet?

Twenty

Dahlia Fury

We are woken up the next morning by the sound of the Rossis arriving in their old Mazda.

'Don't get out. They're just bringing our breakfast,' Zane says, vaulting out of bed.

He pulls on a pair of old track bottoms and heads out to meet them. I move over to where the warmth and smell of Zane still remains and listen to him talking to them. There are no carpets on the floors and I can hear the echo of their conversation. Just when I start to think I should get out of bed, Zane comes back carrying a tray. There is a vase with a rose in it on the tray, steaming mugs of cappuccino and pastries.

I sit up. 'Wow, breakfast in bed. I can't remember the last time anyone did that for me.'

The pastries are still-warm Maritozzis; delicious, yeasty buns thickly filled with fresh cream and studded with raisins, candied orange peel, or pine nuts. Another appropriate name for them would be sugar bombs. I dip my finger in the cream, smear it on Zane's nose, and smile at my handiwork. He looks surprisingly cute.

'Lick it off,' he says sternly.

'Thought you'd never ask,' I say, and resting on my palms, extend my tongue to the maximum and lick him, making it wet and sloppy, the way an overeager hound would.

He jerks back. 'Are you looking for trouble?'

'Take your pants off and I'll tell you what I'm looking for,' I counter.

He puts the tray on the floor and, catching me by the shoulders, rolls me onto my back. I look into his eyes. 'I have to freaking spell everything out to you, but damn you're still my dream man,' I tell him, and clawing my fingers into his hair, I pull his sweet mouth down to mine.

Later that morning, Zane takes me to the ruins of the Coliseum. Of the three concentric ovals only a third of the original stone exterior remains and it is the inner oval that is most intact. The sheer immensity of the structure gives me the unsettling feeling that these ruins were the dwellings of beings much larger than me.

Standing on the moss-covered bricks at ground level I look up at the huge stone stadium, and for a second I get the feeling for what it must have been like to stand in the stadium during ancient times. To hear thousands of people baying for your death.

'Ten years to build, using sixty thousand Jewish slaves with eighty entrances, thirty-six traps doors, accommodating fifty-thousand spectators for festivals that lasted up to one hundred days. During which half-a-million people were slaughtered and a million animals were brutally killed. It is one of the greatest and most unashamed celebrations of human violence. I guess we were all more honest in those days,' Zane says.

'Humanity has come a long way since then,' I tell him quietly.

He sits on the stone seat. 'Don't you see the sheer ferocity that runs your world?'

I shake my head. 'No. I see it run by law and order, by democratic governments.'

He sighs. 'Your government is the biggest example of naked ferocity.'

'What?' I say with a laugh.

'In fact, I'd go so far as to say there is no difference between what your government does and what I do.'

I snort contemptuously. 'That's ridiculous.'

'Why is it ridiculous?' he queries. His eyes are watchful and I realize that he is very serious about what he is saying. As bizarre as it sounds to me he actually believes what he is telling me.

'OK,' I say slowly and go to sit next to him. 'Correct me if I am wrong, but agents of state don't lie, extort money, murder rivals, train and initiate uniform enforcers, constantly go to war with their neighbors to protect their borders, and enforce protection rackets. I could go on ...'

His mouth twists into a smile. Sexy or Cruel? Maybe both. The arrogant tilt to his chin tells me I have walked directly into his trap.

'I hate to break it to you, my innocent little fish,' he says, his voice a sly caress, 'but governments routinely undertake all those activities you mentioned and more. Governments do protect their borders, they lie all the time, and they extort money through taxes. Try not paying your taxes and see how ferocious your government really is. What are extrajudicial killings and kill lists, but the state assassinating its enemies and rivals? Just as I have enforcers they have their police and army to implement their policies. They provide their citizens protection for reasons I maintain law and order on my turf. The only real difference between them and me is my borders are smaller and more fluid.'

I frown. 'It's not the same,' I insist, but as always when he speaks, he shows another side to an argument that I have never even considered might exist.

'There is none so blind as she who will not see,' he says, and taking my hand pulls me to my feet.

He takes me to one of the trap doors through which the slaves and animals that were held underground were unleashed into the arena and I feel a chill in my body. I turn towards him.

'Even if the whole world is violent. Even if the very government we look upon as our protectors is violent, I never want to use that as a justification for my own violence.'

He gazes at me with unreadable eyes.

We have lunch at a sidewalk café and I order exactly what I had the night before. Pasta with cheese and pepper. There are no truffle shavings on it, but it is still incredibly good. Zane has the same.

Afterwards, we go to the Borghese Park and walk in the fallen leaves. It is very beautiful with the changing colors of fall. I look up at Zane and can hardly believe that this is my life. This is the kind of dreamy fantasy existence I expect to find in my favorite books.

We eat *gelato*, soft Italian ice cream, in the fresh air. Then the highlight of our trip: Zane has arranged a private tour for us of the Sistine Chapel.

We arrive as all the other tourists are leaving. A woman in a green trouser suit carrying a clipboard comes up to us. She looks at it and haltingly pronounces our incognito surname.

'Mr. and Mrs. Zhivanescskaya?'

'*Si,*' Zane and I say, and she smiles.

Her name is Claudia. Friendly and chatty, she leads us down the one-way system through

the long corridors of the main buildings towards the Sistine Chapel. Her voice echoes down the empty corridors, and as we get closer she starts telling us about the chapel's eight thousand square feet of restored frescoes depicting stories of Genesis, Moses, Jesus, and the famous Last Judgment.

She informs us that far from being elated, Michelangelo regarded his Sistine Chapel commission from the Pope with the utmost suspicion, because he believed that his enemies and rivals had concocted the idea to see him fail on a grand scale. As far as he was concerned God had chosen him to be a sculptor and not a painter.

Finally we reach the chapel.

She is still speaking, telling us about how the challenge of painting at a height of sixty-five feet required a certain amount of ingenuity with scaffolds and platforms slotted into the specially made wall opening, but her voice has become just an echo. I stand and stare in awe at the ceiling.

Michelangelo might not have thought he was a painter, but he created a transcendent work of genius. It is completely magnificent and grand in a way that no photo can ever do it justice. I could have stood there for hours.

Realizing that her explanations are no longer necessary Claudia falls silent and moves to the door. I turn to look at Zane, and he is watching me. Neither of us says anything. I am not a religious person, but while standing there with Zane in complete silence the power of Michelangelo's painting of God reached out and touched me. I swear I could almost feel his hand in mine.

'Look,' Zane whispers and points to a section of the painting where a robust bearded man is holding a knife in one hand and from his other hangs something that looks like a dripping garment with a sad face.

'See that big figure there,' he says. 'That's Saint Bartholomew. He was skinned alive and beheaded in Armenia, and that's a portrayal of him holding the knife of his martyrdom and his own flayed skin.'

'Oh wow,' I whisper.

'But here's the fascinating thing. The face in that empty envelope of skin is meant to be Michelangelo's self-portrait.'

I exhale my breath at that piece of strange knowledge.

'Why did he do that?'

He shrugs. 'It's a metaphor for the artist's tortured soul.'

I stared at the grotesque skin. It is hideous and yet I'm not sorry I saw it. It adds a fascinating new layer to the stunning beauty stretched out above and around me. I know Michelangelo's tragic and anguished skin will haunt my dreams, but then again so will the splendor of his creation.

I take Zane's hand in mine. 'Thank you for this experience,' I whisper and tears come into my eyes.

He frowns down at me. 'Are you OK?'

My face cracks a wobbly smile. 'Yes. Just happy.'

When it is time to leave I can't resist looking back one last time, knowing that this moment will last in my mind forever.

Twenty-one

Dahlia Fury

Back at the villa we go for a swim in the pool. Splashing and laughing we chase each other like children in the heated water. Afterwards, Zane sits me on the edge of the pool and eats me out while I gaze at a reddening sky and smell the citrusy scent of the lemon grove.

A bird flies overhead as I climax and I feel in my bones that today is special. No matter how long I live I will never forget this day, when I was in a foreign land with a gorgeous man I would have turned myself inside out for.

Exhausted and satiated, I let my palms slide along the tiles until I am lying down. The cool tiles feel so good on my back. Zane pulls himself out of the water and, dripping water on my body, picks me up and carries me to our bedroom. The shutters are drawn closed against the afternoon sun and it is cool and shady. I am nearly dry as he lays me on the bed and with his mouth, tongue, and hands he worships my body. Like I said before, today is special and I will never forget it.

https://www.youtube.com/watch?v=ljDcvhkRuOc&nohtml5=
(Who Wants This Music Tonight?)

That night I persuade Zane to take me back to Luca's restaurant so I can have exactly the same dish I had the night before. He suggests other restaurants but I refuse to give anything else a chance. What else could be as good?

'If you're absolutely sure you don't want to go elsewhere ...'

'I'm very sure. We are leaving tomorrow and I might never come back to Rome in October and there was a lot of *tartufo* left in Luca's hand last night.'

Zane just laughs.

After dinner he takes me to a club called Roxy. It has a mahogany bar front, marble floor, brass fittings, potted palms, and plush, deep-red, velvet rococo style armchairs. The effect is one of uber-luxe sophistication. Populated by the oh-so-chic, perma-tanned men and women in designer shades, it has the definite air of wannabes trying to be cool and trendy, but probably trying too hard to be that.

We are shown to a table by an effusive, smooth talking waiter.

'I brought you here to try the *affogato*. Ice cream with a cup of espresso poured over it.'

'OK,' I agree readily, my senses already open to another new experience.

Zane orders an *affogato* for me and a cognac for himself, while I look around curiously. Next to us two men are playing chess. There is a small stage with a white piano on it, but it is in darkness at the moment. I catch the eye of a deeply tanned man who raises his glass at me. I turn away and my gaze collides with Zane's.

'Making friends?' he bites out softly.

'Nope. I've got all the friends I need right here at this table,' I say with a massive grin plastered on my face.

Something passes briefly over his face, an old hurt, or betrayal, then it is gone. I reach out and touch his hand. 'Hey, trust me. I'm not going to hurt you.' His hand grasps mine hard.

My *affogato* arrives in a little glass dish and he releases my hand. I dip the spoon into the ice cream floating in coffee and taste it.

'Mmmm ... very nice,' I say. 'Want to try?'

'No, there is still a bit of your taste in my mouth and I don't want to lose it,' he drawls lazily.

I blink, my pulse quickening. Hell, this man sure can throw me off guard at the drop of a hat.

Just then the spotlights for the stage come on and I drag my eyes away. A man in a white velvet jacket and a bow tie goes to sit at the piano and the audience claps. He starts playing the piano and a woman with wavy hair in a long red gown comes to stand next to him.

She picks up a mic from the top of the piano and starts singing an Italian song. She is actually very beautiful, in that inimitable Mediterranean way. Her dark and soulful eyes search the room restlessly until they find Zane in the crowd, and fix on him. For an unguarded moment I see her freeze and falter, then she catches herself. Flicking her luxuriant hair she turns her back on her audience and sings the next line facing away from us.

By the time she turns around to face us, she is strong and confident again. Her voice is smooth and her gaze fixed on Zane. She is singing for him! I swivel my eyes surreptitiously to look at Zane, and he has gone completely still. My heart falls like a stone.

On stage the woman drapes herself erotically on the white piano.

Taking a deep breath and trying to look normal, I spoon some ice cream into my mouth. I feel the cold travel into my stomach, and try to stop the sensation that it has all been unreal, just a dream. That I was just fucking with myself.

There is nothing between us, except his lust and my stupidity.

He brought me here knowing she would be here. It's as obvious as hell that they used to be or still are lovers. Why do that to me? Why rub my nose in it? Unless I am here to make her jealous!

I lean back into the plush seat. I can't even get up and leave. I wouldn't know where to go. Plus I am here on a fucking fake passport. I'll just have to sit here like a sour lemon and watch some other woman eyefuck the man I am in love with. I sit stiffly as she finishes her song. It seems to last for hours. I don't look at Zane.

'*Grazia*,' she breathes seductively into her mic, and starts gyrating towards us. I take a deep breath. *Behave, Dahlia. Be dignified. Be the better woman.*

'Zane,' she calls. Even his name on her tongue is like a mating call. She has no eyes for anyone but him. I don't even register.

'*Ciao*, Silvia,' Zane says softly.

She leans down and kisses his cheek close to his mouth leaving behind a lipstick mark. 'I've missed you,' she whispers, but I still catch her words and instantly feel acid pouring into my stomach. How dare they do that in front of me? If I stay here a moment longer I'm going to scratch her eyes out and I've never been violent with another human being before and I really don't want to spoil my perfect record. Well, except that time I tried to slap Zane and that other time I tried to attack him, but I was horribly provoked.

I am about to stand and excuse myself in the iciest voice I can manage when Zane says to her, 'I didn't know you worked here now.'

'Why? Wouldn't you have come if you knew?' she asks lightly, but it doesn't hide her terrible sadness.

She is in love with him, but I don't care. I want to jump up and do a happy dance right here. He didn't know she would be here. He didn't bring me here to humiliate me, or make her jealous. It is just one of those weird coincidences.

She opens her mouth to say something else but Zane says, 'Silvia, meet Dahlia, my wife. Dahlia, meet Silvia, a very old friend.'

The news hits her hard. She blinks with shock and confusion. Reluctantly she turns towards me, her eyes flying to my rings.

'Congratulations,' she says hoarsely. 'You are a very lucky woman.'

'Thank you,' I say.

'I really should go back to my routine,' she says.

'Nice to have met you,' I say.

She nods then turns to Zane. 'I hope you will be very happy,' she chokes.

Zane doesn't say anything, just nods solemnly.

She turns on her heels, goes back to the stage and starts belting out a fast number, strutting across the stage and looking like the consummate professional. Her heart is broken but she has her pride.

The mood at our table has become strange and strained. Zane turns to me. 'We can leave now ... if you want.'

I nod silently.

We walk in the streets still full of people, both of us lost in our own thoughts. Then I slip my hand into his. He looks down at me and smiles. God, I love him. Every day I love him more and more.

Twenty-two

Dahlia Fury

I loved you at your darkest.
-Roman 5:8

We arrive at the villa and as we pass the swimming pool it suddenly occurs to me that I might not have such a good opportunity again, so I turn towards Zane and push him as hard as I can backwards. For a second he hovers in the air, his total bewilderment etched across his face, then he lands in the water with a great splash. I slap my hand over my mouth and try to suppress the hysterical laughter that is bubbling up into my mouth.

His head and shoulders pop out of the water, and he immediately starts peeling off his clothes. There is no swearing, no scolding. In fact, he seems so unconcerned about being in the water it surprises me. I watch him undo his trousers, kick them off and let them sink to the bottom of the pool. Next his shirt. Then he swims to the side where I am standing and hauls himself up so his forearms are resting on the edge of the pool.

He grins at me. 'You're not coming in, *bella*?'

I cross my arms over my chest. 'No, thank you.'

'Too bad,' he says and suddenly his hand shoots out and curls around my ankle.

I freeze and look down at the wet hand encircling my ankle then back to his eyes. They are sparkling with suppressed laughter. 'What's the matter, little fish?'

'Please don't,' I plead.

'Give me one good reason why I shouldn't?'

I say the first thing that comes into my head. 'I'll do something really special for you.'

One eyebrow arches. 'I'm intrigued. Carry on.'

'Show me your thigh.'

Keeping his hand firmly curled around my ankle, he lifts his leg out of the water and rests it on the edge of the pool.

I crouch close to him. 'This is just the beginning,' I say smiling enticingly, and scratch his thigh the way that Stella had taught me to that night at Jamie's. I must have done it right because his eyes widen and underneath his wet boxers his cock is a soldier standing to attention.

'Now let go of my ankle for the rest of the technique,' I croon.

He lets go of my ankle, grabs me around the waist, and chucks me into the water. As I am flying into the water I am actually in such a state of shock I don't even scream. Stella could make a stranger drive her home at breakneck speed for a promise of the rest and I couldn't even get my lover to defer retaliation.

The water is actually surprisingly cold. I emerge swearing and spluttering.

'You've ruined my good dress,' I grumble, treading water.

'You ruined my good suit,' he replies reasonably.

'Now you'll never know what I had planned for you,' I say huffily.

He grins. 'What, after the thigh scratch?'

'You know about the thigh scratch?' I ask incredulously. Stella gave me the distinct impression that it was her own personal invention.

He shrugs. 'Everyone knows about it. It's just a cock tease. Nothing comes after it.'

'What?'

He laughs. 'Yeah, whoever taught you didn't tell you *that*?'

I'm going to knock Stella's head hard the next time I see her. I swim to the side where he is standing with his hands on his hips, and he holds out his hand. I put my hand into it and he grasps it tightly and hauls me out in one smooth move. He kneels down and takes my shoes off.

'Come on,' he says, and we run barefoot and dripping into the house. I leave my wet clothes on the floor and he towels me dry so vigorously that I am quite pink and glowing by the time he finishes. He brings a hairdryer, plugs it into the wall, and makes me sit between his knees while he dries my hair.

'I love your hair,' he says.

I look up at him with a warm smile. 'Yeah?'

'Yeah.' He is silent for a while then he switches off the dryer. 'There. All done. Feel like a hot chocolate?'

I twist around to look at him. 'You're gonna make it?'

'Yeah.'

'I'd love to have a cup.'

I sit on a stool huddled inside a fluffy bathrobe and watch him chop a bar of chocolate into small pieces. Then he pours milk into a glass saucepan and puts it on gentle heat. As it warms he drops the chocolate in and whisks it until it is a rich thick mixture and the delicious smell of chocolate fills the air. He pours the hot chocolate into two mugs and puts a mint leaf into each one

'Now for the secret ingredient,' he says and adds a dash of peppermint schnapps.

We go outside and cuddle up on the outdoor seat that is big enough to be a double bed. The weather is beautiful and the sky is full of stars. He gets on it first and pats the area next to him. I climb in carefully holding on to my mug and curl up to his big warm body. We drink in silence, a delicious feeling of languor spreading through my body.

I put our mugs on the ground and stretch and yawn lazily. I feel safe, cherished and protected, but I want him to feel that too. I know he has demons and I want badly to be that formidable woman who holds them at bay.

'God, I could stay here forever,' I whisper.

I feel his hand tighten fiercely around me. 'I'm sorry about Silvia.'

I look up at him. There is tenderness in his eyes. 'It's OK. You don't have to be sorry. I understand how she feels. I would feel the same in her shoes.'

He looks down at me, his brow creased. 'So why did you push me into the pool?'

He thought I had shoved him into the pool because I was mad about Silvia. Well ... I grin evilly. 'Revenge. Remember when you chucked me into the pool back in England?'

He throws his head back and laughs, a low sexy rumble. 'Remind me never to cross you,' he says.

'Yes, I'd strongly recommend that course of action.'

He touches my cheek as if it is as fragile as a soap bubble. 'You're driving me insane, *rybka*.'

'Good,' I say staring up at him. There are stars behind his head. Heavy lidded he looks at me. Heavy lidded he takes me.

I feel him leave my body and, very gently, so as not to wake me up, slide out of bed. Quietly, he pads across the bedroom and opens the door. The click of the door closing is soft. I breathe quietly. I already know where he is going. I let a few minutes pass then I sit up and go to the door. I open it a crack and listen.

Nothing.

I walk out into the landing and I hear the first strains of music. Quietly, I go down the stairs and sit on the bottom step listening to him playing the piano. I close my eyes and get lost in his dark and brooding music. Oh, Zane. If only you will allow me into your world.

It gets cold but I don't move. I huddle up, eyes closed and listen. I don't know for how long I sit there listening to song after song, but suddenly I feel I am no longer alone. My eyes snap open and see him standing there.

I spring up, one foot on the first stair, ready to run.

'Don't go,' he says.

I stare at him.

'I don't want you to be afraid of me.'

'I'm not,' I whisper.

'Then why are you running away?'

I shake my head wordlessly.

He comes up to me and touches my face. 'You're freezing,' he murmurs.

I realize how cold I am. He lifts me into his arms and carries me upstairs and lays me on the bed. I hang on to his shirt.

'Who taught you to play the piano?' I whisper.

His eyes become bleak. 'Don't get too close, Dahlia.'

'Let me in,' I beg. 'I'm always open and naked for you.'

'If I wanted to hurt someone, the first thing I would do is take someone important to him, his wife, his child, his mother. If I let you in you will become all those things to me. You will also become the target, and I will become vulnerable.'

'Do you know the saying, "just when the caterpillar thought his life was over he became a butterfly"? Why can't you give up this life? We don't have to live in England. We can live here, or we can go somewhere else. I'd go anywhere with you.'

He shakes his head sadly.

'What is the point of all this money and wealth if you're not happy?' I ask desperately.

'But I am happy,' he says and begins to take my nightgown off. He stares at my naked skin. 'You look like the teardrop Beauty shed,' he says wonderingly.

A smile trembles on to my lips. I love this man so much it hurts. 'Really, you're just a musician and a poet at heart, aren't you?'

'If I was a poet I would have said your eyes are two smears of chartreuse in the dark.'

'Exactly my point.'

He moves to kiss me.

I hold his face between the palms of my hands. 'Do you know when your lips touch mine you make me feel like I am flying?'

His lips touch mine. 'Then, fly Dahlia fly. Fly as high as you can.'

Twenty-three

Aleksandr Malenkov

'**M**ama, I wrote a piece of music for you.'

Mama's mouth opens in a gasp of surprise. 'You did *what*?'

'I wrote a piece of music for you,' I repeat.

Mama stares at me curiously. 'Since when have you wrote music?'

I shrug. 'Writing music is easy, Mama.'

'You wrote it for me?' she asks, touching her chest with her right hand.

'Yes,' I say happily. Her blue eyes shine like stars and make me feel proud.

'Let me see it,' she says, wiping her hands hurriedly on her apron.

'I've called it Crying Angel,' I tell her as I hand the sheets over. She takes them as if they are something rare and precious. I see her eyes moving from side to side, and her head nodding slightly, as if she is listening to the music in her head. She reaches the end and looks up at me. 'Oh Aleksandr, this is beautiful,' she says excitedly.

'Shall I play it for you?'

'Yes, but quickly. Papa will be home soon.'

I sit at the piano and open the lid. The keys are yellow with age. Mama stands behind me. I lay my fingers on the ivory colored wood and begin to play. We are both so engrossed in the music we do not hear or see papa arrive.

'What the fuck is going on here?' he roars.

My fingers still, my mother jumps with fear. We turn towards my father guiltily. He is standing in the middle of the room and swaying on his feet, his head is tilted down, his eyebrows are raised and his eyes are wide open. He looks like a bull about to charge.

'I thought I told you never to touch that fucking piano. How are you going to be a fighter if you play a sissy instrument like that?' he rages.

I stare at him mutely.

'What are you staring at you little fucker? Come here,' he screams.

'Wait. Wait. It's all my fault,' my mother says in a trembling voice and moves quickly so her body blocks mine.

'Of course, it's your fault, bitch. I should smash the motherfucking thing to pieces.

Fucking piano. Turning my boy into a weak-willed fucking freak.'

'Please, please don't,' mama begs desperately. 'It's my mother's. I promise I will never let Aleksandr play the piano again.'

He crosses his massive arms over his chest and glares at me. 'I want to hear him say it.'

My mother starts crying softly. I stand up and position myself in front of my mother. 'I promise never to play the piano again,' I say clearly.

'Right. You better not be lying to me. I swear if I ever see you playing that fucking instrument again, I'll smash it to bits,' he says.

Twenty-four

Dahlia Fury

Purely by accident I find the sheets of music two days after we return from our holiday. I go into Zane's bedroom to get the book I was reading the night before, and find them lying on the bed. One look at them and I immediately recognize them as Zane's writing. Zane, I can hear, is in the shower. He must have brought them upstairs with him and left them there while he took a quick shower.

For a few seconds I do nothing. Simply stare at them. Then I move. I don't think, I just pick up the notes and run upstairs to my room. There is a fax/copier machine up there that I sometimes use to copy stuff for work.

I switch it on and wait for the damn thing to warm up.

'Come on, come on,' I whisper, but it slowly takes it time making its bleeps and clicks. The light turns red.

'Come on,' I urge. My palms are starting to sweat.

Finally, after forever and a bit passes, the light turns green.

Immediately, I feed the first page. There is a whirling noise as it starts its slow journey. I never realized how freaking slow this machine is. The paper wheezes out at the other end and I feed it the second page. It goes through at a snail's pace. I open my door and listen. There are no sounds from below.

I feed the next one, and the next one, but I am too nervous to finish. I have four pieces. That should be enough. I collect all the papers and rush downstairs. I don't know what I will do or say if Zane is out of the bathroom, but thank God, he is still there. I replace the sheets on the bed exactly how I found them and run out of the room. My heart is in my throat, and there are patches of sweat on my T-shirt under my arms, but a small secret smile curves my lips.

'Thank you, God,' I whisper as I skip up the stairs back to my room.

I switch off the machine, and hide the photocopies under my pile of unread submissions. Then I call Stella.

'What're you doing?' I ask her.

'Painting my toenails yellow and waiting for the oven to ping,' she says.

'What's in it?'

'Nothing yet. Just warming it up so I can put a pizza into it.'

'What happened to your diet?'

'I decided that diets are not for people like me. There's just no point living if you have to starve yourself all the time.'

I laugh. 'You don't need to lose weight anyway. I don't know why you bother.'

'It's all these damn celebrities and their air-brushed photos. If I lived in America I would sue them for giving me an inferiority complex.'

'Where did you get the pizza from?'

'Antonio made it.'

Antonio works in an Italian pizzeria down the road from Stella's apartment and he makes pizzas to die for. 'What type of pizza is it?'

'Pepperoni with extra cheese.'

'How much longer before the oven is ready?'

'Mmm less than ten minutes. Why?'

'Can I come over and share your pizza?'

'You better hurry then.'

'I'm leaving now.'

Noah isn't around, but Yuri gives me a lift to Stella's.

'Call me when you're done. I'll be at Starbucks across the road,' he says.

'OK,' I say and using my old key let myself into the building and race up the stairs. I open the front door and the whole place smells of baking pizza.

'Fantastic timing,' Stella says, opening the oven door. She is wearing a red tank top, Daisy Dukes, and is walking about barefoot with toe separators attached to her toes.

I go to the cupboard and take out the big pizza plate and two smaller plates. I put the big plate on the countertop and Stella slides the pizza on it. She uses a pizza cutter to slice it into eight parts.

'Are we having salad?' I ask.

'I wasn't going to, but we can if you want to.'

I open the fridge, pull out a bag of salad and dump it into a bowl. Stella smothers it with bottled dressing and we carry everything to the sofa. Stella sits on one end with her feet up and I take off my shoes and sit on the other end. The soles of our feet touch and we smile at each other. Just like old times. Stella picks up a slice and bites into it.

'Oh fuck,' she groans with her mouth full. 'God, I've missed you,' she tells the pizza slice. 'Mmmm ...'

I chuckle and take a bite. 'Mmmm ... Really good, isn't it?'

She wipes her mouth on a paper towel. 'If Antonio wasn't already married I swear I'd marry him.'

'He isn't married, is he?' I ask curiously.

'Yeah, he is. She was there with their kid the other day.'

I take a bite. 'I forgot to ask, has Mark come around with your shoe?'

'Yup, he came by the next day. Funny thing was he brought it to me in a box, which kind of impressed me. Most men wouldn't have known the value of a Jimmy Choo.'

'He's a nice guy. It's sad it turned out this way for him.'

She stuffs the last bit of her slice into her mouth, chews and swallows. She pops open her can of Coke and takes a sip. 'Don't worry about him he's rather dishy. Someone else will snap him up.'

'You know, Stel, I actually wanted to talk to you about something.'

She reaches for another slice. 'You're not coming back to live here,' she says and bites into her pizza.

I smile apologetically. 'Well, if you don't mind I'd like to carry on paying rent for a while and see how things go with Zane.'

She waves her hand. 'You don't have to pay rent while you're not living here, Dahlia.'

'Zane has put a lot of money in my account so I want to. It will make me feel safe and confident if I know I have this place if things don't work out with Zane.'

'Sure, babe. You can have this place for as long as you want.'

'Thank you, Stel.'

She pulls a pepperoni slice from her pizza, pops it into her mouth, and chews. 'Now tell me what you're really here for?'

I grin at her. She knows me so well. 'Well, I wanted to ask you about that composer, Andre Rieu. What's he like?'

She shrugs and looks at me curiously. 'He's a bit like my dad, but he's actually quite friendly. He's a fan of Tintin.'

'So he's friendly then?'

'Yes. I would say so.'

'When is your next appointment with him?'

'Well, he lives in a castle in Mastritch. He only books me when he's touring in England. Why?'

'Oh, so you won't be seeing him soon,' I say disappointed.

'Afraid not.'

For a second I feel deflated then I try another tack. 'Don't you have any other clients who are in the world of classical music?'

'As a matter of fact I do. Andre referred me to this violinist and a cellist.'

'And do you see them often?'

'Actually I think I have an appointment with the violinist, his name is Eliot, tomorrow.'

'Can I come with you? I need to see him just for one minute.'

She looks perplexed. 'Why?'

'I want to show him a few pages from a musical composition I found. Just to know what he thinks of it. What sort of quality it is.'

She frowns. 'Musical composition? Whose?'

'Zane wrote it.'

Her eyebrows rise. 'Zane? Zane? That big scary Russian mafia boss who kidnapped your sis so he could do you writes music? Next you'll be telling me he plays with dolls.'

'Very funny.'

'No, I'm serious. Are you really telling me Zane writes music?'

'I knew he played because I've heard him play and he's really, really, really good, but I didn't know he composed until today. I need a professional opinion of his ability.'

'Why?'

'I don't know. I just think he has more talent than he realizes. I think he could be something great in the music world.'

'Sure, I'll ask Eliot and if he doesn't mind, you're welcome to tag along. And if he doesn't want to do it we'll try Katherine, the cellist. She's very friendly.'

'Great,' I say, and take a big bite of my pizza.

Stella sighs. 'I guess I better get something green into me. Pass me that bloody salad, will you?'

Twenty-five

Dahlia Fury

I'm so glad I put the music sheets into a clear plastic file. My hands are so clammy they would have been soaked right through by now.

'Stop fidgeting, you're making me all jittery,' Stella gripes, glaring at me.

'I can't help it,' I tell her.

We are in the lift going up to Eliot's flat. She turns to me and adjusts the scarf around my neck. 'Will you please relax? *I'm* supposed to be the drama queen, remember. It's all going to be just fine. You'll see.'

'I just so want for Zane to have a choice. To know that he doesn't have to be a criminal when he's so talented. I wish you could hear him play.'

'I'm not into classical music. Puts me to sleep.'

'I wasn't into it either ... until I heard him play. He is truly brilliant with an intuitive feel for every note.'

She smiles placatingly. 'OK, OK, don't get you knickers in a twist, I believe you. Anybody who can make classical music sound brilliant to a person who never used to listen to it must be eye-wateringly good at it.'

I smile back. 'He is, Stel. He *really* is.'

The lift doors open and we walk along the short corridor. Stella turns to me in front of a door. 'You ready?'

My stomach churns and I feel as nervous as I used to feel before an exam that I was unprepared for. I take a deep breath and straighten my spine. 'Yes.'

She places her finger on the bell and looks at me, her face serious. 'Are you absolutely sure?'

I grin. 'You're an idiot, you know?'

She laughs and presses the bell. 'At least I'm not a moron.'

'There's no difference,' I tell her as the door opens.

Eliot is exactly how I imagined he would be. Glasses, nondescript clothes, wispy brown hair, and grave eyes that regard me with unconcealed curiosity.

Stella makes the introductions and he takes my hand in an unexpected death grip. His hands are soft as a baby's, though.

'Come into the living room,' he says, and leads the way into a dark blue corridor. His living room is minimalist and neat to the point of being clinical, with brand new cream leather sofas and a gleaming stereo system. The blue walls display a collection of framed photos of him receiving various awards.

'Have a seat,' he invites.

'Thank you,' I say, and perch at the end of the nearest sofa. Stella comes to sit next to me.

'Would you like something to drink?' he asks.

I look at Stella. I'm not sure whether to say yes or no. Perhaps the offer was extended out of politeness and accepting it would serve only to make this encounter longer and become more awkward, but refusing might make it seem as if I'm only interested in one thing.

'Thanks but I don't drink before a session,' Stella says with a smile.

'I'm fine too,' I add quickly.

'Right,' Eliot says stepping forward. 'Let me see this little composition of yours before you completely destroy it,' he says with a smile.

I realize that I am holding my file so tightly it's almost crumpled into a ball.

'Oh,' I say with an embarrassed laugh and, smoothing it ineffectively, hold it out to him.

He takes the file, pulls the photocopied sheets out, and looks at me warily. 'Why are these a photocopy?'

My fingers twist painfully in my lap. 'Oh, well. They're ... they're ... not my music,' I stutter, suddenly feeling guilty for no reason. I clear my throat. 'I've not stolen them, or anything like that. They're actually my boyfriend's and I didn't tell him that I'm bringing them to you. I wanted to surprise him if ... if you have good news to give me, that is.'

'I see,' he says with a curt nod and looks down at the papers. He frowns. 'This looks like a symphony for a full orchestra.' He remarks with surprise. 'You say your boyfriend wrote this?'

'Yes, his name is Aleksandr Malenkov. I've put his name, address and phone number at the back of the last sheet.'

He doesn't turn to look at the last sheet. Instead, he gazes at the music, then looks up at me in disbelief. 'Did you say he has had no musical training?'

'That's what I believe.'

'He's not a musician?' he asks again. His voice is full of incredulity.

'No. He's a ... um ... businessman.'

'That's incredible,' he declares, his eyes scanning the notes excitedly.

I glance quickly at Stella. She widens her eyes at me.

'Is it good?'

'Good? It's amazing. This is the work of someone extremely talented and accomplished. There are very few people in the world who can compose at this level.'

'Really?' I ask, beaming with happiness.

'I'd like to show this to someone and get back to you.' Eliot looks buzzed and as excited as I am feeling.

'Oh yes, please. That would be just brilliant,' I say eagerly, leaning forward, my whole body straining with joy.

Before Eliot can answer, my phone goes. I take it out and see that it is Mark. I instantly reject the call and put the phone back into my bag.

'Sorry about that. I should have switched it off,' I say as my phone rings again. I flush bright red. I take it out and it's Mark again. I hit reject and smile apologetically at Eliot. 'Sorry. This is such amazing news,' I say, and my phone rings again. I frown. This is not like Mark. Mark has never done that.

'You should take that call. It's sounds urgent,' Eliot says with a grin.

'Thanks. Please excuse me,' I say, and press answer.

'Mark?'

'Thank God I got you,' he says, relief pouring from his voice.

'What is it?'

'Where are you?'

'I'm with Stella. Why?'

'You're not anywhere near Malenkov's house, are you?'

'No. Why?'

'I don't have time to explain right now, but just tell Malenkov that there's a bomb planted in one of his cars. I don't know exactly but I think it's set to go off when the engine starts.'

'What?' I explode.

'Look, I shouldn't even be telling you this, but I promised to be the best friend you have, and this is me keeping that promise. Call him now and tell him to stay away from all his cars today. There's a bomb in one of them. Most probably the one he uses most.'

'Is this a joke?' I ask desperately.

'It's not a joke. It's fucking serious, Dahlia. I can't tell you more at the moment. Just warn him, he'll understand, and please, Dahlia, keep safe. I'll call you later.'

'How do you know this?' I ask, my voice quivering with fear and confusion.

He sighs. 'I'm about to enter a tunnel and I won't have any reception for a while, but I'll explain everything later.'

He disconnects the call.

'What is it?' Stella asks.

I shake my head. 'I'm not sure,' I say, and hit Zane's number on my phone, but it goes straight to answer machine. He always answers my calls. That sends me immediately into panic mode.

'What is it?' Stella asks again, her voice bordering on hysteria.

For an instant I look at her blankly, not really seeing her, then my mind becomes single pointed. I spring to my feet. I can't waste a single moment explaining anything to anybody. Zane is in danger.

'I'm sorry, but I've got something important to do. I'll liaise with Stella and contact you again,' I tell a surprised Eliot.

My body pumping with adrenaline, I turn to Stella. She is staring at me with her famous WTF expression. Maybe later, if this turns out to be a sick joke, we'll laugh about this, but now I'm too frightened by Mark's tone to do anything but run to Zane. 'I've got to go. I'll call you later, OK?' I tell her quickly, and rush out of Eliot's home.

The lift is old and it was slow on our way up so I don't use it. I open the fire exit door and run down the three flights of stairs. Outside, I realize that it is going to take too long for me to call Noah and wait for him to come. As far as he was concerned I was going to wait for Stella to finish her massage and we would be an hour. Who knows where he'd be right now?

As if the Gods are with me, I see a taxi turning the corner into the street and its light is on. I run to the edge of the street and hail it. I get in quickly and give him Zane's address.

'Sorry, love,' he says shaking his head. 'Can't take you there. There's a huge jam in that area. Big accident earlier. People died,' he tells me.

'Just get me as close as possible, and please hurry,' I say to him.

'It'll cost ya,' he warns.

'Charge me whatever you want, but please get me there as quickly as you can,' I say anxiously.

Twenty-six

Aleksandr Malenkov

"Where there is only a choice between
cowardice and violence,
I would advise violence."
-Mohandas Gandhi

It is a winter afternoon. Big, soft, white flakes of snow swirl down from a black sky and fall on me. I quicken my footsteps through the deserted street when a bitter wind starts biting into my face. As I run up the stairs to the second floor and put my key in the door, I have no other thoughts than how glad I will be to get into the warmth of our home.

As soon as I open the door I hear it, the dull thud coming from the kitchen. It is not a good sound. I've heard it before. Many times before. Flesh hitting a hard, flat surface; like a wall, a floor. I fling my schoolbag on the ground and run towards the noise.

My father is kneeling astride mama and he is strangling her.

In the thick, iron grasp of his red, meaty hands, her neck looks as thin and white as a swan's. The sound I heard is the weak thrashing of her legs against the floor. As if he was waiting for me to arrive before the real action starts, he turns his head slowly, a cruel smile creeping across his face. The spooky smile of a madman. Fear slams into my body.

'Nooooo!' I yell and, rushing forward pounce on him.

I rain blows on his head, neck, and back, but he was always a man possessed of extraordinary strength. Like the locking jaws of a pit bull that will not let go even after the dog he's attacking has expired, his death grip cannot be disengaged. My mother's eyes are bulging out of her head. He starts shaking her by the neck like a ragdoll. He is killing her right before my eyes.

I have to stop him. In desperation, I rush to the counter for something to bang on my father's head. Something, anything. I could have come across a heavy bottomed pot, or even mama's heavy rolling pin, but what I see is a knife.

Eight inches of shining steel.

My mother was cutting a chicken with it. The carcass lay decapitated and partly dismembered on the chopping board next to the knife. I swallow back the fear. I don't think. I have to save mama or she will die. With my heart racing and the blood roaring in my ears, I pick the sharp blade up.

The handle has ridges that fit my grip perfectly.

Turning around I swing it downwards directly into my father's broad back. It slices through his clothes and without any resistance at all embeds itself to the hilt into his dirty flesh. My father grunts like a hog in pain, but he does not let go of his quarry.

I grab the black handle with both hands and pull it out. Dark blood rushes out of the wound like a fountain of red. The jet of red splashes onto my legs and shoes as I raise the knife high over my head and, with a shout of blind fury and hatred, bury it into the side of my father's bull-like neck. It makes a sickening wet sound. Squelch. Like when you kill a bug, but a thousand times worse.

Blood sprays everywhere: over my mother, the cabinet, the peeling linoleum, the walls, my father, and me. Everything is scarlet, like the brightest flowers in full bloom.

After that I go crazy. A red mist descends and I stab him over and over, compulsively, until he falls to the floor with a muffled thump. I kick him away and pick my mother off the floor. I cradle her lifeless body in my arms.

I don't rock her, and I don't shake her. I know it's too late. She is gone. Her skin is as pale as a starfish, and her beautiful blue eyes are fixed and vacant. Like stones. Dead. I have never seen anyone dead in real life before and I know nothing will ever be the same again.

Everything I love is gone.

My heart feels like it has turned to stone. I take her hand, still wonderfully warm and familiar, lay it on my cheek, and close my eyes for a moment. In that eternal instant I feel her warm, kind presence again. We should have played the piano together. We should have had a different life.

I hear a sound and turn my head. My bull-like father is still alive. The blood is no longer rushing from him. It is flowing out like a lazy river. He is lying in a pool of his own blood. As a matter of fact, I am also sitting in that pool of cold blood. It feels no different than wet mud.

His expression of suffering is exaggerated by the dark shadows around his eyes, and the pallor caused by being drained of blood. A sick, feeble grin curves his mouth, but the mirth and the triumph don't make it to his bleak eyes. I look down at him, as passionless as an executioner.

'You did well,' he chokes, blood trickling from his mouth.

The man is insane: he wanted to be killed by his own son. I watch as the life ebbs out of him. The flat falls eerily silent. Like a soundless dream. Carefully I lay mama back on the floor. Sitting up against the kitchen cabinet, I pull my knees to my chest and look at my hands. My bloody hands. *I've just killed my father*. No amount of horror can prepare a child for that tearing knowledge. I'm a killer, forever tainted by my father's blood. But I don't scream, I don't cry, I don't break the sacred silence. Mama's spirit might still be around.

I stand, go to the sink and wash my hands until they are clean. I look up and see my reflection in the window. Blood is dripping from my hair onto the collar of my shirt. I hold my head under the running water and rub my hair until the water runs clear.

There is blood on mama's cheek too.

I take a tea towel, wet it, and go back to clean her face. There. Her face is clean. I sweep away the lock of hair that has tumbled over her cheek. Then I close her eyes so she'd have the look of someone asleep and dreaming peacefully.

I exhale heavily. 'Shall we play one last time, Mama?' I whisper.

In my head her voice, happy and free at last, says, 'Yes, *lyubov moya*.'

'Let me open a window first. It smells like the butcher's shop,' I tell her.

I go to the window and open it. A blast of freezing cold air rushes in as I turn to walk to the piano. We kept our promise to my father and it has been nearly a year since I played.

I open the lid and all the old memories rush back. I forget that my parents are lying dead on the floor. I play mama's favorite pieces, and I swear it feels exactly as if she is sitting beside me, her long, white fingers moving on the keys.

I am so lost in the music I don't hear the man come in. It is only when he stands right in front of the piano that I notice he is there. I stop playing and look up at him. He has dark, dark eyes and he is wearing a shiny red shirt, a thick gold chain, and an expensive long black coat.

'I killed him,' I say, shivering in the cold air blowing in from the open window.

'You saved me the trouble,' he replies.

I continue to look up at him.

'Well,' he says finally. 'You might as well come with me. We could do with a good foot soldier.'

I knew he was a bad man, but I left with him. Mama was good, but was no match for bad. I learned that papa was no spy. He was not like James Bond. He was just a member of a group of thieves. Bad men.

From now on I will be bad. Bad always kills good.

I no longer have an appetite for violence

- Aleksandr Malenkov

Twenty-seven

Dahlia Fury

Pay the ticket, take the ride

The journey is excruciating. I never managed to contact Zane despite the fact that I tried his number numerous times. Finally, the taxi arrives a few blocks from the house. The taxi driver was right; the road ahead is chock-a-block with standstill traffic. It is only four o'clock, but it's already dark and starting to rain. I thrust some money at him and jump out of the taxi.

'Please, God. Let me be on time,' I pray.

I start running down the street and realize that the smart heels I am wearing are doing me no favors. I kick them off, and with the cold, wet pavement under my feet, I start to sprint hard, avoiding people on the street. I run as fast as I can, the freezing evening air shocking my throat and lungs as I inhale faster and deeper. There doesn't seem to be enough air as I fly forward. My lungs feel as if they will burst.

The urge to stop and take a rest is overpoweringly strong, but I fool my body into thinking my goal is only until the next streetlight. Just until the next, and the next, and next until finally, just when my thighs feel as if they are burning, my breath is like thunder in my ears, the muscles in my stomach are trembling, and a frightened scream is locked in my throat, I round the corner into our street.

Taking great big lungfuls of air I try to increase my pace, but the muscles of my calves give way and I pitch forward, and almost fall on my face. Thank God, I land on my palms. I push myself up and continue running. I can already see Zane's blacked out Mercedes parked along the kerb on the opposite side of the street about twenty yards away from the house. Fear twists my insides. Something is very wrong. The car is always parked on the side the house is on.

To my horror I see the first car, usually with Anton in it, pull out into the road. I know the security drill. Anton always goes first, then the car carrying Zane, followed by the car with Noah.

That means the Mercedes will be pulling out next!

I'm only a few yards away, but I don't shout because I know no one will hear me. I just increase my speed until it feels as if my feet hardly touch the ground. I reach the car and, grasping the handle with both hands, wrench it open. Gasping for breath, I look at the interior of the car blankly.

There is no one there.

For a second I feel relief then I hear my name being called. I turn and see Zane running towards me.

'Run, Dahlia. Run,' he is shouting.

For a second I freeze.

Great, he's not in the car ... oh fuck.

The adrenaline rush takes over, and I race away from the car towards him. I can see his face lit by the streetlamp. It is white with terror.

I can make it, I think.

I see the light first, flaring out behind me and reflecting as an orange hue on Zane's face as he runs towards me, then I hear the noise – wow, deafening, and finally I feel the heat at my back.

The force of the explosion lifts me off the ground and I feel myself rushing upwards, the wind whooshing by my ears. *Look, Olga, I'm flying*. I see the horror on Zane's face. I open my mouth and start screaming with fear. Then something slams into the back of my head. For an instant it feels as if my entire head is on fire, then it all goes black.

I don't feel my body hit the ground, and I don't see Zane hold my unconscious body in his arms, and bellow, 'No, no, no, no, noooooooo.' I don't see him crane his neck backwards and, with his eyes squeezed shut, howl like a wild beast in terrible pain, the sound tearing from his throat and lifting into the night.

I loved her and she went away from me.
There is nothing more to say.

- Zane

Twenty-eight

Zane

I stand at the window looking down at the hospital's drab car park. It is raining, an icy, mean, diagonally driving mix of sleet and freezing cold rain that pounds the asphalt and breaks up into chaotic splashes of water.

A woman opens her car door, pokes a pink umbrella out of the gap, and unfurls it before she gets out. I kept a woman once who used to do that. I can't remember her name, and I'd have difficulty picking her out of a line-up, but I remember that odd detail. She had hair that would become curly if it got wet. I turn my eyes away from the woman in the car park and look at the sky. It is full of dark grey smudges.

Jesus, how come I don't feel a fucking thing?

I feel like a block of ice. My hands are shaking though. I reach out and touch the

glass. It is cold. Her blood is on my sleeves. I couldn't protect her. All the guards, the twenty-four-hour surveillance, and I couldn't keep her safe. There is not one damn thing I can do for her now. It is completely out of my hands. I'm like a leaf in the river.

Her phone rings and startles me. I take it out of my pocket and look at the screen.

Stella

I feel the name like an icepick to my heart. This is a part of her life, a part I never took any interest in. *What have I done?*

I accept the call.

'Where the bloody hell are you? You bolted out of Eliot's like a bat out of hell and just disappeared. I was worried. I've left like a hundred messages on your phone,' a woman's quarrelsome voice scolds.

'This is Zane,' I say quietly.

For a few seconds she goes completely silent. 'Why are you answering Dahlia's phone?' she asks in a tone that gives me goose bumps.

'Dahlia was in an accident and—'

'Accident? What the fuck are you talking about?' she demands aggressively.

'There was bomb, a car bomb,' I say. Even to my own ears it sounds incredible, implausible and fantastic.

'What?' Her voice is a screech of disbelief, a dagger shoved into my brain.

'It was an accident. She was not the intended target,' I tell her. My voice is quiet and calm as if I don't care, but maybe that is a good thing. It won't do to fall apart now. I have to be worthy of her.

'Target? What are you talking about?' she asks with growing frustration.

'The bomb was meant for me, but she opened the car door and set it off. It was timed to go off thirty seconds after the door was opened,' I explained.

'Where is she now?' she whispers.

'She's in surgery now. If you want, you can come to the hospital.'

'She's in surgery?' she repeats in a daze.

'Yes.'

'How bad is she?'

My jaw clenches hard. I loosen it deliberately. 'I don't know. She never regained consciousness after the explosion.'

She starts sobbing. 'This can't be happening.'

'Shall I send someone to pick you up?' I ask.

She stops weeping, her voice suddenly strong. 'No. What's the name of the hospital?'

I give her the details, ring off, and put Dahlia's phone back into my pocket. I should call her family. I know I should, but I don't. Not yet. It will be better once the surgery is over, and I can give them good news. No need to worry them. There is nothing they can do anyway.

I walk over to one of the couches and sit down. On the wall across from me I see a poster of a human being without skin, all his tendons, muscles and blood vessels exposed. I stare at the image without seeing it. Stella is right. This can't be real. This can't be happening.

'Fuck.' The word explodes out of my mouth as my hand moves downwards in an unconscious striking motion, venting my frustration and fury.

'Fuck,' I shout again.

Noah flings open the door, rushes in, takes one look at me, and goes out quietly closing the door behind him.

'Shit.'

She didn't deserve this. Why the hell did she run to the car and open the door? Why? In my mind's eye I see her face that moment when I called to her and she turned around terrified,

then she saw me and her whole face sagged with relief. Relief that I wasn't in the vehicle. The thought chills me: she knew about the bomb in the car. She thought I was in it and she was running to it to warn me.

Who told her? Who sent her there? I stand up and pace the floor. I stop and run my fingers through my hair.

'Fuck.'

The door opens and Stella walks in. I stare at her. She must have been really close by. Her face is red and her eyes swollen. She strides up to me. 'What the hell is going on with Dahlia?' she demands.

'She's still in surgery.'

She shakes her head as if she cannot understand what I am saying or can't take it in. She is obviously in shock.

'Sit down,' I tell her.

She covers her eyes with her palms, her face contorted. 'I don't want to sit. I want you to tell me what happened.'

'She was with you last. Can you tell me if you know any reason that would make her rush to my house and run to my car to look for me?'

She frowns and tries to remember. 'She got a call from Mark. It was something urgent. I don't know what it was, but it made her run out of the flat we were in.'

'Mark?'

'Yeah, Mark called.'

'What's Mark's last name?'

'I don't know. I can't remember.'

'Wait here,' I tell her and walk out of the door. I walk down the corridor and stand by a vending machine. Taking out her phone I scroll down to the last number received, and hit it.

'Dahlia,' a man says urgently.

'No. This is Zane.'

'Where is Dahlia?' he asks hoarsely.

I can barely hold on to my fury, but my voice is dead calm. 'What did you tell her?'

'Where is she?' he pleads.

'She was caught in a bomb explosion, Mark. It was you who sent her right into it, wasn't it?'

He makes a strange sound of anguish. 'No, no, no,' he says. Hearing him break down makes my heart feel like it will explode. He has no right. He has no fucking right. That's for me to do and I can't do it, because I have to be strong for her.

'Why the fuck did you do that?' I ask, my whole body clenched.

'I know I shouldn't have. I acted unprofessionally, but I couldn't take the risk that she might get caught in the middle of a bomb that was meant for you. I was trying to protect her, warn her.'

'How did you know about it?'

He hesitates. 'I can't reveal my sources.'

I knew then. He was a fucking *musor*. Pig!

'I want to see her,' he says.

'You come anywhere near her and I'll fucking kill you. You've done enough. Stay the fuck away.'

I disconnect the line and grab my head in frustration. Why did he have to call her? Why did she have to interfere? Everything was going so smoothly. I knew what Lenny was planning. As if I'd ever trust a sewer rat like him. I let him make his move and I was about to execute mine. Everything was ready to go. They were about to fall into my net in one fell swoop. Then she goes and foils it all.

Why Dahlia? Why?

I feel the fear building, my breath starting to come in shallow and fast. I can't submit to it. I have to get control. Put it somewhere it cannot seep out. She'll be all right. I know she will. She has to. I've got the best surgeons working on her.

I feel a dull ache in my eyes. I turn around to go back to Stella when Noah approaches me, his face horrified.

'I'm sorry,' he says.

My mind buzzes like an electrical circuit fried by overload. Images get scrambled in my brain. I see her alone running barefoot in the rain as if the hounds of hell are after her. I lash out. My fist swings out hard and lands on his chin. He is not expecting it and stumbles backwards, slamming into the vending machine.

'Where the *fuck* were you?' I snarl. 'You had only one thing to do. One fucking thing. Trail her. Never let her out of your sight.'

He holds his chin in the palm of his hand. 'She didn't want me to come in. It is standard. We always wait for her at the nearest coffee shop, and when she's finished she calls and we go and collect her.'

'That's not what we agreed. You let her decide? Have you gone soft?' I grit out between my teeth.

'We can't follow her into people's homes. She wouldn't let us. This is the first time she left without calling me. There was nothing I could do.'

I slam my fist into the wall. It cracks and bits of plaster and white powder fall to the ground.

A busybody in a nurse's uniform comes towards us. 'Excuse me,' she says sternly.

Both Noah and I round on her with such maniacal expressions of rage that she stops and backs away, a terrified expression on her face.

'I'm really sorry, boss,' Noah says again.

The rage goes away. The ice re-forms. 'Have you picked him up?' I ask, my voice icy.

'Yes, he's in the warehouse.'

'And the rest of them?'

'Pig food.'

I turn from him and walk away. From the corner of my eyes I can see two detectives coming up to me. Well, they'll get nothing from me. I'll be sending them directly to my lawyer.

Twenty-nine

Zane

Dr. Hassan Medhi, the neurosurgeon, comes in. I turn away from staring out of the window and Stella stands. He looks tired and somber. He's been in surgery for the past seven hours.

'How is she?' I ask, my voice tight.

'Come and sit down,' he says moving to the chair opposite the one Stella was sitting on.

Stella resumes her seat and I take the one next to hers.

Dr. Medhi clasps his hands and clears his throat. 'I've done all I could. Her skull was badly fractured and basically the entire left side of her brain was bleeding and covered in blood clots. I'm afraid I was forced to remove ten percent of her brain.'

I gasp, rising to my feet and towering above him.

Dr. Medhi's face twitches. He's afraid of me. Most men are. He clears his throat again. 'It was too risky to remove all the skull

505

fragments. She's on life support at the moment and I've inserted pressure-monitoring devices inside her brain, which will allow us to intervene if the pressure in the brain increases, but I'm afraid you must prepare yourself for the worst. The likelihood of her even making it through is very slim, and even if she does make it, she may never become cognizant. You do understand my meaning ... become aware ... conscious of her surroundings.'

Stella appears frozen with shock.

My throat constricts and my muscles coil uneasily. 'Dr. Hassan I chose you because you are supposed to be the best neurosurgeon in Europe. I don't want to hear anything from you except how you're going to make her better.'

For a few seconds a stunned silence prevails.

Then Dr. Medhi speaks and his voice is filled with a quiet pride. 'I can assure you, Mr. Malenkov, that Miss Fury has received the best treatment she could possibly get, not just in Europe, but anywhere in the world.'

I take a deep breath. The understated confidence in his voice some how soothes me. Yes, she is in the best hands possible.

'The next twenty-four hours are critical,' he says, 'but you will be able to see her in two hours' time. We'll talk again after tomorrow.'

He stands.

'Wait, Doctor,' Stella says, standing up herself.

'Yes,' he says politely.

'I don't understand. Is she going to be OK?'

The corner of his lips turn down in a deprecating gesture. 'God willing,' he says softly. Then he walks out. Not looking at Stella, I walk out of the room. In the corridor I meet Shane.

'I'm sorry, man. I'm so sorry. I just heard from the guys.'

I nod.

'Look, let me take care of Lenny. You stay with your woman. She needs you.'

I look at him and feel as if I finally know the definition of the word bleak. For me, time has stopped. I hear him talking. I see people walking by us, but I don't feel anything. I know I am breathing, and I know my right leg is shaking restlessly, but I can't feel it.

'No need,' I tell him. 'Dahlia's not about to come around for some time. I'll take care of him. He's mine'

He frowns. 'Are you sure?'

'Absolutely,' I say, and walk towards the toilets. I get in there and I vomit my guts out. Then I wash my face, dry it with some paper towels, and go out of the hospital. I stand at the entrance and smoke a cigarette. I have two hours to kill.

Tiptoeing in after washing our hands to see Dahlia is the saddest occasion of my life. She is unrecognizable. Her head is bandaged, an oxygen mask is over her face, there are countless IV tubes coming out of her connecting her to beeping machines. We are only allowed to stay for five minutes.

'You can try to talk to her, if you want,' the nurse says with a smile, but both Stella and I are so horrified we don't say a word.

Once the five minutes are up she herds us out and we stand in the corridor for what seems forever, unable to comprehend that the person in that room is Dahlia.

'Do you need a lift somewhere?'

She bites her lower lip and shakes her head.

It is three o'clock in the morning. 'Come on,' I say to her. 'Noah will take you home.'

She follows me like a lost lamb. We part in the car park. The rain has stopped and I

stand for a few seconds watching them get into the car and drive off. I think I'm putting off the moment I reach home, or maybe I just don't want to leave her here.

The whole street has been cordoned off and Anton has to drop me at the edge of the police tapes before driving away. The blackened car is still there and the place is crawling with policemen and their forensics team. One of them calls to me. He is wearing a cap and holding a clipboard.

'I live there,' I tell him, pointing to my house.

'Right, you are,' he says.

Yuri opens the door for me. He doesn't try to offer any words of condolence because he is like me in that way. He recognizes words for what they are. Ultimately empty. He nods respectfully and disappears into his station.

As soon as he closes his door the house feels like a tomb. There is not a single sound. I walk up the stairs quietly. I open my bedroom door and my eyes glance at the bed. I need a shower. I get into the bathroom and look in the mirror.

That is when I come apart. I lose myself. The ice melts. The pain slams into my solar plexus and I remember the way her face felt against mine, the way she would smile at me, and the tears start falling, at first lightly, then a deluge.

I hang on to the sink and bawl my eyes out like a fucking baby. I didn't tell her that I loved her. I never once told her. She was willing to give up her life for me and I wasn't brave enough to tell her I love her.

'I love you, baby. I love you,' I sob.

I switch on the shower and get into it. The water washes away the sweat, the tears, the blood. I come out, dry myself and pad over to my bed. I lie on it and stare blankly at the ceiling.

She has to come out of it. She has to. I will make her come out of it. I get up, dress, and call her sister. It's not an easy or a short call. A bomb blast calls for a lengthy explanation.

After the call, I go downstairs and Yuri comes to the door. He opens his mouth to say something, but I raise my hand and he snaps it shut.

Without a word I leave the house and drive to the warehouse. I have business to take care of.

I'm gonna show ya, what's really crazy.

Thirty

Aleksandr Malenkov

Lord, have mercy on us
Christ, have mercy on us
-Mozart–Requiem

The early morning air is cold with more than a bite of frost in it and it chills my lungs just to breathe it in. I switch on the music and listen, my ears pricked up like those of a leopard. Even though the stereo is old and cheap, the empty warehouse — well, it's empty except for a desk and a chair — has such good acoustics it makes the individual notes shimmer and sparkle.

Beautiful, soul stirring stuff.

I can remember playing this piece with mama. It was in another lifetime, but the notes are as alive and vivid as goldfish swimming in a pond. The sounds fill my head. I can still see her. As pure as a white swan. *Ah, Mama. Tell*

me of the days to come, when we will walk in
meadows full of wild flowers.

I breathe it into my body, and prepare myself for the task at hand.

He grunts and I turn to look down at him.

Naked. Shivering uncontrollably. Trussed up to a wooden chair. His mouth stuffed with his own smelly sock and taped shut. Tough guy. He makes another sound, frightened, desperate, turkey-like. I start walking towards him. I am furious, fucking livid. My hands are clenched and my heart is racing with adrenaline. I could kill with my bare hands, but I don't hurry.

I stroll. I am a consummate professional.

The music reverberates in my head. I remember the first time I came into the room and found Dahlia sitting on the carpet in front of the fireplace in a toweling robe listening to this piece. She turned her head and smiled at me. 'This is your song,' she told me, and smiled that sweet smile of hers. Like a goddamn angel. She doesn't smile anymore. She just lies there.

Because of this greedy, stupid monster.

I stand over him. 'Hello, Lenny.'

His skin is very white. Without clothes he is no more than a worm, squirming, cowardly, waiting to be squashed. He makes more desperate sounds. He wants to talk. Beg. Plead. Bargain.

No dice.

'Your death will be long and slow,' I tell him calmly.

His eyes bulge with fear.

I kick the chair viciously and he falls backwards, his eyes nearly popping out of his head. Comical, if I had been of a mind to laugh.

With superhuman strength I pick him and the chair up, and effortlessly throw both towards the wall. The chair breaks noisily. His scream is muffled by the sock. I walk up to him and kick his lily white ass with the cold ferocity of a crocodile. Tears start pouring from his eyes. Jesus!

Then I take out my gun, a PB/6P9, Army issue. Sleek. Russian, of course. It's old, 1967, but I like it. I grew up with it. The metal feels cold in my hand, but I know from experience it takes on human body heat very quickly. I screw on the silencer and he looks at me with begging eyes. Silly man. He has no idea. I wasn't called the meanest son of a bitch on the face of the earth for no reason.

With a steady hand I aim the gun at his pale right kneecap. He goes crazy behind the sock. Smiling grimly, I curl my finger around the trigger, and empty my first bullet dead center into his kneecap. A professional hit, fine entry wound and bleeding only from the gaping exit mess behind his knee.

He screams and soils himself.

I take aim and put another bullet into his left knee.

He twists and turns vigorously, but he needn't have bothered. I couldn't have missed if I'd tried.

I gave him a Jesus wound, just above the metatarsals.

He howls and twists even more furiously.

Aim. Fire. A matching Jesus wound on the other foot.

With great precision, amazing really once you consider I haven't done wet work in nearly twenty years, I aim and fire into all his major bones. I reload and aim it between his legs, at the pale shriveled worm nestled there. It explodes into a bloody mess. He is slobbering now, but in fact, he is not in pain. After the first shot, shock releases endorphins into the bloodstream that cause the pain to numb. Like yeast. Pain needs time to grow. In about an hour the wounds will marinate and swell up to the size of grapefruits and lemons.

Then the philharmonic orchestra of pain will play its first note.

I turn and walk away from him and the sickening smell of his shit. I put my feet up on the desk at the edge and listen to the music as I wait. I don't think of her. She wouldn't approve of what I am doing. But she's too good for this world and I'm not.

'Kiss the rain, whenever you need me,' she once said.

'I kissed the rain last night and you never came,' I whisper.

From the bleeding, slowly darkening hunk of meat on the floor comes whimpers, cries, howls, growls, groans, sobs, and screams of pain. When I can no longer bear to listen to his cowardly cries, I walk over to him.

Even without his dick and every major bone in his body shattered he still desperately wants to live. I see it in his eyes.

I point my gun at him and aim.

'See you in hell,' I say, and fire. Bull's eye. Right between the eyes. And you could almost call it a mercy killing.

Thirty-one

Zane

(Coma)

Coma! The word reverberates in the room and my head swims with horror. I feel a cage closing in, all the exits being sealed off. It is not going to be all right. She's in a ... I can't even believe it ... coma.

'Coma,' I echo blankly.

'As bad as it sounds in her present condition it's not actually a bad thing,' Dr, Medhi explains cautiously. 'It allows her brain to essentially rewire itself. In the darkness of the brain the one hundred billion odd cells can find each other again. If enough connections are made her brain will wake up. The human brain is an amazing thing.'

'If?' I ask warily.

'Of course, there is still a chance that she will never wake up.'

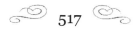

My mouth drops open. 'There is a chance she will never wake up?'

Dr. Medhi's hands open out. 'On the Glasgow Coma Scale assessment she scored 3.'

'What is that? Is it good or bad?'

'The scale assesses the degree of brain impairment or injury and measures the patient's brain functionality. Responses elicited include eye opening, verbal responses and motor responses such as movement. The responses are then ranked on a scale of 3-15 with 3 being the lowest and 15 being the highest.'

I stare at him in horror.

'Well, a deeper coma alone does not necessarily mean a slimmer chance of recovery, because some people in deep coma recover better than others in so-called milder comas. Many factors determine the final outcome, severity of the injury, length of time the person is in a coma.' He spreads his hands out, as if he is a used car salesman trying to convince me that he's just an honest guy. 'It is a thing we still don't understand very well.'

'What are the chances of her waking up?'

'I don't know, but what I can tell you is, research at London's Royal Hospital for Neuro-Disability found that nearly a fifth of the patients studied who were thought to be in irreversible comas eventually woke. Many remember being conscious of what was going on around them but were unable to communicate.'

'How long will the process take?'

'No one knows. It can take days, weeks, months even years. The longest persistent vegetative state is forty-two years. She may be in a vegetative state for long a time, or she may come out of it in the next few days.'

'What is recovery? Will she just open her eyes one day and be well again?'

He makes an expression that can best be described as a facial shrug. 'Recovery usually occurs gradually. In the first days, they are awake for a few minutes and the duration of time awake gradually increases. Some patients never progress beyond very basic responses. Others go on to live a totally normal life.'

'Can she take a turn for the worst and … die?'

'The most common cause of death for a person in a vegetative state is secondary infections, such as pneumonia which can occur in patients who lie for extended periods.'

The more he talks the more cold I feel.

I remember walking out of the little office we were in. I remember heading down the corridor. Using the lift. There are other people in it, but they are like shadows. The doors open. I get out with them. Another corridor. Reception room. People waiting in seats. Then into my view. Stella. She is hurrying towards me.

'What did the doctor say?' she asks. Her voice sounds like it is coming from underwater.

I shake my head and carry on walking.

'What did the doctor fucking say?' she screams at me.

I turn around. She looks quite ridiculous with her red hair and her crumpled clothes. Her hands are held open beseechingly. It's a grand gesture, almost biblical in stature. Dahlia always laughingly said she was a drama queen of the highest order.

'He said she's in a coma that she might never wake up from,' I say. My voice sounds normal, casual even.

Numbly, I watch her sink to the ground. A man goes to help her and I turn around and walk out of the hospital. Noah is outside. He must have seen me because he is holding the car park ticket.

'Where to?' he asks me.

'I don't know,' I say.

We get into the car. 'Want me to take you home?'

'No.'

'How about some food?'

'No.'

'Want a drink?'

It is ten o'clock in the morning and I haven't slept all night. 'Yeah.'

To my surprise he takes me to his home. A large apartment in Kensington overlooking the park. If I had been of a different mind I would have appreciated the luxurious décor and congratulated him on his taste. I would have been happy that all the little deals I passed his way have not been blown away on women and wine. But I'm not of a mind to think those things. I remain numb. From head to toe I can't feel anything. I sit on his couch and watch him pour a large measure of brandy. He walks over and puts it in my hand.

I take it and down it in one long swallow.

'Her mother and sister will be here in eight hours. If you want, I can go on my own to pick them up from the airport,' he offers.

All your sins come back to haunt you. 'No,' I say. 'I'll go with you.'

We drink together in complete silence. Not one word is exchanged. When the bottle is empty Noah opens another. I can feel myself going down and it is a relief. It is a relief to let go and sink somewhere where there is no me and no Dahlia. There is just nothing. It's a good place.

'You'll wake me when it's time?' I ask blearily.

Noah seems totally unaffected by the amount of alcohol he has consumed. 'Yeah, boss. Sleep now. I'll wake you.'

With a sigh I give in to blessed sleep.

Daisy is nothing like Dahlia. She is dark blonde with freckles, a boyish figure and sky blue eyes. I can imagine her smiling. She has that type of face. At the moment though she is not smiling. She is holding on to her mother protectively and looking around anxiously. Dahlia's mother on the other hand looks completely lost and frightened.

I smooth down my freshly showered hair and walk up to them.

'Mrs. Fury,' I say.

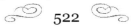

She turns to me with searching, wide eyes. 'Yes,' she whispers.

'I'm Zane.'

'Oh,' she gasps. 'You're the one who's taking care of my daughter.'

I wince inwardly. 'She's still in hospital. If you come with me I'll take you there after you've had a little rest at the hotel.'

'Yes, that would be good,' she says, her eyes confused and uncertain. Now I know why Dahlia is so protective of her mother and treats her as if she is a little kid.

'No, I want to see Dahlia straightaway,' Daisy says. She turns to her mother. 'It'll only take a little while to see her, Mom. Let's go see Dahlia first.'

Her mother nods vigorously. 'Yes, yes, that's a much better idea.'

I turn towards her sister. 'Good to finally meet you, Daisy.'

She nods slowly. 'Yeah. Thanks for taking care of my sister.'

'Right, let's go,' I say, picking up the suitcase. Daisy is carrying a backpack. 'Would you like me to help you with that?'

'No, it's not heavy,' she replies.

We get outside and Noah takes the suitcase off me and the backpack off Daisy. While Noah is putting their luggage into the

523

boot, I open the door, and first Daisy, then her mother slip into the car. I close the door and get into the front passenger seat. We drive in silence. The only sound comes from the stereo system.

We get to the hospital and I wait outside in the corridor while they go into Dahlia's room. They are with her for about fifteen minutes. When they come out both are in tears.

'I can't believe it,' her mother cries.

'I'm very sorry, Mrs. Fury,' I say automatically. 'My driver will take you to your hotel,' I tell them.

'Can I talk to you alone for a minute?' Daisy asks.

'Yeah, sure. If you step this way.' I show her to the door of the stairwell.

'Why is there a security guard outside my sister's room? Is she still in danger?'

'No. No. It's just a precaution.'

Her brow knits and she looks at me suspiciously. 'A precaution against what?'

'Nothing. I'm just paranoid.'

She hugs herself and shivers. 'The bomb was meant for you, wasn't it?'

For a moment the world goes very black. If she only knew how the guilt is eating me alive. I nod.

'Why?' she asks curiously. 'You're not just a businessman?'

'No. I'm a criminal,' I admit flatly. I guess that is what I am.

Her eyes pop open. 'What?'

'Organized crime. That's my game. I run a large and successful criminal enterprise.'

She takes a deep breath. 'What is it that you do?' she asks.

'It's not important. Your sister knew what I did.'

'And she was OK with what you do?' she asks incredulously.

'No,' I choke.

'So why are you still doing it?'

'Because I'm good at this.' In fact, I'm fucking brilliant at it. I'm so good I make it look easy. Lenny couldn't help himself. He thought he could take over my show if he got rid of me.

Daisy stares hard at me. 'Can't you see that you have only reaped what you have sown. You've hurt others and now you are being hurt. You have to stop or this cycle of pain will never end. You have to tell her that you have stopped. You sent her away. You have to bring her back.'

I don't say anything. I just freeze.

'Do you or don't you love my sister?'

'I do.'

'Then go and make it better. Stop what you're doing.'

She takes a step towards me and I have to suppress the urge to step back. I am holding on to my sanity by a thin thread. Her innocence and naivety threatens it.

'We should go,' I say, my voice harsh.

'Yes, run. Run as far as you want, but you can never run away from the knowledge that you can do more for her. Much more. You can bring her back.'

I open the door. Yes, I'm running away. I have to. I can't let her go on. She doesn't know: I've got nothing. There is nothing in me worth believing in. I'm the reason Dahlia is lying there, bandaged, silent, with machines keeping her alive.

Thirty-two

Daisy Fury

'**M**om, do you mind if I just have a moment alone with Dahlia?' I ask.

'Of course not. I'll just go get a cup of coffee,' mom replies, and bustles out of the room.

I go close to Dahlia. Her injuries are severe, but they are all internal. Except for the tube in her mouth, her face is as clean and pure as a sleeping angel. Looking at her I still can't believe what has happened. When I first wake up in the morning and I am still foggy with sleep, the thought of Dahlia being hurt in a bomb blast feels like it must have been a nightmare from the night before.

'Mom and me have to go back this evening, Dahlia,' I tell her, stroking her skin tenderly. 'You know that promotion I was talking about? Well, turns out being management means you can never take time off unless you book it well in advance. I've been told that if I don't go back soon I'll lose my job. We need the money, especially now, with you being ill and not able to send money back anymore. I'll have to support Mom on my own.'

I clear my throat.

'I feel really, really bad, but Stella—I really, really like her by the way—said there is no point in my staying, and that coma, or no coma, you wouldn't want me to hang around doing nothing. Especially since, in her own words, "you're a fat lot of good to her staying here." She's funny, your Stella.'

There is truly nothing to chuckle about, but I force one.

'Anyway, the good thing is Stella said that as soon as you get out of ICU and she's allowed to bring her phone into your room, she'll either FaceTime or Skype me so Mom and me can see you and talk to you.'

I pause.

'Mom really wanted me to leave her here with you, but she looks so lost and frightened, Dahlia. Without me here she'd be an emotional wreck and of no use to you anyway, so I'm taking her back with me. I'm afraid she might go into a deep depression. It'll be better for her to be home with all the things she's familiar with.'

There is no reply but the steady rasp of the machine breathing for her.

'Besides, Zane says we can come back anytime, and he'll even pay for us so we'll both be back real soon.'

I bend down and kiss her cool cheek.

'I'll pray for you. I'll pray real hard, sis. You will get better. I know you will.'

Dahlia makes no response.

I go really close to her ear and whisper, 'I know it was Zane that took me and I forgive him. So there is nothing for you to worry about or feel guilty about. I love you with all my heart.'

I think I must have really believed that she would open her eyes then, but she doesn't. I straighten, and bite back the sob that rises up my throat at the thought of leaving her.

'Bye bye, Dahlia. I love you,' I say, my fingers trailing on her skin.

I go outside and my mother is standing in the middle of the corridor.

'I thought you were going to get yourself some coffee,' I say.

'I changed my mind,' she says, but in such a small voice I realize she was probably too frightened to go and get it in case she got lost in this maze of corridors. She has never been to England before. It's all so foreign and frightening to her. Seeing her standing there makes me feel a bit better about my decision not to leave her behind.

I will have to trust in Zane's love. At least for now.

I call Noah. 'I'd like to see Zane before we leave today,' I say.

'Sure. I'll arrange something with him and call you back.'

Zane

'Do you believe in miracles?' Daisy asks.

I shake my head slowly.

She smiles, a thing that makes her glow like she is lit up from the inside. 'I do. I believe miracles happen all the time. My rescue was a miracle.'

I keep my face expressionless. Her rescue was no miracle. It was a ruthless gamble. A brutal mating technique.

She comes closer and again I have that uncomfortable sensation to move back. Perhaps because she is too pure, too innocent. It's like a sinner going too close to the altar.

 530

'I've been on the net researching comas and there is no doubt that miracles happen. There are all kinds of miraculous accounts of patients coming out of comas even after long periods of time. Some of the stories were about people who woke up after days, weeks and months, but some were truly miraculous. A guy called Terry Wallis spontaneously began speaking after nineteen years in a minimally conscious state.'

She is speaking fast and with suppressed excitement.

'And then this Polish guy had to be introduced to his eleven grandchildren who were all born while he was in a coma! After all those years he woke up. Then there is this other guy who was in a vegetative state for seven years. One day his family was arguing in his room about what to do about an illness he'd contracted. They were trying to decide if they should go ahead with surgery to remove some fluid from his lungs or simply let him die, when he started talking. There were so many cases of people coming out of comas when music was played to them. One girl that the doctors said would never wake up again smiled to Adele's music, and two days later she woke up from her long sleep.'

Her eyes shine brightly.

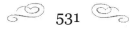

'In another case a man woke up and said, "Pepsi." A lot of the survivors said the compassion and caring of the people around them helped the most. They said that even though they couldn't move they could hear.'

She sniffs and tears suddenly swim in her eyes.

'The reason I'm telling you all this is because I recognized a great strength in you back when we spoke in the staircase landing. A weaker man would have lied, but you told me the truth about who you are and what you do, even though it was brutal and ugly.'

Tears start running down her cheeks, but she ignores them.

'I know I have no right, and it's a very big ask, but I'm asking you here and now, before I leave, to use that strength to help my sister. Please, Zane, don't give up on her, no matter how difficult it seems. She is in there somewhere, and maybe she can even hear us. She just needs some time to find her way out again. She will come out of it. I know it. I feel it.'

I hang on to her words ferociously. In my black cage her words shine like gold, or fools gold. Whatever she's selling I'm buying.

Time passes by slowly, tearing us to pieces. The event is unredeemable,
almost like an ancient and cursed action.

-Giancarlo Signorini

Thirty-three

Zane

After Daisy and her mother leave I spiral into something akin to madness. I become highly-strung, restless, prone to fits of violent rages, and lose all interest in business. When I undertake it, it is without pleasure and reluctantly. I don't even know why I do it any more. Money is wasted on me. I have no real use for it as I have no desire to do anything. I stay away from society, hiding from everyone, and hating everything.

I haven't even played the piano.

I jump when the phone rings and answer it with my heart banging in my chest until I find out the reason for the call has nothing to do with her. When I go to visit her I pause, every nerve in my body trembling, before I enter her hospital room. I'm terrified I might find that she has stopped breathing.

I am shit scared I will lose my little fish.

My home has become a prison, and some nights while I am wandering alone in this vast house I feel like Michelangelo's envelope of skin. Tortured, empty and suffering endlessly.

Once I went to confession.

The priest had an easy answer.

Repent.

'Will that bring her back?' I asked.

'Well, no, but it will save your soul.'

I don't care about my fucking soul. That's irretrievably damned. Everything that is still sane in my body tells me it can't be that easy. Say I'm sorry and wipe out all the pain and suffering I've caused? No, no, no. That's a fool's game. Her sister is right. This is my punishment. A living hell. I walked out of God's house even more desperate than when I entered it.

In the end it is Noah who holds out a rope for me to climb out of my deep darkness. He arranges for me to go to Nimes in France to meet with a very brave Frenchwoman called Bernadette. She lives in a house she custom built, and named *Mas du bel athléte dormant*— the House of the Beautiful Sleeping Athlete.

Her story started when her husband, Jean-Pierre Adams, a famous footballer, went for routine knee surgery to repair a sports-related injury. He never woke up from the anesthesia. He was thirty-four years old and that happened thirty-three years ago.

A part of me doesn't want to meet her. I refuse to believe that Dahlia won't wake up in the next few days or weeks, but another part of me knows that I can learn a lot from her. Dahlia has just been moved out of ICU and I don't want to keep her in hospital a day longer than necessary. I know I can get a better and a more dedicated staff to care for her at home, and I am terrified she will succumb to one of these virulent strains of antibiotic resistant bacteria that exist in hospitals. Dr. Medhi's warning about pneumonia still sends shivers down my back.

Bernadette is seventy-two years old, but her nails are painted red, her make-up is immaculate, and her blonde hair beautifully coiffured. If I saw her in the street I would not have picked her out to be the extraordinary woman who has dedicated her thirty-three years of taking care of her vegetative husband in the hope that he will eventually wake up.

She tells me they met at a dance in the 1960s. The memory makes her smile. 'He was *joie de vivre* in human form' she says wistfully.

Now her husband feels, smells, hears and jumps when a dog barks, but he cannot see, crack a joke, laugh, or dance.

Her day starts before seven. After a solitary breakfast it becomes a mix of changing clothes, shaving, preparing and blending food, feeding him, helping him go to the toilet. Sometimes when he has a bad night she spends the night with him too.

She takes me to his room and something inside me dies. He has hardly aged but for a few white hairs. However, he is a shell of the vibrant *joie de vivre* man in the photographs she showed me. He lies there as still as a breathing corpse. I simply cannot imagine this life for Dahlia and me.

'He can recognize the sound of my voice,' she says looking at my aghast face.

I turn towards her in surprise. 'Really?'

'Yes,' she confirms.

'How can you tell?'

'When you love someone you can tell,' she says with conviction.

'I see,' I say politely.

'Yes, that is why you must keep talking to her. It is love that heals beyond all else.'

At the end of my visit I take her hand in mine to thank her for agreeing to see me, and she grasps my hand with both of hers and says, 'It is worth keeping her alive, Zane. Medical science evolves. If one day they know what to do with her, you will be ready. One day she will come out of it.'

In two hours I am back in England and I go straight to the hospital. I walk in on a nurse washing Dahlia and it is almost too painful to watch. To see those beautiful limbs that had been so full of life and vitality handled as if they belonged to an inert puppet. The nurse looks up at me and smiles in an encouraging fashion.

'I'm going to clean her face now. Often it will stimulate them to open their eyes when we perform intimate things like brushing their teeth or shaving for the men.'

I move closer and stare at the nurse as she squeezes water out of a piece of yellow sponge and gently starts to clean around the life support machine tube. I hold my breath as she lays her thumb on Dahlia's temple and wipes her closed eyes. My heart clenches with hope.

This is it. She is going to open her eyes.

But of course, she does not.

The nurse looks at me, her expression both disappointed and reassuring. 'It can

happen anytime. You know, the best thing you can do by the bedside of a loved one in a coma is to talk to them. They can hear you. Tell them you love them. Let them know you're going to stay with them. You're not giving up on them. Offer them hope.'

The next day I begin to make the necessary arrangements to move Dahlia back to the house.

I hire two twenty-four hour nurses to take turns to watch her and to move her every hour so she doesn't have bedsore or skin problems. I also contact a kinesiologist recommended by Dr. Medhi to ensure her lungs are clear and her muscles exercised to avoid choking and atrophying.

I also hire a professional to come to the house and make a list of everything that needs to be done before a patient with Dahlia's needs can be catered to. He gives us a long list. It runs from a bathroom for the nurses with hot and cold water to a reputable back-up generator for the life support machine in the event there is any kind of disruption to the electrical supply, to the best carbon based air filters on the market.

Going on his recommendation I decide to house Dahlia on the ground floor in the living room with the French doors. Once the location is decided, my secretary organizes a team of workers to come in and build a bathroom in there. They are also told to move the piano from its present location to Dahlia's new room. She wanted to hear me play. She's going to hear me play.

Because I am prepared to pay whatever it takes for quicker service and fly in everything that is needed from any part of the world, the house is ready for Dahlia in five days' time.

Tomorrow my little fox comes home.

Thirty-four

Stella

For a long second I stand outside the door to Dahlia's new living quarters, close my eyes, and take a deep breath. Then I open the door and sail into the room.

'Hello, Sleepyhead,' I call cheerfully.

The nurse stands and smiles. I return the smile. 'You must be Corrine,' I say.

'And you must be Stella,' she says pleasantly.

'At your service.'

'I'll be outside,' she says, and heads for the door.

'You might as well take a break and go to the gym or something. I'll be at least an hour,' I tell her.

'Thank you. I might have a quick swim.'

She leaves and I go up to the bed and give a loud smack on Dahlia's cheek. I run my eyes over her face. Her hair is starting to grow and it has been neatly combed. I pick up her hand

and her fingernails are short and nicely filed, but bare, like a child's. The sight stirs me. She used to love her nail polish.

My chin trembles.

I still can't believe this terrible fate has befallen her. If only I had not forced her to go in my place that evening. I feel the tears sting at the back of my eyes, but I grit my teeth and plaster a smile on my face even though she can't see it.

'You'll never guess what I brought for you. Perfume and makeup. Yes, yes, I know what you're going to say, nobody is going to see you etc., etc., but honestly you really shouldn't let yourself go like this,' I say chattily.

Opening my bag, I take out a brand new container of eye shadow.

'All of this is dermatologically tested so it is kosher for sleepyheads.' Carefully I apply a very subtle amount of brown eye shadow, blend it with a bit of highlighter, and stand back to look at the effect.

'Oh wow. You won't believe how good I am at this.'

I dig into my bag.

'Now this is raspberry pink lip gloss. It's raspberry flavored, just in case you want to have a little lick, or ... Zane does,' I say, and apply a coat on her lips, working carefully around the tube in her mouth. I stand back.

'Oh yes. Ten times better.'

Then I open a box of blusher and rub a tiny amount on each pale cheek. Amazing how quickly she lost her lovely color. I take my hand away and regard my handiwork critically.

'You look amazing. I really am in the wrong profession. I should be a beautician. I thought about getting you nail varnish, but decided maybe that's not such a good idea. You know, the fumes and stuff. If you want to have nice nails, I suggest you get your American ass out of that bed quick.'

She says nothing, just the steady whoosh of her ventilator, so I reach again into my bag. 'Look what else I got you.'

I slip a bracelet made out of organic cotton with little pink love hearts on it that reads HUG ME.

'Hmmm ... it really suits you, Dahlia. I'm really glad I got it now. I found it at a new shop that opened around the corner from us. It was so pretty I got us each one. I'm wearing mine now too.' I hold my wrist out, turning it, as though she is watching.

I put all the cosmetics back into my bag and sit down next to her.

'Mark came around. He's really cut up about what happened to you. He even cried. I was livid with him and I had planned to punch him in the throat when he walked through the door, but I took one look at his face and all my anger died away. He looked terrible.'

I stare at her fingers. For a second I am sure her middle finger moved. I stand and watch it carefully while I speak

'I started to feel sorry for him. I saw how destroyed he is by it all and he did mean well. It must be awful to know you caused the person you love so much damage. Anyway, we went out for coffee, and we talked about you the whole time. It's like we're connected. We're both survivors of a tornado called Dahlia. Both of us connected by our guilt. I keep thinking what if I had insisted you switch off your phone when I switched mine off.'

I am babbling nonsense and staring so hard at her finger I don't even blink.

'He told me everything. How he was part of a police force investigating some guy called Lenny, and while they had him under surveillance they found out that he was plotting to get rid of Zane, and how he happened to see you coming out of Zane's house that time you went in my place. It was a bit creepy but he had such a thing for you, he followed you home, and then, pretended to bump into you at the supermarket the next day. I know how it sounds, but at heart, he's a really nice guy. He is dying to come and visit you, but of course, Zane won't ever allow it.'

I never take my eyes off her fingers, but they never move again. It must have been my imagination. Disappointed, I resume my seat.

'Not that I blame Zane for holding him responsible. I did too. You should know that I've changed my mind about Zane, too. I believe he really loves you. He's like all cold and distant, but I can feel how much he loves you. From what I have seen of Zane, I know now that you're never coming back to stay with me. It's obvious as hell both of you are going to get married and play happy families so I've got myself a flat mate. She's from this unpronounceable little village in Ghana.'

I sigh unconsciously and quickly make my voice bright and peppy again.

'She's all right, I guess. I took her to Jamie's the other night, but she doesn't really drink. She had one glass of white wine all night, and she doesn't like the music there either. So really, I desperately need you to wake up and come for a girls' night out with me.'

Zane

I come into the room and the nurse stands up, smiles politely and leaves. I wait until she closes the door before I approach the bed. I see instantly that Dahlia is wearing makeup. I can only imagine that Stella must have dolled her up. I go up to her. The sight is bittersweet: she looks so beautiful, like Snow White lying in her glass box, but I can't wake her up, take her in my arms.

I go really close so I can feel the heat of her skin, and watch the tiny pulse in her throat beating. She's not gone yet. She's still alive. I just have to reach in and find her.

'You look beautiful tonight,' I tell her. 'Want to listen to some music?'

Of course, she doesn't answer. I go to the piano, open the lid and begin to play for her.

December

Thirty-five

Zane

Our sweetest songs are those that tell of
saddest thoughts.
                                    - Percy Bysshe Shelley

As soon as I finish the call I rush to Dahlia's room. The nurse is exercising her legs, and usually I would come back, but today I cannot wait.

'Could you finish that in a bit?' I ask.

'Certainly,' she says and, placing Dahlia's leg gently back on the bed, covers it and leaves the room.

Dahlia's hair has started to grow back. It is not yet two inches long, but it is enough for Stella to bring some pink clips and get the nurses to decorate it with them. To be honest, I don't like the clips. I've never known Dahlia to wear anything so babyish. She was always a

549

woman thru and thru and now between Olga, Stella and the nurses she's always dressed like a kid.

I run my finger on her cheek. 'Oh, Dahlia, Dahlia,' I sigh softly. 'When will you wake up and come back to me?'

Careful not to touch any of the tubes and lines running into her, I rest my forehead against hers. My lips brush her eyelashes. I close my eyes with the familiar sensation. This should have been such a happy moment, but it feels so sad.

'You did it. You really did it. Guess what you did, my little thieving angel?' I whisper. 'I just had a phone call from the great Andre Rieu. I thought it was a prank call until he told me that a violinist named Eliot Scarborough had called him. I know you went with Stella to a client called Eliot so I pricked up my ears and listened.'

The sharp edge of the plastic juts into my cheek. I lift my head, take off the clip and smooth her hair.

'He said Eliot sent him a few pages photocopied from a symphony I composed that my girlfriend had apparently given to him. It was all meant to be a great surprise. And believe me it was. An unbelievable surprise,' I say.

'Anyway Andre said he wanted to personally thank my girlfriend because during his many years as a celebrity composer and conductor with his own orchestra, he is inundated daily with phone calls, emails and letters from people who have composed arias, overtures or waltzs, all begging him to play their work. Over time he came to the conclusion that a new Johann Strauss or Mozart were things of lore, until he played my music.'

I smile at her. *Please be listening, Dahlia. Please respond to this news.*

'He said he almost fainted when he heard it. He thought it was grand, exciting, romantic, and fabulously enthralling ... and, wait for it, he wants me to send the rest of my notes because he wants his orchestra to play my symphony!'

I stop and put in as much excitement as I can into my voice.

'You did that, little fish. You made it happen,' I say, my voice throbbing with excitement, while my heart weeps with sadness.

She doesn't wake up when I hold her, thank her, touch her or talk to her.

January

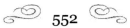

Thirty-six

Olga

It is Dahlia's birthday. I have baked a chocolate cake from a recipe I found in the American cookbook I bought, and the girls have spent the morning decorating her room with lots of balloons. I have also cooked a lot of food for the boys, and Noah has brought in a crate of vodka. The house looks festive, but there is an air of sadness that cannot be erased. She was the light of the house. When she came she brought fun and laughter and noise and now that she has fallen silent the house has become like a tomb.

I saw Zane this morning and he looked as he always looks nowadays: haunted.

I hear the doorbell and I know it is Stella. When she comes in I see that she has been

crying. I open my arms out and she runs into them.

'Oh, Olga. I can't bear to see her like this.'

'Shhh … she will wake up. Give her time,' I say gently.

She pulls out of my arms and dashes away her tears roughly. 'What if she doesn't?'

'I know she will.'

'What makes you so sure?'

'I don't know why I'm so sure. I feel it inside me. Just like I knew when she came to live in this house that she would become the mistress of it one day. I just know she will wake up.'

'Well, you'd better be right,' she says gruffly.

'Do you want a cup of coffee or do you want to go in and see her now?'

She sniffs and blows her nose from a tissue she finds in the pocket of her jeans. 'Thanks. I'll just go see her first.' She wipes her eyes. 'I've got a surprise for her.'

'You do?'

'Yup.'

'Run along then, child.'

'OK, see you later.'

Stella

https://www.youtube.com/watch?v=nrIPxlFz
Dio

I pop my head around Dahlia's door and find both the nurses standing by the window chatting. They turn to look at me. Jane, the older nurse, grins.

'Will you look at this place?' she asks.

I step into the room in wonder. 'Wow! Are balloons a Russian thing?'

She giggles.

'It was that kid Nico. He was like a monkey climbing up the walls.'

I glance at Dahlia. No change there.

'Well, give us a shout when you're finished,' Corrine says.

'OK,' I say taking off my coat.

When they have gone out and closed the door I approach. 'Happy Birthday, Sleepyhead. How are you today?' I ask as I take my computer out of my bag and put it on the table next to her. 'Mark sends regards and birthday wishes. I told him I'll bring him some birthday cake.'

Later I will call Daisy so that she and her mom can wish Dahlia Happy Birthday, but not yet.

'I've realized what is happening in this place,' I say.

'Zane is filling your head with classical music and as much as you claim to like that stuff you must be really missing the good stuff by now.' I take out my iPhone and my Beats Pill Bluetooth speaker from my bag, turn the volume up, and hit play. The sound of the Rolling Stones blasts into the room.

Zane

Everyone is gone. The party is over. I drank a lot, but I don't feel drunk. I pick my way through the streamers lying on the floor and go over to the French doors and stare into the darkness. All that noise and shouting and she never woke up.

My shoulders slump as I exhale.

Suddenly the spotlights in the garden come on. A fox and her two cubs have wandered into the garden. The first thought that crosses my mind is, *I wish Dahlia could see this.* Then the thought: *she will fucking see it if it's the last thing I do.*

I take my phone out and film them sniffing around. The cubs are small, fluffy, and playful, and I know they will make her smile. They came to visit her while she was sleeping.

The creatures find nothing, and eventually they disappear into the area of the garden not illuminated by the lights.

I sit next to her and gently lay my head on her arm.

'I got you a birthday present,' I whisper. 'Two tickets to Beyonce's concert. Stella told me you've always wanted to see her perform. Here's the best part, I've arranged for you to go backstage to meet her. It's next month. The 18th of next month. We're going together. I'm just going to put these tickets right here until the day comes.'

I go and sit at the piano and I play for her with all the pain and passion that exists in my body. I play until the early morning hours. Then I page the nurse, and when she comes I go to bed.

March

Thirty-seven

Dahlia Fury

https://www.youtube.com/watch?v=3YxaaG
gTQYM&nohtml5
(Bring Me to Life)

I am standing very still in a white room.

There is nothing in the room but a white table and six white chairs. The room has no windows, but it is filled with a white light that is very bright but it is not blinding. It has no source, just seems to be everywhere. It permeates everything. Even me. It flows through me giving me perfect peace, perfect bliss.

Time doesn't exist, at least I don't feel it passing. I know I am waiting for something or someone, but I don't know what. I don't feel anxious. I feel peaceful. Sometimes I think I can feel someone touching me. I'm not sure because I can't see that I have a body. A nurse.

She has cool, impersonal hands. A needle pricking my arm. A tube down my mouth, my neck lifted up ... and yet I have no body.

Strange. Bewildering and alien, but I am not afraid. Everything is perfect here.

Other times another touch. A man. I know him very well, but I can't understand what he is doing there. Our fingers entwined. It's familiar and fills me with longing, but I don't know what for.

There are other voices. Indistinct but happy. They reassure me. I'm glad they are there even though I cannot make any sense of what they are saying or why they are there.

Often I hear beautiful music, and there is so much love and sadness in the music. It feels as if it is calling to me but I cannot get to it.

Zane

So what if we didn't make it to the concert. There will be others.

Stella

Oh! My smokehouse! You are not going to believe what happened, Dahlia. This is big. This is *real* big. Mark and I kissed!

April

Thirty-eight

Noah

I rush to Zane's study and knock on his door. Even before he can call, 'come' I open it and enter.

'What is it?' he says springing up in alarm.

'You have to come with me. I have to show you something,' I say quickly. I can barely contain my excitement. My heart is beating in my chest.

His face becomes pale under his tan. 'What's wrong?' he asks urgently.

'Just come with me,' I urge, and start pulling him down the corridor.

He falls into step beside me. Outside Dahlia's door I pause and look at him. There are lines on his face that were not there a few months ago. How much he has changed. I turn the handle and let him enter.

He stops almost immediately. Then he runs to her bed, his hands outstretched. He touches her skin. He stares down at her face. He listens to her chest. Then he turns to me.

'What the hell?' he shouts wildly.

'The new maid accidentally turned off the wrong switch while she was vacuuming,' I say.

He starts laughing. Like a mad man. 'Fuck, Noah. She's breathing on her own,' he shouts.

I start laughing too.

His eyes are shining. 'This is good,' he says. 'It's fucking good.'

I nod and he rushes to me, throws his arms around me and pulls me into a great big bear hug. For a second I am too shocked to do anything, then I hug him back tightly.

When he lets go there are tears in his eyes

'Shit. I'm crying,' he says. He wipes them with the sides of his hands. 'I've never cried tears of joy in my life. I never even knew what the phrase meant.'

'I'm really glad,' I say softly.

'Who took the tube out?'

I point at Jane who is standing silently by the curtain. 'Jane did.'

He turns to look at her. 'Great. Just great. Well done.'

Then he turns to look at me, shaking his head and grinning from to ear to ear. He turns back to Jane. 'Have you called the doctor?' he asks suddenly.

'The doctor is on his way,' she says.

'Well done,' he tells her. He faces me. 'About the maid, give her a bonus, two years' wages, and fire her. Get someone more experienced to clean Dahlia's room.'

'Yes, boss.'

He goes back to the bed and looks down at Dahlia, his eyes roaming her face possessively.

He turns his head to me. 'I can't believe it, Noah,' he says with a big grin.

'I know,' I say. 'I nearly had a heart attack myself when I came in and saw what she had done.'

He laughs again. A deep belly laugh of pure joy

'Right, I'll be outside if you need me,' I say, and leave the room.

Stella

'You may not be able to see me right now, Dahlia, but I'm freaking killing it doing the happy dance!'

June

Thirty-nine

Zane

https://www.youtube.com/watch?v=_Dat9CRV8oo

It's a hot, muggy night, and it's been one of those days when I feel her loss more keenly. As Bernadette told me, there'll be good days and bad days. You just have to weather the bad days and the good days will roll on in.

I decide to go and have a drink at the Matrix.

Not since Dahlia was ripped away from me have I been there. I enter the club and look around. Nothing has changed. I walk to my usual table and sit. A waitress comes to ask what I want to drink. She must be new. I haven't seen her before. I order a large vodka.

'And bring the bottle,' I tell her.

'Yes, Sir,' she says.

She brings a full bottle and a large vodka on a tray. 'Will there be anything else, Sir?'

'I'll let you know,' I say, picking up the glass and raising it to my lips.

She slips away, and I drink. More than half the bottle is gone when a woman's voice asks, 'Zane?'

I lift my head. A woman with curly blonde hair and a tight short dress is standing in front of me with her head tilted and her eyebrows raised. I frown at her. She looks familiar. Yup, I think I remember her. We met through a mutual acquaintance at a Casino. She is Swedish or Norwegian.

She smiles. 'Remember me?' she prompts.

'Vaguely,' I say.

'I'm Abbie, a friend of Zio Tito. We met in Monte Carlo, last year?'

I nod.

'Are you alone?'

I spread my hand out and let it flop down.

She laughs. Low and sexy. Yes, I remember that. Abbie, the consummate flirt. 'Do you mind if I join you?'

I gesture to the space next to me and she takes a seat, gracefully aligning her body so her smooth legs are ever so slightly apart and slanted towards me. She has the kind of golden skin that only true Nordics can have.

'So what's Zio Tito up to these days?' I ask.

She pulls a face. 'Doing time in Italy.'

I smile dryly. Of course he is. 'What's he in for?'

'Some kind of ticket touting online racket.'

Truth is, that is the fate of most criminals. In and out of prison.

The waitress comes and Abbie orders a White Russian. I didn't expect it to hurt that much, but I feel it like a stab in my gut. That's Dahlia's drink. What the fuck am I doing here? We sat here. Right here on this very seat. A deep painful breath shudders through me.

She immediately puts her hand on my thigh. 'Are you OK?'

The shock of having another human being touch me makes me instantly look at her hand. For a second my intoxicated mind believes it is Dahlia's sweet hand. *It is the thigh scratch.* My confused gaze flies up to the face that goes with the hand. And there it is: the invitation to fuck. As clear as daylight.

Do I want to fuck?

Yes.

It must have shown in my face because she moves closer. Her perfume hits me, foreign and thick, and suddenly I am nauseated. Sick to my stomach. I stand up unsteadily. I want to fuck, but not you. I want my Dahlia.

She stands too. 'Are you all right?'

I wave my hand at her. 'I'm fine.'

I weave through the crowd, pushing people out of the way. I don't belong here. I need to get back. I need to keep watch. She may open her eyes and not find me there. I need to get back. I reach the door, and Noah grabs my shoulder.

'Come on,' he says. 'Let's get you home.'

I look into his eyes. 'Yeah, take me home.'

I slump at the back of the Merc with my hands over my eyes. I don't know how much longer I can hold on. I can't go on like this. Something's got to give. The car lurches, and my head hits the side of the door.

God, I'm such a fucking mess.

The car stops and I stumble out. Noah tries to help me but I push him away. Yuri has the front door open and I sway past him. I go down the corridor and open the door to her room. The nurse is reading a book by the lamp. When she sees me, she immediately puts the book down and stands up.

'Go now,' I tell her harshly.

Quietly, she goes past me. I take a few steps into the room and look at my little fish lying on her bed. Fuck, it never fails to amaze me how perfectly still she sleeps. Even if I watch her for hours she will never move a muscle, and yet I know she is in there. I walk up to her still body. I am glad for the silence. I used to hate the eerie rasp of the ventilator. I love watching her breathing. It means she is alive. I touch her face.

'Wake up, little fish. Please. Wake up.'

She doesn't open her eyes. Something tears inside me. I gently push the blanket covering her. She is dressed in a soft loose cotton shirt. I lift it up. She is wearing a diaper. Gently, I undo it. It is clean. The skin around the tops of her thighs is without redness or rashes. Good. The nurses have instructions to check her diaper and turn her once every hour to ensure she never gets bedsores.

I stare at her pubic area. The hair has grown back. It is not trimmed or clean-shaven as she sometimes used to have it. Strange, how totally unerotic it looks. In my head I can hear that nurse say, 'Sometimes when we brush their teeth or shave them they will open their eyes.'

Maybe.

I look at her sleeping face.

Tenderly, I spread her legs and put my tongue into the damp slit. No one sees me. Not even the moon. As soon as my tongue touches her soft flesh my eyes begin to fill with tears. Oh shit. What the fuck am I doing? Tears pour down my face as I lick her. She doesn't even taste the same anymore.

Wake up, Dahlia. Wake up.

She doesn't become wetter. She doesn't wake up, and I just feel worse than the most disgusting pervert. I fix the diaper back and cover her with the blanket. I kiss her cheek.

'I love you, little fish. I really, really do,' I whisper.

She makes no response.

'OK, sleep well. I'll see you in the morning.'

I lurch away from the bed and open the door. Immediately, the nurse gets up from her chair. She goes into the room and closes the door. I trudge upstairs and lie on my bed, but I can't sleep. I am filled with an indescribable restlessness. Eventually, I get out of bed and go to the cupboard. Inside a drawer I find the box. I open it and take the male masturbator out. 'For when I am not here,' she said.

Oh, Dahlia.

I lie on the bed propped up against the pillows. I apply the lube and switch on the gadget. I think of myself licking her, not the way she was today, but the way she was when she first came to me. She had been so full of life and as proud as a queen. God, how different I would have been if I had known then what I know now. If only I'd known how little time there was.

The machine whirls softly. In my head I part her thighs and enter her delicious body. She writhes and moans in ecstasy.

'Fuck me hard, Zane. Fuck me.'

Her eyes are closed. Her body is arched. I take her nipple in my mouth and she groans with pleasure.

'Come inside me, Zane. Fill me with your hot cum.'

I climax hard, my body jerking, crying out for her.

For some time I lie there, too exhausted and defeated to do anything. Then I take the masturbator off and clean myself. I crawl under the duvet and try to sleep. Tomorrow. Maybe tomorrow she will open her beautiful chartreuse eyes.

August

Forty

Zane

I'm just reminding you, little fish, that Andre Rieu's concert is only a month away. I'll be playing at the Royal Albert Hall in front of hundreds of people but the performance will be just for you. There is a box seat waiting for you. Will you please try to come and watch me play, Dahlia? After all, this is your dream …

October

Forty-one

Olga

'At midnight I saw the sun shining as if it were noon.'

-Apuleius, The Golden Ass

I bend down and stroke her hair. 'It's time to wake up,' I tell her, as I have done every single day since she came back from hospital. 'Come on. You can do it.'

All these months I got no reaction, and yet today something is different. I can feel it. I touch her cheek. 'Wake up, brave American eagle and catch your snake,' I whisper fiercely.

Then I straighten and watch her.

There.

A twitch.

Her face twitches.

I clasp my hands together and start praying. I should go call the nurse, but I don't. Instead I will her to wake up.

'Wake up. Wake up. Today is a very important day. You must wake up. Come on. Zane needs you today. You must wake up, brave eagle.'

I wait.

Then.

Her finger ... moves.

I stop breathing. Oh God, please let her wake up.

https://www.youtube.com/watch?v=YQHsXMglC9A

Forty-two

Dahlia Fury

In the beginning I heard indistinct voices, but I could never tell if I was dreaming or not. They seemed to be very close to my ear. I dropped in and out of consciousness effortlessly and without any control. I had strange dreams. Often there were balls of fire. I thought I was a child again walking in a meadow.

Sometimes I'd feel my body being moved around on the bed.

Slowly, I heard the voices of all the people I loved. I understood everything they were saying and I wanted to reach out, oh how much I wanted to talk to them, but I was like a tree, voiceless, unable to move my limbs on my own.

I know that the big concert is today.

Zane will be playing the piano at an Andre Rieu concert. I am so proud of him. No matter what, I cannot miss this performance. I pull my eyebrows upwards with all my might and manage to half-open my eyes. The light is like knives, entering my eyes and piercing my brain. It blinds me and I snap my eyes shut. I feel a rush of movement, then I hear the curtains being drawn closed I struggle again and open my eyes, this time fully. In the dimness of the room I slowly make out a blurry figure. The figure comes closer to me.

'Oh, my darling, darling girl, you're awake!' the person says excitedly.

Olga. That's Olga's voice.

'This is amazing. You woke up today. I knew you would. Zane is playing the piano at a concert tonight. He is already at the concert hall. I'm going to go and call him. He'll be so happy. This is a miracle.'

I dart my eyes to the side and back to her, and she frowns. 'You don't want me to call Zane?'

I move my eyebrows and blink.

For a while she stares at me, then realization dawns. 'You want to go to the concert. You want to surprise him.'

Tears fill my eyes and run down the sides of my face. I move my eyebrows and blink again.

She starts crying. 'You have really learned to fly, haven't you,' she chokes out. 'OK, I'll call

Noah and Stella. They'll know what to do. Stella will make you pretty, and Noah will sort out how to transport you there. Don't worry, between us we'll get you there.'

I wriggle my eyebrows. There seems to be more movement and it was so much easier to perform. At that point I feel myself slipping into sleep again, but I know they will wake me up in time for the concert.

When I wake up again it is because Stella is screaming in my ear. I open my eyes without difficulty, and the room is pleasantly dim. I open my mouth and one word struggles out.

'Kebab.' It sounds high-pitched and strange to me.

'Oh, you big idiot, you,' she says, and hoots with laughter. She grabs my face in both her hands and kisses me on the mouth.

'I love you, Dahlia. I love you,' she sings.

I smile up at her.

'I've called Molly,' she says, 'and she's bringing a dress for you. Two sizes smaller. I'm afraid you've become one of them skinny bitches,' she says cheerfully.

'I ... don' ... t ... want ... t ... o ... wear ... a ... dia ... per,' I say.

'I agree. It's not a good look.' She grins.

Olga brings pillows and puts them behind me so I am propped up. Slowly, bit by bit, the words start forming and exit from my stiff, out of practice, throat. Stella calls my mom and Daisy and both of them sob with happiness. Daisy declares it a miracle, but I know it is something else. Love. Zane's deep love reached out and touched me while I was in that still white world. I was always waiting for him. Always.

After the call I watch in a daze as Stella gives me a manicure and a pedicure. My nails are painted pearl pink.

'Mark,' I say.

And her eyes light up. 'Oh, Dahlia. I think I'm in love with him.'

I beam with happiness. 'Really?'

'Yes, really. He's wonderful,' she gushes.

'Happy. So. Very happy for you,' I say.

At that moment Molly arrives with the dress.

'I'll tell you everything tomorrow,' Stella promises.

'OK.'

The dress is unveiled and it is beautiful: velvet, halter neck, deep green, and long. Both girls help me dress, then Noah comes and gently, as if I am the most precious thing on earth, lifts me off the bed and puts me into the wheelchair that Zane apparently ordered nearly a year ago.

I look up at them all, full of love and gratitude.

'I love you all,' I whisper.

https://www.youtube.com/watch?v=cZXxI2kQwns &nohtml

From my box I watch the musicians come on the stage and take their places. My heart beats frantically as I wait for the pianist to arrive. Finally, he comes into the spotlight. Oh! Wow! How beautiful he looks in his white tie formal orchestra dress code: long black tailcoat, white wing-collared shirt and bowtie.

That there is my man.

I tremble with love for him. He turns towards the crowd and bows stiffly. The audience claps.

Then, as if against his will, his eyes stray towards my box. He does a double take when our eyes touch. Suddenly the rest of the audience falls away. We stare at each other. He shakes his head as if he can't believe his eyes.

I smile at him.

His mouth drops open as his hands rise up in a gesture of incredulity. His eyes move to my left and fall on Noah. Only then does he believe his eyes. A fellow musician touches his arm, and he glances around at the man. He says something to him then immediately turns back to me, as if he is afraid that I am only an apparition. His face full of joy and love, he takes a step as if to come to me, but I shake my head slightly. It stops him.

'Play for me, Aleksandr Malenkov,' I mouth and smile at him.

He nods slowly before going to take his position at the gleaming piano. From there he gazes at me until Andre Rieu comes on stage and he is given a standing ovation.

To my shock he starts telling the audience about me!

About a woman who secretly found her boyfriend's music notes and took them to a fellow musician. He made it funny by adding in the bit about the masseuse connection.

'It's a tale of great love. This brave woman while trying to save him fell into a coma that lasted a year. The doctors thought she might not make it, but against all odds she is here today. Please welcome Dahlia Fury.'

He raises his right hand and waves it towards me. Every eye in that place settles on me curiously as they clap.

Heat flames up my neck and face. How on earth could Andre Rieu know I'd be here? In my confusion and embarrassment I look to Zane. He smiles at me as if his heart would burst with pride. I turn my head to look at Noah, and suddenly I know. *Oh, Noah. Silent, strong and loyal to the bone. You told Andre Rieu.*

'Now … for the first time ever … in his debut performance, ladies and gentlemen: Aleksandr Malenkov.'

The entire audience erupts into applause.

Zane's composition is beautiful beyond words, but so familiar to me it is as if I have heard it a thousand times. Even though I fight the cloak of sleep with all my might, I slip back into unconsciousness halfway through. I have no awareness of how I get home.

I come back again to the blurred sight of Zane sitting beside me in our bed.

'You're awake,' he says, and it feels like no time has passed. Was it not yesterday I took his notes to Eliot's apartment? The rest is fuzzy. I was running. Fast. Nearly falling. There was an explosion. A ball of fire. I flew. Then blackness. I frown trying to remember.

'What is it?' he asks.

'Someone was trying to kill you,' I whisper.

He nods.

'Who was it?'

'It doesn't matter now. It is all in the past. The only true regret I have is what happened to you. Especially since I know it was because of me.'

'No, it does. I need to know. Who was it?'

He sighs. 'It was Lenny.'

'Oh my God. I knew I never trusted him. What if he tries it again?' I ask worriedly.

He looks at me, a hard light entering his eyes. 'He can never hurt you or anyone again. I've walked away from it all. You're all I need now. Thanks to your ingenuity and bravery, I am a musician now.'

'You were wonderful tonight,' I whisper. 'Like I always knew you would be.'

He shakes his head. 'No, you were wonderful.'

'I'm sorry I fell asleep halfway through.'

 587

'Oh, baby. I love you.'

'I know you do,' I say with a smile.

He touches my face wonderingly. 'You do?'

I smile. 'Yeah. I heard you telling me while I was asleep.'

'Good. Did you hear the bit about how worthless life was without you and how much I missed you?'

'Maybe, but tell me again.'

'I want to show you how much, but I'm almost afraid to touch you.'

'Why?'

'What if you fall asleep halfway through? I might never recover from the hurt.'

I laugh gently. 'Oh, Zane. I am so lucky.'

He sighs.

'So are we going to have sex or not?'

'We're going to make love, endlessly. I'm going to rediscover and reclaim every inch of your body again, but not tonight. Let's get the doctor to look at you tomorrow first.'

'But what will we do tonight? I don't think I want to sleep.'

He grins, boyish, beautiful, and irresistible. 'I have so many things to show you and tell you. You missed a whole year.'

'What did I miss?'

He takes his phone out of his pocket. 'To start with, one night while you were sleeping, a vixen and her cubs came to visit. Let me show you.'

I watch him scrolling through the videos he has made for me and I know. It's going to be all right.

https://www.youtube.com/watch?v=bnVUHW Cynig

Forty-three

Aleksandr Malenkov

> Methinks I lied all winter, when I swore
> my love was infinite, if spring make it more.
> -John Donne, Love's Growth

I undress her. Slowly. Dragging each garment across her skin. I'm not going to rush this. I did it wrong before. This time I'm going to do it right. With love. With the kind of love that holds, cuts to the soul, and heals with just one touch, one look. She is mine and I am hers. And this: this is ours. Just ours.

Her top. Her skirt.

'Hurry,' she pleads, her voice low and urgent.

'Shhhh,' I say, but I don't increase my pace one tiny bit. Love is torture. I know.

Her bra. Her panties.

Her impatient gaze meets mine, locks. I let her look at me while my eyes roam her body hungrily, possessively. Let her see what I kept locked away for so long.

This is me, little fish. Adoring you.

Her eyes glaze over as I circle my tongue around one deliciously pink nipple. I draw that beauty into my mouth. My body burns for her.

'Ohhh,' she moans, and arches into me.

We found each other. I suck gently.

She threads her fingers into my hair and makes those little kitten sounds. It's the sweetest thing. God, I've missed them. I move my attention to the other beauty. Her breath catches.

'Oh yes,' she whimpers.

It's been so long. It's been so long.

I raise my head and take her lips. I want to bite on that plump lower lip, ravish her like a caveman, but I don't. I make our kiss slow and soft like butter. Our tongues rolling, lips melding, until I feel her melting under my touch. We burn, merge together, become one.

My hand curves under her ass. Gently, gently I slip a finger into her, and feel the tremor that goes right through her and vibrate in the moan she utters in my mouth. Inside me something is building and growing. Something

I've never felt before. It climbs and climbs. I feel my heart hammering. My soul soaring.

She pushes her body up into my hand, desperate, seeking, wanting. Her eyes blazing with the same lust that is inside me.

'Don't let me come with your finger,' she begs, her eyes half-closed and glazed.

I still vividly remember what I once did to her prone, unresponsive body. She laughed when I told her. 'You should have carried on,' she said. 'I might have become the first person in a coma to have an orgasm.' She only says that because she doesn't know how utterly lost I was without her. How much I cried.

I spread her thighs and feast on the sight before me: ah … my sexy, wet, hungry pussy. Her clit is a little white pearl protruding out of all that swollen flesh. My tongue waters to taste her, but there will be time for that later. I need to get inside her. My cock needs to sink into her tight, hot cunt. Her hips thrust forward. Her sweet sex is seeking my cock.

This is for real.

After all this time I'm going to be inside my baby. Her hand reaches out and curls itself around the base of my dick.

'Holy fuck, I forgot how big you are,' she whispers, her face shining with excitement. Her finger smears the bead of liquid all over my cock head.

I groan. 'Oh, yes.'

Watching her eyes, I spread her legs more open. She positions my erection, hard and hot, between the lips of her sex and rubs herself on it, before pushing it inside her, inch by fucking inch. The old urge to slam into her, to take what I want, doesn't even arise. All I can think about is not hurting her. She is as delicate as a piece of bone china. I'm almost afraid of damaging her. Her breasts are smaller, I can see her ribs, her hipbones protrude, and her skin is so painfully pale.

'Am I hurting you?'

'No. It feels amazing.'

Then she inhales sharply and stops moving.

'Did I hurt you?'

'No. I'm savoring you.'

I know she is lying. I am hurting her. She is too tight after all this time.

'Let me,' I say, and she removes her hand from the base of my cock. I pause and let her get used to being stretched again.

'I love the way you fill me up,' she says, her voice low and throbbing.

'I love filling you up.'

'I'm ready. Fuck me now.'

594

Very slowly, I ease my shaft all the way in, and she rises up to meet me.

'Oh wow!' she breathes.

I set the rhythm. It's not wild and it's not crazy, it's just perfect for two people who have survived being lost. It gives me time to take it all in: her expression, the noises that she makes, the scent of her, the feel of her skin, the sweat that glows on her face. I take it in as a miser collects money, or a magpie hoards shiny objects. Obsessively.

She tires quickly, her hips no longer matching my rhythm, so I come out of her, collect her ankles and push them up to either side of her ears. My pulse quickens instantly. This is what we were before. This will never change. I will always like to see her spread out like this. Her beautiful pussy opened wide for me. I slip my cock back into her slit and press down into that tight, wet channel. The walls of her sex grip me hard and I watch her eyes widen.

'More,' she urges hoarsely.

I push deeper into her. She is tight. Incredibly tight.

'I can take more,' she gasps.

I want to push all the way in, but I can see she is in pain. With a groan I stop and let her adjust to my size. She wriggles her hips and the sensation is like lava in my blood. I almost come.

'I love having you so deep inside me,' she whispers.

I begin to thrust. Sinking into her, deeper and deeper, forgetting myself, until a quick ragged sound tears out of her throat and she climaxes. Immediately I let go, my breath explodes from my lungs, and semen pumps out of me. I come, as I haven't in a long, long time, as only she can make me. Hard and brutal, my neck stretched, a strangled growl rumbling in my throat.

Emptied and chest heaving, I look down at my love. Her skin is flushed and she is taking gasping breaths.

I curl her towards me. 'I'm sorry I hurt you.'

'No, it was the best sex I've ever had.'

I listen to her ragged heartbeat with gratitude. Every heartbeat is a gift I treasure.

'I wanted all of you,' she whispers. 'I've always been able to take all of you, and I wanted to again.'

'You will. When you're ready. There's no hurry,' I tell her. 'We have our whole lives ahead of us.'

Epilogue

Dahlia Fury Malenkov

(Five Years Later)

I open the fridge door and a gust of lovely cool air blows on my face. I reach for a pitcher of lemonade, close the door, and Mark appears at the kitchen entrance

'Hey,' he says.

'Hey yourself,' I answer back.

He comes into the kitchen. He is barefoot and wearing a pair of swimming trunks.

I hold up the pitcher. 'Want some?' I ask.

'God, yes,' he says, and comes to sit down at the counter. He watches me pour the lemonade out. I slide it over to him across the marble counter in a bartender move.

'Fancy,' he says with a smile, and takes a sip.

'So what's going on outside?' I say, plonking myself on the stool opposite him.

'Isn't life funny?' he wonders aloud instead of answering me.

'In what way?'

'I thought you were the one for me. I mean, nobody could have told me otherwise. Like I told Stella, I was completely obsessed. From the first moment I saw you, I actually thought it was love at first sight. I followed you home, for god's sake.'

'Yes, that is a bit creepy,' I chuckle.

'Then I saw Stella and thought, yeah, great body, nice face, but not for me and yet, she is the one. We were always wrong. We didn't fit no matter how hard I tried to make it so. With Stella I didn't have to try. It just flowed like oil out of a jar. You were always meant for Zane and Stella was always meant for me. I can't even imagine my life without her anymore.'

I look at his kind eyes and feel blessed that four years ago I finally managed to convince Zane to accept him into our lives. Before I can answer him there is a shout. 'Uncle Mark where are you?' a voice hollers.

'Anouska wants to torture you. Again,' I say with a smile.

'Oh well. It was too good to last,' he says and stands up.

'Good luck.' I grin at him as he goes out into the bright sunshine.

I look out of the window as Mark hauls my daughter up into the air and onto his shoulders. She clings onto his neck like a little brown spider and they head towards the pool.

I hear a noise and Stella waddles in. She is seven months pregnant. 'Jesus, Dahlia. What the hell are we doing in this confounded country? It's way too hot. I'm just about to melt into a massive puddle.'

'Well, we're all here right slap bang in the middle of a Roman summer. In two months' time you'll be having a baby, and you wanted to come, remember?' I tell her.

'That's true. Somebody pass me a lemonade before I pass out,' she says dramatically.

'It's air-conditioned in this kitchen,' I remind her, putting a glass of lemonade into her outstretched hand.

'Are you trying to ruin a diva's moment?' she asks before draining the entire glass and putting it back into my hand.

'Heaven forbid,' I say, and watch her climb onto the island and lie flat on the cool granite top.

I climb onto the island and lie beside her. 'You always have the best ideas.'

She turns her head. 'Where's Zane?'

I link my fingers with hers. 'Upstairs. Changing Alexei.'

'Oh God. That's another joy that awaits me.'

I giggle. 'It's not so bad.'

'Yeah, right. Next you'll be telling me childbirth is beautiful.'

I grin. 'It is.'

'Thank you very much, but having an eight pound bowling ball shoot out of my vagina is not my idea of beautiful.'

I grin. 'You're a little bit scared, aren't you?'

'As a matter of fact, yes. I'm freaking terrified.'

I laugh. 'Trust me, it'll be worth it.'

'That remains to be seen, but don't you think it is weird to have a little person living in your body, weeing and pooing inside you?'

'Oh, Stella,' I giggle, and squeeze her fingers. They are puffy in this hot weather. 'Only you can say something like that and still look cute.'

'Talking of cute, I forgot to tell you what your little me did yesterday.'

'What did she do?' I ask with a sigh.

'Last week I explained to her that when you get the urge to do something bad it's because the devil is whispering in your ear.'

'Oh, so you told her that,' I exclaim.

'That's not the point of this story,' Stella says impatiently. 'So yesterday I found her happily coloring the wall in my room. Of course, I scolded. "That is very naughty, Anouska. Next time I see you do that I'll have to beat your little butt." She frowned up at me and said, "Is the devil talking to you now Auntie Stella?"'

I burst out laughing. 'Oh my God. My daughter is terrible.'

'I know. It's like she's my daughter. She's got all my traits.'

'She does,' I agree, still chuckling.

'Anyway, when is Noah coming?'

'Tomorrow. He can only stay for a day though. He nearly didn't come, but I twisted his arm.'

'How does one twist Noah's arm?'

'Food.'

'Really?'

'Specifically, date and banana cake. He'll walk miles for a slice.'

'You're kidding. He's seems so impenetrable.'

'No. That's his big weakness.'

She laughs. 'He's still single, isn't he?'

'Yup.'

'Do you think he'll ever find someone?'

'For sure. He has a heart of gold. The woman who gets him will be very lucky.'

I lift my head slightly and Zane is standing there with Alexei.

'Well, well, what do we have here, Alexei?' he says.

'Mommy, Mommy,' Alexei calls, and Zane brings him over and fits him between Stella and me.

His little fingers grasp my face as he plants a wet, gooey kiss on my nose.

'Right. I'm off to see what Mark is up to,' Stella says, trying unsuccessfully to pull herself upright.

Zane holds out his hand, she grasps it and he pulls her into a sitting position.

'Thank you, kind Sir,' she tells him, before waddling out of the kitchen.

'Hello beautiful,' Zane says, coming around to kiss me.

I sit up and hold Alexei in my lap.

Zane leans toward me, bracketing my body by putting his hands on the countertop. 'Happy?' he asks.

'Ecstatic,' I reply.

'I want to take you upstairs, Mrs. Malenkov,' he whispers.

'Like now?'

'Like now,' he says very seriously.

'Why?'

'Because it's our anniversary.'

'No, it's not,' I say immediately.

'Yes, it is.'

'What anniversary?' I challenge.

'The very first time I made you come.'

I grin. 'When I was forced by Stella to go massage the very dangerous Russian mob boss?'

He nods. 'He's not a mob boss anymore, but he is still very Russian, and can be dangerous if provoked. Will you massage him?'

'What about him?' I ask, nodding at Alexei.

'Just throw him in the pool,' he says callously.

'I have a better idea,' I whisper, and thrusting Alexei into his arms, jump down from the counter. I snatch Alexei back and go out into the poolside area where Mark, Stella, and Anouska are playing.

'Can you take care of this little one for an hour?' I say, holding my son out to Stella.

'What am I? Your babysitter?'

'Wait till your bundle of joy arrives and you want some,' I say meaningfully.

'Give me that baby,' she says, holding her arms out.

I give Alexei to her and run.

Yes, I run to my husband.

The End.

This book is inspired by the idea that everybody
deserves a second chance ...

https://www.youtube.com/watch?v=CJsiTpr9 7A&nohtml5

and anybody can change

https://www.youtube.com/watch?v=gt5H- pSsyiM&nohtml5

Coming soon Noah's story:

YOU DON'T KNOW ME

A quick sneak peak into the contemporary romance I am writing with newcomer to this genre, Laura Jack.

THE BAD BOY WANTS ME

GEORGIA LE CARRE
&
LAURA JACK

Chapter One

Tori

'**I** beg your pardon,' Dr. Maurice Strong, London's top plastic surgeon, said with a perfect mix of British snobbery and professional contempt.

Anybody else would have cringed, but not Britney. She had absolutely no problem repeating her certifiably weird request.

'I want you to make my eyes look like a cat's. You know, going upwards, like this.' She laid her forefingers on the outer corners of her eyes, and pulled the skin upwards, as high as her seventeen-year-old skin would stretch.

Dr. Strong glanced at me as if he suspected this was some sort of a schoolgirl prank.

I'll admit it was a feat not to laugh at the crazy scene unfolding before my eyes, but I was damn good. I kept my expression shit-hot blank. It was more than my job was worth to express even a hint of mockery at Britney's frequent forays into lunacy. I was paid by her father to follow her around, fetch, carry, and generally baby her.

How can I describe my job? Well, I guess, it was a bit like the ass-wipers of ancient China. No, I'm kidding. Straight up serious. Apparently, every great emperor had a manservant whose sole duty was to carefully clean his master's ass after he had done a number two, and carry the precious royal droppings away to be disposed of. But here's the best part of this little nugget from the past. You'd think that would have been considered the most horrible occupation a man could have, wouldn't you?

Not so.

Since the emperor was considered a god in human form, direct from heaven itself, it was an awesome job eagerly fought over by many candidates. The lucky guy got to smell and dispose of a god's poop. Unfortunately for me, other than the silent laugh factor to my job there was no such satisfaction in mine.

Getting nada from me, Dr. Strong pushed his glasses halfway down his nose (strange how plastic surgeons never have great noses) and peered frostily at Britney from the top of his gold-rimmed glasses. It was obvious that he thought she needed professional psychiatric help.

'You want me to operate on your eyes to make you look like a ... a ... cat,' he enunciated slowly, the last word dropping like a brick into the frigid air of his consulting room.

'Yes, that right,' Britney confirmed, nodding her blonde head eagerly, and flashing a heartbreakingly happy smile at him.

I could already see what was coming.

Dr. Strong sighed, as if he had done this way too many times, or he might actually prefer the ass wipe job. He clasped his hands on his desk and looked at her sternly. 'I'm sorry Miss. Hunter but I'm here to make people look better not turn them into ridiculous freaks.'

'No, no, no, you don't understand,' Britney launched hastily into an explanation, sheer panic turning her voice into the high, whinny drone that always hurt my ears. 'It will look brilliant.'

'It may look *brilliant*, but I'm afraid I'm not the doctor for you.'

'Oh, but I want you to do it. You're the best,' Britney wailed. He didn't know it, but we were this close (half-an-inch between thumb and forefinger) to a full-blown tantrum.

Dr. Strong looked like he was sitting on a toilet and had not eaten enough fiber to make it a worthwhile exercise. 'Then take my advice and stop trying to ruin a perfectly good pair of eyes.'

'I'll pay more,' she offered suddenly.

Oh! Britney, Britney.

For the first time a flash of anger showed on the good doctor's face. He speared her with a stink glance. 'If there is another issue you wanted to discuss then please do so, otherwise this appointment is over.'

'But ...' Britney cried petulantly. 'You did my nose and my boobs. You *have* to do my eyes.'

'I don't *have* to do anything.'

'Oh please,' Britney begged.

'If you insist on cat eyes no doubt there will be other surgeons interested in taking on the ... project.'

'I don't want to go to anyone else. You're the best.'

He closed the file on his desk and looked at her with cold finality.

'This is so unfair. I want cat eyes. I'm not asking for something unreasonable. And I'm paying. You can't just turn me away,' Britney raged.

'Miss. Hunter,' Dr. Strong reprimanded strictly. 'Kindly do not waste any more of my time.'

Britney jumped up and I quickly followed suit.

'Come on Tori,' she ordered huffily, and proceeded to stalk out of the office with her nose held high in the air.

I shrugged apologetically at the doctor and followed her out.

She ran past the waiting room and rounded on me in the corridor. 'I have to find a way to make him operate on me,' she said desperately. 'Can you help me to convince him?'

'Me?' I asked startled.

'Yes, you. You're always so sensible.'

'To be honest I think your eyes are beautiful as they are.'

She looked at me the way I always imagined Cesar looked at Brutus.

'What?' I asked, bewildered. It's not like we were best friends or anything.

'You don't want me to be beautiful,' she screeched suddenly, and ran off in the general direction of the toilets.

I stared after her for a few seconds before I turned around and slammed into a perfectly solid wall of cologne-scented, honest to goodness, male muscles. Strong, wonderfully warm hands curled around my forearms. I looked up. Okay, long tanned brown throat, unshaven jawline …

Oh! My! God!

Amused, bright green eyes fringed by eyelashes that rightly should have belonged to a girl; straight, black, cocked eyebrows; disheveled hair, and a badass smile curved on the sexiest most deliciously full lips. The kind you just wanted sink your teeth into. *Oh, and just before I faint, a chin dimple just made a late entrance to the party.* This was exactly the kind of man my best friend, Zodie would call, 'a happening guy.' Things happen around him.

'Whoa,' he said.

How can I describe his voice? Warmed up chocolate sauce poured slowly down my naked back. Swoon, my ass, I fucking shivered.

'Whoa, yourself,' I croaked.

He bared his straight white teeth in a grin. It was one of those magic grins that made me want to suck it off his face.

'Was that my sister I just saw bolting into the toilet for a quick meltdown?'

I swallowed hard. This was so not how I expected to meet Britney's famous brother. 'Could be, if you're the rock star brother.'

Cash Hunter's green eyes looked like they were on fire. 'That's me, babe. Rock star brother.'

'Now might be a good time to let go of me,' I croaked.

'Give me one good reason I should?' he countered lazily.

My eyebrows flew upwards. 'My knee's reckoning on an upwards trajectory?'

Grinning, he let go of me and raised his hand up in surrender. 'Looks like I caught me a wild cat.'

My legs played up a little as I took a step back.

He watched me 'Where have you been all my life, Beautiful?'

I gave a fake laugh. 'Are you deliberately using bad lines to save on contraceptives?'

The leather-clad, powerhouse of sexy goodness threw his head back and laughed. That early in the morning the vodka fumes that hit my nostrils were strong enough to make me dizzy.

'What's going to work on you, wild cat? My cock wants to say hello to your pussy?'

'Breath mints might help,' I retorted.

'Damn, you sure know how to suck the juice of out a tender moment.' He rummaged around in his pocket and popped a mint into his mouth. 'Now unless you don't like a long, thick, cock we're good to go.'

I looked up at him with frosty eyes. 'Personally I think size is overrated.'

His eyes gleamed. 'Baby, we're in luck. There's a man on the other side of the corridor who can customize my dong into the right shape and size for you.'

'Hilarious,' I said unenthusiastically.

'I bet I can make you call me Daddy,'

'Thanks, but ... ugh no..'

'Right: change of tack. Not that I'm giving up on getting you into my bed or anything, but want to have dinner with me tonight?'

He was too beautiful to be real.

The door behind us opened.

'Cash,' squealed Britney.

Cash winked at me before he turned his attention to the figure flying at him. He caught her as she wrapped her arms and legs around him like a big kid.

'How did you know where to find me?' she asked.

'Isn't this your second home?' he asked dryly.

'Not anymore. Dr. Strong won't do my eyes,' she grumbled.

'Oh yeah. Why not?'

'He's says I'll end up looking like a ridiculous freak.'

'Hmmm... what did you want done?'

'I want cat's eyes.'

Cash's gorgeous eyes widened. He nodded slowly as she told him about her appointment with Dr. Strong..

'Well, PooBear. I think cat's eyes are a great idea.'

Jesus. Madness must run the family.

'You do,' Britney asked brightly, her whole face shining with hope.

'Absolutely. It's a great look. It'll make you look like one of those beauties from the fifties and sixties.'

'What?' Britney frowned, and climbed off her brother.

'Yeah, you know like Zsa Zsa Gabor.'

'Zsa Zsa Gabor. Who's that?'

'It's from Dad's time,' he supplied with a wise nod. 'Oh, and like ...er ... what was the name of that comedienne who died recently?' He clicked his fingers and looked at me.

'Joan Rivers,' I suggested helpfully.

He stopped clicking and pointed at me. 'That's the one.' He turned towards his sister who was looking at him with dismay. 'Great look,' he said approvingly.

'But they're both so old.'

'So what. They had style. Style never dies, Come on, let's go and see Dr. Strong together. I'll help you to convince him.' He took her arm.

Britney held back. 'Hang on a minute. I don't think Dr. Strong might have been right. I should think about this a bit more.'

'Oh,' he said innocently. 'Are you sure?'

'Yes,' she said lamely.

'In that case,' he turned to me, 'how about introducing me to this lovely creature.'

Britney turned to me. 'Oh, this's Tori Diamond. Dad hired her to be my PA.'

He extended a hand out. 'Hello, Tori Diamond. Cash Hunter, Britney's rock star brother. How nice to meet you?'

I stepped forward and put my hand into his ridiculously strong hands. Jesus, these were some hands. My imagination ran away with me. *One finger inserted deep inside me, and curling to stroke me.* Oh hell! Whew! Was it hot in that corridor or what? Heat crept up my neck.

He smirked. The smarmy bastard.

I cleared my throat. 'Charmed, I'm sure,' I said in the most regal voice I could muster.

Click on this link to receive news of my latest releases and great giveaways.
http://bit.ly/1oe9WdE

and remember

I **LOVE** hearing from readers so by all means come and say hello here:
https://www.facebook.com/georgia.lecarre

Printed in Great Britain
by Amazon

77046583R00371